Philippa East grew up in Scotland and originally studied Psychology and Philosophy at the University of Oxford. After graduating, she moved to London to train as a Clinical Psychologist and worked in NHS mental health services for over ten years.

Philippa now lives in the Lincolnshire countryside with her husband and cat. Alongside her writing, she continues to work as a psychologist and therapist. Philippa's prize-winning short stories have been published in various literary journals. Her first novel *Little White Lies* was published in 2020 and was shortlisted for the CWA John Creasey New Blood Dagger. *Safe and Sound* is her second novel.

Also by Philippa East

Little White Lies

SAFE
AND
SOUND

PHILIPPA EAST

ONE PLACE. MANY STORIES

HQ
An imprint of HarperCollins*Publishers* Ltd
1 London Bridge Street
London SE1 9GF

www.harpercollins.co.uk

HarperCollins*Publishers*
1st Floor, Watermarque Building, Ringsend Road
Dublin 4, Ireland

This edition 2021

21 22 23 24 LSC 10 9 8 7 6 5 4 3 2 1

First published in Great Britain by
HQ, an imprint of HarperCollins*Publishers* Ltd 2021

Copyright © Philippa East 2021

Philippa East asserts the moral right to be
identified as the author of this work.
A catalogue record for this book is
available from the British Library.

ISBN: 978-0-00-846552-0

For more information visit: www.harpercollins.co.uk/green

This book is set in 10.7/15.5 pt. Sabon by Type-it AS, Norway

Printed and bound in United States of America
by LSC Communications

For my sister, Katherine

Chapter 1

Last night, I began to worry about Charlie again.

An appointment letter arrived yesterday, blue and white logo at the top. Maybe it was because of that letter that I lay in bed, unable to sleep, staring at the ceiling, thinking about him. Replaying every one of his actions and movements from the week, checking them in the slow motion of my mind. Did his speech ever slur, did his thinking seem confused or slow, did his emotions wander out of control? I went over it again and again, trying to assess him, and myself, feeling the tightness take hold of my ribs.

This morning, though, in the bright light of day, Charlie seemed absolutely fine. His chatter over breakfast was so clear and clever, and when I got him to reel off everything I'd packed into his schoolbag – my own tiny, reassuring test – he didn't miss a single thing. I kissed him *well done*, feeling ridiculous for worrying.

But even now, as I hurry down the hill from his primary school, I can't quite seem to make the thoughts go away.

*

When I reach the office, Emma is at her desk, her pretty face smiling up at me.

'Morning!' she says, and then a beat later: 'Good weekend?'

It's like throwing a switch. I feel my back straighten; I automatically lift my chin up. I smile back at Emma, though my lips still feel numb from the February cold. Arriving at work each morning, it's like another version of myself that I shift into: my professional role, my competent self. Even my speech comes out a little bit different.

'Oh yes. It was, thank you,' I reply. Even though it was just me and Charlie, the way it always is; the way I tend to keep it. Even though nothing happened but my worries. 'How was yours?' My tone is polite, clipped.

'Oh, you know,' she says, glancing down at her smartphone and up again. 'Busy! I always feel like I need Mondays off, just to recover.' She gives a little laugh.

I nod, as though I know what she means.

'I made you tea,' Emma adds, pointing to my desk. A full mug sits there, still steaming despite the cold; it takes a while for the heating to warm up in this old building.

'Oh,' I say, awkwardly. 'Thank you.' When I get this way – worries in the night – I try to avoid caffeine, but Emma isn't to know that, how could she? I sit down at my desk and wrap my hands round the mug at least, enjoying the heat of it. The room is still chilly and I keep my smart wool coat on while I switch on my computer and open up the files, the allocation that it's my job every day to check.

My list of tasks for this week is clearly set out, little tabs with my name against each one; such a sense of order it brings. A whole framework to contain the day, predictable tasks that fill my head with to-do lists and give so little room for other thoughts. The radiator behind me clicks and gurgles as I pull out my notebook to write out a plan, following the careful system I have, my way of doing each little thing. The Housing Association I work for is a big organization now. We took over from the local authority last year; maybe took on more than we could handle. I've learned the hard way how chaotic this job can potentially get, with all the situations that can arise and the million ways that things can go wrong. But I know I'm good at keeping things running. Most of the time. Ninety-nine per cent of the time.

Outside, on the main staircase, there's the clatter of feet on the laminate flooring and snippets of voices: other people from other offices arriving for their own jobs on other floors, co-workers I rarely see and almost never interact with. Emma pushes herself back from her desk, and drains the last mouthful of tea from her mug. 'Okay,' she says. 'Well, I'm off out – electrician at Trinity Court.' She leaves her desk covered with bits of paper and open files; it's always like that, even over the weekend. I have to fight the urge to tidy. I feel a little more at ease once she's gone. It's harder when she's here; I feel more conscious of how I speak, how I look, keeping up the good impression. I suppose I should be able to let my guard down by now, and maybe I would if she and I were closer. We're a similar age so there's no real reason we shouldn't be friends; she's worked here with me for six months at least. It just isn't like that though.

I look again at my notes for today, unable this time to ignore the unpleasant task that I tried not to think about all weekend, ever since I booked the bailiffs last week. I flip through the folders in my drawer and find the right file, then pull the corresponding notes up on the computer. I triple-check to make absolutely sure there isn't a step we've missed, a reason to allow just a little more leeway, but there isn't. So I'll just have to go ahead.

It isn't an unusual occurrence, a tenant falling behind with their rent or some other payment. We get such a mix of people in the block. I push my chair back over the scuffed carpet – a faded shade of green – and head through to where my boss Abayomi sits next door. I heard him talking on the phone when I came in, his low voice with its rolling accent floating into the corridor.

Now I knock neatly on his half-open door. *My door is always open*, he tells us. He looks up from his desk, with its usual collection of used coffee mugs, his face so open, so non-judgemental that it's almost expressionless.

'Morning, Jenn.' His cheeks lever upwards as he smiles. 'All set for the day?'

I've always liked that about him. We don't talk about emotional or personal topics; we stay focused on the work and the tasks at hand. He is very practical, very pragmatic. I wouldn't like to have a boss who was always asking how I am, wanting to get to know about me outside of work, always considering the ways I might feel. Abayomi keeps things simple. Tight and professional. It feels much safer to me that way.

'I'm going to meet the bailiffs at nine thirty,' I remind him. 'Flat sixteen, Munroe House. Emma is out on visits too, so there won't be anyone in the office to answer the phone.'

'Okay, no problem, I can keep an ear out.'

'Thanks,' I say. 'Hopefully, I won't be long.'

Abayomi rubs at the stubble on his chin. He always looks a bit weary when he first gets in; I think maybe he does a school run, like me, or he has a complicated commute, or maybe he's just not much of a morning person. I've never asked him about it. He certainly drinks a lot of coffee.

'How many months in arrears is the tenant?' he asks.

I check the summary that I printed out towards the end of last week, when I realized we were going to have to do something. We had already sent plenty of warning letters. 'Three months,' I tell him.

The printout has all the details – quite precise evidence. Abayomi nods when I hold it out to him, his sign of approval, and even though it's silly really, a bit pathetic, it gives me a warm feeling just seeing that. There was a period a little while back when I was having some problems with Charlie, and I know I got behind and became disorganized, and since then I've tried harder than ever to be careful and on top of things. My relationship with Abayomi – our working relationship – means a lot to me. I know he thinks highly of me professionally, and I often have to hold on to that at times when I'm not so sure of myself; I suppose quite a lot of my self-esteem, self-worth, whatever you might call it, is tied up with it. Even last year, I never let him see me slip up. I still managed to come in every day, turn up on time, be smartly dressed, make the switch. Abayomi never knew how bad it got; I didn't tell him and he didn't ask, and I'm on top of it now so there's no need to mention anything.

I check the clock above his head. 'I'd better head off.'

'Good luck,' he says, his cheeks lifting again as he smiles. 'I've every faith in you.'

It's 9.20 a.m. now, and back in my own office I check that I have everything I need: the file and its printout, my work mobile that has only work numbers on it, and the master key which will open up the flat, if we need. I even have my coat on already, and yet I somehow don't feel able to head straight out. Instead I duck into the staff toilets to check myself in the mirror. It's me in the glass, of course it is, but this morning, the lines of my reflection seem a fraction out of place; when I move, I have the sense that my reflection moves a millisecond too late. It's fatigue, I tell myself, all that worrying that kept you up and the fact that it was all such a rush this morning. I run the tap, and bend to splash water round my eyes and cool the pouched, raw feeling of lack of sleep. In my handbag I have make-up, things I can use to tidy myself back up. My tube of mascara is running low – I have to push the brush down hard to the bottom – but I get enough to stiffen my lashes and my eyes look brighter after that. I check myself in the mirror again, catching the stray hairs that came loose in the wind and pushing them back into the tight elastic band at the crown of my head. Once that's done, I look all right, I think. Smart and meticulous. My normal professional self.

*

Even so, my stomach tightens as I head out of the office. I don't like this part of my job, I never have: stepping in when people's lives have gone so wrong, seeing all the mess and muddle that they've made. I want to help. In my job, all I'm trying to do is make people safe: getting a roof over their heads; space, security, warmth. I suppose, in a way, it scares me a bit, knowing how easily things can go wrong. How everything might fall apart without you being able to do anything about it.

Outside, I head up the road that rises towards Streatham. Our offices are above a row of shops on Brixton High Street, and the block that we manage is at the bottom of Brixton Hill. Brixton is loud and bright and chaotic: trains on the bridge, buses pushing along the wide road and the pedestrian traffic lights blipping and beeping. The shapes and sounds jangle together, and there's a smell in the air, like scorched tyres. In the street behind me, someone is shouting and I can't tell whether it's in excitement or anger, but I don't look. Most times, it's best not to get involved.

It's better once I get up to the Ritzy Cinema; the space outside here is open and welcoming, with that tree that makes a little canopy with its branches. I'd like to sit down in one of the friendly outdoor seats for a moment and wait until my stomach doesn't feel so tight, but of course there isn't time and anyway the green man at the crossing is flashing so instead I just hurry across the road.

Brixton has got a lot fancier since I came here four years ago, gentrifying in the way people have been predicting for ages. There are more white people now in these neighbourhoods, the kind who eat brunch in Brixton Market and drink flat whites in Café F. I live in a flat halfway up Brixton Hill, ex-local authority and still only affordable because of the deposits that arrive in my bank account every three months. I don't think I could keep living in London otherwise.

When I reach the block, I have to double-check my notes to recall which staircase flat sixteen is on: bottom of staircase B.

These flats near the bottom of Brixton Hill aren't the only ones we manage. There's another block on Effra Road, and another one that we've just taken on from the council on the road that runs from Brixton to Stockwell. The more buildings we take on, the more tenants we have, to the point where there's a danger of them becoming anonymous, less like individuals and more just another number on a spreadsheet.

Outside Munroe House, there are pigeons scuffling around and loose feathers are stuck to the paving slabs leading up to the door. It doesn't matter how often we get bits repaired and the paintwork redone on this block, it always seems to look more run-down than I want it to. At the main doors to staircase B, I let myself in with the security code, punching it into the brand-new system we got installed at the end of last year. It's one of the most secure I've ever seen. There is a back entrance to the block too which leads out onto a little grassy area, and you can get to it from the street via an alleyway that runs up the side of the block. Flat sixteen, if I remember rightly, faces out towards the back.

It's 9.29 now. I close my eyes and take a few careful breaths while I wait in the cramped lobby for the bailiffs to arrive. The handful of other times I've done this, the bailiffs were always punctual, and when I open my eyes a few seconds later, I see them, pushing through the wind. I open the entrance door for them, from the inside, and let them into the building.

They are both quite a bit bigger than me. The thick-set, bald one I recognize. His partner looks younger and has a plain, kind face. Not for the first time I wonder how they ended up in this job. And how it feels to do this kind of work, day in, day out.

I introduce myself – *I'm Jennifer Arden* – and shake hands with them both. I'm careful to make good eye contact, use a firm grip, something I've perfected, over time.

'Flat sixteen is right here,' I say as we head into the building proper. My speech is perfectly articulated, every word pronounced properly. There are three staircases in the whole block: A, B and C, with fifteen flats off each. Except here, in staircase B, there's a funny extra flat, tucked away on the ground floor, number sixteen. The door to it is sort of hidden under the stairs so you could quite easily miss it.

The bailiff with the kind face takes a deep breath and knocks hard on the door. 'Ms Jones? Ms Jones, we are here about your unpaid rent.'

Before I started in this job, I used to picture bailiffs bashing in people's doors and dragging furniture out into the street. Of course, it isn't like that. We've sent this tenant a letter to let her know we're coming. All we want today is to ensure Ms Jones knows about her debts. That's why I'm here. Hopefully, I can agree a payment plan with her, something to bring her out of this mess.

The bailiff knocks again, thump thump.

I think I can make out voices coming from inside, but as I lean closer I hear someone saying *Capital FM!*, and I realize it's just the radio playing. A song comes on a moment later: 'Everywhere' by Fleetwood Mac. If the radio is on though, I can be pretty sure she's in there. We'll keep knocking and hope that eventually she will come to the door, even if she doesn't open it. She has a right not to open it to us, but I really hope we can speak to her today. That way I have a chance to help. We can let things go for a while – the longest I can remember was four months – but we can't just let it go on for ever. Ms Jones is already three months behind. We've sent half a dozen letters, but she didn't reply to any of them, so now it's come to this. If we can't arrange some kind of payment schedule today, the next step is an eviction notice and I would really hate it to come to that.

'Ms Jones?' the bailiff calls again.

There are footsteps on the stairs above. I step back and look up to see who's coming. A neighbour from upstairs, nobody I recognize, a black woman, smartly dressed, probably on her way out to work. There are dozens of people living in this block but now I wonder how many of them speak to each other or even know their neighbours' names. But she must pass this way at least, most days. 'Excuse me,' I call out to her. 'Do you know the tenant in this flat? Is she usually home at this time?'

The woman comes down the last few stairs.

'She's got the radio on,' I say. 'We're assuming she's in.'

The woman pauses next to us and shrugs. 'Her radio is always on,' she says. 'I hear it every time I go by.'

She loiters for another moment between the staircase and the doors to the outside, sizing us up. But she is busy, she has her own life to be getting on with, and no doubt she's learned that it's best in a big city like this not to get involved. 'Sorry,' she offers as she hitches her handbag more securely onto her shoulder and makes her way through the heavy door to the lobby.

We turn back to the flat and the other bailiff knocks this time, his fist bigger, his knock that bit louder. I look down at the file of papers I am still holding against my chest. I wasn't the one who moved this tenant in; in fact, the person who did doesn't even work for us any more, but I've been in the flat before; I checked the last tenant out. I can still picture it. The tiny flat is only a bedsit really, tucked away under the stairs. The living room and bedroom are one and the same, the sofa tucked behind the front door doubling as a bed, and there is a kitchen, but only an archway divides the two, so you could hardly even call them separate rooms. There's a tiny toilet, with a shower attachment that hangs, a little bit crooked, above a plastic bath. And that's it.

The last tenant, I remember, only stayed a few months. They complained about the commercial waste bins that always somehow ended up against the rear wall of this block, even though they belonged to the restaurant twenty yards away. Then the flat was empty for a good while, until this tenant moved in a year ago. Into this flat, now allocated to me.

The song has flipped over and it's another tune that's playing now. I recognize this one too: 'Beautiful Day' by U2. Out of nowhere I get a sort of roiling feeling in my stomach and a prickling up the base of my spine. I hand my file of papers to the bailiff with the plain, kind face and walk right up to the door. I bend my knees so that my eyes are level with the letterbox and lift up the flap. With my cheek against the flaky wood of the door I look through the slat of a gap that has opened up.

I see all the post, a slithering pile of it silting up the floor on the other side of the door. No doubt the letters we sent are among it. The strangest smell reaches me in thin wisps from inside. I let the flap of the letterbox fall and straighten back up. My chest has gone tight. I can't seem to speak.

I find myself thinking back to what happened with the spreadsheet I was in charge of last year and the annual inspection I was responsible for. The bailiffs are looking at me, but I can't find a way to tell them what seems to be wrong. The older one leans down, copying what I have just done and sees for himself what's through that narrow space. He puts a palm on the door, as though to steady himself.

He manages to say something and what he says is: 'Holy shit.'

Chapter 2

None of us can make sense of what is going on yet. At this point, I am telling myself that, despite the radio being on, the flat is empty and the tenant must have left months and months ago for it to be in the state it is now, with all that post piled like a rubbish dump on the other side of the door. All I'm allowing myself to think at this point is that Ms Jones left the flat without telling us and without making any arrangements regarding rent, and for some completely bizarre and unknown reason she's left the radio playing Capital FM. We've had this before, tenants just abandoning their flat, leaving it in a mess, rent in arrears; it's part of the reason we take deposits.

I dig the master key out of my pocket. Under usual circumstances, we would give the tenant twenty-four hours' notice, but in this case we've already sent all the letters we could and it's clear they've all been going unanswered. I have to push hard to get the key to slide into the lock; the mechanism seems gummed up. Behind me, the younger bailiff is still holding the tenant's file as I twist the key and push at the door with the flat of my palm. The pile of letters twists like a doorstop underneath, a great wedge of paper trying to hold us back, but with my shoulder I can lever the door open and it does so, an inch, half a foot. Then it jams completely. That's when I start to feel a bit sick.

I see what's jamming it. The safety chain is stopping the door in its tracks, a safety chain that someone has fastened from the inside. And that's when, behind me, the bigger bailiff of the two, the one who must have seen so many things in his time, says in a voice that has gone low and gravelly, 'We need to call the police.'

*

It feels like for ever before they arrive. It's as though I'm in a dream the whole time that we're waiting. The bailiffs and I hardly speak. I know I should try to contact Abayomi back at the office and let him know what's going on, but I can't bring myself to do it, not yet. I tell myself we don't even know for sure, I tell myself this could all look much worse than it is, and that once the police get here and we actually enter the flat – this flat I'm responsible for, which is allocated to me and no one else – we'll find out it really is nothing, all a big misunderstanding and the worst thing we'll have to worry about is wasting police time.

There are blue lights strobing outside and, moments later, five of us crowded outside the flat in the tiny stairwell. Silently, the younger bailiff hands me back Ms Jones's file.

The first officer – a man – takes one look at the jammed door, the avalanche of post and says, 'You were right to call us.' Those words should be reassuring, telling me that we've done exactly the right thing, but instead I'm suffocated with guilt all over again.

I can't stop it now, what we are about to find. A female police officer is fiddling with the security chain using some instrument they must have brought with them specially, and it only takes a second before there's a crack and the chain falls loose with a shrill jangle and now the officer can push the door right open, backing up all the post behind it.

She pauses on the threshold and reaches into a pouch on her belt. When she pulls out a pair of thin blue gloves and tugs them over her hands, snapping them into place at the wrist, then I know just how serious this is.

The gloved officer steps into the tiny flat. That radio is still playing – God knows how long it's been on like that. I step into the flat as well, and I can feel the two bailiffs crowding behind me. I can just about see past the police officer's shoulder and the first thing that stands out is all the dust and cobwebs. Nothing has been cleaned in here for … what? Months? The whole place is covered with dead flies; a thousand tiny bodies, a thousand tiny wings. And the smell is like nothing I've ever smelt before, heavy, musty, cloying and bitter at the same time, like breathing in wet sand, as if the air in here has swollen into itself. I can see through the arch into the kitchen from here and there's a collection of pretty cups hanging from hooks under the cabinet, pans by the hob, and a little plaque propped against the wall that reads *Family Is The Dearest Thing*. There's a chest of drawers in the corner of the living room – or bedroom, whichever you want to call it – with a mirror on top coated in dust.

When the two officers fan out in front of me, I notice the table. The fold-out table set up against the far wall. It is set for three with plates, cutlery, glasses and a bottle of wine, all thickly dusted as well. Dead flowers in a vase, grey drooping stems and shrivelled brown blooms, and even more dead flies scattering the table surface, dozens of them. I step further into the flat – the five of us now are taking up so much of the space – and that is when I see her.

I clap my hand to my mouth. My whole stomach lifts up on itself, pushing against my lungs to eject everything inside. Fighting the urge to be sick, I clench both hands against my mouth now, trying not to breathe in another molecule of that air – that smell – now I know what it is. My whole body feels as if it is flipping upwards in shock and my mind jerks and jerks, trying to free itself of what I've seen. I stagger sideways, trying to turn away, and instead bumping straight into the large bailiff behind me, caught by his shoulder and brought to a halt. In the press of bodies I can't escape, I can only stand there, gagging myself with my own hands as the male police officer steps past me, into the tiny little kitchen area, and clicks the radio off.

The silence is awful. It makes it so much worse, because now there is no escape from the awful sense of emptiness in the flat, and the realization that I am never going to get that sight out of my head, that crumpled, shrunken shape on the sofa, because no matter how much I try to tell myself I don't know what it is, I do, I do.

The female police officer turns and holds her arms out like a cordon. 'All right, everyone out,' she says. 'We need to treat this as a crime scene.'

Chapter 3

The moments just after those words go blank. They become white squares in which I have no sense of what is happening around me. What I saw has knocked me right out of myself. It feels like something out of a horror movie, but this is real. My tenant should be here, walking, talking. Instead on the couch there is a body, but a body that is so worn away: hair, bones, teeth, all that's left of a person.

I find myself back at the bottom of the stairwell, my breath coming in heaves and gasps, gripping Ms Jones's file against my chest like a shield. Layers and layers of my neat, precise paperwork clipped inside, as though any of that can help me now.

*

The next piece of time is jumbled. I'm aware of the female police officer radioing someone, and then other officers arriving. One of them draws me aside, stylus poised above an electronic notebook, asking for my name and address, and my connection to this flat, this tenant, and where they can reach me, checking that I'll be in the office all day, can they come and find me and take my full statement there?

I can't avoid it now. I will have to go back to the office and tell Abayomi everything.

When they have my details, they let me go. As I walk back up the street towards our office, I feel like a ghost. The wind seems to blow right through me and my whole body feels hollow. It's hard to place one foot before the other and keep walking in a straight line. Those shrunken remains on the couch, that form that was supposed to be a person, how can I unsee that, and what happened, *what happened?*

In the office, my desk looks exactly as I left it, as though nothing has changed at all and the world hasn't just turned upside down. Emma isn't back yet, but there's a message on my personal phone that still lies face down on the desk where I left it. Feeling as though I am standing outside my own body, I swipe to open it. *Please don't worry about what happened this morning. Charlie has settled in fine and is having a good day. If you wish to discuss anything further, please feel free to call.*

I leave the phone there on the desk and force myself to walk to Abayomi's door and knock. When he calls me in, I sit down in the chair across from him without even being asked to. I set Ms Jones's file down in front of me, lining its edges up with those of the desk. I try to find the right words to say it, think what any normal person would do.

'Something has happened,' I manage to tell him. Abayomi lowers his mug of coffee, setting it down on a coaster that bears our company logo. I fight with myself not to let my voice shudder or the muscles in my legs shake. On the inside, it feels as though the whole of me is trembling, as if there's a kind of earthquake running through my core. But on the outside, on the surface, nothing shows. This is my job; this is my work, my profession. This is the proof of my competence in the world.

'We found something,' I tell him, 'in flat sixteen. A body.' Even as the words come out of my mouth they sound ridiculous, impossible to me. Over my shoulder, I catch sight of Emma, back from her appointment and hovering in the doorway. Abayomi glances up and sees her too.

'Just give us a moment, will you, Emma?' He gets up and closes the door gently, ushering her away. When he sits back down again, I clamp my teeth together because it feels as if my whole jaw wants to chatter. 'The police will be coming here soon to take a statement,' I say. But how am I ever going to explain to him, this thing that has happened, in that flat, on my watch?

'The police are at the flat now?' Abayomi asks.

'Yes. The door was ... we had to call them.'

'Okay, good,' says Abayomi. He draws a sheet of paper towards him, makes a note. 'That's the most immediate concern. Alerting them, making sure the scene is secure.' He looks up. Perhaps he sees how ashen my face is because his tone becomes gentle. 'Listen, Jenn, it happens. A tenant dying at home. This isn't the first time and it won't be the last.'

His pen rests against the paper, ready to take down details. 'So, it's flat sixteen?' he says. 'And the tenant's name?'

I open the file in front of me.

'Jones,' I reply. 'Ms Sarah Jones.' I press my finger to the page where it's written, as if to keep my mind in place. On the cover sheet, right next to the name, I see the date of birth. Something knocks at the side of my mind, some thought or memory, but I can't grasp what it is. Instead, my jittering brain does the calculation. 'Abayomi?'

He's still writing.

'She was only twenty-six,' I blurt out.

He looks up now, surprise on his features, his pen hovering. Is he thinking the same as me? *She was young. She was so young.*

He clears his throat. 'Council tenant or private?'

'Private.' Somehow my voice is still coming out steady. 'Assured shorthold.'

'All right, fine.' He inhales through his nose and sits back slightly. 'We'll need to liaise with her next of kin, once the police have spoken with them, so we can arrange surrender of the tenancy. You said an officer is coming to see you later today?'

'Yes, I think so. I can check with them then.'

Abayomi nods. 'Okay, good.'

I look up at the clock on the wall behind him. It's five to eleven. I had no idea we were at the flat for so long.

'And …'

'Yes?' Abayomi continues to speak with that quiet patience he has, and I keep fighting to draw myself together, becoming – on the outside at least – perfectly composed.

'And she had rent arrears. Will we have to settle those too?'

He nods. 'If we can. And once the police are in touch with the next of kin, we can look to arrange transfer of her possessions. Then …' He rubs a thumb across one eyebrow. '… cleaning of the flat. There's a specialist company that we've used once before.'

All these details, all the steps in the procedure should anchor me: knowing that my boss knows what to do and that this has happened before and that there are rules and regulations, a plan to follow, actions we can take.

Abayomi is making it all sound so simple, so routine.

But he doesn't know.

He doesn't have the full facts to hand.

I have to say something. There is no way I can avoid this. All I can do is state it clearly, professionally. Show self-awareness and a willingness to learn from my mistake. My words come out in a rush.

'Abayomi, I have to tell you now. Last summer, I made certain errors. I should have told you but I didn't. There were checks that I didn't carry out. The annual inspection for that flat. I missed it and I didn't tell you. I marked it in the spreadsheet as done. The body – the person …'

I break off, then force myself to continue. 'I think it's been there for a really long time.'

Abayomi's dark skin pales. He lowers his pen. He isn't writing things down any more. There is the longest silence between us, nothing but the scratching tick of the clock above his head. I can see him readjusting his every assessment of me.

'And the police want to speak to you?' he asks again, double-checking everything I've just said.

I swallow down the lump in my throat. 'Yes,' I tell him again. 'This afternoon.'

'All right,' he says, his voice now strangely, almost eerily calm. My punishment hovers somewhere above us, out of sight but surely within reach. 'Go back to your desk,' he says. 'Stay there until the police officer comes. Answer whatever questions they ask. If any journalists contact you, don't speak to them. In the meantime, I need to make a few calls.'

I stand, gathering up Ms Jones's file. The pages are ruffled, creased now. No longer pristine. It takes me two goes to open Abayomi's door, my fingers slipping on the handle, unable to let myself out. I can feel his gaze on my back as I leave.

When I come back into our shared office, Emma stares at me, her mouth open.

'What is it?' she whispers. 'What's happened?'

I wonder if she listened outside the door and actually already knows. I feel as if she's heard everything – as if my mistake is written like a brand across my forehead.

'Nothing … just a … mix-up. The tenant wasn't there. There was a problem, and now the police …' I stop.

Emma is staring at me, her smartphone hovering in her hand, waiting for me to go on. But I can't. I can't bear to tell her and so instead I just take off my coat because suddenly it is stifling in here, and sit down at my desk, staring at the photograph of Charlie in its carved wooden frame, looking anywhere to avoid Emma's gaze. When she switches on her computer, its cheerful little start-up tune feels so out of place. She clatters at the keyboard, her too-long nails getting in the way, same as ever, and I go on staring at my picture of Charlie until my eyes blur, just waiting until the police officer finally arrives.

*

It's the female officer from before. I feel a rush of air into my lungs when I sense the sympathy in her face, and then my chest tightens again. *It's only because she doesn't know yet what you did.* But this is serious, this is the law, and I promise myself I will tell her everything.

She sends Emma out of the room while I'm interviewed. I picture her hovering in the staff kitchen, excluded from everything that's going on, checking her Instagram while she waits.

'She was three months behind with her rent,' I begin. 'We'd had to call the bailiffs. That's who I was with at the flat. We kept knocking, and calling her name but there was no answer.'

The next moments come to me in flashes, disjointed, my mind flinching away from them like a hand from a hot stove.

I describe the sound of the radio playing and the sight of all the post piled up behind the door. 'And then ... and then when we saw ... that she still had the chain on ...'

I stop, break off and reach for Ms Jones's file. All of her details are in here. The ordered facts. The date almost a year ago when she took possession of the flat; the name of the manager who moved her in; Ms Jones's signature for her two sets of keys.

The file I have holds various other forms. Her tenancy agreement, various personal details. I hand them over.

'And when did you last see this tenant?' the officer asks.

I feel the heat climb from my neck to my temples. 'I never did,' I say. The truth. 'Someone else was in charge the day she moved in.'

The officer looks at the papers I've given her. 'This was a year ago?'

I nod. 'Yes. Just about.'

The officer takes longer than normal to write this down in her notebook. I can see all the questions in her head.

'I'll take that colleague's details, if you have them. If necessary, we'll follow up with them.'

'Yes. Of course.' I have the details, right here, in my drawer. A forwarding email, a personal mobile. Look how organized I am. I copy them all down for her.

'Did you have any contact from Ms Jones since then? Were there any repairs she required? Any complaints?'

I shake my head. 'Nothing from her. She never contacted me. And –' I check the file to make sure – 'nothing from neighbours either. It was only when we found in November that her rent wasn't being paid that we had any reason to be in touch. She was a private tenant. She paid her rent to us via direct debit.'

'And what did you do then?'

'We – I – tried to call. I couldn't reach her, her phone seemed to be switched off. Then we sent letters. That's our protocol, to ring and then officially write. We followed our standard procedures for arrears.'

'That's common for your tenants?'

'Not common, but it happens sometimes.' I think about all the protocols we have. A directive for any situation that might arise. But this situation has no real protocol; this situation feels completely unreal.

'Okay, so no rent … But her electricity bills were all up to date?'

I stare at her, wrong-footed, confused.

She speaks slowly, as if I'm not keeping up. 'You said her radio was playing. I'm assuming that she had it plugged in.'

'Of course. Yes. It was. It was playing.'

'All right. So, any explanation for that? Why she'd stop her rent but keep her utilities running?'

The image flashes before my eyes again: that collection of bones laid out upon the cushions. I press my hands to my head, pressing it away, and try to make sense of the officer's question. 'Maybe …' I try to think of the simplest answer: one that won't trigger more questions, more suspicion. 'Maybe she didn't actually cancel her rent? Is it possible that her money just … ran out? And then …' I lift my head. I think I can see it. 'If she'd been paying her utility bills by quarterly direct debit – November to February, that's three months – wouldn't that mean her electricity wouldn't yet be shut off?'

The officer looks at me; she seems faintly impressed, as if I've done well to construct such a theory. Or does she think I've worked this all out beforehand and now I'm just trotting it out to cover something up?

'Well,' she says. 'That we can probably check.' She nods as though she's satisfied for now and I hold her gaze until she turns over to a fresh page in her notebook. 'We don't even know for sure yet that it's her,' she continues. 'Hopefully we'll know from the results of a post mortem. We've taken some personal items from the flat – a hairbrush, toothbrush – that we can hopefully check against bone DNA.'

More details, pressing into my brain. I rest my hand against my temple, as though I can protect myself that way.

'Did you visit the flat recently?' The officer pushes on with her questions and I've promised myself I will tell the truth. I only lied on the spreadsheet, and it was only that once.

'I delivered the last letter by hand. Just through the letterbox. I didn't see her.'

'When?'

I check. 'A week ago.'

'But you didn't go in?'

For a dizzying moment I'm really not sure. I can't remember. I have to check the notes I've printed out, the notes in which I know I didn't lie. I look at them and say, certain now: 'No, I didn't.'

The officer holds my gaze for a moment then looks back down at her own notes. I realize I've clasped my hands together and I am twisting them hard enough to rub the skin raw. 'I have a son …' I begin and stop. How can that be an excuse? How can I expect anyone to understand? All of the problems with Charlie last year were my own, nobody else's business but mine. My voice is small. I am over thirty but I feel like a child again. 'I missed some of the checks. Last year, I was having some difficulties. I didn't carry out all the inspections I should have done. I'm sorry. I am really sorry.'

She writes something in her notebook and I have no idea what it is. No idea what judgement she has made of me.

She looks up. 'Do you know of anyone who might have wanted to hurt her?'

I should have been more ready for that question. Because don't women get hurt all the time? It goes on, it happens, it might have happened to Ms Jones: an attack, violence, a desperate struggle. My heart is hammering. The officer is still looking at me, waiting for an answer. 'Do you know of anyone?'

I shake my head, the muscles in my neck stiff. 'I'm sorry, I can't think. I didn't really know anything about her. I mean … wouldn't her family, her neighbours be the people to ask? I was only the housing manager.'

The officer nods again, but now I'm unsure what that means. I don't know what else they've already found out.

'Could you draw up a timeline then?' she asks. 'Your records of any contact with the tenant at all. Meanwhile, we'll get this statement typed up for you to sign.'

I nod. 'I'll do anything,' I say. 'Anything at all.'

She closes her notebook. There is a silence in the room as she gets to her feet, a silence that feels clogged with my guilt. I've forgotten to ask about liaising with next of kin. I've forgotten everything else I was meant to say. I want to cover my face with my hands, but I don't. I just go on sitting there, hands clasped, back straight, trying to present the best version of myself.

Just before she reaches the office door, she stops and turns back. 'Oh,' she says, 'just one more thing.' She pulls out her phone. 'The shoes you're wearing now, are they the same as the ones you were wearing this morning? When you entered the flat?'

I look down at my feet, my flat-soled ankle boots. 'Yes.'

She makes a gesture with her hand, palm up, a signal for me to stand. I get to my feet, confused as to what she wants.

'If you just step here and turn around,' she says, 'I can take a photo. For elimination purposes, you know? The footprints.'

I turn around, just as she's asked. Now I have my back to

her and I steady myself against my desk, fingertips pressed white against the wooden surface. Standing on one leg, I lift my foot, everything focused on not losing my balance.

Behind me, I hear the camera click.

Chapter 4

I am like a robot for the rest of the day. At three o'clock – the time I usually leave – I go in to Abayomi to ask permission. I feel as though I should ask permission for everything now.

'I'm sorry,' I say to him too. I say it again as I leave his office, but it doesn't seem to make anything better.

As I walk up the hill towards home and Charlie's school, I suspect I am in shock. All I can think is: *This happened on my watch*. That's the fact I can't get away from. Because I didn't do the checks – flat sixteen and other flats too – but still ticked them in the spreadsheet. Which means I am responsible. Because, last year, I wasn't keeping things together.

The brisk walk seems to do me some good though; the early February cold gets the blood moving again in my veins. I cut across the little patch of scrubby grass that takes me onto Endymion Road, past pigeons shoving and pecking at bits of bread in the mud. I head along Elm Park to Charlie's school, glad to be here on time, as I am every day.

I take my place alongside the other parents, women and men with faces I know. Martin, one of the dads, catches my eye – by accident, but I make sure to smile at him anyway, like I'm supposed to. I do try. Every time I'm here, I try to build bridges. Martin smiles back, a sort of automatic reflex, but then another parent touches him on the arm and he turns away, smiling at her instead, smiling with relief, no doubt, glad to detach himself from me.

They don't know what's happened to you today, I tell myself; they can't see. Another mum brushes past me. 'Hello,' I say, because she and I used to be quite friendly and chat quite a bit at the gates. I've always done my best to keep to myself, keep as many people as I can at arm's length, but I used to interact with the other parents in the playground at least; we used to exchange some pleasant conversation twice a day.

'Oh – hello Jennifer,' she says, glancing at me over her shoulder, but that's it; she carries on across the playground to join her little welcoming group, melding in with them so easily, setting off a little laugh that makes my stomach drop. I haven't forgotten what happened last year and neither have they: how it all culminated in that awful moment at Charlie's sports day, in front of everyone, when I couldn't control myself, simply couldn't think straight. Now every exchange here is so painfully awkward. I thought I was getting used to the loneliness, but today it's harder than ever to stand there and pretend I fit in, while desperately trying to ignore the anxiety that gnaws at me. The worst kind of loneliness is when you are surrounded by other people, because then you know for sure that there is no hope, no real solution. Then you know that the problem isn't a practical or physical one; it's the messes you've made that won't ever let you get close.

I hold on to the fact that soon I'll see Charlie. Just the thought of him sends a wave of warmth through me, softening my muscles, slowing my heart. I remember reading once about oxytocin, how women produce it in childbirth, and after, and sometimes I like to tell myself that's what this feeling is: a rush of love hormone for my child. I hitch my handbag up on my shoulder and straighten the cuffs of my blazer. The children are starting to stream out now, boisterous and robust, their feet kicking up shards of gravel from the tarmac. And now I see him, my son. The sight of him still gets me every time, and today too, despite my numbed state, my mind fires out the irrepressible thought: *he is the most beautiful creature to me in the world*.

He lopes towards me, grinning, happy to see me, of course he is. He is tall enough now, eight years old, almost nine, that I can hug him standing up, almost straight. I bend the tiniest amount at the waist as he comes towards me and hold out my arms to him, just as all the other parents do for their own children. My God, he's beautiful, I think. Gladly, he pushes against me, wrapping his arms around my waist. I pull him close, wondering if he can feel my heart still jabbering in my chest as he leans against me, his bird-like ribs pressed to my stomach.

'Good day?' I ask him, my cheek against his hair.

'A good day,' he confirms, turning his face up to me, and my heart calms at once at his words.

It's only as I release him and he steps away that I see it.

His leg.

He looks as if he is dragging his leg.

My bones seem to twist as a shudder runs through me. I remember the appointment letter that came yesterday. I crouch down in front of him, jerking up his trouser leg. I'm looking for a cut, a mark, a bruise.

'Ow!' he exclaims. 'Mummy, what are you doing?'

31

'Did you hurt yourself?' I ask him. 'Did you hurt your leg?'
He twists away from me. 'What? Nuh-uh.'

I stare up at him. He stares down at me. His backpack slips from his shoulder, and I reach out and catch it just before it falls.

The movement brings me back to my feet. I shake my head. I am being ridiculous. 'Silly Mummy,' I tell him. 'I'm sorry.' I set the backpack back on his shoulders and get a hold of myself.

The other parents and children are trickling away now. I reach for his hand. For a moment, he squints up at me, then allows me to take it.

It isn't far to our flat, barely five minutes, and Charlie walks every one of them just fine.

*

At home, our little two-bed flat is reassuringly warm; the heating timer came on half an hour ago and already the radiators have heated it throughout. The hallway, the kitchen, the tiny living room are all so familiar and I am unspeakably glad to be home. This space I've created for me and Charlie, it's so precious. It's what I escaped to London for: our own little sanctuary in the world. For a moment though, as we step inside, I catch that smell again in my nostrils, the smell that was everywhere in flat sixteen – clogged, stale, everything collapsed. I hurry to unwrap Charlie from his clothes and put the oven on to cook him fish fingers, to fill up the kitchen with their smell.

I send Charlie to his room to get changed while I clatter a baking tray out of the cupboard and peas and fish fingers out of the freezer. The drawer is thick with ice; it needs defrosting and I have to yank at it to get it to slide out. It's another thing I must remember to do, and I get my list out of the kitchen drawer and add it on. There are already five other things on there, including the tap in the bathroom that drips and needs fixing and the query with our council tax bill that I need to call up about, and I'll get all of these things sorted, I will, but in the meantime, just having the list puts things in order. I fold the paper up again and set it back in the drawer.

I can hear Charlie singing to himself through in his bedroom, and the thump of his feet on our thin carpet as he hops about.

'Do you want salad or peas?' I shout through to him, and he yells back, 'Peas!' just as I knew he would, but I always ask him anyway; he gets less tetchy when I give him a choice.

I click on the kettle and bang the bag of peas against the counter to break up the lump that's formed in there. The biting cold in my hands feels good, feels like something; a sensation, a pain to keep me steady inside myself. Charlie comes back through in jogging bottoms and a T-shirt with a dragon on it. His arms look thin; he becomes more gangly each time he grows.

'So you had a good day?' I prompt, my voice cheerful and bright as he slides onto his chair at the kitchen table.

He shrugs one shoulder. 'Yep,' he says. 'We learned about the Ancient Egyptians. When you die, they pull your brains out through your nose.' He grin-grimaces up at me and I get another flash of it – the shrunken body on the sofa – and I fight not to think about it: *dying, dead, death.*

The oven is at temperature now; I swallow as I slide in the tray of breaded fish.

'So it was all right, in the end, with Ms Simmons?' I have to lift my voice so he can hear me over the noise of the kettle boiling. Charlie's normal teacher has had to take time off for a major operation and they've brought in a substitute. Charlie was already in a mood this morning; he said he didn't want to go into class, and I could see his temper flaring. I felt myself go rigid, crouching down in the primary school corridor, telling myself he was just a kid, who had a personality, who had moods. Crushing down the panic in my chest, hammering out a promise for him, a bribe, anything to make him stop. Telling him, *Please Charlie, just go in and I'll take you to the park for a whole hour after school. Come on, Charlie, go in, for me.*

And it's only now that I realize, after all the drama and confusion of the day, that I haven't kept my promise to him at all.

I grip the handle of the oven, waiting for his reply.

'I liked her,' Charlie says, sitting up straighter. 'She's funny, she told us a joke.'

I unclench my hand. 'That's good,' I say. 'Really good.'

I slip him my iPad to play with while I cook. To keep him calm; to keep myself calm. He is tired and hungry now, flagging after a busy day at school. Which means over-stimulated. Fatigued. His head lolls as he swipes at the screen. Before I can stop myself, I find myself cupping my hands over his ears, straightening him. Correcting it. Charlie scowls, pushing my hands away.

'Stop it,' he says.

I step back.

I pour boiling water from the kettle onto the peas, scalding the ice off them. I can feel the movement in the joints of my arm. Desperately, I try not to think of bones, the skeleton that lurks just under my skin.

'And what about *your* day, Mummy?' Charlie asks.

I manage to set the hot kettle back down before I have to reply. Charlie is eight years old. He is my son, just a child. I do my best to buy myself time, fiddling with the settings on the hob while I swallow hard, again and again, swallowing away everything I have seen this morning, shoving away those images that keep parading through my brain, forcing them out of our lives.

'Mummy's day was just grand,' I eventually tell him.

On the hob, the water in the pan is already simmering. I turn down the heat – no danger now of it boiling over – and go out into the hallway, where Charlie can't see me. I lean against the wall and take deep breaths. I tell myself to *get a grip*. As an excuse for being out here, I pick up Charlie's school bag from where he's dropped it by the door, the same as he does each time we get home, and take it back through to the kitchen to unpack. Ordinary, normal routines. They steady me.

In among his pencil case and the remains of his lunch, is a bright pink envelope, already open.

'What's this?' I ask as I pull it out.

Charlie looks up from the iPad. His ears look red from my earlier touch. 'A birthday,' he says. 'Molly in my class is having a party next month.'

I pull out the folded paper, bordered with balloons, and it's true. '*Molly invites Charlie*,' it says.

'You're invited,' I tell him, and he nods. 'Yep.'

I check the invite again. No one else has invited us anywhere for months. *Molly*. I haven't heard the name before. 'Is she new?' I say. 'New to your school?'

Charlie nods, and I think, *Well, that explains it.*

Even so, I stick the invite up with the SpongeBob magnet on the fridge, next to that letter with its blue and white NHS logo.

*

When the fish fingers are ready, we sit down together, me opposite him. He grins at me and, automatically, I smile back. I love Charlie. I love him so much, I never want anything to hurt him. Later, I tuck him into bed, set his glow light spinning and kiss his soft, smooth forehead. He is okay, of course he is okay, I can see that now. Look at how peacefully he sleeps. I've been making problems up in my mind.

Hours later, I lie awake in my own bed, the mattress hard beneath me. I lie with my eyes wide open in the dark and finally let myself think about everything that happened today. I find my body shaking with the shock and horror of it. I remember once how a doctor told me that this is the body's way of metabolizing out trauma, and so I let myself shake and don't try to stop it.

I only pray that, this time, it will work.

Chapter 5

Prin, nine years old, rides in the back of the car. She's wearing her favourite dress, the one she kicked up such a fuss about earlier this morning. Mum kept saying it *wasn't entirely appropriate*, but Prin knew how to clench her fists and make her chin wobble and that was when Daddy stepped in, all smiles, and said, *Let's not have an argument about this – why don't we just let Prin wear what she wants.*

So Prin got her way.

The dress is pink with a big flouncy skirt, and the taffeta makes a lovely rustling noise. As Prin sits strapped into the back, the engine rumbling along beneath them, she lifts her feet so she can see the shiny shoes she's wearing, pink as well, with little gold buckles on each side. They pinch her feet a bit; they are getting too small, but Prin likes them too much to tell Mum, who would only want to get rid of them and donate them to *the charity shop*.

She lifts her feet again, higher this time, and they bump into the back of Mum's seat. Mum twists round to look at Prin. 'What are you doing?' she says. 'Stop kicking.'

37

Once Mum has turned back round again, Prin scowls. She has a good scowl; she's practised it in the mirror by herself. But she wouldn't show the scowl to Mum. Or Daddy. Definitely not Daddy.

She stops kicking with her feet and looks out of the window instead. The seatbelt is tight across her shoulder, digging into her neck a bit. She can feel the shiny clip in her hair too, hard against her scalp. None of the scenery outside the window is familiar. She doesn't know where they are, and she can't actually remember the name of the place they're going to. All she knows is, they are going to fetch her cousin – a cousin that Prin has never even met before – who is going to come and stay with them for a bit. There was a whole other bit about today and what it is about; she overheard Mum and Daddy talking about it in the kitchen when she was supposed to be in bed. *Where else should she go?* Mum was saying and, *I just think it's all such a mess*, Daddy said. But then Daddy caught Prin, creeping in the hallway, and she ran back up to her room, hands and feet like a monkey on the stairs, half wanting to giggle and half wanting to scream, until she could get to her bedroom and slam the door tight. In the end, Daddy didn't come in, but she couldn't hear any more of what they were saying either.

Prin likes the idea of having a cousin come to stay. Mum has told her that the cousin is quite a bit younger than Prin, only seven, which Prin is pleased about because it means she'll be able to decide what games they will play or whose turn it will be to go first (it will be Prin's). At school, the other girls don't tend to listen much to what Prin has to say. They pick on her and tell her she's *stuck up*, but Daddy has said it's because they are jealous, because Prin lives in a big house and always has nice things.

The car comes bumping to a halt. 'All right,' Daddy says. 'Here we are!' He checks his watch – the big shiny watch that he sometimes lets Prin play with – and says that they have arrived right on time. Daddy cares a lot about being on time; he gets snappy on school days if they are ever running late.

They have arrived at someone's house. Prin doesn't recognize it. It doesn't belong to anyone she knows. It's quite a big house, but you can tell just by looking that it isn't as nice a house as Prin's. Mum and Daddy are undoing their seatbelts, so Prin undoes hers too. She opens the car door and slides out, careful that the puffy skirt of her dress doesn't catch. The shoes pinch again as her feet touch the ground, but when Mum comes round the car to check on her, she just smiles up at her and doesn't show it.

Mum holds out a hand for Prin and really Prin is far too big now for handholding, but Mum has a funny look on her face, tight and strained, and so she lets herself slip her hand into Mum's.

There's a little paved path to walk up to the house. Prin notices that some of the flagstones are cracked. Daddy knocks on the door and a woman opens it. She has a badge on a sort of ribbon around her neck.

'Fiona,' she says, which Prin realizes is her way of introducing herself, and she holds out a hand to Prin's mum and daddy. Daddy shakes her hand and says, in a very jolly voice, 'Brian,' and then pointing to Mum: 'Susan.'

Prin looks up at the grown-ups. 'And I'm Prin,' she says.

Mum smiles and puts her free hand on top of Prin's head,

her signal that Prin has said something silly. 'Well, that isn't really …'

Mum trails off. Daddy is still just standing there, grinning.

The woman with the badge hanging from her neck smiles and nods and tells them all to come inside. Prin pulls her fingers out of Mum's as they step in through the door. It was only Mum, really, who wanted to hold hands.

Inside the house there's a shiny white kitchen with two people – grown-ups – sitting at what is called a *breakfast bar*. Prin remembers right then that Daddy said they would all go and get ice cream after this. Prin feels much better, remembering how he promised. She really, really, really likes ice cream.

Prin doesn't know who these other grown-ups are, but they look nice enough. Fiona introduces them as Simon and Leanne. Now there are five grown-ups and only one of Prin, but through a big square archway into another room, she sees another girl. She is kneeling on the floor, playing with some kind of plastic model castle, pink and purple.

Her cousin. She is a lot smaller than Prin expected. The sitting room is white as well, with beige furniture in it. The girl looks quite babyish really. Prin reminds herself again about the ice cream that's coming later.

Now Fiona is leaning down. 'Would you like to go and play?' she says to Prin. 'Leanne and Simon have some lovely toys. There are some important bits – forms and so on – that I have to go through with your mummy and daddy, but you two could play in here while we get that done?'

Prin likes the look of the pink and purple castle. She supposes she wouldn't mind playing with that.

She lets the lady usher her forward into the beige and white room. The girl on the carpet looks up as they come through. She doesn't look as if she's been having much fun. There are streaks down her cheeks, as if she's been crying. Perhaps she doesn't much like this house. Prin imagines she'll like their own house much better.

They stop right in front of her.

Prin looks down at the model castle. She can see the collection of plastic characters that go with it now too: a prince, a princess, a dragon.

'What are you playing then?' she asks.

'Nothing really,' Prin's cousin says. 'It's just a castle.'

Prin studies this cousin who she's never met before, who doesn't look like much fun, who might even be a bit boring. Fiona is still standing there, waiting.

Prin's cousin looks up again. 'I like your dress,' she says.

Prin reconsiders her cousin. It *is* a nice dress. She's pleased her cousin said that. She drops down onto her knees, the skirt poofing out around her. The rug under her shins is a bit scratchy, but never mind. Her cousin wipes the back of her hand across her cheeks – a good thing to do. *No tears in this house*, Daddy would say. He says that a lot. *No tears in this house, believe you me.*

The lady with the badge steps back, leaving them to get along with it themselves.

The castle has different moving parts: doors you can open and close, a drawbridge you can wind up and down, banners you can clip on in different places.

Prin's cousin sighs. 'I've done all of those bits,' she says.

Prin looks at her. Is that how she's been playing? No wonder she wasn't having much fun. Prin isn't sure that she likes

41

this cousin much. She glances through to the grown-ups in the kitchen, wondering if she would be better off with them after all. But then her cousin is looking at her so hopefully, so eagerly. So sort of *admiring*. And she did say that she liked Prin's dress.

Prin wriggles on the scratchy carpet, getting a bit closer in. She's made up her mind. She likes the feeling of knowing best. She likes having someone to tell what to do.

'Watch me,' she says, picking up the dragon. 'I've got a much better game we can play.'

Chapter 6

The next day I'm light-headed, dizzy as I get ready for work. I've had a restless night. Every time I fell towards sleep, my body jerked me awake, flinching back from that form on the sofa: that relentless image. I finally fell into unconsciousness at about five and when my alarm rang, two hours later, I dreamed it was the police calling me. They were placing me under arrest.

Charlie is sluggish today; I have to tell him three times to get up. The third time I go into his room, he's sitting slumped on the edge of his bed, loose-limbed, his eyelids drooping.

'I'm tired,' he complains. 'My head is all heavy.'

He goes to lie back down, but I catch his arm, pulling him back upright. The breakfast that I pushed down – a single slice of toast with Marmite – sits in a lump under my ribs. 'We're going to be late,' I tell him. 'Stop messing about.'

And still he flops about in my arms as I tug off his pyjamas, setting more of my anxious thoughts racing, so that I have to fight to cage them away.

He looks chilly without any clothes on though, and maybe the cold wakes him up a bit as he looks more alert. 'Come on,' I say, 'you can dress yourself now,' and he sighs – a put-on, theatrical gesture – and fetches his trousers from the drawer, getting going at last. But over breakfast his conversation is stilted, there are gaps between his words, as though he can't fish out the ones he wants.

'I need my pencil-thing,' he says. 'I need my ... stamp ... my stickers.'

These are things my brain registers, signs my mind is desperate to log, but I refuse, this time, to read anything into it. He's a child, I repeat to myself, and all children struggle at times. I chivvy him along, taking his half-finished bowl of cereal off him and helping push his arms into his coat, making up valuable time.

At the school gates, we join the back of the crowd and I make sure he has his backpack on straight and kiss him on the cheek, wondering whether he's too old for that now, whether it's strange, no longer appropriate. Just as the teacher appears to usher the children in, a girl and her mother come hurrying up, running late. Charlie waves and calls out 'Molly!'

So now I can put a face to the name. Molly's mother looks nice, kind and friendly, and she catches my eye with a lopsided smile, a mum-to-mum moment but one that I'm too anxious to respond to properly. Something that should be so easy to do. Flustered, I busy myself instead with stiffly shooing Charlie inside and just give a stupid, awkward wave to Molly's mother as I rush away, keen to get to work, but really wishing I had said something about the party invite and told her then and there that we'd come.

As I hurry down to the office, I have to walk right past Munroe House and those doors with the code that I know off by heart. It's a wound I can't stop touching. A horror jumping at the corner of my eyes. Nothing in the flat was as it should have been. I saw a home turned inside out; every comforting thing inverted. *The body, the bones.* I turn my head away, trying not to look when the outer door swings open and I glimpse what looks like a forensic team inside. The figures in white coveralls – is that really what it is now? A crime scene.

And then someone pushes past me and I'm pulled back into the crowd again, letting it carry me on down the road.

I'm grateful that I have a full morning of tasks to occupy my jittering mind. There are half a dozen visits on my to-do list, most of them urgent, all of them important. I force myself to focus. First I have to respond to a call that came in early this morning. It is a young family: a working mum and stay-at-home dad with three children.

'Thank Christ,' says the dad when he opens the door to me. 'We tried to fix it ourselves, but it's got worse, it's a proper non-stop dribble now.' He shows me through to the pipe in the shower, pushing a mildewed curtain aside and telling me not to mind the clutter of bath toys. The leak is bad, in danger of turning into a damaging flood, but it's a familiar problem for me to solve. We have a plumbing company who always answer the phone. I go out into the hallway of the flat and dial the number. It's a quick, easy conversation, and then I can tell my anxious tenant that the plumber will be there within the hour, an emergency call-out that we will cover. He's so grateful and I feel efficient, competent, buoyed right up by being able to help. And for twenty minutes, I've not thought about Ms Jones once.

After that I have three inspections to do at the block in Effra Road. The flats here are more modern; the block was only built two years ago and inside the paint is still fresh, not faded and peeling like in Munroe House. As I climb the stairs, I sense a warmth to these flats, something so much friendlier in the atmosphere. But Ms Jones chose that tiny, anonymous flat, tucked away from everything. She could have lived somewhere like this. Wouldn't she have preferred it?

The first flat has no problems. The tenants have looked after it well, kept it tidy and clean and well-aired. Everything matches the inventory as it should. The mum stands in the doorway of the kitchen, watching me as I walk round, a baby balanced on her hip, a toddler busy crayoning at the table in the kitchen. There are family photos stuck up all over their fridge, her husband making up the group of four.

Family Is The Dearest Thing.

But where were Ms Jones's family? Where were her friends?

The frightened part of my mind wants to shut it all out, but with each flat I visit, questions seem to breed, multiplying in the tissue of my brain. I try to tell myself, the police aren't even sure yet if it's her. You're assuming that body on the couch was your tenant, but you don't know that. Maybe someone was squatting there, maybe Ms Jones is elsewhere, totally fine.

The next flat I visit is messy, lived in. There's a family with five children, toys everywhere. My mind flashes back and forth: these living spaces, full of life and movement, and the grim emptiness of Ms Jones's apartment. Lifeless, frozen in time, a mausoleum. Something happened there, but what, but what? The scene lies wrapped in cobwebs, abandoned months ago with *no one ever knowing*. Now her home is cordoned off for forensics, a crime scene, where any kind of horror might have happened.

In the final flat live a couple – modern, young. There are

rows of books on the shelves and artsy prints on the walls, the same as you'd see in a hundred London flats. And Ms Jones's flat too, under the dust, seemed so ordinary. Those cups I saw, hanging in her kitchen – this couple here have exactly the same ones.

And there were plates on the table and glasses and wine for her guests …

And I so want to believe that the body wasn't hers.

*

The visits eat into my lunch break but I don't have much of an appetite anyway, and really I'd rather just get on. I head straight back to the office and when I get there and check my phone, there is a message for me. The police officer I spoke to just yesterday wants to see me again. She's arriving three minutes from now and I hardly have time to take off my coat and scarf before she is knocking at the office door. Emma is out, meaning Abayomi must have buzzed her up.

'Hello again, Jennifer,' she says, coming in. I'm trying to remember her name. Did she even tell me it the first time? If she did, it didn't register, and it feels too late now to ask her. I open my desk drawer and fumble for the timeline I put together before I left yesterday, pleased that I have it ready for her. Here it all is in black and white, adapted from the notes I meticulously kept. There couldn't be an error, I couldn't have forgotten. Not this time. This time, I know what's true, and what was a lie.

The officer closes the door carefully behind her and sits down across from me at my desk. Now I can glimpse her name badge: PC Delliers. Yes, that's right.

47

'Here,' I say, passing her the timeline. 'This is what I've pulled together.'

Honestly, it didn't take long, there's hardly anything on it. The date when the flat was let to Ms Jones, almost a year ago; the date when the gas safety check and the fire alarm tests were done, last March. I've attached the certificates; no problems raised. But then a note of when the annual inspection was due, last June. The one I missed, the one I lied about. The date last November when we sent the first notice about rent, and I've made a note on the page, neatly, to say the rent was always paid up till then. Then here are the dates of our follow-up letters. And the only other thing is yesterday's visit.

There is so much blank space. It looks awful. Anything could have happened in that time. Someone could have done all kinds of things. There could have been mental health problems, a drug addiction, a volatile relationship; but no one was checking, so how would anyone know? And then she lay there, alone, for months and *months*. A fact that's so awful, so terrifying. I always tell myself I care so much about helping people, but with Ms Jones I completely messed up.

'Thank you for these,' PC Delliers says. 'We'll log them and get another statement to say you've provided them.'

'But … do you have any idea what happened?' I didn't mean to ask. I didn't think I wanted to know, but since walking round those other flats, the shock-horror of it has morphed into bewilderment, a kind of despair. I just can't stop thinking about her, about her life. How awful it would be to have it end like that.

PC Delliers takes my timeline and the other papers. 'We'll know much more after the post mortem. Identity, maybe even the cause of death. In the meantime …'

She hands me several sheets of paper, each neatly typed with spaces on each for me to sign.

'Take your time,' she says. 'Read it through and let me know if there's anything we need to change or add or correct.'

It's my statement. My own words stare up at me. *It's not a confession*, I tell myself. *You made a mistake but now you are doing your best to help.* The words are blurry though. There's a declaration too, printed all across the top. It says I'll be liable for prosecution if I state anything that isn't true, and suddenly I find myself thinking, could I actually have gone in there and forgotten? Could I have done something and hardly remembered, hardly realized? Like before? Like back then?

She's holding a pen out to me. I remember lifting my foot, the click of the phone camera.

'But ...' I say, 'I'm not in trouble, am I?'

She looks back at me with a strange, expectant expression. 'No ...?' There's a beat of silence then, as though she's giving me room to say something else.

I tell myself I'm being silly, panicking over nothing. I know myself, don't I? Surely I know the things that I've done. I pull myself together and take the pen she offers. I sign, my hand nice and steady. Easy. Done.

'By the way,' she says as I hand her back the pen. 'We were able to check Ms Jones's bank statements. Turns out you were right about the direct debits and the money running out.'

'Really? I was?' I don't know whether to feel sad or relieved, whether that makes things better for Ms Jones or worse. I suppose right now I'm just glad the officer knows I haven't lied.

PC Delliers nods. 'So at least we've cleared that up. Now,

just one more thing. Do you have details of this tenant's next of kin? We'll need to contact them, as soon as we've ID …'

Of course. We have next-of-kin details here for all our tenants. Ms Jones's file is on my desk. It is a thin file, just the basic forms and nothing more, but it's as neat as any file I keep, even though its corners are a little crumpled now, crushed from that day when we opened up her flat. I flip through the sheets to the relevant page, her email address catching my eye as I do.

'Here.' I turn the document around so that we can both see it. In the next-of-kin space, Ms Jones has written a name, *Peter Duggan*, and a phone number with a London code. Her brother? Her father, despite the different surname?

The officer makes a note. 'Thanks. If it's her, we'll make contact. A relative, someone who knew her. Hopefully they'll be able to shed light on what the hell has happened here. Whether there was anyone else involved.'

I remember what Abayomi said yesterday. 'And you can put her next of kin in touch with us? So we can arrange about the tenancy and the outstanding rent, and her possessions?'

PC Delliers nods. 'Yes, of course. But first things first. Her family don't even know yet that she's dead.'

I feel my cheeks burn, chastised. 'What can I do in the meantime? Isn't there anything else at all I can do?'

PC Delliers shakes her head. 'Just – keep all this paperwork to hand. Someone else may want to look at it. We may have to pass this to CID. A young woman found in a flat like that, there's reason to consider the circumstances suspicious. Other than that, no. If we need anything, we'll let you know.'

*

I wait, hoping the phone will ring or that PC Delliers will come back. But nothing happens. It all just goes quiet. Eventually, I open up my computer files and get on with typing up my notes from this morning. For some reason, I can't stop thinking about that email address in the file: picture_this@gmail.com. Before long I have done all my other tasks for the day too – made the phone calls, sent the letters, booked the visits – and I sit at my desk, staring at my blank computer screen. Emma is out on yet more visits and Abayomi's door is shut; he's on phone calls. As I sit there in the silence, only the clock ticking over the door, all I'm aware of, growing stronger by the minute, is the tug, the pull, towards that flat in Munroe House. There's a feeling, like a compulsion, that there's something I need to be doing, even though the police officer said there was nothing I could do. I just really don't like feeling so helpless.

I still have the keys to the bedsit in my bag from yesterday; the police didn't think to ask me for them. I press my palms down hard on the desk, and it's as if that movement alone lifts me from my seat and then I'm standing up and hurriedly tugging on my coat. There is no one around to notice me slip out.

Outside, through the cold, I make my way to Munroe House. There's a police officer stationed right outside – I admit I hadn't expected that – and through the smudged glass of the entrance doors, I glimpse the blue and white of police tape. I have the code but I can't think of going in, I realize I couldn't bear to. Now that I'm here, I know what I've really come to check, an ugly thought I've been trying to explain. I go round the back this time; Ms Jones's flat faced out the back way. I head down the narrow alleyway that leads round to the scrubby patch of grass.

There's no sign of police tape here, but *I* am here trying to make sense of it. How can a body have lain there all this time? I mean, everybody knows (I can hardly bear to put the thought in my head), *everyone knows* that dead bodies smell. How can her neighbours not have reported anything? I already have the suspicion in my head and when I come around the back it's confirmed. The bins. Those huge bins overflowing with commercial waste. It is February and cold, too cold for the wasps that usually gather round, but even on a day like today I can smell the rank odour. How many people had grown used to this? How many tenants had put up with this and thought nothing of it, just going about their own daily business? In the flat, the smell I breathed in, it was a mixture of everything: the dead flowers, the dust, rotten food and her body itself that was so withered away. A body wouldn't smell all that strongly for long. Maybe only a few weeks, not forever.

Picture this. Picture this. The email address flashes again through my head. I know what I saw in that flat. I saw the post piled up and the cobwebs. I've heard stories – people lying undiscovered for days, weeks, lonely people, old people, people who lived in the middle of nowhere. People who could go days or weeks without seeing anyone. But this is the middle of London and she was young and surrounded by neighbours and she had guests due for dinner, and pretty cups hanging in her kitchen.

I stand out there at the back of the building, my heart sore in my chest, wishing I could have done something, wishing I had known or could somehow turn back time. I desperately try to picture her: how on earth she might have lived before she died. Pieces of litter blow across the tramped, scuffed grass and suddenly a hard, bright memory jolts through me. I can see it quite clearly, I'm sure, and the recollection tips me off balance.

Because I told PC Delliers that Ms Jones never contacted me. That she never made a query or complaint to the office.

And yet ... and yet ... My mind skitters to my desk, to my computer where I see all the neat folders of my inbox. I remember now, I'm sure of it.

That email address – the one from her file: picture_this@gmail.com.

I'm almost certain I've seen it in my account.

Chapter 7

I head straight back to the office. Emma is back at her desk now, typing up her own notes. I tug my chair up to my desk just as she leans back from her keyboard and gives her arms a stretch. 'I'm just about to put the kettle on,' she says. 'Would you like a tea?'

'What?' I shake the computer mouse to get it off standby. 'Tea?'

'Oh, right, thank you.' It's so normal for her to offer; she hasn't realized I never drank the last one she made.

'Coming right up.' She flashes me a smile as she heads through to the staff kitchen. My fingers feel hollow as I log into my computer, so impatient at the time it always takes to load up. If Ms Jones contacted me, and somehow I missed it … If she needed help and I failed to respond … There aren't even that many emails in my inbox – I'm so good at deleting irrelevant messages, or filing the actioned ones away. Out in the corridor, I can hear Emma and Abayomi talking, their voices gently rising and falling. In Outlook, I type her email address into the search bar and hit return. It only takes a moment for the screen to click over.

Your search did not produce any results.

The door of the office swings open, and Emma comes back in, her phone wedged in the pocket of her jeans and two steaming mugs in either hand. She places mine, with a wobble, on my desk.

'Thank you,' I say.

'You're welcome.' She takes a sip from hers as she sits back down, but I just let mine sit there.

No results. Not in my inbox. But I have dozens of sub-folders, all neatly labelled: for complaints, for repairs, for feedback. In each of these are hundreds of emails. So many stories, so many people who have passed through our offices. I draw a deep breath and type the email into the search bar again, picture_this@gmail.com, making sure this time to click the 'all folders' option. The search function begins to whirr its way through, throwing up its results one by one. There's nothing in the first folder, nor the second, nor the third. I watch the search run all the way to the end. But all I get is the same message again – *your search did not produce any results.* And yet somehow my certainty only rises. I cannot shake the idea that I have received a message from her.

I re-type the email address and run the search again. And again.

'Jenn?'

Emma's voice disorientates me. The mug of tea on my desk has a faint scum on top, long gone cold.

'Don't you normally leave at three?'

'What?' I look to the clock. It's already five past. 'Shit.' Charlie. The school run. I've lost track of time completely. 'You're right,' I tell Emma. 'Thank you.'

I push my chair back so fast that I clip my ankle, and I shove everything into my bag in a complete jumble. I get a stitch running up the hill to his school. I make it only just in time.

*

The next three hours are completely taken up with Charlie: his homework, his dinner, his bedtime routine. I try to compartmentalize and put all thoughts of the email away – the way I'm able to with my to-do list in the kitchen drawer – but every other second the thoughts come slithering back. At bedtime, Charlie demands another chapter of his book, and another, even though by now I've read quite enough, the words squirming in front of my eyes.

'Listen,' I tell him, pushing the book into his hands. 'I'll leave the lamp on for you. You can carry on reading for half an hour longer.' Because he's a good reader, a great reader, perfectly capable of reading by himself.

He looks up from the pillows to where I'm standing, already half out of the bedroom door. 'But I want you to read it!' he says.

'Charlie,' I say. 'Come on, that's enough.' He's getting himself so het up. I click off the ceiling light and pull his door shut, my stomach churning. I wait in the hallway to see if he'll cry, or shout for me, but behind the door there is only silence.

I go through to the living room where now, finally, I can pull out my work mobile. I can access all the emails on here as well. Hunched on the sofa, this time I conduct my own search. Manually. I don't trust what the computer said. I open each folder and scroll through the messages, line by line. There are hundreds; the text blurs in front of my eyes. Sometimes I think

I've found it, another email with similar letters. But each time I'm wrong. I go all the way through and still I find nothing, even though I check and re-check.

I exhaust myself. I lie back on the sofa cushions, defeated, my head aching. Did I imagine it then? I've been through every folder, every email, and there's nothing. So was my memory playing tricks on me? Did my guilty mind make the whole thing up? It seemed so clear and real to me, but there is no evidence anywhere in my account. My head is so heavy, pressed at an angle against the cushions. My eyes are so sore. It's not even nine o'clock, but I'm completely worn out. My work mobile slips from my grasp as fatigue crashes into me, like a wave.

*

I must have only dropped off for a matter of minutes, but when my personal mobile rings, the jangle wakes me like a slap. It takes five, six rings for me to overcome the clumsiness of sleep and dig the phone out from the depths of my bag.

When I see who it is, I almost reject the call.

If I do that, though, he'll only call back. I give it two more rings and then I answer. I make myself sound as reasonable as I can, rubbing the sleep from my eye with the side of my thumb and sitting myself upright against the sag of the sofa.

'Hello? Jennifer?'

He always calls me Jennifer, my full name.

'Hi, Dad.'

He's calling to check on me, I know that. There's a part of me that can't help but feel grateful for it. I know he means to help; it's just that nine times out of ten, it doesn't help, it just dredges it all up. Everything from back then.

'I just thought I'd give you a call.' He always makes sure to sound so chipper. Mum won't be there with him, I'm sure of that. She'll be out, or upstairs, watching TV; it's always Dad who rings, by himself. I made a note of the dates, once. It's pretty regular: once every three months. Almost as if he sets himself a diary reminder.

'So, how are the two of you getting on?' he asks.

I feel like there's something stuck in my throat and a head-ache in each of my eyes. Everything I've been through this last forty-eight hours comes welling up, in danger of spilling over, but if I were to talk to him properly, what would I say? How can I just blurt it out to him, this bizarre and horrible situation that I can hardly even make sense of myself? It's been so long since we really talked, years and years since the last time I told him how I really felt. And yet, who else do I have to talk to, and who better to talk to but my own dad?

But when I feel the tears coming, I press them back the way I always have. I press the avalanche of words back too. 'We're fine, Dad,' I tell him. Like I say every time. 'Same as always. Work. School.' I stop there, letting the silence open up between us. If I begin to talk about what has just happened, and what I'm thinking and how I feel, I'm afraid I won't be able to stop. I'm afraid of opening up the door on everything else, on my whole sorry history. I did what I had to do back then, I made it work. I don't want to unravel all of that now.

I make myself ask in return, though: 'How are you?' It's such an effort to make my voice go up at the end.

'Oh!' Awkward laugh. 'Well, you know ...'

I do know. My parents don't get on. They haven't for years. I know it got worse after I moved out and I honestly cannot understand how Dad copes. Why he hasn't left, they way I have. Finally made a fresh start for himself. But he was always too loyal to do that. Too loyal, or too weak. I think about the anti-depressants he takes. Those brittle pills he hides in a drawer in the spare room – my old room. The prescriptions he refills without telling Mum, fearful of her disapproval and the arguments that would ensue. I think about the olive branches he always holds out.

I know there isn't much more to say now. I know where the conversation will go from here.

'I've transferred the money into your account,' says Dad. He keeps doing it, even though I'm ashamed to need it. I tell myself that the money is for Charlie. It isn't for me to deny his grandson that.

'Thank you,' I reply, same as always. 'I've checked and it's come through fine.'

I haven't checked, but I know it will be there.

And I know he and Mum will clash over this later – the fact that he called me. She will want to know everything I said, and he will say to her, why don't you call her yourself? But she never does. Along the way, we've ended up not speaking, Dad in the middle, our loyal go-between. And I give him so little to pass on.

'If you need any extra,' he adds, 'then please do just say.'

'Yes, Dad, I will.'

Though I never do.

Now comes the point where it's time to hang up. We've said everything, haven't we, that we usually say? The opportunity to tell him anything slips away, growing smaller and smaller until I've let it disappear out of reach and it feels as if it was never there to start with.

'Well then …' he says, then lets the silence hang, as though he's trying to force my hand. I press a fist against my mouth.

'Listen, Jennifer, don't you ever—'

But I can't do it. I cut him off. There's no good place this conversation can go.

'Listen, Dad, I'd better get to bed. I was already sleeping when you rang.'

'Oh.' The quiet on the line is disappointed, crushed. 'All right then, Jennifer. I hope you sleep well.'

And we're done, until the next time he calls. No doubt exactly three months from now.

*

Somehow, next morning, we end up running nearly fifteen minutes late. I bundle Charlie into his coat and shoes, and he gives a yelp as I pull his laces tight. I slept badly again and from the moment I woke up, time just seemed to get away from me. As we head out of the door, Charlie tripping on a loose piece of carpet, my anxiety rises up again, but this time I just stamp on my emotions, forcing them down. We arrive at the school at five past nine. Embarrassingly late. I can't even think about what Abayomi will say when I finally reach the office.

We have to knock on the door of Charlie's classroom. All the children look up at us. Ms Simmons comes out from behind her desk, and my hand is hard and flat on Charlie's back as I push him forwards.

My hands are empty now: I've forgotten my gloves. My coat seems to be buttoned up wrong too.

Ms Simmons takes him from me and ushers him to his seat. I turn and hurry out of the door, pretending not to see her look of concern.

*

I walk-run all the way down the hill to work, nauseous at the thought of how late I'm going to be.

When I step inside the office, though, Abayomi isn't even there. Emma says he has been out all morning. She says she covered for me when he rang, told him I was out on a visit to a tenant. I sit down at my desk, at a loss as to how to express my gratitude to her. I have made it so awkward with her that even something like this feels so difficult. I think about the tea she brought me yesterday that again I just left to grow cold on my desk. I walk a line between my craving for intimacy and my desperate desire to keep everyone at arm's length. The result is that it puts people in an impossible position. It makes it so hard for me to accept kindness or help.

'Thank you,' I manage. 'Charlie and I, we were running so late …' Emma looks as though she is expecting more, but I always stop at this point. I see her own face close up. She swivels away, picks up her phone and scrolls through her updates, all those posts to 'like' and comments to read. She told me once that she had over three thousand followers.

The office is silent now except for the hum of our computers and I jump as my phone rings. It is PC Delliers.

'Ms Arden?' she says. 'Can you help me with something?

Can you check Ms Jones's file again, please, and see if there are any other details she has given for her next of kin?' Her voice seems to echo around the office.

I open my desk drawer at the same time as asking, 'Her next of kin? Why? Did the number not work for the person she gave?'

I think maybe, while she's on the line, I should tell her about the email I'm trying to find; I'm worried that I might have lied to her before when I said there'd been no contact, but then I haven't found the email, so would I be lying now if I mention it?

'It's not that,' PC Delliers answers. 'We reached him. But he wasn't a next of kin.'

Her tone is strange. I feel myself go still. 'He wasn't? This – ' I try to remember the name I read – 'this Peter Duggan? Then who is he?'

At the other end of the line, PC Delliers clears her throat. 'Her bank manager,' she says. 'Ms Jones listed her next of kin as her bank manager.'

Chapter 8

I am finding it hard to speak. Her bank manager. Her *bank manager?*

'Can you hold the line?' I tell her. 'While I get Ms Jones's file?'

'Of course.'

I pull it from the drawer, but in the file there is nothing else. Only: *Peter Duggan*. Her bank manager.

'I'm sorry,' I tell her. I'm feeling a little dizzy. 'There are no other next-of-kin details. And I think you have copies of everything else that's there.'

'All right. Well, thank you anyway.' PC Delliers's voice sounds faint on the line now, as though she is standing outside, in the hard February wind.

From her tone I can tell she's about to hang up and before she can I ask quickly, 'What happens now?'

'We'll have to trace her relatives another way. Her parents' details should be easy enough to find. We'll pass those on to the coroner's officer. Or, if we can't reach anyone, it will be up to the council to arrange the funeral.'

A funeral. How could I not have even thought about that? Of course there will need to be a funeral for her. But if no one had missed her in all this time, and no one even knew she had died, then who on earth would be there to attend?

Images flash in front of me. The table set for guests who never came. The broken figure on the couch. And an email that clearly I have somehow imagined.

'... I mean, if it was my daughter, or whatever,' PC Delliers is saying, 'Jesus, I'd want to be there, I'd want to know everything.'

She's right, of course. Any parent would, surely, no matter what had gone before. Wouldn't they? Even if there'd been a falling out, a rift? But I can't help the thought flashing through my mind: *Would mine?*

'I have to go now,' PC Delliers is saying. 'Thank you anyway for your help.'

And before I can say anything else, she hangs up.

*

What happens next is that the police release a statement to the press. I hear it at home that evening, on the local BBC Radio London news. Charlie is in the bath down the hallway; I can hear him splashing. I keep the volume of the radio low.

The statement is very brief. *Police are appealing for information*, the newsreader says, *about an incident that occurred at flat sixteen, Munroe House, Brixton. Anyone who knows the occupant or has a connection with this address should contact* ... and then there's a phone number, and then that's all.

They don't even release her name.

I want to rewind and replay it, but it's the radio and the news just moves on to other things and it's gone. On my mobile, after I've put Charlie to bed, I scan the online news sites for more information, but there's nothing else I can find. Waves of exhaustion roll through me, but if I go to bed, I'm not sure I'll sleep. I sit for a long while in our cold kitchen, questions chasing themselves round my mind, and between them nothing but white space, blank gaps. The kind of blankness my mind can't stand, the kind of not-knowing that could conceal anything.

At ten o'clock, I listen in again to the radio news, hoping this time to glean some new detail. Any tiny crumb I can learn about what happened.

But on this bulletin, they don't mention the story at all.

*

For the next few days, I'm left in limbo. With no next of kin, there's nothing I can do. I try to switch off from it, concentrate on my own life. Reminding myself not to get involved.

On Friday afternoon, when I collect Charlie from school, I finally make good on my promise and take him to the play park before we go home. As we head down into Brockwell Park, I take his backpack and swing it onto my shoulder, pull a pair of gloves out for him from my handbag and make sure his coat is fastened right up to his chin.

Charlie holds me by the hand as we walk, tugging on my arm with each step. It is crisp, the wind chill, and I pull the collar of my coat up, Charlie's backpack slipping a bit as I do.

When we get to the park, Charlie wants to go on the swings, his favourite, and he doesn't need me to push him, he can do that easily himself. I stand beside the swing frame, leaning on the cold, scratchy pole.

'Watch me!' Charlie says, and he clambers onto the seat. 'Watch me!'

I am watching. I am always watching him. Sometimes I am watching him so closely that I'm not even really seeing him. I'm listening so carefully to how he speaks, and scanning every element of his coordination, and trying to judge whether every single one of his emotions seems normal for his age.

When he's set in the swing he turns and gives me a big smile and I give a big smile back.

'Look!' he shouts. 'Look how high I can go!' He leans back, kicks his legs, hangs his head back. On the swing, he looks perfect; it seems impossible to me right then that anything could be wrong. I blink my eyes, trying to clear the fog in my head and clap my gloved hands, a muffled thump in the cold.

'Great job!' I shout as he kicks himself higher still. Look at him, I tell myself. He's gorgeous. He's fine.

Half an hour later, after he's been on the roundabout and the slide, and played tag with a group of other children too, it is growing cold. I can see that – despite the coat and the gloves and the running about – Charlie's lips have a bluish tinge.

I hold out his backpack for him to put on.

'Come on, Champ,' I say. 'Time to go home.'

*

Charlie is babbling away to me as we turn into our own street and I'm looking down, half-enchanted by him so that at first I don't see her. Then I glance up. The stocky woman outside my flat turns towards me and I pull up short, clenching Charlie's hand in mine.

I recognize her. Now I remember.

'Jennifer?' she says. I check my watch. Four forty. I forgot. How on earth could I forget?

She looks chilly, her dark skin paling in the cold. I wonder how long she – Margaret, I remember her name now – has been standing out there, on the pavement.

I fumble for my keys in my pocket, dropping Charlie's hand as I do. I wonder if he recognizes the woman as well and remembers her from last year.

'I'm so sorry,' I say, now that I have the keys in my hand. 'You sent a letter, and I got it and everything … I'm sorry, it just slipped my mind. Please, here, let me open the door.'

The woman moves aside to let me past. Charlie climbs the steps up to the door close behind me.

Inside, our flat is cold, and cluttered. I haven't tidied. They sent the letter, I should have known she'd be here. Maybe, deep down, I'd been hoping she wouldn't come.

Margaret follows me inside. 'In here?' she says, gesturing towards my cramped living room.

'Yes, please, go ahead, sit down. Let me just get Charlie sorted.' I'm assuming she will want to see him too. She did last time. Of course she did, that was what I had kept asking for. Through the doorway, I can see Margaret sitting down, gingerly, on my couch. I wrestle Charlie out of his coat.

'Go and get changed,' I whisper to him. 'Quickly, then come back.'

He frowns, but silently heads to his room.

In the kitchen I hurry to fill the kettle and switch it on,

slopping water as I do. 'Do you want tea?' I call through to Margaret.

She clears her throat. She is pulling a folder of papers out of her bag. My file, I suppose. My notes. 'No thank you,' she says.

The kettle clicks off and I just leave it there in the kitchen, surrounded by the water I've spilled.

I go through into the living room and sit down on the only other chair in there, opposite her. I have to move a pile of laundry out of the way first. I can see Margaret's badge around her neck: Community Psychiatric Nurse, South London Community Mental Health Team. CPN and CMHT for short. I glance towards the hallway to see if Charlie is coming yet. 'He won't be a moment,' I tell her. 'He's just getting changed.'

Margaret looks heavier and more tired than when I last saw her. What was that? Seven, eight months ago? Last summer. Her lids hang low over her eyes. She nods and shuffles through the folders she's pulled from her bag. Clearly she's had a busy day, appointments right up to last thing on a Friday.

Now Charlie appears in his usual jogging bottoms and T-shirt. 'Come here,' I tell him. 'You'll have to sit on my knee.' He wriggles as I pull him onto my lap, his bones sharp against my thighs. The truth is he's really too big for this now. We must look awkward, strange, sitting like this, but I tell myself Margaret isn't here to judge. 'Okay,' I say, 'I'm ready.'

Margaret sets my file on her wide lap and places her hands flat on top. 'Well,' she says, 'it's good to see you again, Jennifer. As you know, this is really just a routine visit, following up on our involvement with you last year.'

I keep my face nice and open and bright. I'm glad I'm wearing my smartest work outfit. The one that makes me look really put-together. Charlie leans back against me, his thin shoulder blade digging into my chest.

'I think you mostly saw our psychologist last year, after your assessment. But I'm still your overall care coordinator, so I hope you don't mind that it's me you've got today. Our psychologist has moved on from the team now.'

I smile and nod, even though my heart drops a bit. The psychologist was so good. Helpful and calm. So many things made sense in her presence. But in the NHS, you don't really get much choice over who you see. Really, it's just whoever is available.

'All right then.' Margaret clasps her hands in her lap, on top of my notes. 'Well. And how have you been? How have things been going with Charlie?'

I'm aware of my son's weight and heat against me. The smell of him; his hair needs a wash. I think about how well I was doing last month and then about the thoughts I've been having more recently, the worries that have been crowding up again.

'Well,' I begin slowly, 'Charlie has been doing well in school.'

That's true. His teachers have told me that. And I remind myself that they would be able to notice things too. If there was really anything wrong. Although – Charlie is in a big class and it's a substitute teacher that he's got right now. I'm the one who knows Charlie best. I remember the video I watched on that website, that said, *Families are experts on their own children, more than any professional.*

'We had a bit of trouble – only a bit – the other morning …'
'Oh?'
'I think … he was just tired. Just … one of those days.'

I really have been doing well. They said I might have a blip occasionally, didn't they, but that doesn't mean I'm back at square one. This month … maybe that's all it is. A blip. With everything that's been going on, you'd expect it … wouldn't you?

'And how are you yourself?' says Margaret. 'How are you eating, for example?'

She is looking at me expectantly. Her face doesn't give anything away. No judgement, but I can't read anything else in there either.

'Eating? Okay, I think.' Although lately I've only really cooked for Charlie. By the time my dinnertime comes round, I tend to have gone past feeling hungry.

Margaret lets out a little sigh. 'And your sleep? How has that been?'

I hesitate. Sleeping. I haven't been sleeping very much at all. Maybe I need to tell her that. How bad my sleep has been since … since … The image flashes across my mind again. Maybe if I tell her, she might have some advice, maybe there are even some tablets they can prescribe. Because I'm sure, honestly, that I would feel better if only I could sleep. I don't think I'd be worrying half as much then.

'There was a situation at work,' I begin. Very gently, I cover Charlie's ears. 'A tenant – one of my tenants – died in her flat.'

Margaret's eyebrows lift, just a little. 'Gosh,' she says. 'How awful.'

'Yes,' I continue, letting go as Charlie jerks his head. 'And the circumstances – they shook me and now … If only I could find out what happened, but the police don't yet seem to know anything, and so I just have it all going round in my head …'

I try to go on. I think I really should say something. Just

so she can set my mind at ease. Not about work – what can she do about that? – but about Charlie. Because I'm not all right about Charlie really. *Reassurance seeking*, they call it, but isn't reassurance exactly what I need? Margaret could refer us back to experts and I know, I know that they checked last year, they did all kinds of tests with him, but the brain keeps developing until the mid-twenties, I read that on the website too, so these problems, these latent, hidden problems, they could emerge at any time. He was fine last summer, but that was months and months ago, and Margaret and her team never really understood, because I never really told them, the true reason that underlay all my fears …

'You're trying to find out …?' she prompts.

'No, I'm sorry. It's not that, I think I need …' But then Margaret's phone rings, a frantic, high-pitched jangle.

'My goodness,' she says, setting my notes to one side and leaning down to her bag. 'I'm sorry.' She pulls out the phone and when she checks the number she frowns. 'I think I'm going to have to take this. I'm so sorry. May I go in your kitchen?'

She is already shifting her weight to get up. There isn't much I can do but nod. She goes into my kitchen, where water lies in rivulets all across the worktops, and closes the door behind her. Now it's just me and Charlie.

He wriggles, and slides down off my lap. There's a board game left out on the floor that we were playing last night. Snakes and ladders, a classic. 'Mummy,' he says, tugging on my trouser leg. 'Come on, it's your turn.'

Muffled, I can hear Margaret's voice next door, sounding stressed out, sounding weary. I slide out of my seat and join Charlie on the floor. Raising my voice to cover Margaret's conversation, which I know I'm not supposed to overhear, I say, 'Okay. Remind me where we are.'

'Okay, well,' says Charlie, '*my* counter is here because I went up the ladder, and now you have to roll and then see where *you* land.'

'Oh yes,' I say. 'That's right. Of course.'

I can still hear Margaret's voice. It's louder now, more tense. 'Fetch the Section Twelve doctor … well then, the police …'

Perhaps there's an emergency; a client in crisis. The last thing she wants on a Friday afternoon. Maybe it would have been better if Margaret had gone outside so I couldn't hear, but it's so cold out there. It's cold enough in the flat. I need to turn the heating up. I take the die and shake it hard in its plastic cup, trying to make as much racket as I can. When it rolls out, I've thrown a six.

'Wow!' says Charlie. 'That's the best!'

But I can see I'm going to land on a snake. My kitchen door opens and Margaret comes back through. She sits down again on my sofa, wincing. I wonder if she suffers pain in her joints, on top of everything else.

'I'm very sorry about that,' she says. 'Where were we?'

I push myself back up off the floor, ignoring Charlie's small cry of disappointment. 'You were asking about eating. And sleeping.'

'Oh yes.' Margaret frowns. She really seems to have lost the thread of our conversation.

The phone in her hand buzzes with a text. She glances at it and frowns again. My file is back on her lap, but she hasn't reopened it. She looks exhausted, and this appointment has already started late.

I want to tell her everything. I want to ask her for her help. But I look at the fatigue that is clear on Margaret's face, deeper than ever since that phone call, and I struggle to get the words out. I hate the thought of being another problem. And then it's so exposing asking for help: displaying all your weaknesses, confessing all your faults. Surely it's better to fix yourself on your own. After all, Mum turned out to be right, didn't she? Eventually, I coped without help back then, so surely I can do the same thing now; save myself all that embarrassment and shame. I think about what's in those notes of Margaret's from last year. Everything they didn't find. All the results that said there was nothing. Instead there are the tools and techniques that the psychologist taught me, all of which I've been stupidly neglecting. I think about all the health-care budget cuts, reported endlessly on the news. I think about how stretched Margaret and her team must be. No doubt there are clients in crisis all the time. And here I am, making a crisis out of absolutely nothing.

I swallow down the words that were lying ready on my tongue and look down at Charlie, my beautiful son.

'I'm fine,' I tell her instead. 'And Charlie's great. Plus work is proving a good distraction. So we're both doing absolutely grand.'

Margaret smiles. She looks so relieved. And I tell myself, it's really just a blip. Really, I am fine.

Margaret leaves my flat five minutes later.

And I am officially discharged.

Chapter 9

BACK THEN

Prin has to remind Daddy about the ice cream. He clearly would have forgotten otherwise. There is so much fussing about getting Prin's cousin into the car, and making sure she has her seatbelt on and that she is comfy, and asking her, like a million times, whether she needs anything.

Prin's cousin doesn't say much, just nodding mostly and saying yes, thank you, she is fine, and it's only once they are about ten minutes down the road, heading home, and Prin has been waiting all that time, arms folded, to see whether Daddy, or Mum, will say anything, that Prin finally pipes up and reminds them about the ice cream.

And then there is a moment where she thinks Daddy *still* won't keep his promise, but then Mum lays a hand on his arm and says, maybe it would be a nice thing to do, and they have nothing they have to get straight back for, do they? So then Daddy catches Prin's eye in the mirror above his head and smiles at her and Prin grins back. She turns towards her cousin who is all sort of squashed down in her seat in the corner of the car, as if she's trying to squash herself away, and asks her, 'You like ice cream, don't you?' And when her cousin answers, 'Yes, I suppose so,' Prin feels so pleased that she made sure Daddy stuck to his word.

*

They stop at the ice-cream shop not far from home. It's the one Daddy always takes her to after swimming: she gets two scoops if she has managed twenty lengths, and three scoops if she manages fifty. Prin never manages fifty, not after that one time when she did so much swimming, Daddy shouting from the sidelines, that she felt too sick to eat anything afterwards, but Daddy got her three scoops anyway, and made her finish it all.

She wonders whether she'll be allowed three scoops today, even though she hasn't been swimming. She skips a bit as they head from where Daddy has parked the car to the shiny glass doors of the restaurant. Inside, there are bright metal chairs and tables; Prin can see them through the tall windows. She heaves open the door, impatiently waiting for Mum and Daddy and her new cousin to catch up. She already knows what flavours she wants. Chocolate, caramel and cookie dough. She's almost sure now that she'll be allowed all three.

Her cousin looks a bit more cheerful now. Not so pale. After all, she likes ice cream too. She stands there in her dress, propping the door open. It's boiling hot outside, but lovely inside, in the cool.

The man on the ice-cream counter recognizes Prin. 'That's a fancy dress,' he says, and Prin does a turn for him. Normally he only sees her with wet hair after swimming, so she's pleased he gets to see how nice she looks all dressed up.

'And who's this?' he says, as Prin's cousin comes up. Prin notices that her cousin is holding her mum's hand, and she feels a strange stabbing sort of feeling go through her. She doesn't like seeing it, though it's hard to say why since, after all, she doesn't much like holding Mum's hand herself. She just doesn't think anybody else should be allowed to.

Prin's little cousin looks up at the man in his white paper cap, standing over all the ice cream on display.

'I'm Jane,' she says, in reply to his question.

Prin frowns, remembering something that Mum and Daddy told her before they picked up her cousin.

She looks at her. 'That isn't your proper name,' she says.

Now Prin's little cousin looks a bit scared, but Mum is still holding tightly to her hand. 'It's *nearly* my name,' she says. 'Mostly it is. Anyway, it's what I want to be called now.'

'But—' says Prin, but Mum makes one of her faces, which means, for Prin, *All right now, that's enough*.

The man on the counter carries on watching them with a sort of smirking smile on his face. Prin wonders if they are in danger of making what Daddy calls *a scene*. Prin wants her three scoops of ice cream. She doesn't want to be in trouble. Fine then. She flips her skirt and closes her mouth. She presses up against the display, her mouth watering at all the flavours in there. Fine then.

Jane.

*

Afterwards, the ice cream sits cold and heavy on the bottom of Prin's stomach. She got three scoops but, like before, it was hard to finish them. She didn't let that show though. She pushed down every last mouthful. Mum and Daddy didn't have ice cream, just coffee. And Jane only wanted one scoop, strawberry flavour, boring.

Back in the car, Jane is pale and quiet and anxious again. It's as if she's upset about something *all the time*, though Prin has no idea what. She hopes Jane will perk up now that they've arrived back home, scrunching up the gravel of the driveway. She can't wait to show Jane her room and tell her it's where she's going to be sleeping. She helps Daddy get Jane's luggage out of the back of the car. Only one little suitcase. Prin tries to remember again how long Mum and Daddy said her cousin would be staying. The size of the suitcase makes it look like not very long, but she seems to remember them telling her that it might be for a *very long time indeed*.

Daddy carries the suitcase into the house, swinging it easily from just one hand and Prin skips after him. The sun is still high and bright in the sky. It's the middle of summer. All the days right now are long and bright and hot. Mum and Jane have already gone inside, into the cool of the kitchen, and Mum is pouring glasses of squash and cracking ice cubes out of the tray.

She sets the glasses out, one for Prin and one for Jane, and tells them to drink up, they need to keep hydrated in this heat. Prin drinks hers down as fast as she can. Jane drinks far too slowly, and Prin tugs at her elbow before she's even finished. 'Leave that,' she says. 'I want to show you my room.'

Reluctantly, Jane sets her glass down. She has wet streaks pointing upwards from the corners of her mouth where the juice has pressed against her skin. 'Can I go now?' Prin asks Daddy. 'Can we go and play upstairs?'

Mum steps towards them, glancing at Daddy. 'Well,' she says, 'shouldn't I come too? Show Jane where everything is, make sure she gets properly settled?'

Prin crosses her arms and turns her mouth down. She looks at Daddy as well, from under her eyelashes. Daddy leans against the counter top and crosses his own arms, like he's mimicking Prin. 'I think the girls will be all right by themselves. And we have a few things to talk through, don't we?'

He's saying that part to Mum, and Mum hesitates for a moment and then nods.

Daddy grins down at Prin, turning the edges of his mouth right up. 'Go on then, off you go.' And he reaches forward to give her bottom a smack, through the dress so that it doesn't hurt, to send her on her way.

Prin is so excited that she finds herself grabbing her cousin's hand in hers as they climb the stairs, pulling her up. Jane is all stiff and rigid. She doesn't seem to be enjoying herself yet. Prin's room is the very first one off the landing at the top. It has her name – her real name that is – on the door in pink glitter letters. She lets go of Jane's hand and pushes the door open. Mum tidied up the room before they left this morning, and it looks perfect! The big double bed with its canopy, the dolls on the pillow, the window seat and the big window that opens onto the roof, the dolls' house in the corner, the desk with all her colouring books, and all her other toys and games stuffed on the book shelves.

Prin bounces on the bed. 'Come *in*,' she tells her cousin. 'You're going to sleep in here with me. We're going to share the same room, like sisters.'

Jane hovers in the doorway. She looks as though she should

be sucking her thumb. 'This is your room?' she says. Prin wonders what Jane's own bedroom is like, back at her own house. Nobody has said anything about that. All Prin knows is that Jane has come from a place called the Isle of White, which sounds like a pretty place to be, even if she doesn't exactly know how to spell it. And that she came over here on a boat, which makes Prin just a tiny bit jealous, because she wouldn't mind a trip on a boat too.

Cautiously, Jane steps inside.

'You can play with anything,' says Prin, 'so long as you ask me first. So I can give you permission.'

Jane trails her way slowly around the room, touching things with the tip of one finger. Prin jumps off the bed; better to show her cousin all her things, and to make sure Jane appreciates them properly. She supposes Jane must have games and toys of her own back home, but she seems to be in awe of Prin's. Which is what Prin secretly hoped she would be.

Jane stops in front of a toy on the windowsill. The zoetrope. Prin hasn't played with it in ages.

'What's this?' Jane asks.

'Haven't you ever seen one?' says Prin. 'You've honestly never seen one of these before?'

She lifts it down from the windowsill and pushes a stack of school books aside to set it on her desk. It's sort of a boring toy really, once you've seen what it does, but she likes the fact that Jane is so intrigued. There's a round cylinder of card, about as wide as a dinner plate, with vertical slits all the way round, and another cylinder of card, with pictures, on the inside, different depending on which inner cylinder you choose. Prin pulls out the desk chair and makes Jane sit down.

'You have to look through here,' she tells her. 'Look at the horse inside, do you see him?'

'The horse? Yes,' Jane says. 'But what does it do?'

Prin sets the zoetrope spinning, but only slowly at first. She wants to keep Jane guessing. 'Keep watching. You have to wait,' she says as Jane squints. 'You have to make sure to look the right way.'

Prin crouches down so she can look inside too, pushing onto the seat beside Jane. She'd sort of forgotten the magic of it, but she's remembering now. She likes this card, the one with the horse, his rippling mane. Right now, he's juddering, flickering, still getting up to speed.

Beside her, Jane is immobile, staring, waiting. She hardly blinks. Their upper arms touch, skin sticking in the heat. Prin can hear the scrape of Jane's lungs, smell the traces of strawberry ice cream on her breath. Downstairs, she hears a bang and what sounds like a few muffled words. She makes the zoetrope go faster now – fast enough.

Jane breathes in, sharply. Prin feels her own skin prickle. They both see it happen: the magical shift when all the tiny pictures blur together, the horse leaping into life, galloping, mane flowing.

'See?' Prin whispers, so glad suddenly of this girl beside her. 'See?'

Jane stays absolutely still. Transfixed. '*Yes.*'

Chapter 10

Charlie does not sleep well that night. I try to tell myself it's only a bad dream, but I'm worried that it's my anxiety rubbing off on him. In the small hours he calls out for me, waking me from some strange, convoluted dream of my own. When I go in to him, he is tense and sweaty, his muscles tight, like knotted ropes, his pyjamas sticking to his skin. The corners of his eyes are crusted with tears.

I sit him up and find him a clean pair of pyjamas. His breath comes in shaky gulps. The fear from the bad dream has sent his body into shivers. He never tells me what these dreams are about. It's as if they escape from him the moment he wakes up, and he's left with nothing but the emotion, in an unarticulated knot. For a while he's rigid when I try to hold him, as if I've become part of his fears too. And then gradually he'll relax, go limp against me. Eventually he'll be ready to lie back down.

I slip the clean nightshirt over his head and help him pull up the clean pyjama bottoms. His breathing has slowed now. He is becoming sleepy again.

He settles back down into the bed and I smooth the pillow beneath his head. I lean down until my cheek is touching his cool forehead, my heart surging in my chest, my love for him swelling the blood in my veins. I sit with him until I am sure he has fallen asleep again.

*

Back in my own room, I dig the crumpled sheets of paper out of the little nightstand by my bed. I haven't looked at these in ages, but I really should have. Some of what's on here I've forgotten entirely. No wonder my thoughts have been running away from me again.

I smooth the papers out on the mattress of my bed. These notes that the psychologist made for me. I make myself read through every word on the pages, until I am sure of myself again. Until I feel strong.

I remind myself that this was how the problems last year began, a stupid mess of my own making. There was that TV programme I watched that put all those anxious ideas in my head, and then I had a few bad nights' sleep, couldn't seem to keep a hold on myself. I have to be on the ball now for *early warning signs*.

Stress can be a trigger.

Maybe I should have insisted on telling Margaret everything that happened at work. Maybe I shouldn't have pretended it wasn't affecting me. But if I *know* I'm stressed, I can protect against it myself, can't I? And look, here I am doing fine with Charlie. I didn't panic this evening when he fumbled his toothbrush and it went clattering into the bathroom sink. I just took a deep breath (*take a deep breath*, it says in my notes) and picked it back up for him and let him carry on. I didn't make him open and close his hand ten times to prove to me that his fingers work fine.

Checking behaviours only make things worse.

Reading these pages has made me feel so much better. I am sure now that I can do this, I can manage. I've got a grip, I've remembered my logic.

When I get into bed, I feel completely fine.

*

On Monday morning, at the office, when Emma goes out to see one of her tenants, I click on Ms Jones's computer file and bring up every record we have about her. I go through every one of my emails again. I can't help myself. It doesn't matter how hard I've tried not to think about it, my mind has been full of her all weekend. I have been involved from the very start and my actions are so tangled up in what happened, how can I leave it alone? She died in one of my flats, I was there when they found her, and it was me who missed her last check. I feel so responsible and the awfulness of what I saw still crushes my chest: those dead flowers, those flies, that radio playing. Every time I picture it, my eyes sting with tears because how, *how* did she end up so alone? There are just still so many blanks, so many questions and *still* I can't shake the feeling that there is something else, some other connection between us, something knocking at the corner of my mind that I've missed. I'm desperate for an explanation, for information, for answers. I tell myself, maybe I didn't look before at everything in her file. Maybe I overlooked something. Maybe there has been a mistake.

I take everything else off my desk – everything except my photo of Charlie – to make space. I undo the tabs on the paper file, the metal clasp catching under my finger, and pull out all the pieces of paper, every single one, and lay them out like a big jigsaw on the desk. There are plenty of sheets of paper – bureaucracy loves forms – but now the closer I look I see just how little information they contain.

A name.

A date and place of birth.

Previous addresses.

Previous landlords.

The temp agency she worked for.

The useless next of kin.

I check the references we received from her old landlord, but there is nothing there that sheds any light. We send out a tick-box form, a simple yes-or-no answer sheet. *Has this tenant ever fallen behind with their rent? Have there ever been any disputes with this tenant? Is there any reason you would advise against letting a property to them?*

For each question the answer is *no*. Ms Jones has never caused anyone any difficulties. She has never fallen late with rent or caused concern, until now. The only thing seems to be how frequently she moved, but then this is London and people who rent move all the time, so is it really that strange?

I have already given all of this information to the police and no matter how many times I flip through the pages or scroll through the information on the computer file, there is nothing else. I try to pull myself together. Despite the lump in my throat, I need to think logically, work methodically. I dig out the neat square of paper that I wrote it down on and call the number for PC Delliers, telling myself that I'm only following Abayomi's protocol, chasing up details so that we can move things forward.

It takes a few rings before she picks up, and when she does she sounds distracted and breathless.

'Yes? Hello?'

'PC Delliers? This is Jennifer Arden ... the housing manager ... the one who was there when they found Ms Jones?'

A muffled pause, as though she is speaking to someone else in the background, then her voice comes back on the line, a little louder.

'Yes?'

'I just wanted ... wanted to ask ... Did you find her proper next of kin?'

'What? Oh, you mean – no, no luck, I'm afraid.'

'"No luck"? But then ... do you understand yet what happened?'

'Jennifer, I'm sorry, I'm not on that case any more. They needed me over in ... Never mind. I think ... the Munroe House case ... They had no reason to pursue it, I think? No evidence of foul play? I guess she was just a lonely kind of person, kept to herself, died alone. They will have referred the case up to the coroner, but the police investigation will be closed now I think. And the local authority will be dealing with the funeral.'

I can't stop her words from stabbing: *Kept to herself, died all alone*. It makes my whole body shudder. 'Closed?'

The muffled background conversation again.

'I'm sorry Jennifer, I have to go. Was there anything else? Did you have any other information?'

'I … No. No, I don't have anything. It's just … it's been quite hard—'

'Well … Oh – I can send you a leaflet on victim support if you need it. You were there when they found her – I remember now. If that has been difficult for you, there is support you can access, if you feel you're struggling …'

That phrase pulls me up. I'm not. I'm not struggling.

'Thank you,' I say. My voice has taken on its familiar strait-laced tone. 'That isn't necessary. I just thought to call … in case there was anything more you might need from me, but if there isn't then—'

'Thank you, Jennifer. Goodbye.'

*

On my phone I open up Google and search yet again. Now, suddenly, there's an article about her, time-stamped late last night. They still haven't mentioned her name though, only *woman found, body found* … They've written about the results of the post mortem. Somehow this journalist has got hold of that. I can feel my jaw shivering as I scan the lines. They traced her dental records and matched the pattern of her teeth to the jawline of her remains.

The pattern of her teeth.

From the dates of the oldest unopened post, the use-by stamps on the neglected food in the fridge, they estimate that she died ten months ago. Ten months. Late April last year. A matter of weeks before my annual inspection was due. So it's because of *me* that she lay there that long. Ten months; almost a year. *Breathe*, Jennifer. *Breathe, breathe, breathe.*

The pathologist hasn't established a clear cause of death. But there were no signs of forced entry. No sign that anyone else had been in the flat. No signs of a struggle. Door locked from the inside.

And now I can't decide for myself which is worse. That someone might have harmed a young woman and kept her death hidden from everyone; that somebody in this world might have done that, and covered their tracks so well that even the police have given up the case. Or that a body could simply lie there, with people passing by every day, a thousand lives going by all around her, *without being missed by anybody at all*.

The wrongness of it all makes me light-headed. Out of instinct, I dial the number for the local authority. They know my name; I have dealings with them all the time, for our council tenants. I manage to get through to the relevant department, and I'm lucky to have a junior person on the line.

'I'm calling about Sarah Jones,' I say. 'About her funeral. I understand you're arranging it?'

'Oh,' the girl on the other end says. 'Yes. We had to. The police couldn't make contact with a next of kin. We step in in situations like this.'

I do my best to keep my voice professional. Not show my emotions, my dragging sense of horror. 'There was no one?'

I wanted information and here it is, though there's an awfulness to it that makes me feel sick. I concentrate on every word, even though the woman's voice through the phone line is faint and seems to jumble in the ringing of my ears. 'They had no luck, tracing her parents, they tried but … and yes, it says here … there were a couple of other relatives, as well, deceased.'

I let my pen fall and put a hand to my head. 'What else?' I ask. 'Is there anything else?'

'No … I'm sorry, I don't think there's … Oh, wait … it says here …' I can hear a rustling of papers and then her voice is louder on the line. 'There *was* someone they did trace, I mean, a living relative but it says …' The young woman on the other end breaks off, becomes flustered. Her voice becomes fainter than ever. She sounds like a ghost, or a figment of my imagination. 'It just says: *refused to respond*.'

I push my chair back from the desk and lower my head towards my knees, trying to stem the nausea I feel. *Refused to respond?* I think of my mother. The fact that we haven't spoken in nearly four years, the fact that she gets angry with Dad when he calls.

'Who?' I manage to say. 'Who was that?'

But now the girl seems to realize her mistake, sensing that somewhere she's broken protocol. 'I'm sorry, I can't, I shouldn't have …'

I can feel that she's just about to hang up. 'Wait,' I say. I sit myself back up, setting my spine straight. 'The funeral then? What about that?'

She hesitates again, like she's recalibrating. Then: 'Yes, that's all arranged. They rushed it through. One p.m., twenty-seventh of February. West Norwood Crematorium.'

As I write the details down, the itch, the urge runs all through my body. I shouldn't get involved, I know that, I should stay here and get on with my job. But I failed once before to show up for Ms Jones and I have the time – my lunch hour – and I have the location. Before I'm even aware of deciding, I'm already pulling on my coat.

Because the twenty-seventh of February.

That's today.

*

There are plenty of buses that run between Brixton and West Norwood, and one comes only a few seconds after I reach the bus stop outside the Iceland supermarket. It is not too full and I'm not going far, so I take a seat on the ground floor.

I have no idea what to expect when I get there. Part of me doesn't even want to think about the realities of going to a funeral arranged by a local authority because they have been unable to find anyone who wanted to step up. It is painfully, painfully close to home. I try to tell myself it would be different for me. Of course it would be different. I tell myself that Dad at least would make sure things were taken care of. I tell myself that Charlie—

The bus jolts over a pothole in the road and my head bumps sharply against the glass of the window. We're right at my stop. I scramble to my feet and call out to the driver. He opens the doors and I stumble off, pulling out my phone. The crematorium is further from the bus stop than it looked on the map and I arrive there only minutes before the ceremony is due to start.

My heart leaps when I make out a knot of people clustered by the entrance: three women and a man. There are people here, after all. As I get closer, I place one of them. The woman from the flat above who passed us on that very first day, as I stood outside flat sixteen hearing the radio play on and on, with the bailiffs, with no idea then what we were about to find.

And the other three must be tenants from Munroe House as well. Neighbours who never reported her absence, who didn't realize she was dead.

I catch the woman's eye and she seems to recognize me too but before I can introduce myself or say anything, the door opens and an usher is waving us all inside.

It is such a small room. They must have chosen this one especially. They must have assumed that barely anyone would attend, because they arranged it so quickly, because efforts to engage relatives came to such a quick dead end. The thought of it crushes the air from my chest. The awful sadness of it, the painful horror. For a moment I really don't know if I can go in, but it would be so much worse to turn away now.

The five of us enter. A single wreath of flowers lies on top of the coffin. The neighbours must have brought it. I am empty-handed. I wish fervently that I had brought a bunch of flowers too. A CD player somewhere pipes Pachelbel's Canon, a default, all-purpose piece of music.

And other than the coffin and the usher and the minister, there is no one else here.

The group of neighbours cluster in one of the middle rows. I don't know what to do with myself, where to sit. In the end, I perch on the end of a row, behind, fumbling in my pocket to switch off my phone.

I have seen funerals in films and TV programmes. I know that people are supposed to get up and speak about the dead person. But there is none of that. The ceremony is a sad, tragic ritual. The minister reads a few short passages from the Bible, though we don't even know if she was religious, and I recognize the lines about ashes and dust. Another piece of classical music plays, as familiar and generic as the first. It's as though she was nothing; she was no one. The minister says a prayer for her, and then the plain wooden coffin disappears from view. We all say the Lord's Prayer together. And then it is over.

I press the heels of my hands into my eyes, fighting to keep my tears at bay. I've told myself I shouldn't get involved, I've tried to keep myself professional, but now the whole thing rises up before me in all its pitiable awfulness. Under the dust, her flat looked so normal, books and ornaments, crockery and clothes. But she just lay in there, dead, with people passing outside every day, the whole of the city oblivious to her, London around her grinding on and on. And now here's a funeral that five people have attended, all of them strangers to her. It's unbearable, but I can't stop thinking about it, I can't stop seeing it, and my chest heaves every time I do.

The group of neighbours are getting up now, ready to make their way out. I wipe away the wet from my cheeks. With stiff fingers, I turn my phone back on; the alert on my voicemail pings. I recognize the number, it's the CMHT, but I don't know why they're calling me. I get up to follow the other attendees, pushing my phone back into my pocket. I didn't find a way to speak to them before but I can't leave now without saying anything, I have to try. I have such a sense of helplessness, when I only ever want to help.

I catch one of them – the man – by his elbow, harder than I meant to. He stops and turns, surprised. 'Did you know her?' I blurt out. 'Did you ever speak to her after she moved in?'

The whole little group have stopped now and are looking at me. 'You're one of the housing managers, aren't you?' one of the women asks, another tenant that I recognize now; I think she lives in staircase C.

I nod, the guilty lump in my throat bigger than ever. 'I was there when they found her. It was so terrible and I feel ... so awful about it. The whole thing is so sad, I just want to understand ...'

The woman I recognized at first – the one who passed me and the bailiffs on her way out to work – shakes her head in reply to my question. 'We just know she used to live on our stairwell. I saw her once or twice when she first moved in, but I didn't know her. Seems no one did. We're only here to pay our respects.'

I knock away a further tear that has crept into my eye. 'It's so awful to think she didn't have any friends, any family. How can that happen? It just doesn't seem right.'

The third woman in the group pulls her coat more tightly around her and I glimpse the cross that hangs at her neck. 'The police told us she had deleted all the numbers from her phone. That, or she didn't have any in there to begin with.'

'She deleted her numbers?' But I think of what I saw in the flat: the table set for guests. It doesn't make sense. None of this makes sense.

The little group are stepping away now, heading back outside. Who am I to them? Just some white woman asking stupid questions and making everybody feel worse. They have done their Christian duty, laid a wreath and paid their respects. They aren't friends or family of the dead girl. The truth is, it's really nothing to do with them. But it feels so wrong to just let them leave, to think of all of us leaving, just going back to our lives. The words come out before I can stop them, as though I can't hold anything inside any more.

'The worst part …' I blurt out from the arch of the church doorway. 'The worst part is that they had to ID her from her teeth.'

Outside, the group of four slows then comes to a halt. The woman I once met coming down the stairs turns around. Her face has softened, and I realize I desperately want her to say something comforting, something to alleviate the horror I feel. Instead, I'm not at all prepared for what comes next.

'Oh yes.' She raises a hand to her mouth. 'She had that gap, didn't she? I suppose it would have been quite distinctive.'

She mimics in the air – drawing a space between two front teeth. And I feel as though I've flipped right out of myself.

The tenant, her age, her email. My imagination that wasn't imagination at all. Suddenly everything clashes together. Suddenly I know, I know, I *know*. I cannot believe I didn't connect it before. How, how could I not have realized?

I'm bent almost double with the shock of it: a coincidence so crazy and improbable and bizarre. I pull out my phone again and open up my email. My personal email account this time. I have to scroll back and back and back, it has to be three years back at least.

But here it is.

The message reads: *Hi Jenn, here's the letter template you needed. Hope that it's come through okay. Stay in touch!*

The email is signed: *Sarah*

And the address is: *picture_this@gmail.com.*

Chapter 11

I knew her. I *knew her*.

Ms Sarah Jones was *that* Sarah. The blonde-haired girl with a gap in her teeth.

I see her, a flash in my memory, three desks along from me, next to the window. Prettier, friendlier, more confident than me. That conversation just before I left, when we exchanged personal emails, because a document needed transferring and all our work accounts were playing up.

The civil service administration office. How long did I work there? Five months, six? Our lives crossed over for a few weeks, little more. The hours were so awkward with Charlie's schooling, and the Housing Association contract fitted so much better. We'd been colleagues, nothing else: until now I hadn't even remembered her second name – Jones, such a common surname, it could have belonged to anyone. People were always coming and going from there; half the office was staffed with anonymous temps, a set-up that suited me just fine.

And I never stayed in touch, because I never did with anyone – school friends, uni friends, colleagues from past jobs. They drifted away and I always let them drift – and so I never spoke to her again. But I knew her, and she knew me.

Sarah from the civil service office. I try to call up other details about her, but all I can see is her sitting with her legs crossed at her computer: the red shoes and blue tights she wore. The picture of her parents she kept on her desk.

Now Ms Jones and my Sarah are one and the same.

And I don't know a single detail of what happened in between.

*

However guilty, however responsible I felt before, now it is so much worse. I knew her, I worked with her, but at the end of her life, she had no one. So many people must have turned away, let her down. And now there's me who never stayed in touch.

I have to do something. I call Emma's mobile and when she picks up, I lie to her. 'I'm not well,' I say. 'A stomach bug, I think. I need to get home. I'll leave a message for Abayomi, but can you let him know as well?'

Emma agrees, the way she always does, keen to please.

I know Abayomi will be out – he has a senior managers' meeting every Monday – but I leave a message on his office phone. Then I take the bus straight back to my flat where I'll have one precious hour before I have to fetch Charlie. On the juddering journey, I check my voicemail. The message is from someone called Freya, a support worker from the CMHT. Her voice on the recording is quiet, nondescript. There's just a discharge questionnaire she wants to run through with me, she says. Sorry not to catch me; she'll try again later. I delete the message with hardly a second thought.

All I can think about is Sarah. *Sarah from the civil service office*. She was just a tiny fragment of my life, but now that connection is magnified a hundred-fold. Our lives crossed only for a moment, but Sarah is so vividly real to me now, not just some name on a form or body in a crime scene. Now I know of other people out there who knew her. People the police maybe had no reason to track down, because there was no evidence of a crime, because the case closed so soon. They released a statement to the press, but with so little detail, how could they expect anyone to come forward from that? And I could leave it all up to the coroner, step away and keep out of it, but how can I possibly let it alone now? All the coroner will rule on is the cause of her death, which won't explain any of the rest of it. But I have the chance to make contacts, find answers, and surely that's the least I can do? I keep thinking of that radio playing in her flat, the three dinner plates laid out ready. There must be people out there who cared about her, who were planning to visit. Who was coming? Who was she expecting? What can possibly have gone so wrong?

I have to find answers and fill in the blanks, I don't know how else to quieten my mind. Maybe I am overstepping here. Maybe I'm interfering where I shouldn't. But there seem to be whole swathes of information that the authorities have missed. And that old email in my inbox burns like a sign.

I need someone else who knew her, someone who can help me. I have to speak to them and find out what they know. All this time with no information or answers. But now, finally, I have a place to start.

When the bus lurches to a halt at the top of Brixton Hill, I stumble off and hurry home, letting myself in with clumsy hands. Without even taking off my shoes or coat, I sit down at the kitchen table, open my laptop and log into my Facebook account. I haven't posted anything on here in months. Sometimes I'll share something from someone else's timeline: one of the random people I've friended, just because I thought their page looked nice. Maybe they had a picture of a cat, or some scenery that I liked the look of. Only that, and posts from the Child Brain Injury Trust.

Even on Facebook, where you are free to make friends with anyone, I don't really have any. The tab at the top lists the number as seventeen. But almost none of them are people I know in real life. But there is a private group on here that, once upon a time, I belonged to – a private Facebook group for the office I worked in. I made hardly any use of it at the time, but now I'm desperate for it still to be there. I have to rack my brains to remember the name of it and I end up putting in combination after combination of words before I hit the right one. And yes, I can hardly believe it – it's still here.

I have to take a few breaths before I can go on. Then I scroll down through the history of posts and comments, names coming back to me, blurry faces, as I'm bombarded by a ticker-tape of memories. I can almost feel myself falling back in time and it's a dislocating sensation. No messages from Sarah, but that's not what I'm looking for. I click through the pictures, the photographs, the memes. To begin with there are flurries of posts, each with dozens of comments. People sharing silly quotes, silly pictures, silly jokes. I click on them, opening up each thread in turn, line after line, the print so tiny. But then over time, the posts dry up, the comments peter out, the group page runs dry. People drift away, losing interest. No one has posted there for – I calculate – eighteen months.

My stomach clenches; I should probably eat something. Instead, I click into the space for a new post in the group. To begin with, I hardly know where to start; I type and delete three openings. What on earth am I supposed to say? The situation is so horrifyingly bizarre, how can I distil that into a post for people I haven't spoken to in years? But I have to write something. There are so many unanswered questions, ones that an inquest is unlikely to clear up. *What happened to you? What happened? How did you end up so alone?*

So I keep going, writing and rewriting, until I've got close enough.

Hello Everybody. I hope you're all well. Not sure if any of you still use this group.

I'm wondering if any of you remember Sarah Jones, who worked with us in 2018? If so, do you think you could contact me?

My number is below, and my email. Please contact me on either of these.

I sit back from the table, my heartbeat thundering. For a moment, I press my hands to my eyes. I can't believe this is happening; it's so unbelievable that I knew her and that I was the one who was there when she was found. But I can't change those facts and there's no way to rewind. I can't pretend that what happened isn't real.

I place my hands carefully back on the keyboard and check the draft of my message, once more, twice more, until I am sure there are no spelling mistakes, no errors. And I'm not doing anything illegal, am I? No police investigation to hinder, no work boundaries to breach? I take a deep breath: lungs full before the plunge.

I read it once more and then I hit 'post'.

*

I sit there for as long as I can before I have to collect Charlie, refreshing and refreshing the page. When I get back from the school run, I check again, and again through the evening, but there's nothing.

For the whole week, I don't hear anything. I try to be patient. At work, I put my personal phone in my desk drawer and try not to look at it, no matter how many times I imagine it rings. I try to limit myself to one check an hour, on the Facebook page, my email, my phone. I try my best to focus on my job. I can't afford to make any more mistakes.

Every evening, as well, I take out the psychologist's pages from my bedside table and read them, trying to ground myself. But I go through them so often that words start to blur and I'm not sure if they are quite making sense. I'm not sure these strategies are right for me any more.

Come Friday evening, I'm wrung out with waiting, my emotional tolerance drained. Charlie is playing up; he keeps crossing his eyes, making them roll in his head and laughing whenever I tell him to stop.

'No *look*, Mummy, see? It's funny! Molly showed me how to do it.'

But it isn't funny to me; in fact, it upsets me so much that I end up shouting at him, and that only triggers a tantrum, which of course only makes everything worse.

'Stop it!' he yells. 'You're always doing that! Always messing with me, always stopping me having fun!'

Suddenly, I'm full of remorse. I wrap my arms round him, trying to get my voice to calm down. 'I'm so sorry. You're right, but it just scares me, your eyes looking like that. I didn't mean anything, and I know you only wanted to make me laugh. Oh, please stop crying, sweetheart, please!'

I have to use every trick in the book to calm him down, anxiety rising in me all the time. I crush him to me until the fight goes out of him. At last he goes limp in my arms, head falling on my shoulder, and then I can kiss him and wipe away all his tears. 'I'm sorry,' I whisper, again.

Later, when he falls asleep, I finally give in to my exhaustion. I have to stop thinking about the Facebook group, I need to try and switch off. Look what a state I got me and Charlie in. I have to do better, I have to get some rest. I run myself a bath, the rarest of treats. This isn't on my list of strategies but now I think, why isn't it? It should be. After all, water has always helped me. The bath is only lukewarm, though; I can't really afford to use too much hot water. I can feel the bumps of my spine against the enamel when I lie back, the ridges of my pelvis too. I wonder if I've lost a bit of weight recently, but really all I care about is closing my eyes. Held in the water like this, maybe I could sleep.

I open my eyes, sure I heard a noise, out in the hallway. Where I left my phone to charge. It is ringing, I'm certain of it. Positive this time that it isn't just my imagination. I push myself up out of the bath, my arms strangely weak, leaving puddles on the floor as I wrap myself in a towel.

My wet hair is freezing on my shoulders as I reach my phone and swipe to answer, standing there in bare feet in the hallway.

'*Hello?*'

'Hello … This is Marianne Fowler.' The voice is brisk, curious. 'I saw your message in the Facebook group. First time anyone's posted there in a while.'

'Oh my goodness … Marianne?' Her face comes back to me in a flash. Cropped brown hair, glasses, a wide chin. Marianne Fowler, lead administrator for the civil service office. Knowledgeable, reliable; I remember how I looked up to her back then.

'Yes. Hello there, Jennifer.'

Even now, she remembers me.

I sink down onto the hallway chair. My legs feel weak, goose-bumped in the cold. There is no going back. I have stepped outside of my small, restricted world, and reached out into the big wide beyond.

'So you're trying to get in touch with Sarah?' she says, her tone calm and business-like.

Of course Marianne doesn't know. How on earth was she supposed to? I've gone looking to her for information, but to begin with, I have to tell her why. 'I'm so sorry to have to tell you this,' I say. I don't know what to do but come out with it. 'Sarah … Sarah Jones … she died.' I wrap an arm around my waist. I'm light-headed as I relay the basics to Marianne. 'She was living here, in Brixton, and she passed away. By herself, in her flat. Nobody missed her for a really long time. Somehow she completely fell off the radar.'

Marianne goes very quiet when I tell her. I wonder if she thinks I'm joking. I shouldn't have blurted it out like this, I realize. This is something that should be broached face to face; a normal person would have understood that straight away. We are practically strangers to each other after all this time, Sarah Jones our only morbid link. How can we really talk about this over the phone?

'Marianne? Could we possibly meet? I'd really like to talk to you. I'm … I'm trying to make sense of things and perhaps you can help.'

'Meet up?' says Marianne, her voice a little breathless. 'Yes, I suppose that might be best.'

She tells me she has a few health problems and isn't managing to get out much. Would I be willing to come to her? 'I can give you my address right now,' she adds.

I've no time to think, and anyway how could I say no? 'Yes – just wait one second. Let me get a pen and paper.' I almost slip as I hurry through to the kitchen, wet feet on bare linoleum. I fumble on the counter, somehow finding a biro.

Now I just need something to write on, but all I can find is Molly's birthday invite, stuck on the fridge. I tug it down and flip it over, blank side up, on the table.

'Did you find a pen?' Marianne says.

The biro I'm holding quivers in my hand; drops of water fall from my hair. Am I really going to do this? Meeting up with Marianne means committing, and it means explaining everything I've done. But meeting up with Marianne is perhaps my only chance for answers. The pen steadies as I press it to the paper.

'Okay,' I say, 'I'm ready. Go on.'

Chapter 12

There is a visitor now who comes to Prin's house. Mum says she is going to come every week.

'What for?' says Prin, and Daddy says, 'To make sure that we are all doing fine!'

He says it just like that, with an exclamation mark at the end; Prin can hear it in his voice. Prin has been learning about exclamation marks in school. They can mean different things, she has learned, like they can mean someone is surprised or that they are excited or happy. Or sometimes it means that they are shouting, but Prin thinks this one is the happy/excited exclamation mark. Daddy is happy and excited about the visitor.

Jane seems nervous though. 'I don't like talking about things,' she tells Prin. 'I don't like it when they ask me questions. It gives me bad dreams.'

Prin doesn't really understand. She likes it when people want to know things from her. She thinks as well about what Daddy said, and about how Jane's mouth tends to turn down. She doesn't think that's the best thing to show visitors. 'Just tell them about all the fun we're having,' she suggests.

Prin's house always looks nice, but on the day the visitor is due, Mum does an extra clean and goes on at Prin more than usual to put her toys away. Prin asks whether she can wear her pink dress again, but this time Daddy says no, that ordinary clothes would be best. So both Jane and Prin dress in ordinary outfits: a skirt and a yellow T-shirt for Prin, and a pair of jeans and a pink T-shirt for Jane. They both look nice.

When the doorbell rings, Prin runs straight to the door, determined to get there before anyone else, even though Mum is shouting her back from the kitchen. She is big enough and strong enough to undo the latch lock, and she pulls it down and tugs the door open. And you'd never guess, but it's Fiona standing there on the doorstep! She is wearing the same badge on a string that she was wearing before, when they went to those other people's house to fetch Jane.

'Hello!' says Prin, and her sentence has an exclamation at the end too, because now she is happy and excited about the visit, just like Daddy.

Fiona smiles down at her. 'Hello again,' she says. 'How are *you*?'

Prin remembers what Daddy said this morning. 'I am fine,' she replies. 'We are all doing extremely fine!'

Fiona's smile slips a little bit, but then jumps back up. 'Well,' she says. 'Is your mummy or your daddy in?'

'Yes, of course,' says Prin. 'Come right through.'

Prin leads Fiona through into the kitchen. Mum is wiping her hands on a dishcloth at the sink. When she turns round she looks a bit flushed as she holds a hand out to shake Fiona's. Daddy gets up from where he is sitting with Jane at the kitchen table. Now *he* is holding Jane's hand, Prin notices. Everybody in the world seems to want to hold Jane's hand! She isn't sure why Jane needs so much handholding.

'Shall we go into your living room?' says Fiona. 'Will the girls be all right on their own for a while, while we talk first?'

Now Prin is confused. This isn't like a normal visit when one of Mum's friends drops round, or Mum and Daddy hold a dinner party, or when Prin has a friend from school come to play. She doesn't know what they are going to talk about. And she doesn't know why she and Jane have to go away and play on their own. She can only suppose that this is one of those grown-up talks that grown-ups sometimes have. Ones she isn't supposed to listen to. But does.

'Oh yes,' says Daddy. 'They'll be fine. Girls? Why don't you go upstairs and play?'

So that's what Prin and Jane do, except that upstairs in Prin's pretty bedroom, Jane doesn't want to do much of anything except stare out of the window, not even trying to have fun, and all of a sudden, Prin finds herself in a mood, one where all her toys and games annoy her, and she is tired of the summer and of being so hot.

She sits down at her desk and pulls out her tray of coloured pencils and opens a colouring book, squashing the pages down flat with her palms so that the spine cracks. Then she picks up one coloured pencil after another and scribbles on the paper, not caring about staying within the lines, not really caring about the picture at all.

After a while, there's a knock at the door, and Mum's head comes poking round. 'All right?' she says.

Prin pushes the colouring book away. 'Can we come down

now?' she says, unable to stop a little bit of grumpiness sneaking into her voice.

Mum smiles and puts her head on one side. 'Very soon,' she says. 'Fiona would just like to speak to Jane for a bit first.' She holds out a hand towards where Jane is still sitting hunched up on the window seat – holding hands again! – and says, 'Will you come down, Jane and have a chat?'

Prin looks back and forth between them. 'And then me? And then it'll be my turn for the chat?'

Whatever these *chats* are, she doesn't want to miss out.

'Oh,' says Mum. 'Maybe! I'll ask her. But for now, would you just stay up here? It looks like you're doing some lovely colouring. Either way, we won't be long.'

Prin looks down at her book. Her colouring is horrible, anyone can see that. But Mum decided it was nice, because she wanted Prin to stay up here and enjoy her pencil crayons and not cause a fuss.

Things get decided like that all the time in Prin's house.

Prin slouches in her desk chair, crosses her arms and kicks her feet. Jane slides down from the window seat and crosses the room and takes Mum's hand, and now Prin wishes that Daddy would come up and sort this out and make it better, but she can hear him still talking to Fiona downstairs, laughing his big jolly laugh, so he is *busy* and Prin knows he won't come and fix this.

'We won't be long,' says Mum again, and then she and Jane are gone. Prin can hear their footsteps tripping down the stairs, and then it's just Prin and her room and her stupid pencil crayons and her huff.

*

And then the visit is over. Fiona says only six more words to Prin before she leaves, Prin counts them. She comes out of her room at the end, when Daddy calls her, and hovers on the bottom step, twining her arms round the newel post while the grown-ups say their goodbyes.

'Look after your cousin, won't you?' Fiona says to Prin. Those are the six words. That's it! And Prin wants to roll her eyes and say, '*Of course!*'

Then there are lots of smiles and shaking hands and then the front door bangs shut and Fiona is gone.

*

That night, Prin wakes up. She has been dreaming of … something to do with stars and jumping, leaping – but now she is awake. Wide awake.

Over in the bed by the wall, Jane is whimpering and moaning. Prin feels a lump in her stomach. She remembers once when she had a nightmare herself, woke up in the dark and was so scared, and cried out for someone to come and help her, because she couldn't move to turn on the light in case a monster gobbled her hand. And then Mum came in and tried to shush her, but Prin was too upset by then, big sobs kept on falling out of her mouth. Then Daddy came in and it was different. He told Prin to stop making such a noise, and then Prin forced herself to swallow the next big sob that was coming – and her crying disappeared, just like that. She lay back down and Mum and Daddy went away and … she supposes that she just fell back to sleep.

But now Jane is crying and making a noise, and Prin knows

Daddy will be annoyed all over again if he has to come in. Daddy can't bear crying, it makes him so angry. He once smacked Prin when she went wailing on and on, unable to stop crying when the school gerbil died. Daddy feels best when everything is fine, and that's why it's always best to be fine, if you can.

Prin pushes back her covers and slips out of bed and goes over to her cousin. She puts her hands on Jane's shoulders and gives her a shake.

'Wake up!' she says. 'Are you having a nightmare?'

But Jane isn't asleep, she realizes. She is awake, and still crying.

Prin lets go of her. 'What's the matter?' she says. 'What is it?'

But Jane just crunches herself up tighter in the bed and goes on letting out big teary noises.

'You shouldn't cry like that,' Prin says. 'Crying is what makes it hurt, don't you see?' She climbs onto the bed beside her. It's a tiny bed really, there's hardly any room. 'Daddy says, if it didn't hurt, you wouldn't cry. So if you don't cry, then it won't hurt!'

But now Jane is saying something. Prin has to lean right in to her to make it out. When she does, she remembers with a jolt the time she was invited over for a sleepover, and in the beginning she was having such fun with the pizza and the films and the games they played, but then it was an hour, two hours after Prin's bedtime and she didn't know the house or the adults in it and she found herself getting panicked, hysterical, crying out what Jane is crying out now.

'*I want my mummy! I want to go home!*'

Prin feels very bad for her cousin then. Very sorry and sad for her. Prin wants to help, she really does.

She goes to the desk, where they left the zoetrope the other day, and switches on the desk lamp so that they can see properly. She removes the cylinder of card with the running horse on it and finds another one, one she knows that Jane will like, the one with the couple dancing. She fits it inside, lining up the slits. She carries it back over to Jane in the bed.

Jane is sitting up now, her thin body jolting with tearful hiccups. Prin tells her to shove over, so she can get in beside her properly. She sits next to her cousin, leaning back against the pillows, and rests the zoetrope on her bent knees. They can see in the light from the desk. Inside the zoetrope, there is a couple dancing

'Look,' Prin says. 'Can you see them in there?'

The couple are so graceful as they waltz around. Prin once saw Mum and Daddy dance like that, ages ago. 'Look,' she tells Jane now. 'There they are, the lovely husband and wife. They can be *your* mummy and daddy, can you see them? Just watch,' she tells her cousin. 'Just watch.'

And so Jane watches, and as she does her breathing slows and her body relaxes and in only a little minute or two, her crying eases, just like Prin hoped it would.

Chapter 13

I have to wait until Wednesday – five whole days – before I can visit Marianne. On Wednesdays I finish work at midday, and it's supposed to be the time when I sort out my life, with a precious few hours to myself before I have to pick up Charlie. I should be using it to go to the supermarket, clean the flat, tackle all those jobs on my to-do list. But instead this week I will use it to travel across London to the address Marianne gave me. Way out along the District line: Ealing Broadway.

I try to hurry through all my work tasks for the morning, but my concentration isn't great; I have to double-check everything and I still find mistakes. There's so much I'm trying to carry in my head, so many question marks and unknowns, like little holes that the details of my work tumble into.

When I see Abayomi come back from a meeting, I go through to his office with Sarah's file. 'Abayomi? Do you have a minute?'

He is still shrugging himself out of his coat and he turns to me with a faint frown on his forehead.

'I need to update you on Ms Jones,' I tell him. I haven't forgotten the protocols he spelled out for me. 'The next of kin … The police still haven't been able to trace anyone, so I'm not sure what to do from here.' I don't say anything about the email in my personal inbox. I have no idea how to tell him about that. And I don't tell him about my own un-protocol'd plan. It feels completely separate from this. It's not like before when I lied about the spreadsheet; this is personal business, my own need to find answers, and it would only complicate things to discuss it here at work. And what if someone here tried to stop me? I'm not sure I'd be able to bear that.

Abayomi runs a hand across his brow. 'There's no executor? No relative?'

'Not that they can find, no.'

'That's … I mean …' He shakes his head. 'But all right. Okay. Then we'll need to write to the Public Trustee. We'll have to sort it out through them.'

'The Public Trustee …' The term is unfamiliar to me. But maybe it's another avenue that could help. 'Okay, well, I can do that, if you just let me know the details and what to do.'

Abayomi hesitates. 'No, it's all right, I'll do it myself.'

I stare at him. 'Why? I can manage.'

'I'd rather handle it,' he says, his voice uncharacteristically firm. He holds his hand out for Sarah's file and I give it to him, a small, hard knot of unease in my stomach.

*

Come twelve, I tidy what is left on my desk and take my coat down from the hook by the door. Brixton Station is mere seconds from the office, and I'm on the Tube within minutes. As the train pulls through tunnel after tunnel, I try to rehearse what to do and what to say when I get there, but my mind keeps running into dead ends. I've really no idea how to hold this conversation. I don't know what to say about the email Sarah sent me or the fact that I missed the annual check, and honestly if I think too much about what I'm doing, I'm in danger of getting off at the very next stop. In the office, Marianne was so efficient, knew everything about everything. And when I first came to London, I was so clueless. I'd never lived on my own before, didn't really know how anything worked. It was Marianne who helped me, setting me straight in her business-like way. Direct debits, tax codes, school applications, the lot. And with the office work she assigned me too, she efficiently corrected my mistakes until I got it, until I could do everything right. I really respected her, I wanted to please her. And … something else too that I never would have said: how maternal it felt sometimes, the way she'd given me advice, guidance. Maybe it was that feeling, on top of everything, that made me hold myself back, worried that if I let myself open up, I wouldn't be able to contain what I felt. So I kept my distance from her, like with everyone else then and everyone since. Thanked her for her help, was so politely grateful, letting her think I'd learned to be quite self-sufficient. Competent, professional, everything under control.

And now I'm going to her with this awful situation, and I don't know what it will make her think. But at the same time I feel such a sense of responsibility: to do something, to find answers, to somehow make this right. My own memories of Sarah are so limited; they don't shed any light at all. And although I don't know what Marianne will be able to tell me -- maybe a lot or maybe nothing – all I know is, at least I'll have tried.

I get lost though, trying to find my way to Marianne's flat. She gave me good, clear instructions over the phone, but in the rush of the call I didn't note them down properly. The app on my phone has got confused as well. I'm not familiar with this part of London and the roads in front of me don't seem to match up with the lines on my map. It's as though the city has turned maze-like, distorting my sense of direction. I find myself travelling in circles, doubling back on myself until eventually I have to ask someone for help. I stop a man with a sharp face who looks at me impatiently while I reel off the address. It turns out that the road I'm looking for is right behind me, and now I finally find the right number – twenty-three – which is Marianne's door.

Outside, it takes me a moment. If I knock, there's really no turning back. I will have really involved myself. My life will have become entangled with someone else's. It won't just be me any more.

I need to be sure I'm ready for that.

When I ring the bell, Marianne is a long time coming. I don't want to ring again, I already fear I am intruding into her life, but I am standing out in the cold and she should be expecting me and perhaps it's just that she didn't hear me. I am just reaching up to ring again when there is a clatter behind the door and then it swings open.

She looks so much older than I remember. I know it's been three years since I last saw her, but in that time she looks as if she has aged ten. Her hair has greyed and she leans on a stick – a grey plastic crutch – and seems shaky on her feet.

'Jennifer,' she says. In person though, her voice sounds just like I remember. There's a warmth in it that was lost on the phone line and I feel a rush of that old feeling, that longing to huddle under her wing.

'Marianne,' I reply, my voice as formal as ever. 'Thank you so much for getting in touch.'

She shakes her head. 'I should be thanking you. If you hadn't messaged, I would never have known.' She holds the door open for me so I can step inside. In the hallway, the flat smells strange; stale somehow. Not unpleasant … just strange.

'Should I take my shoes off?'

Marianne herself is wearing grey slippers. She looks down at my feet, then up again. 'Yes,' she says. 'If you wouldn't mind.'

I reach down and fumble with the zip on the side of my boots, pull them off and place them, neatly, against the wall of the hallway. They look a little incongruous there, in the emptiness. I wonder when Marianne last had a visitor. Now, in my socks, I follow her through into her kitchen. There are brown cabinets on the walls and a stark strip-light above us. Marianne's breathing is a little heavy. 'How long has it been,' she says, 'two years?'

I clear my throat. 'Three,' I tell her.

She nods and lowers herself to sit at the table that presses up against the corner. It seems chilly in her flat. I wonder if – like me – she tries not to have the heating on in the day. I think again of how I remember her: a dozen jobs always stacked on her desk, a source of energy in the office, coordinating everything, always on the go. I'd never thought of her life outside. Yet her flat here seems so bare: the surfaces in the kitchen are perfectly polished, no washing up cluttering the sink. It doesn't seem as though anyone else lives here. I think of my own flat where only Charlie and I live, and we hardly have any visitors either, but our flat feels much more lived-in than this.

She gestures to me to sit down, and I notice now the knots in her fingers. I slip into the seat across from her, precise and upright, the way I used to sit at my civil service desk.

'So,' she says. 'How on earth have you been?'

'Oh …' I shift on the chair. 'Well, fine. I'm still working for the Housing Association, down in Brixton.'

Marianne nods. 'That's good.'

'And … what about you? How are you keeping?'

Marianne gestures to her stick. 'Not so good … as you can see. Arthritis. It forced me to retire a few months ago.'

So now she's here, in this flat, on her own.

'I'm really sorry,' I say. What I told her over the phone must have been such a shock. I regret that all over again; I wish I'd arranged first to meet her and then I could have told her everything, from the beginning, face to face.

She gives a smile. 'And how is Charlie? He must be – what now – nine?'

I blush, touched that she remembered. 'Yes, that's right, almost nine. He's doing – ' *tell the truth* – 'he's doing just fine.'

As though she has just thought of something, Marianne pushes herself up from the table again and fetches two glasses down from a cupboard. She runs each under the tap in the sink and carries them back to the table. 'Here,' she says. 'In case you're thirsty.'

'Thank you.' I reach out and take a sip. As soon as the water touches my throat, I realize she's right. I really am thirsty. I have to stop myself drinking it all in one go. I set the glass back down, still three-quarters full, and curl my hand back into my lap. I realize then that I've still got my coat on. There never seemed to be a suitable moment to take it off.

Marianne lowers herself back down, with a wince. 'I'm really struggling to get my head round what you told me,' she says. 'I mean, this was the Sarah Jones we both knew? And you said she died alone? In her flat? And, what – the police have just closed the case?'

I nod but haven't practised how to say any of this. 'Yes. There wasn't enough evidence of any crime. But … I was there when they found her, and she was my tenant. And when I realized that I knew her from before … The police case is closed and there should be an inquest, but I can't seem to leave it. I'm not sure the coroner will really provide answers. And I just have this … real need to understand.'

I try to think of the questions I rehearsed on the Tube, but they scatter away from me. *Just start*, I tell myself. *Just start*. 'We both worked with her,' I continue, 'but I was only there a short while. I … never really got to know anyone, and Sarah and I only crossed for a few weeks. But you were there so much longer, you maybe knew her better than me? Perhaps she talked to you, about herself and her life?'

Marianne takes a breath that turns into a cough. When she can speak again, she nods. 'She came and went from that job a couple of times. I mean, she worked there on and off, dipping in and out. But I still remember her quite clearly. I suppose I felt I knew her quite well.'

'You do? You did?' I try again to bring my own scarce memories to mind. Her profile against the light of the window. A foot bouncing under her desk … Nothing really more than that. Almost as though she wasn't quite a real person. Or as though it was me who was never really there.

Marianne is gazing at me, but I feel she isn't really seeing me. She's remembering. Going backwards in her mind.

'You know, some people ...' she begins. 'Some people are a little bit different.'

I wait, but she doesn't immediately go on. She takes a sip of her own water, her fingers claw-like against the glass.

'Different ... in what way?'

'Oh,' says Marianne. 'You know.' Her mouth turns up. A smile. Her features soften with it.

'I've seen lots of temps come and go,' she continues, 'but Sarah was ... Well, she was exceptionally pretty, of course, for a start. Those blue eyes.' She looks up at me. 'You remember?'

I can feel my stomach tightening. It's sort of strange, the way Marianne is talking. 'I guess so.'

'Well then, you know what I mean.'

Maybe. I suppose I do. It's true, Sarah was very pretty.

'And she was very outgoing. You know. It was always cheerful in the office when she was around. She got on with everyone. Although ... her main friends were elsewhere. She was part of a big group, outside of work.'

I can feel a hesitation; a little part of me that isn't sure. 'I know I don't *remember* her as shy or lonely. I mean, at least ... she never seemed that way.'

'The opposite. She made friends with everyone. Maybe you wouldn't have been aware of that. You tended to keep yourself to yourself.'

I feel my cheeks flush. She's right of course, and how could I think she hadn't noticed back then? As though she wouldn't have seen that in me, how reticent I was, how closed off. Pretending it was professional boundaries, nothing more. Making out to the world there was nothing I needed.

Marianne leans her cheek into her palm. 'She had a beautiful singing voice as well. That time she sang at the Christmas party … I told her she could have been a professional, but she just laughed it off. She was beautiful and talented, and so lovely with it.'

'Singing? I don't think I ever … If it was at a party, I guess I wasn't there.'

'Look,' she says. 'I got this out to show you.' She lifts something from the pile of papers at her elbow. An envelope, creased around the edges. Its flap hangs open. She pushes it across the table to me and I take it from her.

Inside there's a card. It sticks a little as I pull it out. There's a bright design of presents and stars with *Happy Birthday* written underneath. It's the sort of card you might find in any corner shop. I open it up. There's a message in loopy, swirling handwriting.

Dear Marianne, Wishing you a lovely day, Love Sarah.

I look up. Marianne is smiling again. Her eyes are shining. 'She wrote that for me.'

And you kept it, I think. *You treasured it.* Gently, I slide the card back in its envelope and hand it back across the table. She takes it and holds it in front of her with both hands. I have the sense of something then: how Marianne's impression of Sarah seems strangely skewed. As though she saw her through a rose-tinted lens. But maybe it was just that Sarah had that effect on people.

'But what I don't understand,' I say slowly, carefully, 'is how she ended up so alone. She died – and I still don't even know how – but even worse is that she lay in her flat for so long. That's the bit I'm trying to understand. I mean, I remember her as outgoing too, but there must have been some kind of difficulty she had, some kind of falling out, some kind of rupture with her friends? Her family too … Marianne, she'd removed all her contacts from her phone. Or perhaps she *was* shy really, or she didn't trust people, or …'

But Marianne is shaking her head. 'No, no … That's all wrong. She wasn't like that at all.' She takes another sip of her water. 'She was close to her parents, talked about them a lot. Don't you remember that photograph on her desk? And she had lots of friends, a whole London set. She was very, very popular. But kind as well, generous. Not the sort to fall out with people. She was always happy, always having fun. Going to parties, booking her next holiday. Between her temp contracts, she always seemed to be jetting off abroad. Outside the office, really she had quite a glamorous life.'

Glamorous? I try to grasp the picture Marianne is painting, and hold it alongside what I saw, what I know. That tiny bedsit, covered in dust, the rent unpaid, her door silted up with post. The two images seem whole worlds apart. And yet, haven't I always trusted Marianne's judgement? How many times have I known her to be right? I reach out and take another gulp of my own water, buying time to think of what to say next.

'So then … when did you last see her?' I ask. 'She died … she died months and months ago so, I mean, did she just stop coming in to work?'

Marianne shakes her head again, almost violently. 'Oh no,

she wouldn't do that. She wouldn't just abandon us like that. She got head-hunted. That's what happened.'

'Head-hunted?'

'It must have happened quite suddenly. I didn't even realize she was going, but after all, she didn't have a notice to serve. I had a week off, you see, and when I came back, she'd cleared her desk. The others told me that she got recruited by a big firm, a legal firm I think it was.'

'A legal firm? So when was the last time you saw her?'

Marianne frowns, thinking carefully. 'It would have been … last January. The very end of the month. I didn't get a chance to say goodbye to her. When I came back from leave, she was already gone.'

I try to fit the pieces together. Sarah moved into the flat last February. But a big legal firm was nowhere on her forms.

'I did try to call her a few times but …' Marianne breaks off and gives me a weak smile. 'She didn't answer. I don't suppose she had time to keep up with old friends. She would have been very busy in her new job by then.'

I swallow. This is the moment when I should tell her.

'I'd always known, really,' Marianne goes on. 'She was going to go on to bigger and better things. She was different. That's what I was telling you at the start—'

'Marianne?' I interrupt. 'I need to tell you something … Sarah? She sent me an email. Not recently, I don't mean. It was nearly three years ago, just before I left the office.'

Marianne's hand tightens on the birthday card she's still holding. 'An email? What did it say?'

'She … she was just forwarding a document, from her personal account because the work email was down. And she wrote, *stay in touch*. But you're right, I'm sorry, I always did keep myself to myself and so … Marianne, I never replied.'

Marianne stares at me. I swallow again, harder, ashamed of what I've told her. Afraid of what she might now say. In my awkwardness, I rush to move the conversation on.

'So do you have any idea what might have happened? How she could have lost touch with her family, all of her friends?'

Marianne sets her glass down. It makes a sharp *clack* against the table. 'I don't know. To be honest, since you contacted me, I've mostly tried not to think about it. I think I'd prefer just to remember her my own way.'

I look at Marianne and her words confirm the sense I had a minute ago: *you only saw what you wanted to see.*

Or maybe, like me, Sarah only showed people what she wanted them to know.

Because this picture Marianne is painting … how little it fits with what I saw. That crumpled figure on the sofa, undiscovered for almost a year, those dead flies on the table, the radio playing. And her writing '*stay in touch*' to a nobody like me.

But then I see another picture: the plates laid out on Sarah's table. And she *was* pretty, really pretty, and there *was* something about her, wasn't there? Even I can see that when I think of her. So whose version is right? The one I've been carrying, of someone troubled, isolated, struggling, alone, or Marianne's image, of someone so vivacious, so popular, always ready to reach out for new friends? I feel myself fracturing between the two, unable to mesh the narratives together.

I get up. I already have my coat on and I think I need really to go. 'Thank you for talking to me,' I say. 'I'm sorry I can't stay.'

Marianne just nods. She still has Sarah's card in her hands. I wonder how many times she has held it.

'You've been a lot of help,' I tell her.

She glances up at me. 'Have I?'

I nod. 'Of course.'

But the truth is I feel more off balance than ever. Marianne knew her, and says she knew her well, but what she has told me isn't the real truth about Sarah. It can't be. None of the pieces fit together. It only seems to have pushed them further apart.

She's looking up at me, as though coming to a decision in her mind. 'You know,' she says, 'I know someone else who might be able to help you. If no one else from the Facebook page gets in touch. Help you more than I have, I mean. There was an old boyfriend she talked about sometimes. I have the details somewhere, I once wrote them down for some reason. When I find them, I could text them to you. You could speak to him. Perhaps there are things he would know that I ... don't.'

I feel a rush of gratitude towards her, for acknowledging that there could be something she missed, and I feel that warmth towards her all over again. 'Thank you. I think that would ... really be helpful too.'

She has done her best. I can't ask her for more. This has been hard enough for her as it is. 'Thank you,' I say again. 'I really am grateful for this and ... and for everything you did for me back then. No, you don't need to get up,' I tell her. 'I can easily let myself out.'

It's been a good meeting, I tell myself, overall. I'm glad that I've come, really I am. It's been lovely to see Marianne, despite how she's changed and despite the awkwardness of our conversation at times. I've always admired her, always respected her.

And she's really tried her best to help and I promise honestly to keep in touch. I smile down at her as I do my zip up to leave, but then I see that she needs to say one last thing.

'Jennifer?'

'Yes?' I hover there, the zip cold on my neck.

'About the email she sent you.'

'Yes?'

'I wouldn't have done that. If it was me Sarah emailed, I would have replied. I would have stayed in touch.'

I'm standing above her, but I feel so tiny. 'I know. I know you would have.'

And although my head is aching, it's as though these words make a pact between us: acknowledging the error I've made, and my responsibility to put this right.

Chapter 14

At work the next day, I surprise myself with my own efficiency. My thoughts feel clearer, and my concentration is so much better than it has been these last few days. A sense of clarity is coming back.

At lunchtime, I tell Emma I'm heading out. 'Do you want me to get you anything from the shops?'

Emma looks up from the desk, her face bright. 'Um ...' she says. 'Would it be all right if you got me a KitKat?'

'Of course.'

She goes digging in her purse for some money and I stand there awkwardly. I want to tell her not to bother about money, but then I worry she'll feel she owes me and try to return the favour some time, and that just doesn't feel right. She hands over a two-pound coin. 'That'll be plenty, right?'

'Oh,' I say, 'more than enough.'

Once I get outside, I head into the Sainsbury's right next to the Tube station. Along with the KitKat, I buy myself a sandwich. For the first time this week, I actually have some appetite. I still only have those two items though, so I go to the self-scan checkout and bip them through with my contactless card. Now you can shop for most things without having to talk to anyone at all. Just a computer voice to tell you what to do and, *Thank you for shopping at Sainsbury's.* I add a plastic bag in too, even though it costs 5p. It just doesn't feel right to put Emma's KitKat straight into my coat pocket, where it might melt or get crushed.

It is a little warmer today, and I think maybe it would be nice to sit outside, in the sun. I've got my coat on, enough to keep warm. I head to the open area outside the Ritzy Cinema. They have all these seats here, scattered in little groups. A way of encouraging community, people coming together to talk. It's nice. Quite a few are empty, so I sit down on one while I eat my sandwich.

When I'm done eating, I pull out my phone and check in case Marianne has messaged. I check my email and Facebook too, even though there's nothing.

Then I just sit for a while, enjoying the sunshine. I know I can do with the Vitamin D and I can feel my muscles easing, the blood flow opening up. It makes me realize how tense I've been lately. I close my eyes against the sun's rays. I can hear the buses and the car horns and the traffic lights. But today they don't bother me. Today it's okay.

After a while though, the cold seeps in, even through my coat. The clock on the town hall chimes the half-hour: time to go back. I get up, a little stiffly, from the seat, and drop my empty sandwich carton into a bin. Back at the office, I push in through the main entrance doors, back into the warmth, and it warms me further as I quickly climb the stairs, the little bag with Emma's KitKat swinging from my wrist.

But when I open the door to my office, I jump in surprise.

There's no sign of Emma, but Abayomi is standing right by my desk.

'Jennifer,' he says. 'Do you have a moment?'

'Yes …' I tell him. 'Sure.' I set the plastic shopping bag down carefully. My desktop looks unusually dishevelled. Not ordered in the way I normally like. Did I really leave it like that before lunch?

I reach out to tidy up, clearing space for us, but instead Abayomi says, 'Will you come along to my office?'

I stop. 'Of course. I mean, just one sec.'

I pull Emma's chocolate bar out of the bag and put it on her desk along with her two-pound coin and a little Post-it note for her. *It hardly cost anything*, I write, *don't worry*. And then quickly, at the bottom, I add a little *x*.

Then I follow Abayomi to his room. He closes the door behind us and asks me to sit down. Instinctively, I realize I don't want to. But Abayomi sits and so I have to do the same. I find myself holding on tightly to the arms of the chair.

'Jenn, I apologize in advance for this. It's a little difficult to say, to be honest.'

I look at him without replying. My mind has suddenly gone quite blank, like switching off a TV screen. I'm just waiting for what comes next.

His words come at me with a sort of echo in them, distorted in my ears.

'I need to ask you to take some time off. A few days maybe. A couple of weeks at most.'

I stare at him. 'Why?' My voice comes out barely above a whisper and I can't get the cheerful tone to come.

'There's going to be a bit of scrutiny on us,' he says. 'From higher up. I think it would be easiest if you were out of the office for a bit.'

'You're suspending me?'

Abayomi removes his glasses and rubs the divots in the corners of his eyes. 'No … No. We can call it a leave of absence.'

'So … pretend I'm off sick or something?' I can feel myself clutching for some kind of resistance, as though there's a way to stop the slide.

'There won't be any interruption in your pay.'

I feel my arms grow weak; there's a hollow feeling in the pit of my chest. How can I explain to Abayomi what this means? That work, my job, feels like so much of what keeps me sane? The routines, the order of it, the repeating structure of each day. Enough contact with people to stave off loneliness, but always professional, never too much.

I fight to keep my voice steady. 'Please, Abayomi. Surely this isn't necessary. I can help. What if the police call here, what if they need me to answer more questions?' I'm grasping at straws, I know I am.

'Emma or I can answer those.'

'Please,' I say again. I'm cold with shame. 'I know I was off sick the other afternoon, but it won't happen again. Please. I really don't want to take time off.'

Abayomi shakes his head. 'I'm so sorry, Jennifer. But it won't be for long. A few days, a week at most, I'll make sure of it.'

I look at him, see the tension in his face, and feel something inside of me give. He is only trying to do his job. Having me in the office puts him at risk. And he's only trying to give me time to pull myself together. He can't know he's only pulling me further apart.

I stand up slowly. Abayomi doesn't say any more. I sense he's as embarrassed as I am.

In a gesture of kindness that almost breaks me, he holds the door open for me as I leave.

*

Outside, in the cold of Brixton High Street, I feel as though I've gone into some kind of free-fall. It's as though there's no pavement, no concrete under my feet, and very little right now holding me together. I don't know where to go. I don't *have* anywhere to go, except home, to my empty flat. I've walked these paving slabs hundreds of times, but suddenly they seem completely unfamiliar. What happened? I keep thinking. What just happened? Halfway up Brixton Hill, I sit down on a bench in the cold, my knees letting go of me. As they did a fortnight ago, pigeons gather round me, bumping each other and cooing. Their bobbing heads tilt up at me, waiting for food, but I've nothing to give them. I just sit there, defeated and ashamed.

I'm still sitting there when my mobile shrills. When I pull it out, I recognize the number of the CMHT. 'Hello?'

'Hello?' comes a soft voice in return. 'Is that Jennifer Arden?'

'Yes?'

'This is Freya,' the woman says. 'I hope you don't mind me calling again. It's about the feedback questionnaire, I think I said in my message.'

Freya. 'Yes,' I tell her. 'I remember. I'm sorry I didn't get back to you. I did get your voicemail, but ... there's been a lot going on.' I press a hand to my temple where a deep ache is growing.

'That's all right.' Freya's voice down the line is warm and

friendly, like a little anchor grounding me. 'I always planned to ring you again.'

'You said you're a support worker?'

She hesitates. 'Well yes,' she says slowly. 'For now. But I'm only going to be here a few more months. I've got a place to train as a clinical psychologist.'

'A psychologist?' I picture the psychologist I saw last year. She was so kindly. The tarmac under me feels a little more solid.

'Yes. It's been ... very competitive. It's taken me a long time to get on the course. But it's happening now and it's really very important to me. To help people. Honestly, that's all I really want to do.'

'Oh,' I say. 'Well, that's good. That's great. Sorry – you called about ... a questionnaire?'

'Oh yes,' she says. 'It's a bit of a new thing. More data they want to collect, but it shouldn't take more than a minute or two. Is that okay? I'm not interrupting you with anything else?'

'No,' I reply. 'I'm just ... heading home.' As I say that, I get to my feet. It's far too cold to sit out here. 'I can answer the questions while I walk, if that's okay?' Even though my legs feel wobbly, as though I'm crashing from an adrenaline high.

'Yes, that's perfect. If you sure you're okay with that? All right ... well then ... first question. On a scale of one to ten, how satisfied are you with how quickly your referral to the team was processed? One is "very unsatisfied". Ten is "very satisfied".'

'Ten,' I tell her. When my GP saw the state I was in, panic attacks happening daily by then, she didn't wait around and neither did they.

'Ten … Okay. That's good. That's great. Um … question two. On a scale of one to ten, how satisfied were you with the convenience of your appointment? One is "very unsatisfied". Ten is "very satisfied".'

There's a roar in my ear as the wind gets into the phone's microphone. I hope she can still hear me. I want to give good answers, the best answers. I want to let her know I've appreciated the help. 'Ten,' I tell her again.

'Yep, okay. Good. So, question three. How useful did you find the input you were given? One is "not at all useful" and ten "extremely useful".'

I step sideways to avoid a deep crack in the pavement. I think of the pages of advice in my bedside drawer. They have helped me, haven't they? I've been anxious lately, worrying so stupidly about Charlie again, but I can cope with that, can't I, with the help of those pages? 'Ten,' I say again. 'I'm sure that would be a ten.'

And yet my voice sounds really shaky.

'And … on a scale of one to ten, how much do you feel you've improved as a result of the input? One for "not at all"; ten, "a great deal".'

'Oh …' This hill seems so much steeper than normal, I can't believe how hard it feels to climb. 'Ten,' I tell her, just like for all the others. *Ten ten ten.*

'Well, that's great,' Freya is saying. 'I'm very pleased to hear that. I won't keep you much longer, I just needed to run through these, but that's pretty much everything now really, except …'

'Except what?"

'Oh …' Freya hesitates. 'It was just … I wasn't even sure

if I should mention this. I hope you don't think I'm crossing a line.'

I don't care. I don't mind. She can cross all the lines she wants. 'How do you mean?'

'Margaret presented your case in our team meeting – we discuss all the cases for the whole team, every week. She mentioned ... that a woman had died in one of your flats. That you were trying to find out what happened. Margaret sort of skipped over the whole thing, but I thought, my God, that must have been awful for you. I mean, I can't imagine the shock of it all.'

Suddenly, I can feel something wet at the side of my nose, and I try to pretend that it's only the wind making my eyes run, but honestly, I know that it's not. I can't remember when someone last thought about me like this, putting themselves in my shoes, expressing such honest concern for how I feel. I never let anyone get close enough to ask, and Freya only called for some questionnaire data, she doesn't even know me, but she's already understood. I'm nearly at the top of the hill now, so close to home, yet suddenly the words come tumbling out of me, as though Freya's kind voice has opened up a channel.

'Freya? The woman ... my tenant ... She had this table ... these three plates set out, she was expecting ... somebody, friends, guests, but no one came and I don't understand what happened. So I'm trying to trace friends of hers, anyone who might know. I was just trying to get answers but now everything seems to be such a mess, and I'm not sure I'm coping as well as I should ...'

On the other end of the line there's a silence, stretching,

opening a gap up under me. And then: '... Jennifer, I didn't know whether to say anything. I mean, I know you've said ten to everything on the questionnaire, and I didn't mean to intrude but – you don't sound too great.'

A thick lump catches in my throat. But I've been discharged, haven't I, so what can she do?

'I know,' I say. 'But it's fine. I'll be fine.'

All Freya called for was some stupid questionnaire. At best, she will tell me to book an appointment with my GP, go back through appropriate channels, explain everything from the beginning, get myself referred all over again.

I loosen my grip on my mobile. I'll hang up before she can tell me that, I won't make her say it, she doesn't need to, I'll just go. But just as the handset is slipping from my ear, I hear her:

'I think I should come and see you,' she says.

Chapter 15

I'm expecting Freya to visit at any moment, but for the rest of the day there is nothing. The next morning, I call up the Community Mental Health Team and leave a message on the automated voicemail. Maybe someone passed it on to her or maybe they didn't, but either way, no one calls me back. When I try to call Marianne, she doesn't even seem to have her phone switched on.

The reality of my suspension sinks in. While Charlie is at school, I'm completely on my own.

I have nothing to do and nowhere to go. It isn't good for me to be alone like this. I don't do well when left with just my own thoughts and without anything real to attach myself to.

I try to get out, give myself some structure. I get on a bus from the top of Brixton Hill and ride it to the other end of London and back. From the upper deck, I can see thousands of people, every conceivable colour, shape and size. But I don't know a single one of them and being among all these people makes me lonelier than ever. I've been in London for nearly four years and haven't made one single friend. There is no one I could get off and talk to, no one I can call up to go for coffee with, no one who might call round unexpectedly. No friends, and my family never visit.

I have a desperate urge to go to the office, to march in there against Abayomi's orders and sit myself down at my desk and refuse to move. But I would only humiliate myself even further. Abayomi has a wife and three children, a whole family at home, I've seen the photograph on his desk. He doesn't know that Charlie is all I have in my life. How can he know I have nothing else to do with my time? Instead, I go to the cinema – the Ritzy. I buy a box of popcorn but I barely eat any of it. I sit through some strange art-house film, trying to understand what's going on, and I get back home feeling sick and dizzy. Saturday passes in a strange sort of blur. On Sunday, I manage to take Charlie to the park.

But – except for the school runs – I don't go out at all after that.

I spend the next two days balled up on the sofa underneath a blanket. There's just nothingness, a vacuum, that fills up with my thoughts. I'm so ashamed; I keep picturing Abayomi sitting across from me with such a look of disappointment on his face. I go over and over the mistakes I've made. I try not to panic about the trouble I might be in. The hours until I can go and collect Charlie crawl past like snails, so much slower than the rushing of my mind; I punctuate the empty time by making cups of tea that I don't drink. I try to make myself forget about Sarah, my need for answers, but I find myself checking my phone again and again for Marianne's text. Sometimes I think I'll manage to nap, but if I close my eyes, all that happens instead is that images play like a film on the ceiling above me. I see Sarah, before and after, I see myself in her flat, I see myself picking something up from the floor – something soft and square – a cushion? I see Sarah lying below me, I see Charlie, I see my own hands—

I jerk myself up. Lying in bed only makes me feel worse. It makes me feel as if I'm not coping, when I am coping, of course I am.

By Wednesday afternoon, though, I am wrung out. Charlie is already fractious when we get back after school. I haven't been near the supermarket and we have run out of all the things he likes for dinner. The only option is cheese on toast, but he hates cheese, he tells me, which isn't even true, but he is in a bad temper. I stand at the grill and pull out the toast, which I have managed to burn at the edges. More than ever now, despite my efforts, I can't get Sarah out of my head. I feel the questions crawling round my skull, like insects. I can't stop going over everything Marianne said, all the other fragments I've collected about Sarah. Every tiny thing I remember about her. Sometimes the pieces look as though they might come together but a moment later they all unravel, nothing to hold them in place; then the whole process starts all over again.

I set the grill tray down and take a deep breath, forcing the branches of my lungs to open. I have to focus, I have to set my questions aside, lock them up at the side of my mind. I give Charlie ketchup and his favourite drink and it's enough, this time, for him to accept the sorry dinner I've made.

After he's finished eating and I've washed up his plate and cutlery, we sit together on the living-room sofa, so I can help him with his maths homework. He has a book of arithmetic to work through, two pages of sums and subtractions.

Charlie is okay at maths usually, but this evening he is rushing the questions, making silly mistakes on problems I know he can easily solve. Can't he?

I watch him hesitating over the numbers, not seeing the obvious solutions.

'What's wrong?' I finally blurt out. 'You know you can do these.'

But what if he can't? What if something has changed, slipped within him? Could it happen like this? I try to think about what I have read online, but all the information has tangled up in my head. I can't seem to sort it out.

Now Charlie is getting angry, emotions bubbling up within him, and my heart cries that the fact he isn't controlling his temper is another sign.

I pull the workbook out from under his hands, his pencil scratching a streak across the page. I set it on my own lap and flip back through the pages, right back to the beginning, to the problems I know he could practically do in his sleep.

I set the book back down on his knees, pushing the pages back under his fingers. 'Here. Show me.'

He looks up at me, a mixture of anger and anxiety twisting his features. He knows it's a test.

'These ones,' I say. 'Show me. I need to see that you can do it.'

I don't feel in control of myself. The anxiety has distorted me in its grip. But I'll feel better, I'll *be* better, if I can get proof. I just need to check. I pick up the pencil and push it into his grasp. He stares down at the page. Most of the sums are filled in already, but there are the optional extras we don't usually bother to do.

'Show me,' I say again. He presses the pencil to the page. For one awful moment, I am terrified that he can't do them. He is taking so long. It is excruciating, watching him fill in

136

the answers. Is he really finding it that hard, or only going slowly to spite me?

He finishes the first one and I pull the workbook towards me to check. With a rush of relief, I read his answer: correct. I tell myself, *let that be enough*. I bend over the workbook and turn to the original page of his homework. I fill in all the answers myself, each one correct, perfect. If I've missed something, if there really is a problem, then at least no one at school will know. The homework is done.

Charlie slides from the cushions, stands up. The way he is looking at me …

'I'm sorry,' I say. 'It's just that – we were taking too long. If you want, we can look them over together in the morning. I'll rub out what I've written and you can do them again, by yourself.'

I sit there, holding the workbook out towards him. He is taller than me, standing up like that, and his face is so angry and stiff. For a second, I fear he's going to hit me, lose control absolutely, and I'm aware of myself rising to my feet, and I can't even say what I'm about to do when—

My mobile pings.

We both jump at the noise. I lower the workbook and pick up my phone from the couch. When I see the number, I reach a hand out to Charlie. I manage to take him by the shoulder. 'I'm sorry,' I tell him. 'Let's leave it for now. I have to get this.' He takes the closed workbook from me, silently, and goes through into the kitchen. I hear him scrape a chair out from the table.

My fingers are shaking as I key in my password to open the screen properly.

Sorry, Marianne writes, *for taking so long to get back to you. I couldn't find the details I was looking for. I don't have a number or email or anything, but I remember his name and where Sarah said he worked.*

Then a little gap and the next message: Alastair Matthews, and the name of a hospital in north London. And a last line: *Please let me know whatever you find out.*

*

I should probably stop. I should probably leave it. But what else do I have to do with my time? I want to be working, I want to be helpful. And I'm desperate for something on which to focus my mind.

So, late that night, I find myself sitting with my laptop, all my senses amplified: the feel of the keyboard under my fingertips, the sound of the laptop fan whirring, the smell of soap from the shower I've just had.

I type the name of the hospital into Google. And still I wonder what on earth I am doing. Again, the words echo through my head. *Don't get involved. Don't get involved.* But look what happened to Sarah when no one got involved. When no one thought it was any of their business. When everyone assumed she was doing fine, better than fine. When everyone else was too busy to know. And there's that email in my inbox. And there's Marianne, needing to know.

On the hospital's own site I type his name into the search bar exactly: Alastair Matthews. The search functions spins but then the screen comes back with nothing. I switch over to Google: *Alastair Matthews, hospital, London*, but nothing comes together. I try all kinds of different spellings of his name, but even than none of my attempts bring up any results. I search and search, but can't find any details. I don't even know what his job is there. Doctor? Nurse? I don't even know what he looks like. And hospitals. The very thought of entering one makes the nausea rise up, flashes of memory cascading through my mind. The sirens, the panic and all the hours in that claustrophobic ward. It makes the breath catch in my throat.

I let my fingers slide from the keyboard. I don't have to go, I could stop all of this now. I know logically that I could. But I don't feel sure that I am operating that logically any more. I feel as if something deep within me has come to the surface. Under the new rawness of my skin, there's an itch, an urge, a burning need to know. As if piecing together Sarah's story will allow me to piece together the whole story of myself.

A voice whispers to me, so clear it doesn't even seem like my own thought: *Why don't you just go there?* it says.

*

I sleep on the idea. Or at least, I lie in bed awake and think on it, over and over. Charlie sleeps peacefully next door, untroubled, fine. And I am fine too, despite everything that has happened. I am sure I am. It's just that there's so much going round in my head. Around 3 a.m., I give up, get up instead and pull on some clothes.

In the living room, I lay out sheets of paper on the coffee table and try to organize what I have learned so far about Sarah. I scribble on the blank pages everything I have gleaned.

The estimated dates of when she died, the time when her life crossed paths with Marianne's, with mine. When she sent me that email.

According to Marianne, she used to have a boyfriend, she had a job, and friends and colleagues. Somewhere in that time, though, something went wrong. A reason to leave her job, a rift with her parents. A reason to remove all her contacts from her phone. And yet, she must have still been in contact with someone. More than one person. She had guests due, she *wasn't* all alone.

I place pieces on my map, I draw lines between them. I sketch out hypotheses, possibilities, ideas. They make patterns, shapes, they fill up the page. I run out of paper and go through Charlie's stationery box to get more. I must end up with ten, a dozen sheets in all, spread out all over the living-room table. It doesn't seem to matter if I'm not reaching a conclusion. Just the process of it absorbs me. I feel as if I'm making something, constructing something. I'm not looking at the clock or aware of the time. I'm completely absorbed in my task. I feel a strange giddiness, a sort of fluttering happiness. I feel wide awake. I should be tired, in fact, I should be exhausted, but instead now it's as though I've broken through something and I don't even feel the need for sleep any more. I have an energy I can't seem to burn off. Is it because I feel this sense of purpose?

Or is it simply because in filling my head with questions and possible answers about Sarah, I am leaving no room for all the other thoughts and anxieties that usually haunt me? Whatever it is, this mission has taken me out of myself. I feel clearer, freer, happier than I ever usually do.

Around five, I drift into a fragile sleep, right there on the sofa, still dressed, and when Charlie shakes me awake the next morning, my back, my neck, my whole body is stiff, but everything seems a whole lot clearer. The hospital won't be so hard to get to from Brixton. I can take the Tube and change at Euston, or there is even a bus that will take me almost straight there.

'Mummy,' says Charlie, 'what are you doing?'

I smile up at him and open my arms. 'Silly Mummy,' I say. 'I was watching TV and I just fell asleep.'

He looks at the pages scattered in front of me, but he doesn't say anything about them, doesn't ask. 'Can I have breakfast?' he says instead, and I get up and pour his favourite cereal.

The morning unfolds quite normally from there.

Still in the clothes I tugged on last night, I hurry Charlie to school, kissing him goodbye at the school gates, his cheek cold under my warm lips. Then I duck back to the flat to put on a much smarter outfit and do my make-up properly and get my own breakfast. I've got into the habit of skipping it of late, but today I really should get some fuel inside me. When I pull the bread out from the bread bin, though, it's mouldy, and there's so little milk left it's not worth a bowl of cereal. I tell myself I'll pick up something on the way instead, put the milk back in the fridge and throw the bread away.

I put on one of my smart work suits, re-do my hair and touch up my make-up. I check I have everything – wallet, phone, keys – and I'm just in the hallway zipping up my boots when the doorbell rings.

I freeze, balanced on one leg. Who is calling? They're right there, on the other side of the door. Carefully, I lower my foot and stand up straight. When I put my eye to the peephole in the door, there's a woman standing there, smartly dressed like me, official-looking. Suddenly I have a strange, irrational dread that sets my head spinning and my ears ringing. My mind flicks back to the moment of PC Delliers photographing my shoes. And then that nightmare I had that night, of the police coming to arrest me. Because what if there are all kinds of things I don't remember? Despite all my scribbling, despite all my notes. I didn't remember about Sarah's email, so what if there is something huge, terrible that I have forgotten, something I did and then simply painted over, my mind erasing it like whitewashing a wall?

I'm struggling to breathe as I grip the handle and tug the door open, forcing the fear back, forcing my mind down.

When the woman on the doorstep says her name, it feels as though my whole body goes limp.

'Jennifer? I'm Freya.'

Freya. She has come to visit me after all. My muscles relax, my lungs expand.

Her smile and eyes are as kind as her voice. I stand there in my coat and half-done-up boots. 'Yes. Hello.'

She hesitates. 'You're heading out?'

'No … I mean, yes … I …'

'Could you possibly hang on five minutes?' She holds up a paper bag with the logo of some fancy coffee shop on it. 'I brought cupcakes,' she says, and I feel as though we're in one of those American TV shows where friends drop in on each other, bringing treats.

'Oh,' I say. 'Thank you.' Underneath my suit, my stomach rumbles.

'So … should I come in?'

I'm still so off-guard that I automatically say yes. I open the door wide to let her step in, and her soft coat brushes my hand as she passes.

I hurriedly tug my boots and coat back off, and follow her inside, into my own flat.

'Through here?' she says, pointing towards my kitchen.

'Yes, okay …' I still feel a bit dizzy. It already feels so different from Margaret's visit. That one was so formal and … brisk. I think about what Freya said over the phone, about what Margaret presented in their meeting: *She just skipped over it …*

And I didn't have the nerve to tell Margaret anything, because she seemed so weary and stressed and worn out.

But here is Freya, bright-faced and smiling, with cupcakes.

She hovers over the sink, drawing the cakes out of their sticky paper bag, little crumbs scattering on the draining board. I rummage in a cupboard to find plates we can use.

'I was going to ring you beforehand and let you know I was coming,' she says over her shoulder. 'But then I was so nearby anyway, I didn't mind stopping in on the off chance. I'm just sorry it's been a while since we spoke. It was partly because Margaret had already discharged you. I had to sort out reopening your case.'

I shake my head. 'It doesn't matter. I've been all right.'

She pauses to look at me. Her kind eyes have the question in them: *but have you, honestly?*

And honestly, it's hard for me to tell. Have I ever been the best judge of my own mind, my own sanity? But maybe Freya can help me with that. This is her job, her profession, isn't it? She's going to be a clinical psychologist, for heaven's sake.

She gives the cupcakes a little shake then places each one carefully on the two plates I'm holding out. She leans against the worktop and takes a deep bite of hers. The pink icing is taller than the cake itself. I look down at mine and my stomach shrinks. 'I haven't had much appetite lately,' I tell her, setting the plate aside. 'Thank you, though, it looks really nice.'

Freya lowers her own plate. 'You haven't been eating?'

I look back at her. Her eyes are hazel, I see now. Everything about them speaks of concern. 'Not very well, I suppose.' I never said any of this to Margaret. With Margaret, I didn't know how. But Freya has arrived like a friend instead of a professional. Warm-hearted, casual, open-minded: it works so much better to put me at ease.

'Or sleeping either?'

It's as though Freya already knows how I am. 'Or sleeping,' I confirm, more honest with her than I have been with anyone in a very long time.

Perhaps by now she knows all about my case – or at least everything I chose to tell the team at the time. Which was never everything: never the worst part. Perhaps she has asked Margaret to go through what details they have. If so, then she knows what happened last year with Charlie. How it all started with me watching that TV documentary, the one about kids with cerebral palsy, and getting those awful fears in my head. The anxiety that turned into panic attacks, which then started happening all the time. And then that awful, awful incident at sports day when everything came to a terrible head. Charlie in the three-legged race and me watching his every movement like a hawk, my chest crushed with anxiety, a panic attack threatening to explode at any moment. Charlie was out in the lead, winning the race, but staggering and stumbling against the other boy, looking so monstrous, such a lurching mess. I rushed onto the field, unable to bear it, snatching him to me, fighting to rip the ties from his leg. And Charlie shrieking at me, screaming at me because he had been *winning*, Charlie lashing out with all his might, hitting me and catching his elbow as well on the little boy next to him, splitting his lip, bruising his face …

They called an ambulance for me in the end. Because when the panic attack took hold, it honestly felt as though I was dying. But also because I'd completely lost it. Because I'd seemed completely insane. When they came and checked me, and checked the little boy, nothing turned out to be as bad as it looked. It really was just a panic attack, they told me. And the little boy would be just fine, he was more upset about losing the race.

But no one from school looked at it that way. And they have avoided me and Charlie ever since.

'The truth is,' I tell Freya now, 'I still struggle with Charlie sometimes. When he does certain things. When he looks a certain way …' Freya holds her gaze steady on me as she listens. 'I love him so much, you see, I never want him to not be okay. I just know, sometimes, it's me that makes him that way. It's me creating the problems in the first place.'

Freya nods, a gentle nod. 'It isn't easy,' she says, swallowing her cake, 'caring so much. Wanting things to be perfect and right. You're doing your best. I can see how hard you're trying and how much you love him. Just from how you speak, I can tell.'

The balloon of tension eases from my chest. 'Yes,' I say. 'Thank you. Thank you for saying that.'

Now I manage to pick up my cake and take a bite. It tastes strangely synthetic, but I don't mind. As I swallow, I glance at the clock. The five minutes she suggested have already rushed past. Part of me wants to just sink into her company, but I'm worried that if I don't get on that bus to north London now, then in another few minutes I'm going to lose my nerve.

I put the cake down. 'I'm sorry, Freya, I didn't realize – I have a … a meeting. I'm sorry, but I really should go.'

'Yes – I'm sorry.' She tries to dust the crumbs from her hands. 'You told me you were heading out.' She puts her own plate down on the worktop but then her eyes move past me, catching on something. 'What's that?' She pushes past me, back out through the hallway. 'Jennifer, what's all this?'

She is looking through the doorway, into the living room. Where the coffee table is strewn with pages, spilling over onto the floor.

'This? It's nothing really.' But Freya steps forward, right inside the room now, and when I follow her in, close on her heels, I can't help seeing it the way she does. A mess of paper, a spider web of notes. Like in the films when someone has scrawled all over their bedroom walls. She is staring at them and there is such intensity in her gaze. My words come out in a rush as I try to explain myself. 'It's just the thing I told you about. The woman who died. I've traced one of the people who knew her and I'm writing out what she told me about her, along with the other bits and pieces I know. She thought … she had no idea, but Freya, something must have gone so wrong somewhere. It doesn't add up, how Sarah – the tenant – lived, how she died. I'm simply trying to piece it together.'

I scoop all the papers up off the table and pick the loose sheets up off the floor, ordering them in my arms until they seem like just a neat stack. Organized, sensible and sane. I step round Freya, heading back to the door. 'Listen, thank you for the visit and your help and the cake. Don't worry about this, I know how it looks, all lying out in a mess like that, but honestly – it's just a few thoughts. It's been good for me, really,' I ramble on, aware of my need to convince her. 'At least I'm doing something, not just being holed up in this flat on my own. I mean, I didn't tell you before, but I'm suspended from work, just while they make some internal enquiries, and this whole thing has given me a focus, a purpose.'

We're back out in the hallway now.

'Jennifer,' Freya says, 'I really think we ought to …' But I've already manoeuvred her back to the door. 'I'll call you, shall I,' she says, 'make a proper appointment? And you know you can come to me, any time.'

I give a little, light-hearted laugh. 'Honestly, Freya, you don't need to worry. You just caught me on a bad day before, when you called. I mean, you can come again if you like, in fact, that might be nice, but honestly, Freya, it isn't that bad.'

And as she turns reluctantly to go, I tell myself I've misread the look in her eyes, the one that says: *But maybe it is.*

*

As soon as she's gone, and I've got my coat and shoes back on again, I head to the bus stop on Brixton Hill, the one just outside the prison.

As I wait for the bus my brain tells me, *You can go back, go home*. But I don't. Because I have to try at least. I read the text from Marianne again: *let me know whatever you find out*. And it's true what I told Freya, I need something to focus on: a mission, a project. I haven't heard anything from Abayomi and when I rang the office yesterday and Emma picked up, her voice bright and naturally friendly as always, she didn't know any more than I did. Just that some people from head office had been by the other day and had looked on the computer system and at some files. 'But hopefully,' she added, her voice full of optimism, 'you'll be back soon.'

The bus is here now. Like I usually do, I take a seat on the top deck, and there's a space free at the front, best place for views.

On the journey, I try to think of what I can say to Alastair if I find him. It was hard enough with Marianne, but this will surely be harder still. I try to imagine how it would feel if someone told me out of the blue that someone I once loved had died in such circumstances. It would be so painful, such a shock. How careful I am going to have to be.

The traffic is thick in London today; it is never much else in a city as full as this. People get on and off along the way, and for a while two women push in next to me, one right beside me and one across the aisle, each clutching a pile of bags. From their conversation, I can tell they are mother and daughter – grown-up daughter. They've been shopping together, a good day out. Their connection seems so strong, so easy. And then there's me, and the three-monthly phone calls … I turn away and look out of the window. Before long, the two women get off.

It isn't long before we reach the stop for the hospital. My legs are shaky as I step down off the bus. To my relief, from the outside the building looks completely different to that other hospital I know, the one lodged so firmly in my memory. Different stonework, a different shape and much bigger. I try to tell myself that, teaching my brain the differences between then and now. But it's still a hospital, a place that normally I try so hard to avoid, and I suddenly wonder whether I can really do this. I can feel my mind skittering, tugging like a dog on a leash towards the past. I have to stand at the bus stop for a moment, pretending I'm studying the return bus timetable, before I feel ready to go on.

There is a path from the bus stop through the car park to the hospital entrance. When I step inside, I expect to meet the hospital smell I remember, one I would recognize anywhere, but instead the only scent I get is that of coffee from the Costa's in the entrance area. It makes this easier.

I check that my hair in its bun lies perfectly smooth against my scalp and that the buttons on my blouse run straight down my front. I only wish I'd thought to bring a work badge as I walk up to the efficient-looking woman on reception.

'Hello,' I say. 'My name is Jennifer Arden. I'm here to meet Alastair Matthews. I understand that he's working here today.'

She looks me up and down: the smart blazer, the neat hair, the lipstick I've so carefully applied. Underneath my smart blouse, I'm aware of my armpits, slick with cold sweat.

'Children's ward,' she says. 'You'll most likely find him up there.'

And it is as simple as that.

'Thank you,' I say. She is pointing to a sign on the wall behind me, with directions to the different wards and departments, and I can see the children's ward clearly marked in bright pink.

The children's ward.

'Take the lift,' she suggests. 'Down there, at the end of the corridor.'

I take a deep breath and follow the direction of her pointing finger. My heels click on the polished floor as I walk. I find the lift, and ride it up to the second floor. When I step out, the hospital smell hits me. It takes me straight back and I have to force myself not to turn around and leave.

This children's ward is light and bright and noisy. There's another reception desk up here, and I go up to the nurse on duty and say the same thing as before. He looks at me more suspiciously than the woman downstairs.

'Do you know Alastair?' he asks. I shake my head, racking my mind for some better way to explain myself, but the smell is in my nostrils, all tangled up with my fear and shame from the past.

And all the lies that were told.

Before I can think of anything, I hear a voice behind me. 'Are you looking for me?'

Chapter 16

BACK THEN

Prin climbs out of her bedroom window in nothing but her nightie. Neither Mum nor Daddy knows that she can do this. She only worked it out herself a few months ago. She has to shimmy right to the left-hand side of the window to reach the flat of the roof below with her feet. But she is big enough, tall enough now to do it. In the summer it gets so hot in her bedroom. But at night-time, she can come out here where there's a breeze and it's cool and she can look out over the whole world.

Or out over the back garden anyway.

It's a very pretty garden. Mum does a lot of the gardening herself, but Daddy also pays for people to come and make it look extra nice. Daddy likes things to look pretty and perfect. Prin thinks about the word Mum used about him once, talking to a friend of hers in the kitchen with Prin secretly listening from behind the closed door. *A narcissist*, Mum said, *I read about it. I think that's what he is*, and it made Prin think about the flower they learned about in school, *narcissus*, which meant a sort of daffodil, a very pretty flower.

Prin feels the roof below with her toes, warm and gritty. She lets herself drop down, then slips across onto the flat of the roof next to it. This is where she can lie down and look at the sky.

Tonight, even though it's very late, the sky is still turquoise along the horizon. Turquoise there, and then deep ink-black on the other side. Prin knows that the sun sets in the west which is why one side of the sky stays light longer. She learned that in school, and her Daddy confirmed that it was right.

Prin's nightdress feels light and thin now against her skin. She was so hot in bed before, kept kicking the covers off her and turning her pillow over and over trying to find the cool side. On the bed Mum set up for her against the far wall, Jane was fast asleep, seemingly unbothered by the heat. She's only seven, Prin remembers. Prin remembers going to bed earlier and sleeping more herself when she was as little as that. Jane was so fast asleep she didn't even stir when Prin lifted the sash window.

Now Prin lies herself down on the roof. It is hard under her back; she should have brought a blanket or something out here, made herself a little bed. She closes her eyes and imagines lying on a feather mattress, like the princess in her storybook, who lay on that whole tower of mattresses!

Up above her, faint stars circle. She can see all kinds of pictures that they make. Daddy taught her about the *constellations*. Plus Prin has made up constellations of her own.

She is just about getting used to having her cousin here. She's getting used to sharing her room and her toys. She hasn't even minded giving some of her old clothes to Jane, because it turned out there really wasn't very much in just that one little suitcase she brought. Prin counts off the weeks on her fingers. They've had three weeks of summer holidays so far, which means there are another three left. Such a long time, ages and ages, really. She wonders whether Jane will go home then – at the end of the summer. She did try to ask a couple of days ago, as they all sat round the bright breakfast table in the sunshine and Daddy made pancakes for everyone, and there were strawberries and blueberries too, Prin's favourite. She brought it up then, but Daddy turned round from the cooker and said, '*Shush*,' and he was smiling, but it wasn't his normal smile and then Prin's mum put a hand over her own mouth and the other on Prin's head, in that way that made Prin want to sink right down through her chair, and Prin knew then that somehow, again, she had said the wrong thing.

And the whole time, Jane just sat there, pushing one blueberry after another into her mouth.

Now, as she lies there on the roof, Prin hears the scrape of the patio door below her. Someone – Mum or Daddy – has stepped out onto the patio below. Prin lies still as a statue, quiet as a mouse. She wonders suddenly, for the first time since she's been coming out here, what would happen if Daddy put his head round her bedroom door in the night to check on her unexpectedly. What would happen if he did that and saw her bed empty, the covers kicked off onto the floor? What would she do? She would be caught red-handed, and she wouldn't be given a chance to explain. In future, Prin thinks, she will stuff pillows under her covers, the way she read about once in a book. She will trick Daddy into thinking she is in there. Everybody, really, can be tricked.

Now Prin hears a scraping sound, and a moment later she

catches the smell of something on the air. A bitter, smoky smell. She recognizes it, but how strange! She doesn't know what this smell is doing here.

Very quietly, Prin sits up. She can't see any of what's happening below her – she'd have to stick her head right over the edge to look and then whoever was down there would see her, and then, boy, would she be in big, big trouble. Instead she focuses on the tree branches that make criss-crossing silhouettes against the sky and stretches both of her ears to listen.

For a while there's almost nothing but silence, just a tiny kissing sound, a tiny crackle and sounds of breathing.

Then she hears the patio door scrape open again, and her Daddy's voice saying, 'Susan.'

Prin draws her knees up to her chest and wraps her bare arms around them. It sounds a little bit mean the way he says it. He's speaking the way he does when he's telling Prin off.

Now Prin hears another voice. It must be Mum's but it doesn't really sound like her. It's a low stream of words, sort of mumbled, when normally Mum speaks quite slowly and clearly. She's so mumbly that Prin can only make out little bits and pieces: … *my sister… do that … horrible.*

Then comes Daddy's voice again, even harder this time: '*Susan.*'

Now there's a silence; complete silence this time. Then the stream of words becomes something else, turns into another sound, a very awful sound to Prin's ears, one that makes her stomach grow *uh-oh* cold despite the heat, like it's chock-full of sticky ice cream again. The smell of cigarettes is stronger than ever now too, and it makes Prin feel sick. She really feels as if she might throw up, like when she had that stomach bug last winter.

Now Prin almost doesn't care if they hear her. She just wants to get back inside. She slides off the roof, back onto the lip below her window, pulls herself up and back inside. Over by the bedroom wall, Jane is sitting upright in bed, awake now. She gives Prin quite a fright as she comes in. Her round face is as pale as a moon.

'What is it?' she whispers. 'What's happened?'

Prin shuts the window behind her, cutting off the cool breeze from outside, trapping herself and Jane back into the heat. She gets back into her bed, her feet dropping crumbs of grit into the sheets, and pulls the stifling covers back over her.

She lies on her back, eyes wide open to the ceiling. 'Nothing,' she tells Jane. 'You're supposed to be asleep.'

And it must be nothing because there's no tears in this house!

So Prin lies there and closes her eyes and refuses to listen to the voice in her head that tells her:

Mum was crying.

Chapter 17

When I turn around, a tall, slim man with sandy hair is standing there. He is pushing a wheelchair with a boy of six or seven in it. For a moment, I have the strongest feeling that we have met before, but we can't have. And I have no idea how to handle this situation. Despite my time on the bus ride, I still have no idea what to say. So I just come out with it.

'I'm Jennifer Arden,' I say. 'You don't know me. But I've come about Sarah Jones.'

*

The worst of it is, he hasn't heard. I blurt it out, right there by reception, in front of the little boy and with no warning to Alastair. He goes pale. That's a cliché, I know, but he really does. He's very good, though; he doesn't lose his composure. His first thought is clearly for the boy in his care. In that gesture, I can tell at once the kind of person he is. Nurturing. Responsible. Protective. And then, here I am.

'Will you give me twenty minutes?' he asks me. 'I'll be on a break then. Will you wait here until then?'

There is a little line of chairs by reception. I point to them.

'Can I sit here?' The nurse on reception is watching us the whole time. 'Will that be okay?' I ask him too, and he just shrugs.

Alastair and the boy head through the main doors to the ward and they fall closed, snicking behind him. I sit down and place my handbag on the chair beside me, sliding my hands between my thighs. I try not to think too hard about where I am. I should have eaten something before I came. I'm feeling light-headed. But I will wait for Alastair and then we will talk. It's all right, I tell myself. It's all right.

On the clock on the wall above reception, the hands seem to move very slowly. The reception phone rings; the nurse on duty answers it and there's a murmured conversation. From where I am sitting, I can see through the doors with their big glass panels into the main ward inside. There's one bed in particular, with blue and red balloons all around it. Maybe just to say get well, or maybe for a birthday. When children are in here long enough, I imagine all kinds of dates come and go. There is a girl in the bed with a tube in her nose. I have no idea what she might be in there for, but what I see is her family gathered round her bed. I can see a woman who looks to be her mother sitting at the head, a man in a chair on the other side. And I see a couple, what looks to be grandparents, by the side of the bed.

The memories come, as I feared they would. I try to push them down but they keep rising, ballooning into my mind. The shock and the panic, arriving at the hospital. The medics rushing up to us, me, Mum and Dad, then rushing away with that little body in their arms ... And how later they came back, they came back and told me—

I jerk round at the hand on my shoulder: Alastair, here beside me. 'I'm free now,' he says, 'if you want to talk.'

We go to the big hospital canteen, which reminds me of the one at my old high school: low ceiling, strange smell. I mention this to Alistair, trying to ease the tension, trying to let him know a little more about myself. He just smiles tightly and nods in reply.

We order our drinks: him a coffee and me a green tea. As we queue, it feels as if we're on some strange, terrible date. We each pay for our own drinks though. I put three sachets of sugar in mine, hoping it will stabilize my dizziness. I've dressed smartly to come here, but in the mirror this morning, I could see I looked unwell.

We find a table in a corner. It's private enough, but the canteen is noisy, every clink and clatter echoing off the walls, voices rebounding all around.

I suppose all hospital canteens look similar, with their clusters of families grouped at the tables. There's a family of five not far from where we're sitting: a mum and dad, a teenage girl and two younger boys. I wonder who they've come here to visit. A grandparent maybe? Another sibling?

I look across the table at Alastair, trying to concentrate only on him. 'Are you a nurse here?' I ask, and Alastair shakes his head.

'A porter. I take the children round the hospital, wherever they need to go.'

'You were working here when you knew Sarah too?'

Alastair shakes his head. 'No. Before that. I knew her from university.'

'You were at university together?' I don't know why this

should be a surprise. Why I'd imagine Sarah wouldn't have had a degree. 'Where?'

Alastair hesitates for the tiniest moment. 'Middlesex,' he says. 'But I wasn't—' Over my shoulder, someone drops a piece of cutlery and it clatters against the floor. I can't help glancing round.

Alastair pushes aside his paper cup. 'I'm sorry,' he says, 'I'm not making sense of any of this. You say Sarah died, and you're trying to trace old friends …'

I breathe slowly, carefully. 'I was the housing manager for the flat where she lived. I wasn't the one who moved her in, but the flat was on my caseload and … I was there when they found her. I don't know if you saw the story in the news – about the woman in Brixton and how – and how …'

Alastair is looking at me. Steam from our drinks blurs the air between us. He says, very quietly, very slowly: 'That was Sarah? My Sarah?'

'Yes.' It feels as though the room around me is spinning. I wish that I had slept more last night. I'm not at my best at all.

'You're going to have to give me a minute,' Alastair says.

The canteen suddenly seems busier, noisier than ever. The racket sets my body on edge. I should tell him about the email Sarah sent me and the fact that I knew her, years before, but suddenly I find that I can't. Suddenly, I feel horribly, horribly responsible. The look on Alastair's face is awful.

'I'm sorry,' I say. 'I'm really sorry to have come here and told you this.'

Alastair shakes his head. 'I'd have wanted to know. I'm just … it just … I feel so awful. I mean, I feel sick. I think I'm in shock.'

I don't know what to do. Didn't I know this might happen? I try not to move a single muscle. Maybe he will simply want me to go away. Maybe he will get angry with me, shout at me, tell me I'm a terrible person for coming here. I clench my jaw, preparing myself for any possibility. But in the end, Alastair just lets out a long, shaky breath.

'We got together,' he says, his voice a little unsteady, 'when she was in her second year. She would have been – what – twenty then? I was twenty-two. She was my first ... proper girlfriend.'

'I'm sorry,' I say again. 'She must have really meant so much to you.'

He gives a small nod. 'She did.'

'Can I ... can I ask how you met?'

'Oh ...' Alastair smiles, faintly. 'In a coffee shop. She was at the till and twenty pence short for her hot chocolate. I lent her the change. We started chatting ... and that was that. We saw each other all the time from then on. We were together eleven months in the end.'

'You were so close. And eleven months ... You know, I'm glad. I'm glad she had someone who cared about her like that.' My voice sounds waterlogged, thick to my ears. 'And ... her friends? Did you meet them, the other people in her life?'

'I don't ... I mean, we ... hung out in different groups. And then once we got together, she seemed to want to spend all her time with me. At my place.' He gives me a shaky smile. 'I didn't mind that.' He rubs the palm of his hand across his eyes. 'I liked it. We'd spend all the time we could together. We talked ... we talked all the time about the future. We had all these plans. She'd describe where we would live when she'd graduated and we'd saved enough money, all these different places we would travel to. She loved talking like that. She had this way of making everything feel so real.'

I swallow, a scrape of dryness passing down my throat. I can see the bedsit again, that shrunken body on the sofa. I don't know if I'll ever stop seeing that form.

'But it never happened like that? And afterwards, you never kept in touch?'

I realize as soon as the words have come out that they sound like a horrible accusation. Alastair's expression is so pained and hollow and I have spoken so clumsily. 'I'm sorry,' I say quickly. 'I didn't mean it that way.' I am suddenly caught by the rushing shame of what I'm doing. Coming here, asking questions, hurting this man who has done nothing wrong.

'I'm sorry,' I repeat, 'I shouldn't have come here, I'm upsetting you, it's awful of me, I'm sorry.'

What am I doing, messing about in other people's lives? I don't have the right, how could I have thought that I did? I push my chair back, half get up.

But Alastair reaches across the table. 'Please don't go,' he says. 'You can't come here with news like this and not give me any chance to talk about it. I'm not in touch with anyone else who knew her and right now I'm full of memories and questions, and who am I going to go home and talk to?'

I stare down at him. He's right, of course he is. His hand on my arm is so strong, so warm. I'm involved in this now. I can't just run away when it's painful or uncomfortable. I have to stick with it. My spine aches as I sit back down again, the chair legs scraping on the hard canteen floor.

I breathe out, curling my hands round the edges of my seat,

holding myself steady. 'So what happened?' I ask. I make my voice as even as possible. 'What happened between you?'

'I asked if I could meet her parents. She'd met mine by then and they liked her. Really liked her. It seemed like a natural thing to suggest. We'd been together over nine months by then. I was serious about her. I'd thought she was serious about me. But her parents ...' He gives me a wry smile. 'It all went downhill after that.'

There's a reason. There is always a reason.

'After a week and a half,' Alastair goes on, 'she sent me an email.' He draws in a deep breath and I copy him, realizing how empty my own lungs are. 'She broke up with me in the email. No proper reason. She just wrote, *I can't see you any more.* I tried to email her back. I wanted her to explain. But my email bounced back. She never replied. I couldn't get hold of her at all. She'd changed her mobile number and closed her email account. Or else she was simply blocking me. So no, we didn't keep in touch.'

His words sit heavily in the silence between us, and I feel echoes of the emotions he must have had back then. Everyone carries wounds, I realize. Everyone gets things wrong. *But not like you have,* a little voice whispers. *Not like you, because yours wasn't a mistake.*

'I'm sorry,' I manage to say to Alastair. 'I'm so sorry it happened like that.'

Our drinks are barely lukewarm by now.

'I did get another email though,' he says, 'two months later. I didn't recognize the account it was sent from and it only had two words in it: *I'm sorry.* I think it was probably from her. It helped to tell myself that it was, anyway, but I'll never know for sure. I tried to forget about it, move on. After a while, I think I forgave her, mostly. She must have had her reasons, even if she couldn't find a way to tell me.'

I think of the funeral, all those empty seats. The parents who simply never showed up.

On the table, our paper cups rest a few inches from each other. I have a vision of reaching out to touch him. Maybe I'd touch the back of his hand. Maybe I'd put my whole hand in his. The thought of it makes me feel dizzier than ever. When did anyone but Charlie last touch me?

Instead I see Alastair glance at the clock on the canteen wall.

'Do you have to get back?' I say.

'Yes, but here, let me give you my number.' Alastair fumbles in his jacket for his phone and I dig in my bag for my own. He recites the digits and I type them onto my contacts. A few weeks ago, I had no more than a handful of names in there. But now I have two more than I did. I call him, briefly, so that he has mine too.

'Thank you for coming to tell me,' he says. 'Honestly, thank you.'

Alastair has just enough time to walk me back to the hospital exit before he has to return to the children's ward. We don't talk as we make our way out, but strangely, silence doesn't hurt. There are clues, I know it, in what he has told me. I can't join the dots yet, but I feel I've caught a glimmer of something, and now I have one more person willing to help me.

At the exit to the hospital, the sliding doors open back out into the cold. Stray leaves have blown in at the edges. Alastair and I shake hands to say goodbye. It could have felt too formal, but it doesn't. His palm is so warm and he grips my hand in both of his. 'You'll keep in touch?' he says. 'You promise?'

I manage to nod. I can't help thinking of how it echoes Sarah's words.

He lets go and I slip my hands into my coat pockets, ready to face the cold outside. Over his shoulder, I glimpse again the family of five that I saw in the canteen and watch as the mum curves an arm around the shoulder of her daughter.

'Okay, than,' says Alastair, 'I'd better go.'

He gives me a wave as I head out of the doors. I know it's time to leave, but at the last moment, I turn back, words crowding up at my throat.

'Alastair!'

He hesitates in the atrium of the hospital, lit up by the strip-lights. Gusts of cold wind tug at my hair. I don't want to keep him, I've already taken up so much of his time, disrupted so much of his day, his life. But I can't seem to leave without asking him this one last question. 'The children on your ward,' I call to him, 'they all have people who visit them, don't they? Family who come to see them? And the families, the parents – if they need it, they can have help, can't they? Support if they need it, say? And no one would blame them, would they, no one would judge?'

But the sliding doors close shut between us before he can answer, and then someone approaches him, rushing him away, and so I never get to know what this kind and forgiving man might have said.

Chapter 18

All the way home on the bus though, I feel warm; it feels like a sort of internal glow. I pull out my phone and call Marianne. It goes to voicemail and I wonder now whether she has a landline I should have got the number for; whether she is one of those people who never really checks their mobile.

I leave her a rushed voicemail instead.

'Marianne … I met Alastair. He was her boyfriend, you were right, back when they were both at Middlesex University. He said … it all fell apart when he asked to meet her parents. Her death was such a shock to him too, but he was … he was so kind about it. Marianne, he was lovely. I'm on my way home now, but you can call me back whenever you want, whenever you get this message.'

My ear is hot as I tuck my phone into my trouser pocket, my breath light and high in my chest. *You can call me back whenever you want.* I would never have said that three weeks ago. And that, surely, can only be a good thing. Is it possible that something good might come of all this?

The ride home goes by in no time. Before I know it, I'm back at my flat. Home, safe and sound. It is still early, barely one o'clock, still hours before I have to collect Charlie. I nip out to the corner shop on Elm Park to pick up bread and milk, then settle myself on the sofa, flick through the TV guide and put on a film. A rom-com, something totally safe. I think how long it's been since I relaxed like this. Let my mind wander, just zoned out. I can feel my eyelids drooping, I yawn; I think for a little while I doze.

I'm so much calmer than normal when I go to collect Charlie and, back home, the whole afternoon and evening seems to flow. No fights, no squabbles; Charlie seems quite happy. I make us beans on toast and we sit down together in the kitchen to eat it. The heating is on and the flat feels cosy, our little private bubble of home. I think of the stack of papers in the living room. Later this evening, I'll go back to them, add on what Alastair too has shared. For now, though, I look across at my son as he licks beans off his knife.

'I love you,' I tell him.

He grins. 'Love you too.'

We spend the rest of the evening playing snakes and ladders. Charlie wins three times, me two. Then it's bath, pyjamas, clean teeth. He's yawning now, leaning against me. I switch on his glow lamp as he clambers into bed. When I kiss his forehead, his skin is warm, clean. It's these shimmering moments that I treasure, try to keep.

It's just as I'm tucking him in that it happens. I'm pulling up the blankets, pressing them tight when my mobile buzzes in my trouser pocket.

I pull it out to see a new message waiting. A red circle on the text icon, blossoming there like a tiny drop of blood. From Alastair maybe? Or Marianne?

When I unlock my phone, the number is withheld, and the preview only shows blank space.

Charlie looks up at me sleepily, yet curious too.

'What is it?' he murmurs.

I shake my head as I swipe open the text. The bright white of the screen seems to light the whole room, like a spotlight, blinding. In its glare, the space around me upends. It feels like the phone is burning my hand. I stare down at my son, so small, so innocent.

'Nothing,' I tell him. 'It's nothing,' I repeat. I manage to kiss him, switch out his lamp. Get out of his room and close the door behind.

I lean against the wall of the hallway, gasping. I can hardly bear to look at my phone again, but eventually I force myself to do it.

In the middle of the screen are seven stark words:

Jennifer Arden, I know what you did.

Chapter 19

I drop the phone and it bounces on the floor. I can't breathe. My whole chest has gone tight, become a cage. The air wheezes in and out of my lungs. I stumble into the bathroom and wrench open the medicine cabinet, pushing aside boxes of plasters, packets of paracetamol, Sudocrem. A new toothbrush, still in its packaging, goes clattering to the floor. I scrabble in the cabinet and finally my fingers close round it. My inhaler. I shake it, close my mouth round its mouthpiece, push the button, inhaling, inhaling. It doesn't seem enough, it doesn't seem to help. I sit down on the stool by the bath, cracking my hip on the bathtub as I do so. I lean forward. I try to hear the sensible words in my head. *Slow down, calm down, breathe, you* can *breathe.* Gradually, gradually, the attack eases. Tiny airways open up again in my lungs, tiny slivers of air find their way through. I grasp the edge of the sink and pull myself to my feet, fumbling to turn on the tap. I cover my face with stinging cold water, filling my cupped hands again and again.

I KNOW WHAT YOU DID.

Slowly, shakily, I lift the inhaler back into the cupboard.

But that message. What is it talking about, what does it refer to? I think of the police officer photographing my feet.

Have I forgotten something that somehow, in a haze, I have done? I wasn't well last year, I know that. And Sarah's death happened around that time, didn't it? Isn't that what the news article said? Last April. When things had already started to go wrong for me, building to the summer when I missed the checks, lied in the log sheet, because I wasn't coping, but was doing my best to look as though I was.

And who would have my personal number? Who would be messaging me like this? I have so few people in my contacts, and the number was blocked. *But you put your phone number in that Facebook group*, I think. *When you posted your message about Sarah.*

Is that what this is about? Sarah, her death? Or – is it about something from longer ago? From back then? Another time when I wasn't well, and hardly knew what I was doing? Is there someone out there who knows about that, who has chosen now to hurl the accusation at me?

But who then? And who would think to message me like this?

I stare at my reflection in the bathroom mirror. I don't look well. *I don't look well.*

I force myself to think rationally.

If you did something, I tell myself, the police would know. Abayomi would know. You wouldn't hear about it in a message like this. And if it's to do with what happened back then, why would anyone bring that up now? And still the shock of those words closes all of my questions down. I have been so curious, so set on investigating, overturning stones, finding everything out. Now all I want to do is crawl into a corner, hide, disappear. Make sure no one can see me. Make sure nothing about me can be seen.

I turn the running tap back off. I dry my face with a towel, pressing the soft material into my skin, tangled in a storm of memories: hands pulling me away. Blue skin. The ambulance's scream. I breathe in the smell of detergent and try to ground myself. Eventually I'm able to go back through into the hall-way and switch on the light. My bones feel so stiff as I crouch down to pick up my phone. Hands shaking as though I'm trying to snap a lead on a dog that has just bitten me, I swipe at the text and delete the message.

Next door in his bedroom, Charlie is cosy under his duvet. We're both here, in our home, and he's sleeping sweetly.

And nothing here feels safe any more.

*

The next morning, it's so hard to walk into that freezing playground, but I force myself to get Charlie into his school clothes and I concentrate on not clenching his hand as I walk him to school and on keeping my smile up while I stand at the gates. I make myself wave as he trots inside, even though my mind is like some creature trapped in a cage, rushing in panic from one end to the other. Did one of these mums or dads, a parent of some classmate of Charlie's, send that message? Has someone managed to join the dots? But that doesn't make sense, I realize when I manage to think straight. Why not come out with it straight to my face? *So who then?* My brain goes skittering round and round. *Who, who, who?*

In the cocoon of our home, no one can see us, but now it seems the monster of my anxiety has grown so huge that even back in the flat with the door closed again against the world, I am unable to stop myself from shaking. Maybe it was nothing but some stupid prank, some joke. There are tenants who have my personal number, don't they? It could easily be one of them, annoyed with something, having a go. Am I just reading craziness into this, guilt colouring everything I see?

Really, though, I can't shake the dread that this is all tied up with Sarah. The text message was only one line, one brutal, damning line. The rest was blank space, so much room for me to fill in the gaps: *Leave this alone.* And still it comes back to me in a sickening wave: that image of Sarah's body on the couch. Months and months passing with no one missing her. The horror, the absolute horror of that.

I go through to the bathroom to dowse cold water on my face again. As I do, my phone pings, then pings again: two texts from Alastair, of all people. I can see from the time stamps that there was a space of a couple of minutes between when he wrote them.

It was good to meet you yesterday, the first says.

And then:

I wondered if, some time, we might meet up again? You seemed such a nice and thoughtful person.

I don't reply to him. I can't. All I can do is stare at myself in the bathroom mirror, hands gripping the edges of the sink, thinking, *Am I? Am I? Am I?*

I have no one to turn to, to give me perspective on this. Because how can I bear anyone else trying to make sense of why someone would send me a message like that? How can I answer the very first question they would ask: *But Jennifer, Jenn, what on earth do they mean?*

*

I know I have to pull myself together. I'm full of anxiety, guilt, suspicion, and I cannot let myself get like that again. If someone doesn't want me asking questions about Sarah, then I'll stop. It seems I should never have tried in the first place, because look at the toll it's taking on me.

All of my old anxieties re-triggered.

But I know something that will help. Something that will help me put all of this behind me. I go into my bedroom and pack a bag. I have to dig in the back of my wardrobe to find the flimsy black costume, but eventually I pull it out, and find an old towel in the bathroom to take as well. This idea isn't on any of the pages in my bedside drawer. It's another kind of strategy, one I discovered all by myself. Now it feels like returning to an old friend.

It is as cold as ever as I walk down the hill to the centre of Brixton. The light is so clear, it makes the edges of everything look razor sharp. As if they would cut me if I held a finger up to them. I pass under the rail bridge and turn right along the pedestrianized road where there are a few stalls selling household goods. A row of checked tea towels flap in the wind, a whip-crack of a sound.

Inside the big brown building, the smell is exactly the same as ever: chlorine. It's well heated inside, warm after the chill of my flat. It's an open session and it's during the school day so there won't be lots of kids, but Brixton Pool is busy whatever time I've come. I am sure today it will be busy enough.

The changing rooms need refurbishing and the latch on the cubicle door I choose isn't working properly, but it is all so familiar that I don't mind. I pull off my layers – so many layers in this cold weather – and pull on my swimming costume and fit my swimming cap over my head. My hair is that much longer than when I last came that it's hard to fit it all under the tight rubber now. I have lost weight too since I last came here, it's quite obvious now: my hipbones jut through the Lycra.

I stand under the showers at the edge of the pool, feeling the needles of water scratch their way down my back, then lower myself into the shallow end. The water is cold at first and my breath hitches a couple of times in response. There are two lifeguards on duty today. One is watching the baby pool where a few toddlers bounce in armbands and inflatable rings. When Charlie was a toddler I used to take him to the pool. All babies can swim, the memory of being in the womb still so fresh for them at that age. I took him only once, though, that was it. The thought of him underwater, mouth and nose blocked like that, I couldn't keep going. My anxiety was too much, even then.

The other lifeguard – a man with a beard and yellow flip-flops – is sitting halfway along the length of the pool. He's relaxed in his chair, not worried about anything. Trusting the swimmers to know what they are doing. The pool is about as full as I expected. Plenty of people doing lengths up and down. And there's a wide space on the far side without lanes, where people can swim however they want. It's best, though, I have learned, to stick near the lanes.

I check that my swimming cap is on tightly enough, then push off from the shallow end, ducking my head under the water. I start with breaststroke, swimming like a frog, letting my face dip under the water with each pull, melding into the flow of swimmers. To the lifeguard I'm just another woman in a black swimsuit and blue cap. Quite ordinary. After a few lengths the water doesn't even feel cold any more. My goose-bumps have gone; my shuddering has stopped. It's only that I am a little out of breath. I come to a pause at the deep end and hook my arms over the side, my heart running fast. I wait until my heart and breathing slow, then I slip under the lane ropes until I find a little space just off to the side. I look as if I'm just floating, taking a rest from doing my lengths.

I haven't done this in a long time. I have been going too easy on myself.

I float in the water and breathe out slowly, letting each ounce of air out of my lungs. You can do this to calm down: expelling the carbon dioxide out of your system, letting that stale, anxious air release. You can do it for that.

I empty my lungs.

Then I sink myself under the water. Right down to the bottom of the pool.

It is very quiet and peaceful down here. I cross my legs, anklebones hard against the floor. My body is heavy with no air in it and I can sit, like a buddha, right on the bottom.

For a few seconds at least, it doesn't hurt. The oxygen from my previous breaths lasts a little while. But with empty lungs it doesn't take long for the suffocating feeling to start.

First it sets the blood pounding in my head. Then my body twitches with the frantic desire to draw breath, my ribcage jerking in a series of desperate hiccups. I don't give in. The pain centres me, sets the world to rights. It is a show of my love to put myself through this. It's a way to express the deepest empathy I know.

I count the seconds. Normally I can last no more than thirty.

Today I force myself to forty-two.

I am gasping when I reach the surface. I turn to the poolside, hiding my face. No one has noticed, they never do. After all, I'm only down there for half a minute, not much more. Not time enough for anyone to worry. Most people wouldn't empty their lungs before going under. The rush of air back into my lungs feels like such a sweet relief, and like a betrayal. I have done it though. I have levelled the balance. Like drawing a thick black line through my head, ordering the chaos of my mind.

I feel so much better afterwards. My head is so much clearer. It's as though that suffering beneath the water washes away the shame and guilt, and I can be my ordinary, clear-headed self again. *Your anxiety, your paranoia*, I remind myself, *it's driven by guilt, it always was*. I've made this link before, but somehow, along the way, I've forgotten it. I never quite told the mental health professionals the truth. They had their formulations and I had mine. I – we – never told anyone. *But if you address the guilt*, I remember now, *then all the anxiety melts away*.

When I check my phone in the changing room, there are two missed calls and a voicemail from Freya. I simply delete them: one, two, three. She doesn't need to call me or visit. There's no reason for her to worry about me now. I won't be pursuing Sarah's case any more.

Outside the swimming pool, it's striking how much better I feel. My damp hair, crackling with chlorine, makes my head sing with the crisp cold, and the air, the sounds, the whole world around me feels clearer, as though cotton wool has fallen from my ears and a film has been washed away from my eyes. I can breathe right to the bottom of my lungs.

The mind is so powerful. *Anxious people constantly need proof that things are okay. Normal people start from the assumption that everything is fine.*

I remember someone telling me that once. *Assume things are fine.* The secret, then, of how to be normal: if you don't know, if everything sways one way then the other, then you can make the choice.

You can choose to be sane.

On the way home, I stop off at the supermarket and load up a trolley with all the things I should have bought these last two weeks. I carry the bags all the way up the hill, their handles carving deep runnels into my arms. Back at the flat, I take a shower to wash the remains of the chlorine out. I clean the whole flat, I do three loads of laundry, I tick off every single task on my to-do list. From the living room, I throw away all my scrawled pages of notes.

Then that afternoon, almost like a reward, Abayomi calls on my work mobile. The ringing is like an alarm going off in the flat; the phone trembles where I left it on the kitchen table.

When I answer, the conversation doesn't take long. There's only one thing he's calling to tell me.

They are ready for me to come back to work.

Chapter 20

BACK THEN

Prin and Jane are playing in the bedroom with the curtains closed. It's August, and the hottest day of the year so far. It is midday and far, far too hot to play outside. Daddy has said that later, once the sun has gone down a bit, he will set the sprinkler up on the lawn. Prin is looking forward to that. She's excited to show off her cartwheels to Jane. She can almost do them with her legs straight now. She has been practising.

For now, though, Prin and Jane are inside, playing with Prin's dolls. Prin has a whole story in her head for them to act out, but Jane isn't keeping up. She seems more interested in making the dolls sit upright, with their legs together and their skirts straight. 'It doesn't *matter* how they sit,' Prin keeps telling her, but for some reason, it matters to Jane.

Despite the closed curtains, Prin is still hot. Both of them are wearing shorts and T-shirts, but even that feels to Prin like too much. The curtains aren't really thick enough and the sun is slanting through, making the carpet warm under the window seat, close to where they are sitting. The air in the room is thick and muggy. No breeze. No air at all almost, it feels.

Prin picks up one of the dolls. She has a whole scene in her head, ready to act out. 'Don't!' cries Jane, which is stupid, because it's Prin's doll, she can do whatever she likes with it. But Jane has just spent the last five minutes arranging this doll *just so*, and now she's upset that Prin has barged in on all that.

Prin lifts the doll towards her. Jane makes a grab for it and gets her by the skirts. Prin is holding the doll by its soft head. Jane tugs, Prin pulls, both of them refusing to let go. It's a hot, frantic tug-of-war.

Jane pulls again and Prin pulls back even harder. Then she hears it. A ripping sound. She looks down.

Jane is holding the doll in her hands.

And Prin is holding the head.

*

Prin almost falls headlong as she rushes downstairs. She is already shouting out as she runs. She's managed to wrestle the doll's body off Jane, and now she holds both pieces in her hands. She has left Jane sitting in the hot room above, eyes huge, arms wrapped round her knees, knowing she has done a bad thing and is likely to get in quite a lot of trouble. Prin is going to tell on her. It was all Jane's fault, that's what Prin needs to say. She is furious with Jane for breaking one of her toys, but as she runs downstairs, the tears come too. It wasn't a favourite toy but it was *very upsetting*, seeing the doll rip apart like that. The sheer violence of it releases another flood of cries from Prin, anger and upset and hurt and shock. She shouldn't be crying, she knows that, but it was so horrible the way the head just *came off*!

She bursts into the kitchen, clutching the ragged pieces of doll in her hands.

Mum is standing at the kitchen sink with her back to Prin, her shoulders shaking. When she turns around, Prin's own tears die in her throat.

Mum is crying. She is crying.

There isn't any doubt this time. Prin can see the wet streaks all over Mum's face.

'Mum?' Prin stops short in the middle of the kitchen. The word comes out small and uncertain. Her own eyes suddenly feel quite dry. She takes another step forwards, then stops again. As she stands there, holding the broken doll, she sees fresh tears well up in Mum's eyes. 'Mum?' she says again, and she cannot help but feel frightened this time.

Then there's a noise behind her. It's Daddy. He was standing on the other side of the room, hidden by the door when Prin came in, but now he steps forwards, right up to Prin. He crouches down in front of her and puts his hands on her shoulders, turning her a little bit, so she can't see Mum properly any more. Mostly, she can only look straight into Daddy's eyes

He cocks his head. 'What happened?' he asks.

Prin looks down at the pieces of doll in either hand. She looks up again at Daddy.

'We had a – me and Jane ...' Prin stops. 'Why is Mum crying?' she whispers.

Daddy smiles. 'She isn't,' he says.

Prin looks up at Mum again. She is busy wiping the wet from her cheeks.

'But,' says Prin, her voice louder now, 'she *is!*'

Daddy shakes his head. 'No,' he says. 'She's cutting an onion.'

Prin looks all around the kitchen. On the table, on the draining board, on the granite island in the middle. She can't see an onion anywhere. 'Where?' She is still holding the pieces of doll.

Daddy stands up; he's very tall when he stands up straight. He goes to the fridge and opens the door. It looks so nice and cool in there. Mum is still standing by the sink. Daddy pulls out a clear plastic bag and sets it on the draining board beside Mum. Prin can see that there are onions inside: four of them, brown and crackly. Daddy takes one out, then lifts the chopping board from behind the toaster and sets that down next to Mum too, the onion on top. And he takes a knife out of the knife block. 'There,' he says, when it's all laid out. 'Do you see?'

She looks back and forth from Daddy to Mum and back again. Grown-ups know things, Prin understands this. They are always trying to teach you lessons, and Prin always tries to be quick to learn. And here it is: another lesson. *No tears in this house!* And she knows just how much Daddy likes things to be fine. And suddenly Prin sees, it, just like Daddy said. It's as though all the little pieces come together. It's just like the zoetrope, and playing with the dolls, and all the stories she writes in her head. She gets it! *Why*, she says to herself, feeling more grown-up than she ever has before, *it's just Make-Believe! Who would have thought? Make-Believe is a grown-ups' game too! They Make Believe and then it's real. How clever!* she thinks. *How clever is that?*

She smiles up at Daddy and he smiles back. He stands next

to Mum with his hand on her shoulder. 'Now,' he says, 'what is it you were hollering about?'

Prin looks down at what she's holding in her hands. She brings her left hand and her right hand together. Body and head join back up. 'Oh!' she says. 'Nothing. I can hardly remember. I think everything is just perfect after all.'

It feels very strange, and new, but very clever.

Daddy smiles down at her, his big crinkly smile, and Prin smiles up at him, right back.

*

Back upstairs, Prin sets the doll down on the floor with the others. If she lies it down, it looks just fine. She tells Jane not to move that one. She'll think up another part for that doll in her story. *Sleeping Beauty*, something like that. Jane is just happy not to be in trouble. She's quite happy to play Prin's story-game now.

And later that afternoon, Daddy sets the sprinklers up all over the lawn. The sun is slanting in the sky now and there's a breeze. Prin does her cartwheels and she's quite sure her legs are straight. She only has to believe it, and it's true! She and Jane jump through the sprinklers, just as planned.

There are rainbows caught in every single one.

Chapter 21

It feels like months, years even, that I have been away from work. When I check the dates, though, it's only been a little over a week. I don't have any clean tights; I haven't washed any since the last day I was in the office. I spend all Sunday evening sorting myself out.

On Monday morning, when I pack my handbag, I put my inhaler inside just in case. I haven't needed to do that in ages – nearly a year, probably – but now I just feel better having it with me. I know the medicine in it isn't real; these symptoms are psychosomatic, nothing more than my body remembering things that I've been unable to come to terms with, expressing feelings I'm trying too hard to submerge. But to my mind, having the inhaler helps; with it, I can convince myself that when I feel the tightness in my lungs, it's nothing more than a winter flare-up, one that will settle down soon.

When I pull on my work clothes – a simple blouse, plain black trousers – the waistband is ridiculously loose. In the back of my wardrobe, I find a belt. With that clipped tight, you can't see the extra inches.

In the bathroom, I put on even more make-up than usual. Powder and blusher as well as foundation, eyeliner, eye shadow, mascara, the lot. I blow-dry my hair until my scalp burns, then wrap it into a glistening bun. Heels this time, instead of my ankle boots and a tight hold on that thick black line I've drawn in my head.

I practise a smile in the bathroom mirror. I've even remembered to clean my teeth.

On the walk down Brixton Hill, though, despite the blue sky and golden sun, I can't shake the sense of a façade; I can't shake the sense of something crouched darkly behind it. I jump at car horns, feel clawed at by the wind. But I keep my chin up so no one would know.

When I enter my old familiar office, Emma is there, same as always, tucked in at her desk.

'Hey!' she says. 'Really good to see you! Listen, can I get you some tea?'

Because to Emma, tea is the answer for everything.

I nod, because it's easiest, but at the same time I'm asking the same thing I'm asking about every single person in my life now, those few people that there are – was it her? Did she send that message?

But her face is so open and she is so friendly and normal with me, a bit sorry about everything that happened, that's all, that it just doesn't seem possible to suspect her. She is such a kind, straightforward person. Surely not someone who could wish me any harm.

Abayomi wants to see me first thing, of course. While Emma makes tea, I go to his office. It's warm and smells of coffee. He stands up as I come in and comes round the desk to pull out a chair for me. As if, in my time off, I have become some kind of invalid.

'Good to see you, Jenn. How are you?'

I rest my palms carefully on my lap, one on each side, just so. It helps me confirm that I am sitting up straight. I reply to him calmly and professionally, in my neatly articulate voice. 'Good to see you too. And I'm fine.'

He hesitates for a moment, as though he's expecting me to say something more. I keep my hands in my lap and wait for him to continue.

'I really appreciate,' Abayomi says, still with that hesitation in his voice, 'how good you have been about all this. I'm sorry again for how it's been.'

'No,' I say. 'I completely understand.' Even though I didn't really have another choice.

'We've had an internal investigation. I explained to them that although some checks weren't done, the safety checks were complete and everything else is up to date. We could provide the certificates for those. I had to explain to them, though, about the annual inspection.'

'Of course. And can I say again how sorry I am about that. It won't happen again, I can assure you. I really appreciate you having me back.'

Abayomi's dark skin flushes. Now it is his turn to say, 'Of course.'

I know he's sitting only across the desk from me, not far away at all, but it's a little like looking down the wrong end of a telescope. To bridge the gap, I give a smile, one of the many smiles I've practised.

'You'll have to work for a while under closer supervision,' Abayomi is saying. 'I've been asked to keep an eye on you. We'll be making changes to a number of the ways we do things, and there will be a report. An official one. Beyond that, I think they'll be willing to draw a line and move on.'

I nod. 'All right. That's fine. I understand.' My breathing is so light, I can hardly feel it.

'All right then.'

Abayomi coughs and pushes his chair backwards. I follow his cue and get – a little unsteadily – to my feet too. I'm keen to get started. I honestly feel quite all right about everything.

I'm just turning to leave when he says:

'Jenn?'

I stop. My turn to hesitate now. 'Yes?'

'You are sure, are you?'

'About what?'

Abayomi touches the photo frame on his desk, an unconscious move with the tips of his fingers. 'Are you sure that you're okay?'

I'm wearing lipstick and eyeliner. I'm wearing blusher and heels and the belt, for heaven's sake. I can't feel a single hair out of place.

'Yes, absolutely,' I tell him.

I don't let my smile move an inch as I step towards the door, and I close it as tightly as I can when I leave.

*

The rest of the day all goes so well. I'm back in the swing of it so easily, as if I've never even been off. Within hours, my files are all up to date. I go out on appointments in the afternoon, and I complete them all without a hitch.

Being back here is such a relief. I've returned to my ordinary life; I can put all the rest behind me. When I check my phone, there are missed calls from Marianne and the sight of them gives me a pang in my stomach. But after a minute, I make myself delete them. Haven't I made up my mind about this? I need to concentrate solely on my job, and on Charlie. I can't keep getting mixed up with anything else.

Then just as I'm about to leave the office for the day, my scarf already half tied around my neck, my work mobile rings. This time it's a call from a London number. When I answer, a voice says, 'Ms Arden?'

'Yes?' I say.

A pause. There have been so many strange phone calls lately, but I don't recognize this voice at all.

'Yes?' I say again.

'Sorry, hello, my name is Mike Bernard. I'm calling on behalf of the coroner.'

'The coroner?'

'Yes. Regarding Sarah Jones and the forthcoming inquest into her death.'

I have to close my eyes. I should have known. I really should have expected this.

'We would like to gather a further statement from you, as a witness.'

I tug at my scarf to loosen it; it has got wrapped so tightly around my neck. Coroner's court, the inquest. I can feel the whole thing opening up in front of me again, as though I haven't put any of it away at all. I sit back down in my chair and pull off my gloves. Even when I try, I can't seem to turn away. Instead, it feels as though I'm being picked out for this. It feels as though, even if I wanted it to, this awful tragedy just won't let me go. *I knew her*, says my own voice in my head. *She sent me an email*. When friends and relatives didn't want to know.

'What will you need from me?' I manage to ask. My neck stings from the rub of scratchy wool of my scarf.

'We are simply collecting all the details regarding the circumstances of Ms Jones's death. Along with the police report, her medical records suggest natural causes. She – ah – had severe allergies. The state of the body though – it's difficult to know. Our aim at the inquest is to provide a legal ruling.'

'I understand,' I say, while my mind races: natural causes? Allergies? Something as preventable as that? The new information lodges in my head, scattering new images, new shards of sadness, new guilt. 'But … am I under scrutiny?' I blurt out to this man on the phone, this man I have never met; I feel completely at his mercy.

A pause again.

'I understand your Housing Association has admitted a degree of … negligence in relation to the case. But – ' I think I can hear him shuffling papers – 'I understand this was not directly related to the cause of death. Only to the delay – the extreme delay – in the discovery of her body.'

'And you want a statement from me?'

Somewhere on the floor above, I hear a security alarm sound shrilly and then cut off.

'We would, yes. If you can let me know a correspondence address, I can send you the full details of what to provide and where to submit it to? It is quite straightforward, nothing really to worry about.'

'All right. And the inquest itself? Will I have to attend?'

'I believe that will be unlikely. We will of course inform you if we wish to summon you as a witness. But it's more probable that we'll simply include your written statement as part of the submitted evidence.'

'But … even if you don't call me, will I be allowed to attend?'

'Yes, of course, Ms Arden. Inquests are public hearings. Any member of the public may attend.'

'Thank you. Then can you send the correspondence here, to the office?' I rattle off the address. 'Please do that. I will help in any way that I can. I want as much as anyone to make sense of what happened.'

'Of course,' Mr Bernard says. 'Thank you for your time today, Ms Arden. I'll send you the information out right away.'

As a courtesy, he gives me his number to write down, then hangs up.

And I fumble in my bag for my inhaler, firing sharp puffs to ease my gasping chest.

*

Charlie is walking with Molly when he comes out of school. For a moment, I think they are even holding hands. Then she runs off towards her father, and Charlie is running across the tarmac towards me. His movements look smooth – coordinated, even. I make myself bend down and open my arms. He runs right into them, hugging me tight.

'Did you have a good day?' I turn my smile down towards him.

'The best!' He wriggles free and looks up at me.

Assume it's fine. Always, always assume it is fine. And Charlie really *has* had a good day at school; Ms Simmons comes out to the playground especially to tell me. 'He did really well in our maths test,' she says. 'He said he'd been practising with you.'

My son is looking up at me, his face open, eager, hopeful. Kids need praise like flowers need the sun, I know that. Genuine praise, loving praise.

'That's great. I'm so pleased,' I say, smiling at both of them, my son and his teacher. 'It's lovely to hear when Charlie is doing well.'

I stoop down and take his hand in mine.

My perfect, flawless, healthy son.

*

To prove it to myself, I take Charlie out to eat for dinner. We walk right across Brockwell Park and down to Herne Hill, where there's a fish and chip restaurant that Charlie has loved ever since we came here for the first time a couple of years ago.

We go out to eat like this so rarely, trying to get by on my single wage. And because being out in public like this puts me so on edge. But I'm remembering something else the psychologist told me last year. *You have to test your fears. Really test them, push them far enough to really prove them wrong.*

When we get to Ollie's fish restaurant, I let Charlie order whatever he fancies. He wants the children's portion of cod and chips, and I choose the same, only adult-sized. I know I need the calories. Once we've ordered our drinks, Charlie busies himself colouring in the paper placemat. I try not to let it remind me of the tests they gave him, paper and pencil exercises, tests of function and intellect.

Lately I've been letting my mind run away with me. These worries about Charlie. I need to get a hold. Mike Bernard's call has restarted everything – everything I thought I could let go. How did I think I could just walk away? After the way I let Sarah down before? And now am I going to let Marianne and Alastair down too? And anyone else out there who knew her, who cared? I told myself I wouldn't leave it up to the coroner. How can they answer the questions we all need answered? But if I'm going to keep investigating Sarah's death, then I need to be sure that my mind is clear, strong. Sitting across from him, I steady my breathing. I sit there, hands in my lap, concentrating – in-breath, out-breath – until my heart beats a slow, steady rhythm. I time it for a minute, then one minute more. I know how to do this. I knew that I could.

Once I'm sure that I am okay, I pull out my phone and dial one of the few numbers I have stored in there. Marianne sounds surprised but glad to hear from me.

'I've been trying to get in touch,' she says. 'I got your message the other day, but when I tried to call you back, you didn't pick up.'

'I know, I'm so sorry. I was called back to work. I am really sorry for not answering your call.'

The waiter brings our drinks and sets them on the table. Charlie lifts his with both hands, as I've taught him. Nice and steady, no slips.

'But you said you managed to find him,' asks Marianne. 'This Alastair?'

'Yes. Yes. At the hospital.' I take a sip of my own lemonade, the bubbles painful against my tongue. I don't think to tell her about the text message, the threat. I simply write it off in my mind. Some anomaly, some prank, some miscommunication. 'He had no idea she'd died, Marianne. They were a couple at university but it seems they hadn't spoken in years.'

'So I knew her more recently than he did.'

'Yes. He had no way of knowing. When they broke up, she completely cut him off.'

'Why?'

'I don't know … He doesn't really know. But he mentioned her parents … Marianne, there was surely something wrong there. As if … she was embarrassed by them? Or they were … ashamed of *her*? She changed her email address, phone number. He tried to contact her, but it was like she'd blocked him.'

There's a pause while Marianne digests this. 'Well, there must have been a reason.'

There is always a reason. 'Like what?'

Marianne's tone is so sure. 'Something he did to make her act that way.'

I hesitate. 'That *he* did?' Charlie stares up at me, wondering what I'm talking about. I hand him another crayon and nod at him to keep colouring. 'I don't know, Marianne,' I say. 'I don't think so. He really seemed like a nice person.' And I think of what she said herself: how after Sarah got 'head-hunted', Marianne couldn't reach her either.

'He seems really hurt by it all,' I add. 'Still.'

On the end of the line, Marianne goes quiet.

'I meant to ask you,' I say. 'Those times when she wasn't working with you, where did she go then, do you know? You said she dipped in and out.'

'Well, holidays, I assumed, like I said. Perhaps she sometimes took other jobs.'

'But what if she didn't?' I say. 'What if she was just … at home, on her own?'

'No,' says Marianne. 'I can't imagine that. I just can't.' She goes quiet again. Then: 'Well, now what?'

'I don't know … I've been trying to map it out and make sense of it, the little bits and pieces we know, but I still really don't have any answers. Alastair was honestly in such shock when I told him, and we didn't have long to talk really at all, he was only on a break. I think maybe—'

'Yes? Maybe what?'

I look at Charlie, colouring across from me. I think of how it's always only me and him.

'I think I need to see him again.'

As the waiter arrives with our meals, I tell Marianne I have to go, promising again to keep in touch. Properly this time. When the waiter sets our plates down, my portion looks gigantic but I force myself to eat, pushing each mouthful down. I need to take better care of myself, I know that. As Charlie eats too, he chatters to me about his day. Just like any ordinary kid. He's happy, relaxed in himself. Content. No emotions bouncing off the walls.

If you look for it, you'll find it. So don't look.

I let my ears tune him out ever so slightly, blurring my eardrums the way I'm able to blur my eyes. Charlie is doing great. And I am doing fine.

I take a few more bites of my meal, managing most of the mushy peas at least before I push my plate aside. While Charlie finishes up his, I click open my mobile again. In the messenger app, Alastair's texts are still there.

I read them again, three times, until I'm sure.

Then quickly, before I can change my mind, I text him back: *Yes*.

Chapter 22

But first there's something I have to check.

When we get home from the restaurant, I put Charlie to bed early. Then I open up Google again.

I don't know why I didn't think of doing this before. There's this piece of the puzzle I haven't chased until now. Her parents. How much they seem to have to do with it all. There's no way of knowing whether they'd be willing to speak to me and yes, I know the police couldn't trace them before. But it was me who tracked down Marianne and Alastair, and what if the police just didn't look that hard?

As a housing manager with links to the local authority, there's a special register I can access. We use it sometimes for our deeper ID checks, when we're worried that something doesn't quite add up. I have Sarah's details and I can start there. We can find birth certificates here. Marriage certificates too.

I log into the register and type in Sarah's details. Her full name, her date of birth. I'm lucky: the other Sarah Joneses have different middle names so, incredibly, there is only one result.

And here it is: her birth certificate. I find myself reading it holding my breath.

Here they are, the names of her parents. Suddenly they are a hundred times more real. Sarah's mother, Sarah's father. I'm getting closer, step by step. I plug their names, together now, into my search. The database works hard for me, offering up new leads.

Now a marriage certificate appears. And with it, an address. The place where, back then at least, they lived. Somewhere a long way away from London.

My brain feels as though it's tingling. My whole body is tense, on edge. Through this database too, you can find other addresses. You can check the other places people have lived – still live. It's a function I'm not technically licensed to use. Maybe the police never even went this far. But these are exceptional circumstances, surely. And if I don't tell anyone that I've looked, who would know?

I tell myself I'll only look so far. There are other searches I could run, other databases, even. But I won't. I'll go as far as I can here, then I'll stop; I'm already stepping over a line. Even with this one address, it might be enough. And in fact, when I run their names through this feature, no other homes come up. Which means the address from the marriage certificate is where they're still living – unless, of course, they've moved out of the country: Scotland, Northern Ireland, Wales or abroad.

My hands are shaking as I log out of the database. I've only been in there two minutes at most. Now I plug the postcode into Google, a search engine anyone's entitled to use. When the map appears, I click straight onto Street View. The stretched images appear, disorientating at first, but then I spot the road sign: I'm in the right place.

I scroll my way up the road, checking the house numbers. It looks like such an ordinary street: the houses on either side are uniform, modest. It looks as if such ordinary people live there. Is this where Sarah used to visit them? *You can go there*, I think. *You could knock on their door*. It's not impossible. Not a totally crazy idea.

The Street View is glitchy, every transition a jerk. Thirty-five, thirty-seven. I need forty-one. When I reach the right place, though, I can't believe it. I have to scroll back and forth to check. Number thirty-nine is there on one side. And there's forty-three, but …

Number forty-one should be right in between. Instead there's nothing. Only a blank. A flattened plot of land that someone's tried to concrete over.

This is where they were supposed to be living.

Instead Sarah's parents' house has been torn down.

*

I close the laptop. My hands are really shaking. Something about this runs so close to home, hooking onto all my suppressed fears. Moving me to do things I never normally do.

The TV clock says it's almost half past nine. Late, but maybe not too late. I pick up my phone, the impulse a compulsion, and take it through to the kitchen. I know the number off by heart, though I could count on two hands the number of times I've dialled it.

I can't remember the last time I did this. Clumsily, I type

the digits and press call. Six rings, seven. Maybe they aren't in. Maybe they no longer answer the phone at this time.

Then: 'Hello?'

I hesitate just a moment. 'Dad?'

'Jennifer?' His voice is surprised, pleased. I never call him. He always calls me. 'How are you? I mean … is everything okay?'

'I'm fine,' I say, because that's what I always, always say. But even as I say it, tears are sliding down my cheeks. I let my whole body slide down the kitchen units to sit on the cold kitchen floor. 'I'm fine,' I say again, somehow managing to stop my voice from cracking. 'I just thought I should call, for a change. I'm all right, I'm quite okay. And Charlie – ' my voice sounds strange, high-pitched in my ears – 'Charlie is great, he's really doing fine.'

'Oh good. That's good.'

My words are like a runaway train, gathering speed. 'You know, he's almost nine now. He's a lovely boy, really he is, and he's growing up so fast.'

'Okay,' Dad says. 'Well, that's really great. Listen Jennifer, just let me …' A pause on the line. 'I'll just take this downstairs – will you hang on a minute?'

'Wait – Dad?'

'Yes?' I can picture him, hovering at the top of the stairs, one knobbly hand on the polished banister. I picture my mother, sitting in the upstairs living room, stiffly upright in her chair, eyes on the TV, but listening to everything going on.

I've started now and I don't seem to be able to stop myself from rushing on, breaking protocol. Before I can stop myself, I've rushed even further, right into the one area I never meant to go. I don't know why I'm even asking, it's as though I'm deliberately trying to hurt myself. Or maybe I'm just feeling so desperate that I don't care.

'Dad … is Mum there?'

'Jenn—' Dad says again, in a voice that says, *don't you know better than to ask?* but I cut him off, pushing forwards as though I can beg him into changing his answer.

'Could I speak to her? Can't you get her to come to the phone?'

Dad's painful awkwardness floods the line. It comes back to me, the thing he once said to me, trying to explain how much worse it became when I moved away. *She took it as a slap in the face.* And now, again, I have put him in such an awkward position. I can picture that room behind him, the pristine sofa, the stack of coasters that must always be used, every prized cushion placed just so, the rug Mum used to hoover and hoover as if she was trying to hoover the whole floor away.

But Dad tries, he really does. 'All right … let me see. Wait just a sec, Jennifer,' he says.

I wait for what feels like a hundred years. I lean forward and press my forehead to the sharp bones of my knees. It's as if I'm praying or bowing or waiting for some kind of blow to the head.

A rustle again at the handset.

I sit up.

'Jenn,' says Dad, 'I'm sorry. She can't come to the phone right now. Another time maybe, it's just, right now …'

He is still talking, sorry about everything but I lift the phone away from my ear. My whole body feels cold and rigid.

Whatever had opened or softened before has closed up again. I'm almost disgusted with myself, letting myself get in a state like this. All these years I've shut this part of my life down, and now I'm the one ripping open the wound? It doesn't make sense. *I'm not making sense.*

Very carefully, very quietly, I hang up.

Chapter 23

Four days later, on Friday, I've arranged to meet Alastair during my lunch break. It's the only time I can do it, I've explained, I have my son with me all the rest of the time. During the working day, though, he's at school.

'I don't mind at all,' Alastair replied. He has all this week – and next – off work. He's happy this time to come and meet me close to my office. Closer to home – I've told him where that is. My world this time, instead of his.

He must have Googled a venue, because he suggests Brixton Market, the place where everyone from outside Brixton thinks they should go. I have forty-five minutes for my lunch break. Enough time to get a coffee and maybe a sandwich together.

At twelve forty-five, I head down the stairs. I have my smart work suit on, flat shoes this time, but my smartest jacket. I re-did my make-up at my desk before leaving. The streets of Brixton are heaving; I have to side-step constantly and, as I pass the narrow section of pavement under the railway bridge, my handbag gets shoved off my shoulder.

I find Alastair standing at the entrance gates to the market. Part of me was worried that I wouldn't recognize him, but I do, of course. He looks just the same. And then something happens that I wasn't expecting: a heat in my chest, something flipping in my stomach. Those kinds of feelings. I swallow hard, pushing them away.

When I come up to him, I don't know whether to shake his hand or what, so instead I just stand there, both hands holding tight to the shoulder strap of my handbag, my arm like a barrier across my chest. He has a bag slung over his own shoulder with what looks like a bundle of files inside.

He smiles at me. 'Shall we head in?'

The covered market is swarming with people too; it always is. The avenues are narrow in here, everything crammed in together, shop fronts pushing out right into the walkways, sandwich boards set every which way to catch your eyes.

'Any place you'd recommend?' Alastair asks. I try to think of some trendy place that he might like, but I never come here and there's nowhere I can think of to suggest. There are smudged skylights above, columns of flags hanging from the rafters, banners, shop signs. It's colourful, vibrant, crowded, claustrophobic.

'Anywhere,' I tell him. 'Anywhere you'd like.'

'Here?' he says a moment later, pointing to a simple coffee and sandwich bar.

'Sure,' I nod. I kind of just want to sit down.

As we pull out chairs, I catch sight of my reflection in the window, a see-through outline, barely there. I try to glimpse what Alastair might see.

You seemed a kind and thoughtful person.

I try to read that somewhere in my silhouette, but instead what looks back at me is someone who looks thin and skeletal, stretched and elongated in the glass.

'Here's the menu,' Alastair says, lifting the plastic cards from the little wooden table block they stand in. 'It seems nice, and they have special lunch-time options. Not too pricey.'

'Sure,' I say. 'Sure.'

We sit down at the slatted table in the covered avenue outside the café, even though it isn't very warm. The table rocks, one leg too short, and the slatted wood of its top risks things sliding through. There's a flower, a single stem, in a little glass on the table between us: pretty, but when I touch it, I discover it's not real.

It's not a date, it's not a date, it's not a date.

Alastair hands a plastic menu to me.

'Thank you for coming to see me the other day,' he says. 'I would never have known about Sarah otherwise.'

I am glad that he has come straight out with her name. Labelled the point of us meeting again like this. I lower my menu and make myself look directly across at him. I wonder if he might be as nervous and awkward as me. There's no real template for what we're doing, bonding only through a woman who died.

I clear my throat. It takes a few goes. It really feels as if I have something stuck in there. 'I got a phone call the other day. There's going to be an inquest. I need to submit information for a statement. But I'm still trying … to piece it all together.'

Alastair lets out a breath. 'I stopped by … Munroe House before coming here,' he says. 'That's the place, isn't it? Where she was living. Where she … died.'

The name of the block makes me flinch. 'How did you know where it was?'

He looks back at me. 'I looked it up. Google Maps.'

I shake my head. 'Of course. Yes. She had the bedsit there, on the ground floor.' I get a flash of it: that cramped space under the stairway; the radio playing; the lifting of the letter flap.

'Did you think of anything else?' he asks me. 'After we spoke? Have you found out anything else that you should tell me?'

'Only that … through this, um, work database, I managed to trace her parents' address.'

'Their address?' An expression I can't read slides across his face.

'Yes. And then I looked their house up online. But it isn't there now. It's been torn down.'

'What? You saw that?'

'On Google Street View.'

He is staring at me. I haven't told Alastair about the message in my email inbox. And now I can't help testing him, checking.

'Maybe I shouldn't be looking into all this. Maybe there are people who think it isn't my place. Maybe I shouldn't be getting involved after all …'

I watch him, carefully, for his reaction. Alastair lays his menu to one side and rests his wrists on the edge of the table. For a second I worry about him getting splinters, but when I feel with my own fingers, I can tell the edge of the wooden table is quite smooth.

He shakes his head. 'Don't say that. I'm glad you came and found me. We can't stop now, not after everything you've told me. I keep remembering all sorts of things. Nothing that would help us though. Just … how happy she seemed.'

How happy.

'Her parents though. There was an issue there, wasn't there? They were … estranged in some way? The police, they couldn't reach … and then at the funeral. Alastair, there was no one there.'

A waitress interrupts, come to take our order. I start by saying I only want a black coffee, but when Alastair orders a whole meal, I pick up the menu again and make myself order a sandwich.

When the waitress leaves, I realize Alastair is frowning at me. 'What do you mean, "estranged"?'

'I thought … because …' I stumble over my words. 'You said she didn't want to introduce them to you.'

Alastair lets out a short, painful laugh. 'But that was because of *me*. It must have been. Sarah was so close to her parents. My God, Jenn, you've no idea. That was what made it so much worse. She absolutely adored them, went to see them all the time. Practically every month, she'd disappear off there. Always calling them on the phone in between. She absolutely loved them. They adored her. The way she talked about them – like they were the best parents in the world.'

'Then … then why weren't they there when she died? They didn't come, Alastair. They weren't at her funeral.'

Alastair is shaking his head, looking down at his menu again. 'I'm telling you, when I knew her, they weren't estranged.'

There's an awkwardness that has come over us. Because I'm so confused by what he has said. Because all this information isn't adding up. That image of the house torn down. And yet … and yet … I press my fingers to my temples. Didn't Marianne say exactly the same thing? *She was close to her parents, talked about them a lot. Don't you remember that photograph on her desk?* And that pretty placard in her flat. *Family Is The Dearest Thing.* When Alastair knew her, she saw them, visited them, spoke to them all the time. Did something change since then – so suddenly? Did something happen so close to when she died?

The waitress brings our drinks and food. My coffee and a Coke for him. Now I find myself, stupidly, wondering why he doesn't drink. Wondering if maybe he has a problem with alcohol; it's not as if he's working today. I can feel myself trying to pick faults in him. Discredit him just because he's been nice. The smell of the food catches in my throat. For a moment, I have to cover my nose. As Alastair lifts his cutlery he looks at me and I pick up my sandwich, ignoring the greasiness of the bread on my hands. I pinch off a corner, swallow it down.

Alastair takes a few mouthfuls of his – some kind of health-food salad – then he lays down his knife and fork.

'Can I show you something?' he says.

I swallow another pinch of my sandwich. 'Of course.'

He reaches into his pocket. I wipe my hands on my napkin and watch as he pulls out his phone.

'Just a moment,' he says, 'I need to find it.' There are red patches high on his cheeks. Whatever he's about to show me, it's important that I get my reaction right. 'Here.' He holds the phone out so that I can see the screen. It's a video. He presses play.

She is moving, smiling, talking to the camera. It's her. It's Sarah, I recognize her at once. She is singing. *Singing.* What is that tune? I recognize it. Her voice is high, clear, childlike; I remember what Marianne said about her voice. She's singing to the camera. To Alastair.

And Alastair still has no idea that I knew her. Because I never told him. Because I held that back.

You are my sunshine, my only sunshine. It's supposed to be pretty, but all the hairs on my neck stand up. She approaches, closer and closer, as if she's about to step right out of the screen. A shudder runs right through me, my mind flashing on that body on the couch, because I can't escape a sense of horror, seeing her so alive on this video and then her death, that carpet of flies in her flat. My stomach heaves; I have to look away. I pick up my napkin and press it to my mouth where sour saliva is welling up. 'Sorry,' I say. 'I'm sorry.'

I push my plate away and sit back in my chair. I cannot get that image out of my head: her dead on the sofa, all her features worn away. My breath is coming in short, tight lungfuls. I lean down to my bag and fumble in it for my own phone. 'This isn't making sense,' I tell him. 'What you've said about her parents. Something must have happened. But we can check. I know who I can call.'

I dig in my bag again, this time for the scrap of paper that I wrote Mike Bernard's phone number on. The coroner's officer. I set it on the slatted table, holding it tight under my fingertips so it won't blow away. The varnish on my nails is chipped, flaking away like everything else. I type the numbers into my phone and press call. Mike picks up almost immediately.

I'm breathless as I try to explain why I'm calling and remind him who I am.

'Yes,' he tells me, 'Jennifer Arden. I certainly remember. Is there something I can help you with?'

I set the phone down on the slatted table and put it on speakerphone, so we both can hear. Alastair's eyes are locked onto mine. There's an echoing racket around us, but we can still hear Mike's voice. I wrap an arm around my waist and lean down to speak into the phone.

'I'm here with a friend ... someone else who knew Sarah. Please can you help us clarify ... the situation with Sarah's parents? A woman from the local authority said police couldn't ...' I'm reaching back in my mind, trying to remember the exact words of that conversation, which feels like it happened so long ago.

They had no luck, tracing her parents, they tried but ... there were a couple of other relatives, as well, deceased.

'... that they couldn't reach them?' I manage. 'I'm sorry, I don't know if any of this is appropriate, I don't even know if you're allowed to tell me ...'

I squeeze my arm more tightly around myself, pressing it against my ribs.

'Jennifer, I'm sorry. According to my notes – one sec, let me get them up. Yes, here ... her mother in 2001, father in 2003.'

And what Mike says next unravels the careful design I've made, all the little stitches I've embroidered for myself; I feel the threads coming loose, my sense of reason fraying.

'Jennifer, I'm sorry, but both Sarah's parents have died ... Almost twenty years ago.'

Chapter 24

Alastair scrapes his chair back from the table. A knife goes clattering to the floor. The shock on his face is a mirror of my own. Not *as well, deceased* but *deceased as well*. That young woman from the local authority had given me the facts – and I had completely misunderstood.

I hang up my mobile as Alastair bends forwards and clasps his hands in front of him, elbows pressing on his knees. I think I can actually see the tremors running through his legs.

My own heart is thundering. My own stomach is in knots.

He goes on sitting like that, head bent towards his knees. 'Alastair?' I manage to say. 'Are you okay?'

People are looking at us. He clenches his hands tighter. 'I'm sorry, I think … I think I'm having an anxiety attack.'

For a moment, I don't know what to do. I have never seen someone else like this. I only know it of myself. *Then what would you want?* I shout at myself inside my head. *All those times you felt your mind was fracturing, what did you need right then and there?*

I manage to push my own chair back, get up and go round to him. I crouch down beside his seat and place a hand on his arm. Steady and kind.

'Try to breathe more slowly,' I say. 'Honestly, just focus on your breathing.' I say that, and just keep holding onto him.

He takes a shuddery breath in, lets a shuddery breath out. 'I'm sorry,' he says again. 'I get these attacks. It's been ages … since the last one … but what the man said just then, it's another total shock.'

'Can I get you some water?' I say. 'Or anything else?' I make sure to keep my hand on his arm, grounding him. That's the most important thing. I'm quite amazed at how calm I am being, how well I manage to seem in control.

'If we can get out of here,' Alastair says. He's managed to lift his head a bit. 'The noise … and it's so crowded … is there somewhere we can go, a bit of space, a park, anywhere like that? That's what has always helped me before.'

'Yes,' I say. 'Of course. Can you stand up? I know a place, it's only a few minutes, if you can walk there with me?'

'Yes, thank you. Jenn, I'm so sorry.'

'It's fine. Honestly, please don't be embarrassed.' I'd hate for him to feel the shame I've felt. I let go of his arm, just for a moment, to dig some money out of my bag. I push all the cash I have – a ten-pound note and a five – under a plate on the table, in among our unfinished meals. Alastair has got his bag now too. He's upright now, if unsteady on his feet. His face is so shockingly pale.

Instinctively, I hold out a hand to him, the way I would for a small child. With Charlie. Just as instinctively, Alastair takes it, gripping almost more tightly than I can bear. At the same time, the contact of our palms sends little shocks through me, my skin tingling, nerves singing, my system so starved of human touch.

Brockwell Park is really no distance away. We zigzag our way up the road together, his hand in mine, my hand in his. I lead him through the little entrance gate on this side and, as soon as we enter, I can feel Alastair relax. His hand loosens its grip on mine – though doesn't let go. 'Thank you,' he says. 'Yes, this is perfect. I'll be all right in a minute, I swear. I just need … to get a proper breath.'

'We can sit down? Here, or keep walking?'

Alastair points to a bench a little way up the hill. 'There. Let's walk to there, and then sit down. Thank you. God, I can't tell you how embarrassed I am.'

'Please, honestly, it doesn't matter. I've been there … I understand. I've had anxiety attacks before.'

Alastair nods. 'Thank you for saying that. Here, okay, I'm going to sit down.'

We both sink down. The bench is warm from the spring sunshine. I can feel the heat soaking into my legs. Somehow, we are still holding hands.

'I'm sorry,' he says again, and now finally slips his hand from mine. He rests his palms on his knees. His legs don't seem to be trembling any longer, and his breathing is slower, deeper. 'I'm feeling better. It's passing. Open space – it always helps.'

I don't know what I should say now. I feel so calm on the outside, and yet my heart is racing in my chest and my hands feel cold – anxiety of my own. I try to match my breathing to his – long, slow breaths.

I still can't believe what Mike Bernard said.

A cluster of sparrows comes hopping up to us, darting near us, then flitting away. Gradually, they grow braver, less timid. Watching them calms me. Soon Alastair seems calm enough as well.

'I'm sorry,' I'm the one to say now. 'I swear to you, I had no idea. I'm as shocked as you are.'

Alastair gives his hands a shake. I understand the gesture: shaking away the pins and needles of adrenaline. 'I just can't believe it,' he says. 'The way she talked about them ...'

'You never suspected?'

'No. She was always telling me stories about her family, her childhood. Silly things that happened to her at school, stuff she got up to with friends, family holidays, all of that. She was ... a natural storyteller. She was studying Creative Writing, did I tell you that?'

He looks over at me, smiling, though his eyes are wet at the corners.

I smile back, despite the weight of sadness in my chest. 'No, you didn't.' And I think: did he tell me what he was studying at university?'

'Yeah ... English and Creative Writing. She showed me some of her pieces once. I wasn't much of a judge, but I thought they were good. Really vivid, you know? And we had a whole pattern set up in our lives. This bread shop that we'd always go to. Stupidly expensive, neither of us could really afford it, but they did these pancakes that she couldn't get enough of. And then, sometimes, we'd just take a bus across the city. Sit on the top deck, people-watch, make up all these stories about who we saw. Or make up more stories about ourselves, all this stuff we would do, all these places we would go. I keep remembering all these things about her. Like how, when she was annoyed, she'd push her tongue against her teeth ... she had this gap in her front teeth and she'd push her tongue against that gap. We spent *all this time together*, I really thought I knew her. But now I realize, I never really met any of her friends. I never met her family, we never went to any of these places she kept talking about. So did I really not know a single thing about her? Can I really have been that stupid? When she knew every single damn thing about me.'

I glance across at him, sharply. A harsh note has crept into his voice. Bitterness … or something else? All of a sudden, I can't quite read him and little hairs on my arms stand up.

'It's so hard,' he goes on, 'to give you a proper sense of her, Jenn, when you didn't ever know her or meet her.'

You didn't tell him, I think. *Right at the start, you didn't tell him, and how would it look now if he finds out you lied?*

Alastair leans back now against the bench, looking so much more relaxed. He closes his eyes. 'This is a nice park. What's the name – Brockwell?'

'Yes, that's right.'

'You're lucky to have this on your doorstep. It took me a while to get used to all the hustle and bustle when I first came to London. How did you find it, coming from Brighton?'

I look across at him. 'What?'

He sits up, opens his eyes again. 'What?'

'How did you know I grew up in Brighton?'

Alastair frowns. 'You told me. When we first met. I thought you went to school there.' He smiles. 'Listen,' he says. 'I can see a café just up there. Will you let me buy you a tea, a coffee or something? To say thank you? I mean, it's hardly anything in return, but can I?' He has already got to his feet. He really does seem completely fine now.

I smile back at him, his figure a silhouette against the sunshine. 'Sure,' I say. 'Tea, please. That would be great.'

He heads off and I'm just about to shout after him *decaff!* when my mobile rings. When I pull it out, it's Marianne's name on the screen. I take a couple of breaths to steady myself. Should I tell her now, over the phone, about Sarah's parents? After what it did to Alastair? Should I wait to visit her, or will that take too long; would she want me to tell her as soon as I could?

'Marianne?' I say when I answer. 'Marianne, you'll never guess—'

But she is already speaking over me. 'Jennifer, you said you were going to see Alastair again?'

'Yes? Why?'

'I did some research. You said he and Sarah were together at Middlesex. A friend of mine works in the admissions office there. I had a hunch, I just wanted to check. I called to find out when they attended. It's true, Sarah was there. She studied English and Creative Writing.'

'Yes, I know. Alastair told me.' I can see him at the open café, giving his order at the counter.

'He told you?'

'Yes. That's how they met. That's where they went out. Marianne, what is this about?'

'Jennifer. He was never there.'

'What?' I can see Alastair heading back towards me, two takeaway cups of tea in his hands.

'He's not on any of their registers. Jennifer—'

'I'm sorry, Marianne, I have to go.' I let the phone slide from my ear. *He lied to you*, says the voice in my head. *Yes*, I reply. *But I lied to him too.*

'Here you go.' Alastair is looming over me, holding out the steaming cup. Automatically, I reach out to take the drink he has bought.

'Are you okay?' he says. 'Jennifer, what is it?'

'I'm sorry,' I say, stumbling to my feet. My bag slips from my shoulder and I yank it back up. 'It's just the time. I have to get back to the office. I'm late, I'm sorry. I really have to go.'

'Will you let me walk you back then, at least?'

I force a smile. 'No, honestly, I'm literally going to have to run. You stay here. Enjoy the sunshine. I'll call you later.'

And I hand back the tea and leave him there, standing in the park, staring after me as I rush away.

*

At the bottom of the stairs in our building, I hold onto the banister and force myself to catch my breath. I didn't eat more than two bites of my sandwich, but my whole stomach feels swollen and distended, crushing up against my lungs.

I'm on my own in the stairwell. Nobody can see me here. Gradually, gradually, I fight through the panic. In my mind, I comb back through the conversations, trying to find explanations for the parts that don't add up. How did he know I grew up in Brighton? Why did he lie about being at Middlesex? *Think, think, think. You have to remember.* I take it, line by line. Our first conversation in the canteen. I made that comment, didn't I? About my school canteen. That must have been when I mentioned to him that I went to school in Brighton. And what did he really say about university? Did he really say he went there? Or only that he knew Sarah when she did? Is that all it is? Misremembering and forgetting and hearing my own interpretation of what he said? Just like on that call to the local authority? It's fine, I tell myself. Maybe he wasn't straight up about everything. *But then neither were you, Jennifer. Neither were you.*

Finally I'm able to pull myself up the staircase, legs weak and tingling as the blood fights to get round them properly. By the time I get to the top, I am steadier. Confident that I can trust my judgement. I find that I can stand up straight. And by the time I open the door to my office and sit back down at my desk, anyone looking at me would see I'm just fine.

Chapter 25

BACK THEN

It is boiling hot in the car. The sun comes beating down on the sunroof and the air con hardly does anything. Prin can't wait to get to the beach, into the biting cold of the water. She kicks her feet, careful this time not to clip the back of Mum's seat. Across the car, Jane is strapped in too, gazing out through the hot window glass. She's wearing jelly shoes and shorts and a T-shirt and, like Prin, she's got her swimming costume on underneath.

Prin is so hot that even though she's nine years old, she can't help herself. 'Are we nearly there yet?'

Mum twists around in her seat. She is wearing big round sunglasses and has her hair tied up in a messy bun. She's wearing a big long floaty sundress. Prin thinks she looks very pretty.

'Not far now,' she says, and smiles.

Daddy is driving and he looks in the mirror above his head to catch Prin's eyes. 'Are you excited?'

'Of *course!*' says Prin. 'Aren't you?'

Daddy is good at getting excited about things. Daddy is good at having lots of fun.

Prin swings her feet again and looks out of her own window. She tries to work out how long Jane has been with them now. It must be a month, at least. She still isn't sure whether Jane will go back home at the end of the summer holidays. Mum and Daddy haven't really said anything about that. Although, she thinks she heard them talking about Jane coming to school. To the same school that Prin is at, though of course she wouldn't be in Prin's class. Prin thinks she wouldn't mind if Jane stayed longer. She thinks she wouldn't mind if Jane never went back home.

Prin squints against the sunshine. It's coming right in through her window, right into her eyes. She wishes she had sunglasses like Mum's.

Prin has got quite used to having Jane live with them. The only thing she doesn't like is when Jane has those bad dreams. Then Prin has to get up and make her stop: get into bed with her and show her the zoetrope. That lovely couple dancing. She explains to Jane about the Make-Believe, how she only needs to picture it, and it's real. She thinks Jane is beginning to understand. Prin spins the zoetrope at just the right speed and tells Jane to imagine anything she wants. Then Jane calms down and soon enough they fall back to sleep.

It makes Prin a bit sleepy just thinking about it now and she leans her head against the car window. In fact, she must have actually dozed off for a bit then, because the next thing she knows, Mum is opening Prin's car door, smiling down at her and saying ,'We're here!'

*

It's a little bit of a walk to the beach, but Prin doesn't mind; she knows it will be completely worth it. Daddy gives them each something to carry from the car boot. Jane gets the buckets and spades, and Prin takes the big waterproof bag with all their towels in it. She is quite big and strong enough to carry that. Mum looks after the bag with the sunscreen and the important items like wallets and keys, and Daddy carries the big cooler box that has their lunch and snacks inside.

Jane says she's thirsty when they get to the sand, and Mum fishes out cartons of orange juice for her and Prin. She rubs sunscreen on them both while they drink and Prin shifts her feet about impatiently in the sand.

Once that is done with, the first game they play is Jumping Over The Waves. Prin can swim, but Jane can't, and Mum insists that they stay in the shallows. Some waves are small and some are big, but Prin can jump over all of them. Jane doesn't do much jumping; she mostly just stands there, arms out, letting the water crash against her shins. After a while, Prin gets bored of doing all the jumping herself, and anyway it's time for lunch. Mum is already laying the food out on a blanket.

'Come on,' says Prin to her cousin. 'We're supposed to go and eat.'

Lunch is delicious, all of Prin's favourites, even if there's sand in some of it.

Afterwards, Daddy lies down on one of the spread-out towels and Mum says they are both going to have a little rest.

'Don't go far,' Mummy tells Prin and Jane, lifting her sunglasses back from her face. The hidden skin underneath looks pale. 'Don't go back in the water for now,' Mum says, 'and don't go anywhere where we can't see you.'

Prin wriggles and squirms while Mum rubs more sunscreen onto them both. She already knows what they will do. She remembers this from last summer, when they came to this exact same beach. As Mum caps the sunscreen and puts her sunglasses back on, Prin takes Jane by the hand.

*

Prin is running now, up the beach, pulling Jane after her. Jane stumbles a bit in the jelly shoes she's wearing, a size too big, but she runs fast enough to keep up. Jane is actually quite good at running.

Only a tiny way along the beach, there is a funny little rock formation. It makes a little cliff above the sand, not high at all, honestly; the top is only a foot or two above Prin's head. Not even so high as last year, because Prin is three whole inches taller now. To the side, more jagged rocks make a sort of staircase, so it's easy-peasy to climb right up.

And then, from the top, you can jump right off. And it feels like flying.

Prin comes to a stop at the bottom of the cliff and checks back over her shoulder. She can still see them, Mum and Daddy, little wavery flat shapes in the heat. She can see Mum's arms, holding up a book, and the slash of Daddy's bright red towel.

'Come on,' says Prin to Jane. She scrambles her way up the rocky staircase, Jane trailing after her. Prin climbs slowly, for Jane's benefit. Jane goes very, very slowly, only moving one hand or foot at a time. It's silly really, there's no danger of falling. The rocks are almost like normal steps.

Halfway up, Jane comes to a halt. She is holding onto the rocks very tightly, and seems to be breathing quite fast.

'Prin?' she says, and Prin expects her to say she wants to climb back down, that she is too scared to climb all the way to the top, that she wants to go back and just sit on a towel. Prin twists round so she is crouched on the rock looking down at Jane, jelly shoes gripping tight.

'What is it?' she asks.

Jane looks up at her, her face like a little monkey's. Despite the sunscreen, her nose is already growing pink in the sun. 'Why do they call you that?' she says. '"Prin". Instead of your name?'

Prin gives her hands a clap. She isn't holding on at all. 'It's a nickname!' Daddy's name for her. 'Short for something – can't you guess what?'

Jane gazes up at her, her face blank. Just waiting for Prin to tell her the answer. Instead, Prin turns away and scampers up to the top of the cliff. It's not really a cliff; more just like a little platform. Now that she's taller, Prin is almost disappointed with how short the jump really is. But she still wants to show Jane – Jane who is still climbing so slowly, one foot, one hand at a time, picking her way up the rocks.

Prin stands up as tall as she can. She can see such a long way from here. She can see Daddy and Mum easily. Daddy is up on one elbow, sort of leaning over Mum. Mum sees Prin and sits up, waving at them: a series of quick, sharp waves. Daddy turns to look over his shoulder. Prin waves back.

She looks down at Jane, who is almost – just about – at the top.

Prin puts her hands on her hips. 'It's a nickname,' she tells her. 'My daddy's nickname for me. It's short for Princess,' she says, holding out her arms. 'I'm my daddy's princess.'

Then she bends her knees, and jumps.

*

The sand below is so soft to land on, feet and bottom. Like a pillow. Prin falls onto it, still feeling the rush of the fall. Jumping like that, it's the best feeling in the world: there's the heat and the sun and the crashing waves and the feeling of soaring, flying.

Prin lies there, staring up into the blue, absorbing it all. She feels giddy with the thrill.

Then she gets to her feet and scampers back up the rock to the top.

It's Jane's turn now.

'Don't look so scared,' Prin tells her. They are both standing at the top again now. 'You saw me do it.' She tugs Jane's arm, pulling her closer to the edge. 'Imagine you have wings. Big, shiny wings. It feels amazing, you'll love it!'

Jane's feet slide over the rock in their too-big jelly shoes. She pushes her weight back against Prin's chest, shaking her head. She's gripping Prin's wrist so hard that Prin can tell she'll leave red marks. What a scaredy-cat!

'Hold your arms out,' Prin tells her. 'Like this! Like they're your wings! Why don't you use your imagination?'

And then Prin isn't exactly sure what happens next; whether Jane jumped or just slipped or whether Prin's elbow nudged her, but the next moment she is tumbling from the cliff, a whirl of arms and legs.

Prin scrambles down the staircase, her stomach a big knot. What will Daddy say if Jane is hurt? What if Jane has broken her leg, her arm, *what will Daddy say?* At the bottom, Jane is all crumpled on the sand and she's making a funny keening sound. Prin rushes up, but Jane is already pushing herself upright. Her face is red, her wispy hair sticking out all round her head.

'I thought of it,' she pants, grinning. 'Just like you said.' Her face is all taken up by smiles. 'Make-Believe! I was in the air and you were right, it was just like flying! Come on,' she says. 'Let's do it again!'

*

After that, they jump and jump, again and again, each time better, each time higher than the last. Eventually they collapse on the warm sand and lie next to each other, breathless. From along the beach, Prin's mum is calling for them. Lying on her side, Prin squints against the sliding sun; Daddy is coming for them across the sand, a big, tall, handsome shape. Mum's voice continues on, high and bright in the summer air.

Just before they stand up to run to Daddy, Prin rolls over and props her chin on her hands, looking down at her cousin. 'If you had one real wish,' she asks her, 'what'd you wish for?' She thinks about what she'd wish for herself: a horse, a trip to Disneyland, a TV in her bedroom. Wings so that she really could fly.

But Jane's answer, when it comes, takes her utterly by surprise.

'I'd wish for a lovely mummy and daddy,' Jane says, 'just like yours.'

Chapter 26

I am fine, and I'll call Alastair – and Marianne – again soon.
With everything that has been going on, though, I've completely forgotten about the party.

It's Charlie who reminds me on Saturday afternoon,
pointing to the gap on the fridge where the invite should be.
SpongeBob hovers there, empty-handed. I remember now
taking it down to scribble Marianne's details on it, but I can't
think what I did with it after that. I hunt through all the piles
of paper in the kitchen but don't find it anywhere. It doesn't
matter, though. Charlie has already memorized the details. He
has a wonderful memory, how could I have questioned that?

It's already half past one and the party is at three. I find
him a pair of smart trousers and an ironed shirt to wear. He's
so excited, he can hardly stand still. We have to dash out to
the corner shop to find a present, hoping there'll be something
decent in the limited selection.

Charlie rakes through the items on the shelves. 'What about
this?' he says, holding up a set of paints and paintbrushes.
'Molly likes it when we do art at school, I think she'd like to
have something like this.'

I look down at my son, struck by his thoughtfulness, his

empathy. The paint set is hardly the fanciest of presents – the paint looks cheap, the colours garish – but it means a lot that Charlie knows what Molly would like. I grab some wrapping paper, some ribbon too, and all together, it doesn't look so bad.

We're running so late that I book an Uber to take us to Molly's house. Charlie recites the address to me and I type it into the app. It costs more than I expected, but I go ahead and book it anyway. How often do we get to go out like this? And isn't that what the money from Mum and Dad is for anyway? For Charlie? I make a note to myself to transfer the amount from my savings fund once we get back home.

The taxi comes so quickly and gets us there so fast that in the end we arrive outside exactly on time. We scramble out of the taxi and I remember to rate and tip the driver. It's a really nice house, Victorian terrace, flower holders on the windowsills, so different to our own flat up a flight of concrete stairs. I can see helium balloons tied to the front door, so I know we're at the right place. Charlie has got the details spot on. The balloons bounce on their strings in the gentle breeze, and Charlie bounces with them. He's a ball of excited energy. I stop and turn him towards me, straightening his shirt collar, which has got crooked from all his hopping about.

'Okay then,' I say, 'here you go.' I hand him the present so he can be the one to give it to Molly.

Other parents and kids are arriving now. Their faces are familiar; I have seen them hundreds of times at the school gates. I recognize Rachel and Martin and Sally. I make myself stand up straight and smile because I can see on their faces that they are surprised to see me here. *But Molly invited everyone*, I want to say to them. *Everyone in the class, including Charlie.*

I relax my shoulders, smile and wave. I'm realizing now that it's really only me that has been making things difficult. I must come across as so stiff and awkward at the school gates, no wonder people tend to avoid me. I probably have some look on my face, embarrassed or preoccupied or fierce, and of course that's going to put people off. They've simply all been taking their cues from me. I need to be sure to do things differently now. They need me to show them that I'm okay. And I do feel okay, I mean, I'm so much better now. And, for today at least, I will put Sarah out of my mind. I wave again, and Charlie gives a little jump at my side, pulling on my arm.

Martin smiles back at me and lifts his own hand in response. He has both of his sons in tow, one Charlie's age and one a little younger. I smile down at them both as they come up. Rachel is holding her daughter Lara's hand, and Sally has Erin. We make a happy little bunch.

And then the door to Molly's house opens and we are ushered into the warmth inside.

Molly's mum has gone all out. There are balloons *everywhere*. There must be a hundred at least, all different sizes and shapes. The colours seem so bright; it's as if everything has a little shimmer to the edges, so vivid and pretty. As I balance myself against the wall to slip off my shoes, I almost expect to feel a little spark. Sally and Rachel are kissing Molly's mum on the cheek, their voices fluttering around them. In another room a child screams with laughter, a waterfall of giggles. As I pull my ankle boot off, I notice there's a ladder in my tights, starting at my big toe and running right along the side of my foot. I pull the material round so none of it shows. The rest of my outfit looks just fine: a smart skirt, a pretty blouse.

Charlie has already found his way to the centre of things, handing his present to Molly along with the other kids. Seeing him next to the other children, I realize he must have had another growth spurt. He's one of the tallest among them now. His hair shines under the lights. We washed it properly in the bath last night, for the first time in what felt like a while. He knows these children: they are his classmates, his friends. It's totally natural for him to fit in.

I find myself standing next to Martin and Sally. My eyes feel dazzled by all the spotlights in the ceiling. We've each been given a slice of chocolate cake on a paper plate. It looks huge, dark and sticky, like something I could fall and get stuck right in, and the paper plate feels almost too flimsy for the weight. When I take a bite, the burst of sugar makes my teeth ache. I don't think I've been brushing properly of late. But the cake is delicious, it really is, and I've almost eaten the whole thing before I know it.

Martin and Sally are talking about something, a television programme they both saw last night, some adaptation of a Harlan Coben novel. Their voices sound exaggerated somehow: Sally's a high-pitched flickering, and Martin's very loud, booming in my ears. My mouth is too full of chocolate sponge for me to speak, but I look back and forth between them, nodding and smiling.

It's lovely to be here, it really is. I'm so grateful to Molly's parents for inviting us.

Now Molly's mum is setting up a game of musical chairs. The chairs screech as she drags them across the living-room floor to line them up. All the colours and the movements, it looks like something from a carnival parade. The music from the stereo seems to come from all around us; the whole air seems to vibrate with it. I smile and move my head and nod as Sally and Martin continue talking. Now Molly's dad is coming over to join us. He looks so like Molly, lanky and tall, there's no way you could mix up who he is. He holds out a hand to me – only to me, because he already knows Sally and Martin, I realize.

'Molly seems very taken with your son,' he tells me as I shake his hand. I can feel Martin and Sally both looking at me. I swallow the chocolate cake that's filling up my mouth. 'Oh,' I say, smiling brightly. 'Does she?'

He's very tall, Molly's dad; I feel like I'm tipping backwards as I look up at him. 'They sit next to each other at school – did he say? She tells me he has been very kind to her. She can be quite shy, and of course, she's new here.'

I keep nodding, my head floating loose on my neck. 'I think that Charlie really likes Molly too. He talks about her a lot.'

The music for the game has started now and it's loud. Really thumping. A headache buds at the back of my skull but in front of me everything is lovely and bright. I'm trying to see past Molly's dad, to keep an eye on Charlie. The children swivel and tilt themselves as they circle the double row of chairs. It's like an animation, a Disney *Fantasia* of movement. There seem to be arms and legs everywhere; it's almost hard to see where one child ends and another one begins. When the music stops, the children tumble themselves towards the chairs, elbowing each other. Charlie gives a shriek of delight. Through the swirl, I glimpse him sliding neatly into a seat and I want to clap; maybe I even would if my hands weren't taken up with my crumb-strewn plate. I feel almost giddy with how happy I feel.

I'm aware of Sally and Martin looking at me and I realize Molly's dad – I haven't even got his name – has asked me another question. 'I'm sorry,' I say, 'what was that?'

The music starts again, a new bouncing, high-pitched song. Pharrell Williams, is that it?

'I was just asking when Charlie's birthday falls,' Molly's dad repeats.

I smile up at him, wider than ever. 'First of May,' I tell him. 'May Day. He was a beautiful May Day baby.'

Molly's dad and Sally and Martin smile and nod, but my eyes slide past them, back to the children, and I lose the thread of what anyone is saying. The music clicks off again; the children scramble for the few remaining chairs. Arms and legs and bodies tangle. The scene seems waterlogged to me, dreamlike. All of a sudden, everything grinds down to the slowest of slow motion. A boy shoves Charlie, thrusting him aside, sliding past him into the last empty chair. My blood feels as if it has jammed in my veins. Charlie is the only one left standing, spotlighted in the middle of the room.

His whole body turns rigid, a scarlet stain burning across his cheeks. My stomach plummets, seems to fall right away. An ugly shudder runs right through my son, as though he's having some kind of seizure; he's hardly able to focus his eyes. In the vacuum of silence he opens his mouth, and now his voice is a roar, his mood completely out of control, flipped. His tongue is huge and swollen behind his teeth and he stutters, he *stutters*:

'That's not *f-f-f-air!*'

My God, *my God*. Everything has stopped, everyone is look-ing: parents, children. Everyone has seen. I thrust my crumpled paper plate into Sally's hand. My voice sounds disembodied as

I say, 'I'm sorry, excuse me, please take this.' My ears have gone dead, like I'm underwater – or like Charlie's roar has burst my eardrum. I feel stripped naked, completely exposed.

I push through the crowd and grab my son by the arm, my sticky hand creasing and smearing his clean shirt. I drag him clear of the circle of chairs and children and elbows, even as he fights and twists in my grasp. I can see Molly's mum stepping forwards, concern written all across her face. But all I can focus on is getting us out of there, getting *him* out of there.

It feels like sports day all over again, but this time the voice in my head is pounding, *It's real, it's real, it's real. It isn't your anxiety, your paranoia, your crazy brain, because you weren't anxious, you were happy when you saw it, heard it. Happy and calm and clear in your mind and it* still *happened. His rage, his eyes, his stutter; you can't keep pretending. Something's wrong in him, you know it is, you've just been ignoring it while you obsessed about Sarah. But this is happening, you've been right all these months, and so you need to get him out of here right now.*

I don't stop to say goodbye to anyone. I don't even thank Molly or her parents for the balloons or the games or the cake. I drag Charlie down the hallway, wrestle him into his coat and shoes. He pretends he has no idea what is happening. 'Are we leaving, Mum? Are we going?'

'Yes,' I tell him, already swiping for a taxi on my phone. 'Yes, we're leaving right now.'

'No!' he cries. '*No!*'

I just manage to get him outside, into the cold and away from the house before he bursts into tears.

*

As soon as we get home, I strip Charlie out of his party clothes and put him into his pyjamas. I get the thermometer from the cupboard in the kitchen and push it under his tongue. When I pull it out, I read the gauge without showing him.

'You aren't very well,' I tell him. 'You have a temperature.'

He's weak now, exhausted. I pull the big duvet off my bed and drag it through onto the living-room sofa. I put the television on, gentle cartoons, the volume low, and make him lie down. I make him hot milk, scalding myself in the process, and give him Calpol. I sit beside him on the sofa and smooth his glossy hair, my hand a steady rhythm. But when fifteen minutes later I place my palm on his forehead, his skin still feels hot, and he twists and fidgets under my hand. I give him a second dose, praying this one will soothe him. I just need him to be still. I just need him not to move, or try to get up or speak, because every movement, every word is like a trigger and I just need some space to *think*.

When he falls asleep, as I'd hoped he would, I get up quietly. The slice of birthday cake sits like a rock in my stomach. I go through to the bathroom and quietly, almost silently, make myself sick.

Then I take my laptop into the kitchen and open up the webpage I promised myself last year never to go on again. They told me back then that it would only make things worse. *You'll just confirm all of your worst fears, you'll convince yourself of everything you read. It's a confirmation bias*, the psychologist told me. *It doesn't help*. But now I can't help myself. I tell myself I just need to know.

The address comes up as soon as I start typing it into the search bar. The Child Brain Injury Trust. I've been to this site so many times before. On here there are pages and pages of information. Fact sheets on everything you could ever want to know. Videos of a dozen different children and their families.

I click on a fact sheet about damage in infancy. I click on a video about the developing brain. *It's impossible for any health-care professional to predict the outcome for a child … some of the effects may not come to the surface until years later* … Through in the living room, Charlie is sleeping soundly on the couch. I love him so much and yet he terrifies me. I want to hold him, crush him to me, and yet at times like this, I can hardly bear to go near him.

As I scroll through the site, I do everything I can to read the words properly, not to let my mind pick and choose, but it's as though my reason has no balance any more. From anywhere, everywhere, random words and phrases leap out at me. *Word-finding difficulties, issues with coordination and speech, information-processing problems, frustration and anger.* It's all in a jumble, no organization to it at all. I am not checking properly what might apply and what couldn't possibly. It's as though my anxiety acts as a magnet, drawing every frightening idea to it, and I haven't got the ability to filter it any more and I've no longer got the strength to push it away.

One recollection after another leaps into my brain, again and again the monster bites. The maths problems. *He couldn't do the maths problems.* And he couldn't find his words the other morning. And these tantrums, growing worse and worse, plus how many other mental, emotional signs have I missed?

I feel like crying. I feel so lost, so confused. I am an intelligent woman, a professional, thirty-one years old, but I can't tell which way up my world stands. I try to tell myself, *They don't add up. What you've been noticing, what you've been seeing, it doesn't fit with how signs would present.* I repeat it, over and over to myself, but the words are like water, they just run away from me, slipping and disappearing through the holes in my reason. There is nothing here I can hold onto. Nothing feels solid any more in my head. I try to focus on nothing but my breaths, I try distraction, Mindfulness, counting in sevens, anything that can steady my mind.

But the voice in my head only repeats: *It's true, it's true, it's true.*

*

When Charlie wakes that evening, around nine, I give him another dose of Calpol and tuck him into his own bed. Miraculously, he sleeps through the night, but it's another night when I don't get a wink. My creased bed sheets need changing – I haven't done it, even though it's written on my list in the kitchen – and the mattress feels as hard as a rock. Whichever way I lie there's a bone that sticks out: the back of my pelvis if I face the ceiling; my hipbone if I lie on my side. When I try to curl up, the edges of my kneecaps bruise together. I don't seem to have any cushioning any more. I cannot stop thinking about Charlie. And I can't stop reeling either from the truth about Sarah's parents. It feels as though pieces of reality have fallen out of the world, and taken a whole piece of my own mind with them.

And if I can't calm myself, I don't know how I'm going to get it back.

When I get up on Sunday morning the world feels unreal,

flimsy, as though everything around me has been cut out of cardboard. Charlie wakes up ravenous, demanding breakfast, a bowl of Frosties plus two slices of toast. He gulps it all down, telling me, 'Honestly, Mummy, I don't feel ill at all.'

When I take his temperature again though, I tell him that he is. Charlie is confused, complaining, but I put the TV on for him and tell him to watch whatever he wants.

I do the only thing I know to do to keep safe. I retreat from everything, cut off from everyone. It is light outside, a bright February day, but I don't open any of the curtains in the flat and I keep the blinds in the kitchen drawn. I can't bear the thought of anyone looking in. In the gloom, Charlie channel-hops, still in his pyjamas. We pull the big duvet through onto the sofa again and this time I climb in beside him. I hold him to me, knowing that I am holding him too tight. Alastair rings and texts, and rings again. I let it go to answerphone each time.

Every few hours, I give Charlie more Calpol. I don't check the pack, but I tell myself I can't have gone over the dosage. The Calpol makes him compliant, sleepy. Every so often, I make him hot milk. I can lie with him on the sofa, warm and huddled.

I tell myself, even if there is something wrong with him, no one needs to know. What if I kept him here, with me, for ever? Just the two of us, like this? We could do that, we could manage, we could create our own little world. Even if his mind was falling apart, I would look after him, it wouldn't matter. We wouldn't need anyone else. Together we'd be safe. Together, both our minds could be sound.

Chapter 27

BACK THEN

A week after the day at the beach and it is *still so hot*. There is only a little bit left of the summer holidays now, but it isn't getting much cooler. It's been a very long, very hot summer.

Today, Prin and Jane are playing in Daddy's potting shed. It's shady in here, dusty with old dried dirt, and there are soft cobwebs in the corners of the ceiling. Prin doesn't mind the cobwebs. She knows spiders are more scared of her than the other way round. She and Jane are wearing sandals and their toes are dusted brown from the scatterings of soil that line the floor.

They are trying to plant some seedlings. Prin discovered some seed packets on the back of one of the shelves, and Mum agreed they could have them, along with a mossy bag of compost and some brown plastic flowerpots.

They are allowed to play in the potting shed, so long as they don't touch Daddy's tools. That's the rule. But that's fine; they can plant the seedlings with their bare hands, so long as Jane isn't a baby about getting a bit of dirt under her nails.

It's cool and quiet in the shed. Mum and Daddy are busy

in the garden too. Mum is weeding in the flowerbeds – Prin can see her through the open doorway, her elbows rising and falling – and Daddy is mowing the lawn out front.

Prin crouches down and lines up the empty plant pots. They've got six of them, all the same size. To be honest, they look a bit plain and boring, and one of them has a crack in the bottom.

'Whatever,' she says out loud to Jane. 'They'll do. Now we just have to fill them up.'

The compost from the bag is crumbly and smells funny. It seems very dry; these seedlings are going to need a lot of water. Prin digs out a handful and presses it into a pot. Mummy said, once planted, it would take at least a month for the seedlings to grow. Prin didn't think of that before. She can plant the seeds, but the pot will still look pretty much like it does now, not the riot of flowers she'd pictured.

Still, Prin fills another pot. She might as well; she can't think of anything else for them to do. She and Jane have exhausted all her games and toys. She's bored of colouring, bored of dolls, bored of practising cartwheels. Actually, she's just *bored bored bored*. Prin's skirt hangs across her knees. She's probably showing her knickers a bit, squatting like this, but who cares? It's too hot and, anyway, it's only Jane who would notice.

And Jane isn't even looking.

Instead she's gazing up at the cupboard stuck up on the wall where Daddy keeps his tools. There's a saw in there and a hammer and a chisel and a whole set of screwdrivers, all different sizes, all ordered neatly on their own little pegs. The catch on the door has come loose and Daddy hasn't fixed it yet, so the doors are hanging open. They look a bit like they're panting in the heat.

Jane goes on staring at the cupboard. 'I know a game,' she says. She gets to her feet and peers right into the tool cabinet.

Prin sighs. 'We aren't supposed to touch those. They're Daddy's.' She adds another dry handful to a pot.

But Jane doesn't listen. Instead, she stands on her tiptoes and reaches up. Prin goes still. Watching her cousin, she can't help but feel a sickly fascination. *Breaking the rules*. She glances out of the picture-frame of the doorway. Mum still has her back to them. Prin brushes the clumpy soil from her hands and gets to her feet to stand beside Jane. A little sharp tug, and the hammer slides off its peg.

'Oh,' says Jane. 'It's very heavy.' Her arm dips with the weight. Prin feels her skin tingle with the thrill. She was bored, but she isn't now.

The hammer looks huge in Jane's small hand. 'Well, what now?' says Prin.

Jane gives the hammer a tentative swing. She wraps both hands round the handle and swings it again, wider this time.

'The game is … when I hit you, you fall down. But then the game is, you get back up.'

Prin wrinkles her nose. 'What? What kind of a game is that?'

'It's *my* game,' says Jane. 'I want to play it.'

'It sounds stupid.'

'But I *want to play it*.'

Prin looks at her cousin standing there, clutching the big hammer, her shoulders hunched up, her face tight. Prin glances out through the doorway again. Mum has moved round the garden now, out of sight.

Prin gives another, huffy sigh. She's pretending to think it's silly, but somehow she can't help feeling that tingle. They aren't supposed to be playing with dangerous tools, but why not? After all, it's only pretending. And Prin is so bored. 'So I fall down, then jump back up again? Like I'm dead and then I'm alive?'

'Yep. Just like that.' Jane swings the hammer again, a wider, higher arc this time, her small body twisting in the wake.

'Okay ...'

'Stand there then.' Jane points to a clear space where there's room for Prin to fall on the floor without hitting anything. Prin's dress is already dusted with soil so she doesn't much mind getting dirty. In fact, the more she thinks about it, the more she likes the sound of this game. She can think of lots of dramatic ways to fall over. She can think of lots of impressive ways to come back to life. She can be like a Disney princess. Yes, it can all be very dramatic.

'Ready?' says Jane. She plants her feet apart and lifts the hammer up to her shoulder.

Prin gives her skirt a flip. 'Ready!' She's already worked out her first effort at collapsing. She's picturing just what she'll do with her arms.

'Three ...' says Jane.

Prin closes her eyes so she can imagine it clearly. She's going to do a really big swoon. She can hear Jane shuffle her feet on the floor.

'Two ...'

There's the buzz of Daddy's lawnmower over the way. The smell of the warm wood slats of the shed. Prin lifts her arms up ready and cracks an eye open, just in time to see Jane lift up her own arms.

'But – ' she giggles – 'you aren't going to *really* hit me!'

'*One!*'

A crack, a burst of pain.

And Prin falls.

*

When Prin opens her eyes, Jane is crying. Really shrieking.

Mummy is bursting in through the doorway, her face a horror-show of concern. 'What's *happened*?' she's shouting. 'What's *happened*?'

Lying flat out on the floor, Prin puts a hand to her cheek. There is blood on her palm when she pulls it away. She wants to cry, but she doesn't of course. Jane, though, goes on shrieking. 'Get up!' she's crying. 'Now you're supposed to get back up!'

Now Daddy is in the doorway too. The lawnmower isn't going any more. He takes one look at Prin and pushes past Mum to scoop her right up. Prin feels herself swung into the air and carried outside.

'You're fine,' Daddy says to her as he rushes her across the lawn. 'It's just a tiny graze, I promise.'

As he rushes her away, Prin watches back, over his shoulder. Inside the potting shed, Jane is still crying, tears everywhere, when she isn't even hurt. Prin is being so brave, not crying one bit, even though it feels way worse than a graze.

But Jane is crying fit to bust.

And Mum is holding her, hugging her. All the things Prin wants someone to do. Prin closes her eyes and goes limp in Daddy's arms.

And feels the jealousy twist in her guts.

Chapter 28

Safe and sound, I tell myself. *Safe and sound*. But I know it can't go on like this.

Charlie has to go to school.

I have to go to work.

There are tenants relying on me and it's my job to help them.

And then there's Alastair and Marianne. And Sarah.

On Monday morning, I haven't got a choice. I lever myself off the sofa at 6 a.m., letting Charlie sleep another hour. In the kitchen, the lights feel overly bright, as though I'm moving in a stage set. I compose a text on my phone to Charlie's teacher, telling her what happened, asking her to document any other signs she sees. I read it back – and then just delete it, not ready to face the realities yet. Instead I steady myself with order, routine. I already have Charlie's breakfast on the table by the time I wake him up. This morning, I do everything for him: pour out his cereal, fill his glass with juice. I pack his bag without asking him anything. I don't want to set any tests he will fail.

He makes a weak effort to push me away. 'Mummy, I can do it myself!' – but he's too sleepy to fight me, or maybe he's just learned that it makes it worse to fight. Either way, he stands by as I take charge of everything, and I'm so quick that we are up and out of the house faster than we have ever been.

The fresh air is good for me, sharp against my cheeks. There's a normality in the familiar walk, the familiar scene, and we arrive at school early, making up for the recent times I've been late. I promise myself that, soon, I'll speak to Ms Simmons.

But right now, there outside the school gates, someone is waiting for us.

I spot him as soon as I cross the road, holding Charlie's little hand in mine. Alastair. He has his back to us, but I recognize him even before he turns around.

As he comes towards us, I tighten my grip on Charlie's hand, feeling as though every cell in me is trembling. But his eyes are still gentle, his face is still kindly. And the other day, I answered all those doubts, didn't I? Marianne's suspicions and my own, they each had answers. Everything adds up?

He comes to a stop in front of me. He looks cold, as though he's been standing out a while. 'Jennifer, hi. I hope you don't mind me coming. I wasn't sure what I had done wrong,' he says. 'In the park, I know it was awkward, embarrassing … my anxiety, I just – you rushed away so suddenly.'

I can feel Charlie's hand hot in mine. He is staring up at this man he doesn't know.

'But how did you know this was where Charlie went to school?' I ask.

Alastair steadily holds my gaze. 'You told me,' he says. 'When we were arranging to meet.'

My brain feels slow, gummed up, but he's right. I remember that now too. So many things that I'm not keeping hold of properly. Obviously I told him, because here he is, standing right in front of us at the school gates.

'I thought I'd come, even just on the off chance,' Alastair goes on. 'I just wanted to know that you're okay. That we're okay.'

Charlie is looking back and forth between us. 'Charlie,' I say slowly, 'this is my friend Alastair.'

'Hello,' says Charlie.

'Alastair, this is my son.'

Now that I pay attention properly, I think my trembling is only fatigue. He works in a hospital, I tell myself, he's good with children. Alastair smiles down at my son, glances back up.

'You're all right, then?' he says to me.

I nod. My neck is stiff. But I'm better already for being out of the house, better already for having someone to talk to. I tamp down my thoughts, really pull it together. 'Yes, I'm fine. I'm sorry I was so rude. I'm sorry that I made you feel awkward.' I draw a breath. 'Sometimes I get anxious too.'

Now Alastair's face breaks into a smile. There is a blush too, on his cheeks. The trembling in me dies down. I glance down at Charlie, who is still gazing upwards with big round eyes. I think about all the times he's asked me: *I have a Daddy though too somewhere, don't I?* All the times I've wondered about Luke.

'Listen, Jennifer, the reason I kept trying to ring you – I mean aside from checking you were okay – was because I think I've found another contact. An old school friend of Sarah's. Chloe. Sarah had this old postcard from her, with her phone number on. It ended up in a book I lent Sarah, she used it as a bookmark. I spent all of yesterday looking, and I know it sounds weird, but I actually found it. I still have it – the postcard. Chloe might have changed her number since then but ... maybe not.'

Now Charlie is tugging at my hand. 'Mummy, what are you talking about?' he says.

I shouldn't be talking about Sarah in front of him. Not least because it's still making my head spin. 'It's nothing,' I tell him. 'Don't worry.' To Alastair, I say, 'Did you call her? This school friend – Chloe?'

Alastair colours up again, shakes his head. 'I wasn't sure ... I thought it might be better if you did it. A strange guy calling her, out of the blue? Saying that he has her number? She might find it a bit, you know, too weird ... But if you rang her? If you were able to explain?'

He pulls something from his jacket pocket, and I realize it's the very postcard he mentioned. The cardboard is worn and crumpled, the ink all faded. It looks years old. On the front is a picture of a harbour, the word *Portsmouth*; on the back, the writing is almost faded away. But Alastair is right. You can make out a number.

Before I can stop myself I reach out my free hand and take hold of it.

'And you'll let me know, won't you, anything you find out?'

People relying on me. Behind us, the school bell is shrilling. I nod silently, then say, 'Yes.'

I push the card into my bag and look down at Charlie. 'All right then, you need to go in. Time to say goodbye to Alastair.'

Charlie looks at me and I see his face fall.

Alastair glances at me, sensing the awkwardness. 'Oh wait! Here.' He digs in his pocket and pulls out a little green tub. 'I don't really know if you're into this,' he says, squatting down in front of my son, 'but the kids on the ward love this stuff.'

It's Silly Putty. Such a fun, innocent thing. From the start, didn't I know that Alastair was a kind person? A good person. He came to find me, to check I was okay, and he knew I'd be with Charlie so he brought him this toy.

Charlie looks up at me, checking it's okay. I nod to him: *go on.* He takes the little present from Alastair shyly.

'It was nice to meet you, Charlie,' Alastair says, getting back to his feet.

'Say thank you,' I tell Charlie. 'Tell him thank you before you go.'

Charlie doesn't have a father in his life, and so he does far more than that. He puts his arms right around Alastair and hugs him. I rub my eyes, feeling so exhausted.

And I watch as Alastair hugs him right back.

*

I feel steadier after that, though. At least I think I do. And so when I get to my desk in the office, I don't even wait to switch on my computer before I try calling the number on the postcard. I can still hear the voice in my head: *Forget all this. You're getting in too deep,* but it's like an addiction, I can't stop. The further reality seems to retreat, the more desperate my need for answers grows. I tap the numbers from the back of the postcard into my phone and press dial.

I don't think I seriously expected it to ring.

I don't think I seriously expected anyone to pick up.

So when the voice comes on the line – *Hello, Chloe speaking* – I nearly lose hold of the phone in surprise.

'Chloe?' I repeat.

'Yes – who is this, please?' Her voice is soft but very clear. She could be standing right next to me.

'My name is Jennifer,' I say, 'Jennifer Arden. You don't know me, but I'm a ... a contact of your old friend Sarah Jones.'

Of course there's a silence then on the line. '... *Sarah?*'

'I understand you knew each other?'

'Yes. We were ... at high school together. Excuse me, who did you say you were?'

'I'm sorry ... I was ... I am the manager for the flat Sarah rented. And I also knew her, very briefly, through work.' I switch the handset to my other hand. 'Chloe, I'm sorry, but could we meet up? I'm not sure I want to explain this over the phone.'

'Explain what? I'm sorry, I'm not following. I'm not even sure how you ... even have this number.'

I draw a deep breath, and I know that I have to tell her this much, because otherwise, why would she agree to speak to me, some stranger, getting in touch about someone from years ago? 'Chloe ... I'm ... really sorry to have to tell you this. I was the housing manager and ... and ... I'm afraid Sarah died ... a little while ago. Your number was on a postcard ... An old postcard you sent her. I'm trying to contact all of her old friends. I'd like to meet up, if we possibly could?'

In the silence that follows, I wish I was able to see Chloe's face. I can't tell what kind of emotion she's going through.

'I know this is a shock,' I rush on. 'I do know it's difficult. It's just ... we're all still trying to make sense of what happened.

You were friends with her, weren't you? If we could meet, if I could speak to you, it would really help …'

'She died? But how?'

'She … I … I'm sorry – it would be best, honestly, if you can, for me to explain face to face …'

'You want to meet up? I don't … I mean, where even are you?'

'In London, Brixton. Is that anywhere near you?'

Chloe gives a barking laugh. 'Right now I'm in Scotland. About to fly to Dubai. And I'm really not sure you understand. High school, Sarah …' A gap. 'That was not a happy time.'

For the first time, I register the pain in her voice. Not just shock and hesitation, but pain. Now it's my turn to pull back. 'I'm sorry,' I say. 'I'm sorry.'

Now there is only a silence between us. I can't push her, not after what she's just said. All I can do is listen, and wait.

'You said she had a postcard I sent?'

'Yes,' I say. 'She kept it. She was using it as a bookmark.'

There is silence again.

'She didn't forget you,' I add. 'She must have thought of you a lot.' I wait three, four beats. Then I brave it. 'Do you think we could possibly meet?'

She lets out a long breath. 'Well … but, like I say, I'm in Scotland.'

I press a hand to my head, trying to think. How can I possibly get up there? There is no possible way I can.

'Wait,' says Chloe. 'Could you get to Gatwick?'

'Gatwick?'

'It's where I'm flying out of. To Dubai. I'm getting an internal flight down from Edinburgh on Wednesday.'

Gatwick.

I know my way there. Of course I do. It sits on the train line between here and my parents' house. I have travelled past it dozens of times in my life. And Wednesday is my afternoon off. 'Then I could …' I can hardly believe I'm saying this. 'Then I could meet you there? At the airport?'

Another silence. All I can hear is the bang of my own heart, the panting of my own breath. For a moment I think she's dropped the line entirely.

'Chloe?'

'Yes, I'm still here,' comes her voice. 'And – yes – you could.'

*

After the call, I feel strangely elated. Buoyed up. Focused. I look at the photo of Charlie on my desk and force the tension out of my chest.

I have another visit to do this morning: a pair of tenants, and reports by their neighbours that they have vandalized their flat. I need to go and inspect the damage, start to make an estimate of costs. It's one of the worst kinds of jobs I could have, but today, even that doesn't bother me.

The tenants are out – in fact, I think they've done a runner – and as I walk round the property, I feel a strange sense of detachment. The place is in a terrible state: cracks and holes in the walls, burns on the carpet. In one bedroom, a door has been completely ripped off. I have no idea what happened here: a fight, a bad trip, a blind fit of rage? It isn't for me to guess, only to note everything that I see, marking it against the neat inventory I've made.

It takes me a little over an hour, but when I'm done I head back to the office, relieved. A difficult duty well executed, a sad job well done. As I reach the bottom of Brixton Hill, a bus drives past me through the puddle at the pavement's edge, and I jump aside to avoid getting splashed. As I do, I have a sense of someone turning their head towards me through the window, but by the time I look up, the bus is already behind me, lumbering away up the hill. I pull my coat more tightly around me, against the damp wind that whips around my neck. I've forgotten my scarf and my neck feels bare. Little sparks flash at the corners of my vision.

As I cross at the pedestrian lights outside St Matthew's Church, I hear the click of feet on the pavement behind me, someone hurrying up from behind. The sound makes me pick up my own pace, pushing on against the wind. It feels as if I'm racing them. Or hurrying to get away. Not far to the office now, but the streets are busier at the bottom of the hill, the narrow pavements of the High Street crowding people all around me. Yet still, over all the noise, I can hear those clacking footsteps. I can hardly tell whether I'm really hearing them, or whether they are a figment of my own mind.

I glance back, quickly, over my shoulder, but I can't make out anyone I recognize in the scrum of bodies. I push on, hurrying forwards, a sudden panicky need to get inside, through the familiar doors and up the familiar staircase to my office, where everything is organized and predictable and safe. I glance backwards again, just a glimpse over my shoulder, the scene blurred by the pricks of light in my eyes, but I'm sure of it this time; a figure is burrowing their way through the crowd, following me, trying to catch up with me. I try to hurry on even faster, but there are people in my way, like a sheer wall in front of me. 'Please,' I blurt out, 'let me through, *please*,' as I try to push through, my hands like claws, the panic climbing in my chest; but no one notices, no one hears me, and then I feel a hand on my arm.

*

'Jennifer!' She lets go of me. 'I'm so glad I caught you. I saw you from the bus. I jumped off. You were walking so fast, though, I had to run to catch up.'

It's Freya. I can feel myself staring at her.

I don't know what to say. I try to smooth back my hair, push the windblown strands into their bun, but they just seem to keep flying loose.

'Listen,' she says. 'Can I buy you a quick coffee?' We are standing on the street, right outside the Starbucks that's tucked in next to the Tube station. People are bumping past us on all sides.

'I have to get back to work,' I say.

'I know, but just quickly. You have a few minutes, don't you?'

I look up at the clock on Brixton Town Hall. Still only a quarter to eleven. It's true, I do. And I don't want to be rude or let her see how flustered I am. I don't want to give her a reason to think I'm not okay.

'I could …'

'Come on then,' she says. 'We'll be really quick.' And before I can say anything else, she is already pushing her way inside, squeezing past the crush of people coming out. I follow her, not knowing what else to do.

'What do you want?' says Freya. 'My treat.' I wonder if she'll try to buy me another cupcake.

'A black coffee,' I say. Then louder, because the coffee machine is making such a racket, 'A black coffee. No sugar, no milk.'

There's a tiny gap in the morning rush and we find ourselves pressed right up against the counter. The cakes and biscuits look huge and the smell of doughnuts turns my stomach. I don't want to be here, I want to get away, but how can I just leave without making Freya worry? Without her following me with even more concern?

'When we last spoke,' she says, 'we talked about your ... situation at work.' She has to half shout to be heard over the noise. 'Is all of that ... still on your mind?'

Now that I can look at her, close up, she doesn't seem quite as young as I remember. Around her eyes are tiny, feathered wrinkles. I draw a hand over my own face. My skin feels dry, my lips cracked and raw from winter cold.

'I mean it is, but only because I've traced some other people who knew her.'

'So you've kept on investigating, is that it?' Her voice sounds stricter: a note of disapproval. I can see in her hazel eyes what she is thinking. *She is concerned about you.* She has come all this way to see me, never mind that when I last saw her, I told her I was fine. And all those tens for her question-naire. *Completely satisfied.* Completely okay. I put a hand on the counter to steady myself, gritty grains of sugar under my palm. I try to explain, to justify myself. 'There are all kinds of parts that don't add up. She lied ... Sarah lied about her parents ... I found out yesterday ... They're dead and I thought

249

they were alive.' I make myself stop. I sound crazy. I can hear myself. I sound a real mess.

'Jennifer?' Freya is leaning towards me. 'Don't you want anything to eat?'

I shake my head. 'No. No thank you.' The very thought of it makes me feel ill.

'All right. Fine. But just wait there.' She turns aside to place our order, stretching foward to speak over the counter. As she pulls out a payment card from her wallet, another card slithers out with it. I see it tumble to the floor, flipping over and over, and it lands right at my feet. It takes me a moment to recognize what it is. Pale pink, with a photo. My body gives a strange shudder.

Freya isn't looking, she's too busy paying. Hardly thinking what I'm doing, I crouch down and pick up the driver's licence, my knees cracking as I straighten up again.

Freya turns to me again and I slip the card into my coat pocket. She has two tall paper cups in her hands and holds one out to me. I swear I can feel the warmth of it from here. I can see her mouth moving; she's saying something else to me. 'What?' I say. It's so noisy in here, so crowded, more people are pushing in all the time.

'Jenn,' she says. 'I'm sorry, but I'm worried about you.'

My hands are in my pockets. I can feel the plastic card there, right under my fingers. There's a sea of people between me and the door. *I'm worried about me too*, I want to say. *But I just need answers to all of this. Then I'll be fine.*

'I want to …' I'm suddenly so aware of the state I'm in: my untidy hair, the bags beneath my eyes, all the hesitations in my voice, all the weight that I've lost. Freya only needs to ask me one more question, with that probing concern, those observant hazel eyes.

She is standing there, hardly a foot separating us, still holding out the coffee to me. Despite the noise, she speaks so softly. 'Here, Jennifer. Why don't you take this?'

I look down at her, straight into her eyes.

'Take it. Listen, Jennifer ... I think you need to stop all this.'

I feel as though she can see right into me. As though I can't hide a single thing from her. Part of me desperately wants to reach out and take the paper cup from her. But I'm quite frozen. I shake my head.

'I'm sorry ...'

'Please, Jenn. For your own sake, come and sit down. Don't you think you should just sit down?'

One is completely disagree, ten completely agree. Ten, I want to say. Because she's right, isn't she? Look at what has happened to me since the day we found Sarah. But I so desperately need to make sense of what happened, and so I need to leave Freya thinking I'm fine. I can't give in to her, I can't stop all this now.

My voice comes out not much more than a whisper. 'I'm sorry, Freya, I have to get to work. Thank you for the coffee, but I haven't ... I can't ...'

I step backwards, bumping into someone behind me, their sticky coffee slopping onto my hand. I leave Freya standing there, holding out our drinks.

I hear her last words, called out to me as I turn my back and scramble away through the crowd.

'Just know that I warned you. I really did my best!'

Chapter 29

It turns out it *was* just a graze in the end.

But that night, Prin wakes up because Jane is crying out again in her sleep. Big fat wails that are sure to wake Daddy and Mum. Prin slithers out of bed, her feet finding the hot floor below. The night is so warm she can hardly breathe. She goes over to Jane's bed and puts both hands on Jane's shoulder, giving her a shake.

Jane is awake, Prin is sure of that, but her whole body is shaking, and it reminds Prin of the gerbil who died in its cage at school, just lay sideways on the floor, jerking and quivering and it didn't look right at all. *Don't look at it*, their teacher cried. *Don't look!*

But Jane is right here in Prin's bedroom. She can't help but look. Jane is crying and shaking and it's all getting a bit scary for Prin. The house is big and both Mum and Daddy sleep soundly, but the way Jane is going, how can they help but hear her?

So Prin runs to the desk and grabs the zoetrope, the trusty zoetrope that always calms her cousin down. But this time when Prin offers it to her, Jane pushes the toy away; in fact, she knocks it right out of Prin's hands and it falls on the floor with a crack.

When Prin picks it up again, it's all dented and bent out of shape.

Jane is pressing her hands to her eyes. 'I can see it!' she keeps saying. 'I can see it all happening. Please make it stop. Please make it go away!'

The zoetrope is on the floor and broken. Jane's sobs are getting louder and louder. Prin just wants to stop Jane crying and she can't think of what else to do. Until she remembers at the beach: how Jane was laughing. And remembers Daddy in the kitchen, with the onion.

She grabs her cousin's elbow and pulls her out of bed. Maybe she pulled her a little bit hard, but she needs Jane to come with her. 'Come *on*,' she says. 'I know what will help.'

Jane still has one hand pressed to her eyes. 'It's like the zoetrope!' she says. 'The pictures! They just keep going round and round!'

'Come *on*,' says Prin again. She shows Jane how she can lift up the sash window and how they can clamber right out. Jane is smaller and shorter, but with Prin's help she can do it too.

In their games, Prin always takes the lead and Jane follows. Like always, it is so much cooler out here. Better for Prin and better for Jane.

'Isn't it better?' she says, and when Jane doesn't say anything she tells her, ''Course it is!'

She helps Jane climb up on the flat piece of roof. They are out under the stars now. The sky above them feels like a great dark blanket, lifted up to give them room beneath. 'Look,' she says to her cousin. 'Look.'

She points up to the stars wheeling above them. It's better than any silly, broken zoetrope. You can see anything you want in the stars. Horses, angels, whatever you like. 'Look up,' she tells Jane. 'What do you see?'

They are both sitting on the gritty roof, but they could be floating in mid-air. This could be a magic carpet ride they are on. Jane only has to look up, and then she can see whatever she wants. Forget her nightmare and the pictures in her head. There are far better pictures in the sky.

'What do you see?' she asks Jane again.

Jane draws in a shuddery breath. She puts her hands down from her eyes and looks up. 'I see a man. And a woman,' she says.

'Like in the zoetrope!' says Prin.

And Jane says: 'Yes.'

'Well, what are they doing?' Prin asks next. 'Dancing?'

Jane shakes her head. 'No. Not dancing.'

Prin kneels up on the flat of the roof. If she tilts her head back, it makes her dizzy. She opens her mouth to the cool night air. 'I can see horses,' she tells her cousin. 'Dozens of horses.'

Now Jane gets up on her knees too. 'They want me to go to them,' she says.

'Who?' says Prin.

'The handsome daddy and the beautiful mummy. The ones there, in the sky.'

Prin looks across at her cousin. Jane is actually standing right up now, and she isn't that far from the edge of the roof. 'Do they?' Prin says slowly. 'How do you mean?'

'You said … if I imagine hard enough, it's true. Like the flying …' says Jane. 'On the beach. With our wings.'

'That's right. You can imagine,' Prin says. 'Anything you want. Anything at all, you can make it real.' She's just about forgiven her cousin for the hammer – and the zoetrope.

Jane holds out her arms. 'I can reach them,' she says. 'I really think I can reach.'

She looks so funny to Prin, balanced up there. In one part of Prin's mind, she knows very well what could happen. The part that pictures that is the hard, mean part of her, the one that remembers the feeling in her stomach as Daddy carried her away from the shed, Jane crying in Mum's arms behind them.

And then, with another part of her mind, it all feels so *true*. The stars, the dancing couple, the dream of flying, the magic of it all. And maybe it really can happen, the flying, if she just imagines, maybe if they both imagine really hard …

When she gets to her own feet, Prin finds she is standing just behind Jane. Her hand comes to rest on her cousin's elbow. Jane's skin is soft and dry and warm. The night feels so magic. If she could just have a tiny lift … she really does look as if she can fly. And there are parents waiting for her, up there in the sky, a mum and a dad that Jane can have for her own …

Prin thinks this, but only thinks it, she's sure. She's sure the thought never entered her hand …

But one moment Jane is there, on the edge of the roof …

And the next she's fluttering into the black.

Chapter 30

After my run-in with Freya, I work solidly right through lunchtime, trying to get on top of everything with all my boxes ticked, but somehow the work seems a slippery pile. I can't quite seem to keep track of where I am up to or what I'm supposed to be doing. It takes such a mental effort to get everything in order.

At twelve o'clock, the school lunchtime, I call and ask for Ms Simmons. When she comes on the line, I tell her I need to check on Charlie. 'He was a bit ... poorly over the weekend. I just need to know if ... he seems all right.'

Ms Simmons's reply is tinged with surprise. 'He was poorly? Well, today he honestly seems right as rain.' A little silence hangs. 'Was there something particular you were worried about?'

I hesitate. *Assume things are fine.* 'No ... No, thank you, I just needed to check. But you're saying he's fine?'

'Yes ...'

I feel stupid, but I can't *not* say it. 'But if there *was* anything ... anything you'd noticed —'

Ms Simmons's voice is direct now, a tiny bit impatient. 'We'd always let you know if there were any concerns.'

'Yes. Yes, of course, thank you.'

Clumsily, I make myself hang up.

At one o'clock, I go downstairs to collect the post, holding tight to the banister as I navigate the steep steps. There are various letters that come in to the office, most of them routine, occasionally one that's harder to deal with: a complaint, a bill from a plumber that's ended up far steeper than expected, some government notice of some policy change.

This afternoon there's the usual collection, plus one addressed directly to me. I carry the whole stack carefully back upstairs and go in to give Abayomi the ones he needs to deal with.

Then I take that one letter back into my and Emma's office.

It's a plain envelope, with my name and office address handwritten, in neat block capitals. With my thumb I prise it open. The envelope is thicker than I realized, and the flap slices the edge of my thumb. It's a small cut, but deep, and it bleeds badly. I should go to the bathroom and get a paper towel to stop the bleeding, but I don't. I just curl my thumb into my palm and try to stem the blood that way.

The document inside isn't very long, but it tells me everything I need to know: when the inquest hearing will be and where. It also reminds me to send over what information I can provide. The date is only a few weeks from now, far sooner than most inquests take place. Mike Bernard writes that Sarah's case has been brought forward, a space opening up in the schedule because of delays in another, more complicated case. I stare at the details, the words blurring in front of my eyes. The inquest. The place where all kinds of questions are meant to get answered.

I think of everything people have told me about Sarah, all the pieces of the jigsaw I am trying so hard to fit together in my mind. The pieces are slippery too, though, with edges that slice at my fingers when I try to grasp them. I pull up all the notes I made before, the details and timeline I compiled for PC Delliers. I pull up a new Word document and place my hands on my keyboard, but I can't seem to think of anything to write. *She lied about her parents when they were dead the whole time. I had an email from her but I never kept in touch. She lay in that flat for ten whole months and not a single friend or family member came to her funeral.* The picture these pieces are trying to make feels overwhelming. My brain jams, freezes. All I can do is stare at the blank page. I have to stop, pushing myself back from the desk, taking in gulps of air, my heart pummelling my ribs, skipping beats; my pulse is so irregular these days. I want to help, somehow tell Sarah's story, find some kind of answer to make it all right. I'm trying so hard to tie everything together, but what have I got really? So many disjointed pieces of information. So many questions that still lead to blanks.

The blank page is waiting, the coroner's court is waiting. It feels as though even Sarah is waiting.

But I have no idea what to say.

*

But then it is Wednesday. My afternoon off. My chance. The Tube from Brixton to Victoria, then the Gatwick Express that runs every fifteen minutes.

I'm so far into this now, there seems to be no way to turn

back; even if there were, I don't want to. I want to know. As I leave the office, one minute past twelve, I text Chloe to tell her I'm on my way. There's no text in reply, but I didn't expect one. If the timings are still right, she will be above me now, flying thousands of feet in the air.

I press on.

I know this train line so well. But it's been years since I travelled it, or since anyone travelled on it to see me. Victoria to Gatwick. And on to Brighton.

Brighton. So close to where my parents live.

The whole thing feels like some crazy coincidence. But I agreed, didn't I, to meet her here? I knew that I would have to take this train. So am I setting this all up for myself? I remember calling home the other night, that strange impulse that overtook me. I'm supposed to be finding out what happened to Sarah, but the further I go with that, the deeper I look, the more it seems I'm trying to trace back what happened with me.

It's too messed up, too weird. I press my forehead hard against the glass window of the carriage. I close my eyes and try not to think of anything at all.

In a matter of minutes, we arrive at Gatwick. The train shudders to a halt and, all around me, people with bags and suitcases stand to get off. I only have my coat and handbag, but I get off and follow them too. I can't remember ever being to this airport before. There have been only two times in my life that I have flown anywhere, and both times I was a child, and can hardly remember.

As soon as I step off the train, I feel disorientated. I don't know where to go or what to do. People rush past me, focused, determined. Businessmen and -women who must do this all the time. I search for the signs that say 'Arrivals'. Chloe has given me the number of her flight, and said that I can meet her there. She'll come out through the gates, and then we'll go to some airport café, and order coffees and be able to talk. That's what we'll do.

There are long corridors that I have to walk down, bright lights and rivers of passengers in both directions. So many signs, and my eyes don't seem to be working very well. But I find the Arrivals area at last. There are monitor screens showing the flights and I scan them, the letters blurring. Someone knocks me with their suitcase, clipping my ankle, right on the bone.

I scour the boards until I find it. Flight 128, Edinburgh to Gatwick. The plane is twenty minutes delayed.

I find a seat and shakily sit down. My legs ache these days if I stand too long; it's as though my blood can't get round them properly. I know I should buy lunch, but I'm worried that if I go wandering off, I'll miss her, and we have even less time now, with her incoming flight delayed.

I realize I don't even know what she looks like. She can't know what I look like either. I pull out my phone and scroll through my photos; but I don't have a single one of myself. There aren't really photos of anything except Charlie. I hold the phone up in front of me and press the button. The click; I look at what I've taken.

I hardly recognize the person looking back at me. She's so thin, the skin under her eyes so bruised. I could take another, try to make myself look better, but I fear they will all come out the same. And Chloe will see me in the flesh anyway, exactly as I am. I send the picture, with the words: *This is me.*

I check the Arrivals board again. Now her flight is due in just five minutes. Time seems to somehow have skipped. I push myself to my feet and make my way to the barriers. I can see the sliding doors that she's due to walk through. I hold on tight, feeling as though I'm swaying. I really, really should have bought some food.

A few moments later they announce her flight. Streams of passengers begin to pour through the doors. I scan every one, looking for anyone whose appearance might match her voice on the phone. There are so many people, surely more than can have all been on one flight. Beside me, there is a family, hugging, reunited after who knows how long. I hold the edge of the barrier more tightly, my palm slippery on the greasy metal.

A woman is coming towards me now. She is scanning the crowds as well. She must be around my age, younger probably, but her dress, her style somehow makes her seem older. She wears a boxy skirt suit, and I can see a work badge pinned to her lapel. She is wheeling a squat, black suitcase behind her. I didn't picture her quite like this but I think this is her; I think this is Chloe. I raise a hand and she catches my eye. She recognizes me from the picture I've sent.

'Jennifer Arden?' She stops opposite me, on the other side of the barrier.

'Chloe?'

I have found her. She is here. I know we don't have long.

*

Her flight was delayed, and it has taken up even more of her time coming out into the Arrivals lounge to meet me. We head

261

to a café where I buy myself a flapjack, dense with dried fruit, a cup of decaf tea and a bottle of juice. More calories in one go than I can remember eating in a while.

Chloe hesitates then orders a black coffee. Then a sandwich. Then a piece of cake too.

We sit down on bright plastic chairs, Chloe's squat suitcase pushed in beside us. Her movements are heavy, awkward, like she isn't comfortable in her own skin. Our bodies, our looks, are very different, and yet I can relate to exactly how she feels. I tighten the band in my hair, the ponytail high on the crown of my head and, as I lift my arms, I catch the smell of myself: sharp, vinegary. Sweat under my arms.

I run through it again, the reason why I'm here. It feels like a well-rehearsed script by now; I have said it to Marianne and Alastair before, and I'm repeating myself now again for Chloe. Maybe I'm rushing her, but I'm just so aware of the time.

'If you could just explain how you knew her. Anything you remember about her, no matter how small.'

Chloe toys with her sandwich. Perhaps she's uncomfortable eating in front of me. I try to take the lead, twisting the cap off my orange juice. The smell is strong: citric, sharp. I press the bottle to my lips and make sure to take a sip.

'I knew her from high school,' Chloe says. 'I would have been twelve, thirteen. She joined halfway through the year.'

'And you ... became friends?' I do try to tread carefully, not say the wrong thing.

'Yes. I didn't ... have many friends back then. So I suppose I was grateful for her attention.'

'You hung out together?'

Chloe shifts in her chair, pushing the palms of her hands

down the length of her coarse skirt. 'Only in school. Our backgrounds were different.'

'How do you mean – about your backgrounds?'

'Well, she came from a very privileged home. She had a horse that she rode at weekends. She went on dozens of holidays abroad.'

Chloe looks up at me, something pained and sad in her eyes. 'I, on the other hand … didn't have a happy home life.'

From across the table, I can now read her name badge. Managing director, it says, and the logo is for a huge company that even I have heard of. I recognize something in her then. She is high up, successful. But personal life and professional life: I know so well how they don't always match up. Despite the smart work suit, the professional competence she so clearly has, I can see the struggle to keep things together.

I fumble in my bag and pull out the postcard that Alastair gave me. I slide it across the small table to her.

Chloe picks it up, turns it over.

'Do you recognize it?' I ask.

She nods slowly. 'Portsmouth, my God. I had to stay there, with my dad. Three months before my mum got custody back.' She stares down at the words she wrote years ago, the ones I've read too, again and again. *Missing you. Really wish you were here.* And the telephone number, so Sarah could call.

'You can keep it, if you like,' I say, but she shakes her head.

As she hands the creased card back to me, I catch sight of the watch on the inside of her wrist, the seconds ticking past. The second hand seems to move much faster than it should.

'And – back then,' I press on, 'as a teenager … what was she like? What kinds of things do you remember?'

A look crosses Chloe's face. A sort of pained nostalgia. 'I mean, it was great. For a while, at least. I'd never had a friendship like that. She had a way of making me feel … very special.'

'What about her family?' I say, doing my best to keep my tone casual. 'Did she talk about them?'

Chloe laughs, that barking laugh I remember from our phone call. 'Her daddy was a great success and very handsome and her mummy was beautiful and the best in the world.'

It sounds as if she is quoting word for word. 'Is that what she said? That's how she described them?' The saliva glands in my mouth cramp up. I put the juice bottle down again.

Chloe shrugs. 'That was sort of the way she described everything.'

Do I tell her the truth about Sarah's parents? Why do I get the feeling she already knows?

'There was another relative too,' Chloe goes on, 'a stepsister? No – wait – a cousin. I'm trying now to remember her name; maybe it would help you. Sarah talked about her all the time; she carried around this photo of the two of them together.'

A photo? So … could this person be *real*?

'So … so what happened between you?'

Chloe pushes her sandwich aside, reaches for her coffee instead. 'You have to understand how much I believed in Sarah. How much I *believed* – full stop. She made me think there was such a thing as a happy home, a happy family. I suppose I dreamed that, one day, I'd be invited along. I would get to do all of those things too. That was so much of what got me through. And in the beginning, I had no reason to doubt her.

I'd read books, I'd watched TV shows. I knew there were kids who had all of those things. And, like I said, I wanted to believe her. But the more time I spent with her, the more I started to notice … Little things. Her stories got more exaggerated over time. And there were little errors she sometimes made. I made the mistake, once, of catching her out. She said she was going on holiday to Spain, but I bumped into her at the bus stop when she was meant to be away. She yelled at me then. She was furious. I quickly learned not to do that again. And she could be so quick to explain things away. So I noticed it, but I just … ignored it. I didn't want to look at what was really going on.'

Chloe pauses, takes a breath. She has said so much all at once. I take a sip of tea, the liquid scorching my mouth. 'And what was that?'

'I just … there was something really wrong with her, I think.' Chloe looks down and shakes her head. 'She was lying, Jennifer. All the time. This whole life she was supposedly living. The parents, the holidays, the horse. She'd made them all up. She was always pretending. And I went along with it. I just let her lie, until …'

The tea and orange juice curdle on the floor of my stomach. 'Until, what?'

'Until one lunchtime when I couldn't find her. We had a place we usually hung out, outside. But that day, we'd had another falling out and she'd sneaked off to the art room. Our relationship was sort of … unravelling by then.'

I don't say anything. I don't want to interrupt.

Chloe coughs into her hand. 'Someone told me where she had gone, so I went looking. I still didn't have … anyone else to hang out with. When I got to the art room, I could hear voices. There was a group of popular girls who often hung out in there.'

Above us, there's an announcement over the airport Tannoy. The flight to Dubai. Chloe's flight. I can feel the pull of it, pulling her away from me. I want to put my hand around her arm, hold her back until she gets to the end.

'Voices?' I prompt.

'Behind the door. There was Sarah's ... and these other girls. Three, four of them, I wasn't quite sure who.'

'Did you go in?'

'I couldn't. They were ... talking together, giggling.'

My chest aches as I picture her. Awkward. Alone. 'So what happened?'

Chloe gets to her feet, heaving her luggage up off the floor. I get to my feet as well, my head spinning from the effort.

'I stood out there in the corridor until the bell went, waiting for her and the girls to come out. I suppose I was going to beg her to take me back.'

They call Chloe's flight again, and I steady myself with a hand on the back of the cold plastic chair.

'She was shocked, of course, to see me there. But then she smiled. Told me she was ready to make up. Maybe she didn't realize how long I'd been standing there. Maybe she didn't realize what I'd heard. And seen.'

'Seen ...?' My mind flashes to those three plates, set out. Empty, waiting, speckled with flies.

Chloe fastens her jacket around her. It's too tight; it pinches her frame. 'Seen what was in there.'

My head rings. The hollowness in my stomach expands. 'You mean, *who* was in there.'

Chloe lets out a sigh, shaking her head.

'No, I mean *what*. Inside that classroom? Jennifer, there was nobody else there.'

Chapter 31

All of these falsehoods, all these charades. It's as if I'm peeling back layer after layer, and what is it I'm finding underneath?

Chloe tells me that Sarah was in foster care; that was what she'd later found out. *Foster care.*

So much for *Family Is The Dearest Thing.*

All these impressions of Sarah I've collected, how much of any of that was real? Marianne admired her and Alastair loved her, but now it seems there was an entire fabrication that Sarah wove around her whole life; what she presented to the world was a smoke-and-mirrors game. I'm shocked, dazed and yet ... and yet ... doesn't it somehow all begin to make sense? The image I've held of Sarah has *never* joined up with what I saw in that flat, and in the face of Chloe's words it begins to fracture, disintegrate. Making way ... for what? What was she running from, what was she hiding? Underneath the façade, what on earth was going on?

They are giving the last call for Chloe's flight; she has to go, and I need to get out of this claustrophobic airport. Chloe says she'll text me if she remembers the cousin's name, but I can't help thinking that will end up being a lie too. I leave her in a hurried, awkward rush and head back to the train station, everything I've learned spinning round in my head.

I stand on the platform, knowing full well which way I should be going. Back towards London and Charlie. Already they are announcing the next train. The trains are so frequent though, there is always a next one. It should be so easy just to head back home.

Instead I cross the station to the other side. To the platform opposite, where trains run the other way.

Truth and lies. Deceptions and pretence. Sarah's story cuts closer to the bone than ever. It feels like a compulsion, a craving, a violent urge. I can feel my own history pushing up to the surface, swelling against my lungs. Dad has called me, without fail, every three months. And every time I have kept our conversation short, never letting it develop into anything. So am I any better than Sarah, avoiding everything, never facing up to the truth? Living inside my own little bubble? I'd thought it was easier that way. I'd thought it made it better. To hold a cleaner, kinder story on top of everything. A story that wasn't so hard to look at and that allowed you to feel better about yourself.

But the truth, the reality, is that it hasn't helped me. *She* hasn't helped me. And I need her to name it now. I know that's why I'm taking this train. I think deep down, my father has always been trying to give me a way in. But it was *her*, always her. And now she's the one who I need to say it.

It's only a couple of stops. Twenty-five minutes, thirty at most. I have time, don't I, to get there and back? I can still be there when Charlie comes out of school. My parents' house is such a short walk from the station, and look, the train towards

Brighton is already pulling in. My legs cramp as I step up into the carriage, straining with the effort. I hold the top of each seat as I walk up the aisle. Here's an empty seat, a whole table to myself; I can buy my ticket when the guard comes round.

We pull out of the station, heading further south, towards the town that I know so well. Sea and sunshine and quaint little beach huts. The perfect, don't-scratch-the-surface kind of place. Is that why I came to London then, with Charlie? Because London doesn't feel so false? Because London wears its mess in the open. Grit, grime, dirt, shame. In London, maybe the streets aren't so clean.

My parents don't even live in Brighton proper. They live on the outskirts, Preston Park; my stop is the one before we reach Brighton itself.

Twenty-eight minutes later and I feel the pull forward in my seat as the train brakes, slowing down, and it's as if standing up is no more than a continuation of that forward motion. I hardly feel as though I've made the decision, it's more like my body is getting up of its own accord, a Pavlovian response to the station name, and before I know it I'm standing on the platform.

*

I know the route to their house so well, it's like walking there in a dream. I don't have to think, I hardly have to feel. My feet carry me there, all on their own. The sun is bright, dazzling, but the air around me is still freezing cold. It's colder than ever here, nearer the coast, and there's a violent, whipping wind. I pull my coat around me as tightly as I can – there is more loose material than ever to wrap round. How long is it since I've been here? Three years, four? All this time, keeping away, the whole thing too painful, too awkward. The truth always sitting like a mean dog between us, and always wondering who it would bite first.

I follow the corners of the streets, turning left, right, then left again. I'm almost there. The roads look just the way I remember them. Nothing here seems to have changed. I come up the back way, approaching the house from the rear. There's a fence at the end of their garden: a green picket fence, the paint shiny. It looks as if it was painted just days ago. I bet they get it painted every few months. Keeping up appearances. The recycling bin is out on the pavement. Wednesday. Bin day, I remember. There's so much I remember about living here.

And then, over the fence, I see him. My dad.

He looks so much older than I recall. Maybe something has changed after all.

He's bent over, levering at the hard lawn turf with a spade, trying to dig out a clump of weeds. Behind him, on the washing line, great white sheets crack and flap. My father's hair blows sideways across his head, revealing the baldness underneath. He hasn't seen me; he's facing away. I put my hand on the fence, the sharp post digging into my palm.

'Dad,' I call, into the wind. 'Dad.'

He straightens up. Sees me. All kinds of emotions ripple over his face. Surprise, at me standing there. Shock, perhaps, at how thin I am. And happiness. Happiness, above all, to see me.

I fumble at the little gate in the fence. The bolt feels so small in my fingers, but I manage to pull it open, and step into the garden. The white sheets lift up as if in welcome as I cross the muddy lawn towards him. He drops the spade. Holds out his arms. I walk right into them, shrinking to a child again. I feel him plant a kiss on my head, where my scraped-back hair has grown so thin.

'What are you doing here?' he says. I can feel his cheek against my temple. His skin is cold. It really is freezing out here.

'I was … I was just passing.' I swallow to stop the tears welling up. I just want to keep standing here, sheltered in his arms.

From behind him, I hear the back door of the house open. We break apart. My mum is standing in the kitchen doorway, her face red from the rosacea she suffers. I know her hands, if she touched me, would be chapped and dry.

'Hello, Jenn,' she says. 'This is a nice surprise. We had no idea you were going to visit.'

The sheets on the line lift again, cracking like a whip in the wind.

'Why don't you come in?' says Dad. 'Come in and have tea?'

'If I'd known,' says Mum, 'I'd have been more prepared.'

I look at her, standing there in the doorway, like a gate-keeper. Like some obstacle I would have to get past. I push my hands into my pockets and shake my head. I can't go in there. Not now. Not yet. I feel as though if I step inside, I won't be able to keep my mind straight. In there is my mother's domain. Where everything is controlled by her. The cushions on the couch, the pictures on the walls, the plates in the cupboard. And reality. Reality is controlled by her in there too.

So instead I stay out here in the cold, almost daring her to step down out of the warmth and come over to me. She doesn't, though. Of course she doesn't. We're trapped in this hopeless triangle of my dad, my mum and me.

'I don't need to come in,' I say. 'I just need to ask a question.' My lips are numbed, thick to move. 'Just one question, and I'll go again, don't worry.'

'Really, sweetheart,' says my dad. 'It's been ages since we've seen you. And you really need to come in and get warm.' He reaches out for me, but I shrug him off. If he hugs me again, I'll completely lose my nerve.

I turn towards Mum again. 'Why did you say what you did, at the hospital? When the doctors asked you what happened, you didn't let me speak. You answered them before I could say anything. And I never understood why you said all that.'

My mother's face is wary, bewildered. She is trying to understand why I'm asking. What I need. What she can do to defend herself.

'You're angry with me?' she says.

No doubt she hates that we're doing this here, in the garden, practically standing in the middle of the street. Outside, where all the neighbours can see us. She'd want us to be sitting down inside, properly, talking this through calmly and safely. But my body still shudders at the thought of stepping in there.

Now Mum comes down, one step, two, from the kitchen doorway. The white sheets twist and writhe on the line. 'Are you angry with me, for what I did? For showing you I loved you? For being a good mother?'

'Come inside, love,' Dad says again.

Is that what I am? Am I angry? Is that what is driving me to all this? I try to scan my body and make sense of my emotions, but I can't grasp anything, only the cold ball in my stomach, the hollowness in my legs, the scrabbling of my heart. I have no idea whether it's anger or not.

'I just want to know why. Why you said that.'

'Oh love, is this about …?' My dad looks back and forth between us. 'Jennifer, sweetheart, we don't have to do this. Not like this, not right now.'

'You know though, don't you?' I say to him. 'Come on, Dad, deep down, don't you know? That it wasn't true, what Mum said. When she told them that I fell asleep, that I wasn't keeping an eye on him. You know that, you can feel it, can't you? It never happened like that.' I turn back to my mum. 'So I just want to know, why did you have to lie? Why did you think you had to pretend?'

'What "pretending"? For heaven's sake, Jenn, it was my job to protect you. And you were already hurting so much by then. You were so unhappy when you came home from university, and then … everything that happened with Luke … How could I let things get any worse?'

My mind is torn, because in one way she's saying all the right things, and yet at the same time, it just isn't what I've come here to hear.

'When I found you,' she goes on, 'I knew at once you never meant it. You were unhappy and confused, and so it was an accident and that's exactly what I said.'

'An accident?' Mum is closer than ever to me now. And I realize then, *Dad can't protect me.* Not physically, not emotionally, not at all. He's standing there, right next to me, and he should be able to help me, his daughter. But I realize that if it really came down to it, me against her, he would be forced to take her side.

And so I can't do it. I can't stand there and let her touch me. She's my mother, but I don't feel safe. I feel as if there's a pit

274

I'm about to fall into. Because she still hasn't acknowledged it. This is the closest we've ever come; this is the first time I've said these kind of words out loud. But she is shaking her head, her face so closed down. She won't allow either of us to come clean. And all I hear her say is:

'I did what was best. I was protecting you, protecting Charlie. I stepped in, didn't I? I kept you both safe.'

It isn't an admission. It isn't enough. The truth is still buried there, covered over by all her words: what she did. All I can see is her face, Dad's confusion. Those white sheets. Pure. Pristine. Not a single mark on them. My reply is on the tip of my tongue, but no matter how I try, I can't get it out. The words are welded into my mouth. All I can do is say it into the empty chambers of my mind.

I didn't need protecting. I needed your help.

The green picket gate behind me hangs open, exactly as I left it. I turn and escape from the garden, the house, from them. What had I expected? A happy ending, a perfect confession? The righting of everything that went wrong back then? I should never have come. I was so stupid, so desperate. I'm not thinking rationally. I'm barely thinking at all.

Charlie, I think to myself. Get back to Charlie. He needs you, what on earth are you doing here? You have to go home. You have to get back to him.

My shoes bite my feet as I run back to the train station. I feel the blisters swelling beneath my tights. I reach the station and scan the departures board. And then it's as though I've swallowed my heart.

The next scheduled London train has been cancelled.

And the next one, and the next.

Chapter 32

I keep staring at the board as if the facts will change, but they don't. I ask a station guard but all she can tell me is the exact same thing. I'll have to wait almost fifty-five minutes. I am here, stuck, and Charlie is miles away in London, at school, and I won't be able to get back in time and no one will be there when he comes out.

I send a text to the school, frantic with apologies, explaining. *I'll be there as soon as I can*, I say.

I have never done this to Charlie before. I have always, always been there to pick him up, never late by more than a few minutes. I have done everything I can to be so reliable. Because when there is no one else, who can we rely on? But now I have gone off on an obsessive mission of my own, for Sarah, for myself, thinking I was fixing the whole world. And instead all I've done is let Charlie down.

I try and control my breathing. I go into the station toilets and splash water on my hot face, trying not to cry. I mentally send a million apologies to Charlie.

My phone blips. *We can supervise him only until 4 p.m.*, the school texts back. *Please ensure someone collects him by then.*

I have to find someone to help me. But who? Who? I think

of all the other parents: Sally and Rachel and Martin. Molly's dad. Any of them would do, but when I scroll through my phone, I see I haven't stored any of their numbers. I know there is a sheet of paper from the school that has all their contact details on it. But that is shoved in a drawer in my kitchen, and not an ounce of good to me now. I stare at my contacts list, so short, so limited. I don't know what to do, I have no idea who to call.

Except maybe one person.

I can feel the wariness still lodged inside me, but what other choice do I have? For Charlie's sake, I have to reach out. I open his number, desperately praying that he will be there. I pause, my thumb hovering over his name. I have to, don't I? Despite the knots in my stomach?

I press call. And Alastair answers.

It comes out in a garble, the predicament I'm in, but it's fine, he reassures me. He's not at work, he can get there. I grow weak in the wave of relief.

Just text the school my details, he says, tell them who I am. Charlie has met him, he has the Silly Putty to remember. And Alastair is a good person, he works with children; surely he will be able to keep Charlie safe.

I hang up. I text the school again, giving them Alastair's name and my permission. *Please tell him just to walk Charlie straight home. Charlie has his own key and I'll be there as soon as I can.*

It's okay, I tell myself, in the scratched mirror of the station toilets. My face is so thin with worry and guilt. It's all right, I say to her, this woman that I'm trying so hard to be kind to. The school knows what to do and Alastair will be there.

Back out on the platform, I sit down on one of the hard benches, lean my head down between my knees. It will be okay. This happens to everyone at some point, I tell myself, and you've always done your best. Don't be hard on yourself. Don't be too hard.

*

When a train eventually arrives, racing up from Brighton, my journey home is only forty-two minutes late. As I climb aboard I do the calculations over and over in my head; this long on the train, this long on the Tube to Brixton, this long to run, as fast as I can, up the hill. I think I can get home by five past four at the latest, and earlier if I'm lucky and if everything flows on time. Charlie will only have been waiting half an hour and he'll have someone with him all of that time. He will be okay. He will forgive me. I keep telling myself that, trying to calm down, even while all the way back on the train, I am counting every second.

The half-hour it takes to get back to Victoria feels like an eternity, each minute stretching my nerves to the limit. I pull out my phone to text the school again, but when I press the button to light the screen instead it gives a painful bleep and switches itself off. No battery. The phone is old and doesn't hold its charge and like a fool I've not brought my charger with me. I can't update Alastair, I can't update the school. All I can do is sit rigidly in my seat, willing the wheels of the train to turn faster.

Still miles away from Victoria, I pull my bag up from where it lies tangled with my feet, leave my seat and go and stand in the vestibule, so I can be the first one off. Hopelessly, I check my phone again, but now it won't even switch on. I'm just glad I managed to send the texts I did before it died.

Victoria Station is heaving, but I push through the crowds. Each step takes me closer and I luck out in the Tube, stepping onto the platform just as the train for Brixton is pulling in. I head down to the end and find space in the last carriage.

Ten minutes later, the Tube train jolts to a stop, the blips sound and the doors slide open. We're here, my home stop, Brixton.

I run up the left-hand side of the escalators, take the steps to the street two at a time. My coat is thick and cumbersome for the cold weather and my handbag with its too-short straps keeps slipping off my shoulder. In the shoes I'm wearing, I risk wrenching an ankle, but I make myself run all the way up the hill, only slowing near the top, my side wrenched by an agonizing stitch. But I am so nearly there, and it's barely five to four. I have made such good time, Charlie will still be at the school, with his teacher. I can relax; it's going to be all right.

I take the back street off Brixton Hill, the one that leads straight to the school. When I make it to the playground, one minute to four, there is no sign of Charlie, but then of course, they wouldn't be waiting outside. It's too cold for that. I push at the front doors of the school to head inside. I know where Charlie's classroom is, it's one of the first off the main corridor. I know exactly where he will be.

But the outer doors jolt against my hand. Locked. I can't get in.

I try again, shaking the handle, but it really is locked, the school is closed. Now I can tell – there are no lights on inside. And there is no sign anywhere of Charlie.

Home then. Alastair must have taken him home. He must have arrived early, before four, and why would a teacher wait past then? I turn to head to our flat and, as I do, in the staff car park I see a little blue car, just leaving. It stops when the driver sees me and the woman inside – I recognize her now as Charlie's teacher – rolls down the window.

'I'm so sorry,' I say. 'I couldn't … my train … and then my phone …' I stop and take a breath. 'Has Charlie gone home?'

Ms Simmons smiles at me. 'You didn't get my text? Your friend came … Alastair. Charlie was fine and went with him.'

'All right, thank you. I'll head straight there. Thank you, I promise, it won't happen again.'

I stumble-run up the road, my legs shaky beneath me. Ms Simmons shouts after me. When I look back, she's pointing – *they went that way!* – but that doesn't make any sense. Every second feels too long, but I am nearly there, I am nearly with him. Here is my flat, and I already have my key in my hand as I run up the steps. I shove open the door, half falling inside, calling out for them. 'I'm here!'

But there is no answer. The flat is warm, but the flat is empty. There is nobody inside.

I check all the rooms. Nothing, nothing, nothing.

Alastair has taken Charlie. Pins and needles of terror shoot up and down my arms. There was no sign of them at the school, there is no sign of them at home. I have to bend over, the pain in my throat and tightness in my chest is so excruciating. The words rush through my head, *Oh my God, oh my God, oh my God.*

What do I really know about this man? Alastair, who I first met barely two weeks ago. Alastair who works with children, who sat across from me at a café and told me things about his life. I trusted him because he seemed to like me, because he said I was *kind and thoughtful*, because he made out he had anxiety too, because he gave my son Silly Putty.

Really? I inwardly scream at myself. *Really?* When Marianne told you he had outright lied?

I force myself to stand back upright, muscles wrenching in my chest. Think. *Think!*

They went that way. I can see it in my mind: Ms Simmons's pointing finger. That way ...? Towards the park?

I hitch my stupid bag back onto my shoulder and slam the door of the flat behind me. I'm really running now, zigzagging through the streets. I've been this way a million times with Charlie, I could walk it in my sleep and now I cannot bear to think what I will do if they are not there. I shove my way through the entrance gate to the park, catching my fingers in the cold iron. I run towards the swings, the place I go to with Charlie all the time.

If they're not here, the words, the blood pounds in my head. *If they're not here* – and I can't even finish the thought.

Because they *are* there.

Two figures, spinning slowly on the roundabout. From here, they could be father and son. Alastair waves at me as he sees me coming, and Charlie jumps off the roundabout, stumbling as he lands, his face split by a smile.

I should want to hug my son. I should say thank you to Alastair. But instead fear has hijacked every cell of my mind. Somewhere, there's a part of me looking down from above, wise and rational and quite in control. But down here, running across the cold ground, I'm like a wild animal, all teeth and claws, fight and flight all scrambled up inside me, so that when Alastair comes up to me, Charlie following just a half-step behind, I swing my bag at him as if it's a weapon. Alastair raises his arms to protect himself, but I can't seem to control myself, I can't seem to stop.

You're having a breakdown, that wise person above me says. *A total breakdown*. I can see it happening to myself, quite clearly.

I keep hitting Alastair, again and again. All the confusion and horror of these last few weeks has come bulging out of me. I have become violent, enraged, hysterical, helpless.

'How *could* you?' I'm shouting at him. 'How *could* you? How dare you take him off somewhere like that, my son! You had no right, you had no right!'

'I'm sorry!' Alastair is trying to say. 'I sent you a text! Charlie couldn't find his key. We came here to keep warm. Charlie said he comes to this park all the time. We knew you were coming, and I sent you a text!'

He's repeating himself, in the face of my madness.

'I thought we were friends,' Alastair is saying. 'I thought we trusted each other. I was glad that you asked for my help!'

My arm is too weak to keep fighting and swinging. My bag drops like a leaden weight to my side. There's the tiniest, tiniest moment where it can all be so different. If Alastair would only step forwards right then, wrap his arms around me, hold me tight until I know that I'm safe. But I have scared him too much, how can he approach me? So instead I grab Charlie's arm and then we are running, me and Charlie, away from this man that I've become so terrified of, and my head feels as though it can't contain what's inside it any more; so many questions and falsehoods and mirages, each one of them shredding another part of me into nothing. We run across the cold, muddy grass, out of the play park, Charlie stumbling and crying beside me, and I can feel myself leaving that wise version behind me, floating loose above me, and I think to myself, if you run out of these gates like this right now, there might be no way you will ever get her back.

*

When we get home, I give Charlie Calpol again. He cries and shouts at me – he doesn't want it, he hates it – until in the end I have to half-force it through his lips, hand over his mouth to make sure he swallows. I don't know how else to manage him or myself.

I put him to bed, weak with relief when he falls asleep. I plug my phone in to charge and drag open my laptop. I type everything I can think of into the Internet search bar. What happened to Sarah's loving parents? If they are dead, then how did they die? It feels as if this piece is the answer to everything. The thing that will bring my sanity back. The woman at the local authority, the coroner, they never told me this. Maybe they didn't even know.

I type in Sarah's name, her surname, her date of birth. I keep going and going, trying to find something to piece reality back together. Everything about Sarah was false; her whole world was constructed upon lies and pretence. And at the centre of those lies was the fantasy about her parents. Seemingly the root of it all. The person who sent that terrible text: is this the secret they didn't want me to know?

I don't know how I manage, but I find them.

The newspaper reports, from eighteen, twenty years ago.

I know as soon as I see them, this is it.

Sarah's mother died in 2001.

Sarah's father died in 2003. In prison.

The dates are connected, not a coincidence. It is one final horror on top of all the others.

As the pieces come together, I feel the last thread of my mind stretch to breaking point.

Sarah's dad was in prison for murdering Sarah's mum.

Chapter 33

BACK THEN

There are lots more visitors to Prin's house now. All kinds of people *traipsing in and out*.

Jane has gone again. Not back home. For some reason (as Prin is starting to pick up now), she can't go back to her own house or her own mummy and daddy. Something happened there. A very bad thing. So now that she's been allowed to come out of the hospital, Jane has gone to another house, to stay with another family for a while. Just until all of this mess can be sorted out, Daddy says.

Meanwhile a *psychologist* wants to talk to Prin.

They actually have to go to her office for the talk, to a big building forty minutes' drive away. Prin and Mum and Daddy. The building is grey and the lady's office itself has toys in it, plus loads of paper and felt-tip pens. Prin supposes this is because this lady talks to lots of families, and the toys and pens are to keep the children busy.

The lady says she first wants to talk with all of them together. Mum and Daddy and Prin. Then she will talk to

Prin on her own. She asks whether Prin would like to play with anything. Prin asks for the paper and pens.

To begin with, Prin just lets Daddy talk. He's the best at talking in their family.

'No,' he tells the lady, 'we didn't tell her what happened. We thought it best not to tell her any of it. Prin – she ... our daughter would have just thought her cousin was coming to stay for the summer. We didn't tell her any more than that. I mean, would you?'

The lady's face looks rather serious at these words. Prin lowers her head back down and carries on with what she is doing, which is drawing a picture.

'Did you think that would be best for her?' the lady asks. 'Not to tell her anything at all?' She is asking Daddy, but both Mum and Daddy answer.

'No,' says Mum, just as Daddy says, 'Yes.'

There's a pause then, in which all Prin can really hear is the squeak of her felt-tip pen. She puts that pen – a red one – down, and picks up a blue one. Red for the roof and dark blue for the sky. She wonders when it will be her turn to talk.

Daddy puts his hand on Mum's arm. 'Yes,' he says again.

The lady nods. She appears to Prin to be thinking hard. 'What about with – ' she glances at her notes – 'Jane? How much did you talk to ... Jane about what happened between her parents?'

Another silence.

This time it is Mum who breaks it. 'Very little,' she says. 'We weren't sure ... we thought it best—'

And then Daddy jumps in to explain it all to the lady. He gets her to see how it is, very simply.

'That's not how we do things in our house,' he says.

Now it is Prin's turn. Mum and Daddy are sent out of the room, though Prin has a feeling they are still watching her from somewhere. Maybe from behind the big mirror in the wall. The lady rests her elbows on her knees and leans down towards Prin. Prin wishes now that she wasn't sitting on the floor. She pushes the paper with her drawing away. The roof, the sky, the girl, the wings. She isn't sure why she decided to draw that.

'Thank you for coming to chat with me today,' says the lady. She has quite a nice face, Prin supposes. She looks old, but she is smiley. 'I'm keen to know a little bit about you. You and your family and … your cousin.'

'Okay …' says Prin slowly. 'What do you want to know?'

'Well. How about you tell me how you feel about your cousin. Did you like her? Did the two of you get along?'

Prin wrinkles her nose. These are sort of silly questions. 'Yes. We shared a room. I let her play with all my toys. We played lots of games together.'

The lady waits as if she's expecting Prin to say something else then. But Prin doesn't.

'Were there any games you liked to play most?'

Prin isn't sure how best to answer that. She isn't sure what she's supposed to say. They would play with dolls, and on the grass under the sprinklers, and jumping games like the one at the beach. Then the hammer game that they got into trouble for. So which was the right answer out of all of that?

'I have a zoetrope,' says Prin. 'Jane especially likes that.'

'A zoetrope?'

287

Prin looks up, checking. 'You must know what that is?'

The lady nods.

'Oh,' says Prin. 'Well, that's good.' She shifts her legs. All this kneeling is giving her pins and needles.

'So you got along, and you liked playing together. But tell me, was your cousin ever sad? Did she cry, for example, or sometimes get frightened?'

Prin wants to laugh. She wants to say, *All the time!* But she doesn't want to say mean things about her cousin, plus she remembers what Daddy has always said: *No tears in this house!* So: 'No,' Prin tells the lady. 'She was always very happy.'

'Oh … I see. And what about the night on the roof,' the lady says. 'Was Jane happy then?'

Prin feels a rush of feeling in her chest, remembering it all again. The breeze and the stars and Jane's eyes gleaming and the silhouette of her against the sky just before … just before …

Prin sits up straight. 'I didn't push her,' she says. Prin feels it's important to say that right straight up. She even repeats it. 'Not on the rock and not on the roof. I didn't.'

The lady's face looks so serious that Prin can't help wanting to laugh.

'So what did happen?' the lady says.

Prin opens her mouth, then closes it again. She thought all the words were there, but they seem to have run away from her. It somehow isn't so clear when she has to explain it aloud.

'Jane *was* a bit scared,' she says, slowly. 'And the zoetrope wasn't working. I took her up to the roof. I liked going up there before, by myself.'

The lady nods. 'Yes?'

'She wanted to fly,' says Prin. 'We had done it before. Flying.

288

At the beach. She loved it. It made her happy. And she saw her parents up in the sky. She said, I'm imagining it, I'm imagining it. Things can come real, you know, like that.'

'Become real?' Now the lady is frowning.

'Like the onion,' says Prin. 'You can say something, and you can imagine it, or wish it, or picture it happening, and then it goes that way. It's just *true*.'

The lady makes a careful note on her page. 'And so ... on the roof?'

Prin goes still. She looks up at this lady, right into her eyes. She feels something cold and soft move on the bottom of her stomach. When she looks at the papers the lady has laid out on the table in front of her, she sees the names in there.

She sees *Sarah Jane Jones*.

And she sees her own name too. Her real name.

'It was Make-Believe,' she whispers. 'And Make-Believe is just real.' She doesn't know why this lady can't understand that. She thought this was a grown-up game. She thought this was a grown-up rule.

'So was it real to you?' the lady asks. 'What you were doing up there on the roof?'

Now Prin feels a stubbornness well up inside her. 'Of course it was!' she says. 'She held her arms out, she made the wings, she only had to jump and she'd do it. We were both imagining. Imagining really hard!'

'So what was it you imagined? That she would fly?'

'Yes! I imagined that because it's what she wanted, because I really, really wanted her to stop crying and because her mummy and daddy were up there waiting!'

The lady looks at her for a long time, very still. And very serious. 'But you know the difference, really, don't you? Between what's real and what's imaginary? What's true and what's ... *Make-Believe*?'

Prin shakes her head. 'I didn't push her,' she repeats. 'She jumped and she flew.'

'But – ' the lady leans right down close – 'but do you see that it *wasn't* real? No matter how hard the two of you imagined, it was only ever pretend?'

Prin looks up again. Her stomach clenches. She realizes it then, like a cold douse of water. This lady knows things. She is a *psychologist*. She knows better than Mum, she knows more even than Daddy. This lady is clever.

And this lady is right.

*

A few weeks later, everything seems to be back to normal. Prin is back at school and Mum's fine and Daddy's back at work.

Sarah Jane isn't living with them any more.

The zoetrope never did get mended. The dent was too bad: it doesn't spin any more. So Prin decides to cut it up. She can use the little pictures for something else. She goes through into Daddy's office. She knows he keeps a sharp pair of scissors in there.

When she opens his desk drawer and lifts out the scissors, underneath she finds a piece of paper. With her name on it.

Prin sets the scissors down on the desk. She pulls out the piece of paper. It is stapled to three, four more sheets. Prin's name appears on them all. Sarah Jane's name appears on it too.

Prin can read the words in the report, even if she can't understand what they all mean. But there is one phrase she can make out quite clearly.

... potentially in great danger, if she should go on living with this child.

Very carefully and slowly, Prin slides the report back into the drawer. Feeling very cold and very hollow, she takes the scissors back to her room and sits on her bed, hands clasped very tightly.

She thinks for a long time about what she's read in those pages. What it says about her. She sits there until the sun moves round and her room grows dim, the blades of the scissors digging deep runnels into her palms. And she promises never to do it again.

Chapter 34

It's only a few hours later that it happens. A bang against the front door of our flat. The squeak of the letterbox opening. And a sound like an avalanche, something falling like slurry into our hallway.

I wasn't asleep; I never seem to sleep. I'm wide awake when I hear the sounds and feel my blood turn absolutely cold. Before anything else, I go through into Charlie's room. He's awake as well, sitting up in bed, woken by the noise. I crouch down next to his bed and turn on the lamp, covering us with bright, white light. I stare at my son in the harsh light and he stares back at me. My fingers are raising red marks on his arms where I am gripping him so hard.

I have no idea what this is.

'Stay here,' I whisper. 'Don't move from this bed.'

I let him go and push myself back to my feet. My legs feel like paper straws under me. I stand there and listen again for any other sound, but now there is only silence.

I step out of Charlie's room, pulling the door shut behind me. Keeping him safe or trapping him in. The hallway outside is pitch black. I listen again. Nothing. But there was something and I have to turn on the hallway light and look at what has happened. Someone was here, right outside our front door. Someone has shoved something through our letterbox in the middle of the night.

I take another two steps into the hallway, sliding my hand in an arc across the wall to find the light switch. The whole thing has such a nightmarish feel to it. My fingers catch on the switch and I feel the nausea rise in my throat as I count silently to three and flip the hall light on.

There are papers everywhere. Someone has dropped a whole stack of papers through our letterbox. Silted up under the door like that, they make me think of that mountain of post behind Sarah's door.

From here I can hardly make them out; all I can see is that it is pages and pages of typed sheets.

Has someone come here to give me answers? Are these about Sarah, documents, notes that reveal the ultimate truth?

I unfreeze my feet from the bare floorboards. The flat is icy, but I don't even seem to feel the cold any more as I walk forwards and crouch down. They are flipped upside down, they are scattered in a mess. I pick up one sheet, two. At first I can't make head nor tail of them.

And then I see the logos.

And then I see my name.

'Mummy!' Charlie cries out for me from his bedroom, his voice muffled by the door closed between us.

'Stay in there,' I tell him. 'It's all right. It's just a letter that's come for me.'

The pages are a mess, their order broken apart, but I can see from the dates that they go a long way back. All the way back to eight years ago.

I try to scoop them all up, but they keep slipping from my hands, the thin edges slicing at my fingertips. I know what these are. I know. And then I see what I was meant to see all along. It's a page with just nine words on it, set out in capitals, in thick bold marker pen. It says:

STOP LOOKING

YOU'RE CRAZY

LEAVE HER ALONE

I drop the papers I have just gathered up and they scatter all over the floor again. I feel as though I have been burned, scorched.

Charlie calls out again. 'Mummy! I'm scared!'

Frantically now, I crouch down again, choking back the sobs in my throat. This time, I manage to scoop all the pages up, a tangled bundle in my arms. I stagger through into the kitchen and drag out a recycling bag from under the sink. Behind me, I hear Charlie's footsteps. He has got out of his bed, out of his room. His eyes are huge in the white of his face. 'What is it, Mummy?'

I cram every one of the pages into the see-through bag, crushing them down.

'It's fine,' I tell Charlie. 'It's fine.'

I knot the handles of the bag, so tightly that nothing could ever get out. I force myself to smile at Charlie. 'It's nothing,' I tell him. 'A letter came, but it wasn't important. Look, it's so unimportant that I'm throwing it away.' I hold up the bag, the papers like weird, flat creatures inside.

YOU'RE CRAZY. YOU'RE CRAZY.

I must be. Look at me. Charlie is standing in the doorway of the kitchen, a black ghost in the hallway light. I know what it says in those awful pages. I know what's written down about what I did.

'It's nothing,' I tell him. I put him back to bed, but I am still up, pacing the flat, thoughts racing. *Who has done this? Who has done this?* My mind scrolls from person to person. Marianne, Alastair, a parent from the school, or some stranger that I don't even know – the same person who sent that awful, blaming text? But I can't answer any of my own questions, so instead I simply, desperately try to block it out. If I try hard enough, I can tell myself that it was nothing but a dream. If I never open that kitchen cupboard again ... that cupboard where I've stuffed that bag of papers. As I pace the flat, outrunning my own thoughts, I have the strangest, weirdest feeling: the idea that I sent those notes to myself, that it was another version of me outside the door, pushing those papers through the letterbox. Maybe even, if I were to open that cupboard now, there would be nothing in there, and I would prove to myself that the whole thing was nothing but a product of my fevered imagination. The hallway is entirely bare now. Not a shred of evidence left.

Assume it's fine. Don't look.

I repeat the words to myself like a mantra. A spell to make everything okay.

*

But two hours later, or three, Charlie is crying out in his sleep. He is wailing, a nightmare. I push back the duvet, my skin flinching from the cold night air of the flat. I must have somehow made it to bed; undressed myself and crawled under the covers. Now I don't even stop to pull on my dressing gown, I just run straight through to his room.

He is crying, moaning, his voice so shrill as he writhes in his bedclothes. When I get close to him, I can feel the heat coming off him. He is burning up. A fever? Is he ill? He shrieks again, a heart-slicing sound.

I kneel down by his bed and try to wake him up. 'Charlie! Charlie!' His room is so dark, lit only by a blur of orange from a streetlight outside and I can hardly make his features out. He could be anyone, anything, some creature thrashing and moaning in my son's bed.

'Charlie!' I reach out. I don't want to startle him but I have to wake him up. I lay my hand on his shoulder and shake him. He jerks as he comes to. He is still crying, fearful, sobbing tears.

'It's all right,' I tell him. 'Calm down, it's all right.'

I reach out and snap on the bedside lamp, bathing the room in white, chasing every dark shadow away. This should help him, he should come to now, but instead, in the glare of the light when he sees me, he gives another cry, pushing himself up to a sitting position. 'No! Mummy! No!'

'What is it! I'm here.'

'Don't hurt me,' he cries again. 'Mummy, I don't want you to hurt me.'

'Charlie! Stop it, you're having a bad dream!' I grip him by both shoulders now, twisting him round, forcing him to look at me. I can see it in his eyes, a brutal tangle of fear and desperation, needing me, fearing me. I hold him tighter, trying desperately to contain him and all the time thinking, *I can't do this, I don't know how to cope with this any more.*

He is shaking. Even with how tightly I'm holding him, he

is shaking. Is he cold? Frightened? What is it? His whole body seems to be going into spasm. He was hot before, but now he is freezing. He carries on shaking even when I lie him down, tuck him in. The shaking won't stop. I press the covers down tight across him, *safe and sound, safe and sound*, but it doesn't help. He doesn't say anything, he isn't even making a noise. I can see the muscles clenching in his throat. What is wrong with him, what is he doing?

He's having a fit, my mind tells me. *Can't you see, he's having a fit, brought on by fear, brought on by terror. You know that his brain is weak, damaged. And this is it. This is how it breaks.*

Now his eyelids flicker, it looks as though his eyes are rolling back in his head. I'm totally at a loss as to what to do. The very sight of him terrifies me, I can't cope with it, I can't bear it. 'Charlie! Please stop it!'

I have to calm down. I'm only making it worse. *Get help*, I think to myself. *Get help*. He needs me to be steady. He needs me to be sane. I run back through to my room for my phone, then through to the kitchen, pulling that letter with its blue and white NHS logo out of the drawer where I shoved it. There is a number on there that I can call. I have never used it before, never had to, but I have never felt as desperate as this.

My hands are shaking as I dial the number. When I go back through, Charlie is still shuddering in his bed. The number rings, rings, rings again. I don't know if anyone is going to pick up. And then someone does. There's a voice on the line.

'Hello, South London Crisis Team.'

My words come out in a mess, a garble. I try my best to explain what is wrong but I don't feel as though I am making much sense. 'It's my son,' I tell them. 'I think he's having some kind of fit, but I'm not sure and I don't think I'm thinking straight. I have anxiety, terrible anxiety about his health, I think things sometimes that aren't true at all and I can't tell right now if something is wrong with him or not.'

'Did you say your son?'

'Yes, he's eight, he's nearly nine, I'm frightened that he's having some kind of seizure. He keeps shaking, but I don't know if that's just me, I can't tell if it's just all in my mind.'

'Is he hurt physically?'

'I don't know! That's the thing, I don't know!'

'Are you having thoughts about hurting him? Are you having thoughts about hurting yourself?'

'No, no, of course I don't want to hurt him! He just keeps shaking, he won't stop, but is it all in my mind?'

'I can't – I'm sorry – over the phone like this. But if you say he's shaking … Do you think maybe you should take him to A&E?'

I feel a wave of relief. 'Yes, yes, I'll do that, thank you. If you're saying that's what I should do.'

'Well, I—'

But I am already hanging up. Charlie's shaking seems to have calmed now. He is limp. He looks as if he's just sleeping. But I can't be sure. 'Charlie!' I whisper to him. 'You have to get up. I have to take you to the hospital.'

He groans sleepily, opens his eyes.

I pull him from the bed, stand him upright. I drag day clothes out of his drawers, strip him out of his pyjamas and push him into trousers, a T-shirt. On my phone, I bring up the Uber app. With my other hand, I pull Charlie to me, holding him tight against me. Tiny tremors still run through him.

It's no distance at all from here to King's College Hospital in Camberwell. Too far to walk but, once the taxi comes, we'll be there in ten minutes or less. We can go there, I can get the help I need. Charlie can get the help he needs. But even as I type the details into the app, I'm overcome by a wave of nausea. The thought of that blank A&E waiting room, the sense of illness and injury all around. The wait, the endless wait, and I am so fearful of wasting people's time because what if it *is* only all in my head? I can't do it. I cannot go there, even though the woman on the phone said I should. I'm too confused, I can't seem to explain myself to a stranger. I need someone who knows, who understands, with whom I don't have to start from the beginning.

There is only one person I can think of. Someone who has been right all along. I know now that I never should have got involved in Sarah's death. I should have left everything to the police and the coroner, not gone poking my nose in where it wasn't wanted. Wasn't needed. There are secrets in all this that someone doesn't want me to discover. And all I've managed to do in searching is unravel my own mind. And she was right, she tried her best to warn me, for my own good, for my own sake, and I wouldn't listen, but I need her now. My mind is splintering, I can feel it. I've completely lost my way, and I have Charlie here in my arms, but I need help to protect him.

He is exhausted, lolling against me. I carry him through to the living room and set him down on the sofa. In the depths of my coat pocket, I find it. It's still here. I pull it out; the tiny pink rectangle of plastic stares up at me. Her photo, her date of birth. Her address. I carry it in shaky hands back into the kitchen, set it face up on the worktop. I type the details into the Uber app: our destination. The driver will be here in less than five minutes and I hurry to my bedroom to get dressed. I pull on crumpled jeans, an unwashed jumper. The armpits smell of sweat. My hair is greasy. I am a mess. But Freya will set me straight, I have to believe that. If only I had listened to her from the start.

YOU'RE CRAZY. I KNOW WHAT YOU DID.

My phone pings: the taxi is here. I put Freya's driver's licence into my bag. My back wrenches as I lift Charlie from the sofa. He is like a dead weight in my arms. Outside, I lock the door behind us. It feels as if I am locking us out, as if we might never return here again.

The taxi is waiting just down the steps, in the street below us, its engine growling. I open the back door and set Charlie in, pulling the seatbelt and fastening it round him. I get in the other side. The clock on the driver's dashboard says it's almost 5 a.m., the last hour of true night, the point when you know that dawn is not far away.

The driver repeats the address I have given him and I nod to confirm it. The smell of me, the sweat from my clothes, seems to fill the whole of the car. Charlie is awake now, alert. He doesn't ask me where we are going, though, not yet. Maybe this seems to him like nothing but an extension of his dream. Maybe to him none of this seems real.

The taxi slides away from the kerb and we are off. It is warm in here, womb-like, with the radio turned on low, a soothing babble, the soft seats, the dark outside as we glide along the streets. The gentle rocking is so soothing.

I could sleep, I think suddenly. I could just go to sleep and not wake up for days. Maybe that is all I really need. To sleep, and let my brain become whole again. I let my eyes close, but they won't stay shut, they jerk back open, like every other time I have tried.

If only, if only I could sleep. I press my hands to the side of my head, as though I can crush my mind back together, make the pieces join up again and work. Beside me, Charlie stares out of the window, watching the city flicker by. 'Where are we going?' he whispers now. I am sure that he has stopped shaking.

'To visit a friend,' I tell him. 'A friend who will help us.'

Just the thought of it brings a strange peace to my mind.

The lights outside are mesmeric as they glide by. We are heading east, an area of the city I rarely go to. The sky above us is still pitch black, but not for much longer. I keep telling myself that. *Not for much longer*.

The very earliest shops have lights on in them. The city is beginning to wake, people beginning their days. Another day, like the last. You can stop all this, I tell myself. You'll go to Freya and she will help you, you'll get sleep, get rest, and she will let you know if Charlie is okay. You just have to make it to her address; you just have to knock on her door. It's five in the morning, and surely she will be there, it's just that you will have to wake her up. But it's all right, it's all right, she'll understand. You'll just tell her how desperate things have got. She is trained not to judge and she's already been so kind.

The taxi driver pulls up to the kerb. Above us there are thick high-rise buildings. Tower blocks.

'Here you are,' he says. He cranes round in his seat to look at us. 'Sure you'll be all right from here?' He's concerned for us – a dishevelled woman and a young, exhausted boy, travelling across the city in the middle of the night. He doesn't know that we've come here for help. I make myself smile at him. 'We'll be fine, thank you.' I fumble in my purse for a tip, find a couple of fifty-pence pieces and hold them out to him, forgetting that I'm supposed to use the app. He takes them silently, his eyes still on Charlie. I hurry to unstrap my son and get him out.

I take Charlie's hand as the taxi pulls away, its red tail-lights disappearing up the street. I pull out Freya's driver's licence and squint in the dim light to check the address again. Charlie is the one gripping my hand now. There is no one around. The night is freezing. I realize that neither of us have coats. Inside Freya's flat though, it will be warm, I'm sure of that. And look, there's a map here, to show us where to go. The block we need is just on our right. For a moment I worry that we won't be able to get in. There'll be some sort of security system, won't there? And if I have to ring a bell, will it even be working? Will Freya hear it? Would she come down when I tell her who it is? Haven't I seen a hundred times in books and movies that scene where the patient turns up at the professional's home inappropriately, crazily, breaching all kind of boundaries? Isn't this exactly what I am doing?

It's for Charlie's sake, though. For Charlie's sake. And Freya told me to come to her, any time.

We are in luck. The door to the block isn't properly latched. I push our way inside, pulling Charlie after me. Inside, there's a wide, echoing staircase leading upwards. I check the flat number; it looks as if Freya lives many floors up.

We start climbing. The stairs zigzag up and up; the wall on one side of the tower is a floor-to-ceiling window. As we climb I feel a dizzy vertigo, as though the stairs, the walls are tilting, as though I could fall right out of that huge window. As we climb higher, I can see right out into the city. London is out there. Somewhere, across the river, lies my flat; empty, waiting for us to come home. Somewhere out there is the bedsit Sarah lived and died in; somewhere, Alastair is asleep in his bed. Charlie trips on the stair beside me and I jerk up my arm to wrench him back to his feet. I can't stop now to analyse his clumsiness, I can't be the one to find the answers any more. I just have to get to the top, and to Freya. We are nearly there; the numbers rise with every floor we reach and we are nearly there at Freya's door. This high up, I can see a smear of light low down in the sky, in the east. The sight of it brings such a sense of hope. The dawn is coming, the night is almost over.

And now we're here. The ninth floor, and here is her flat, number twenty-four and the sight of it almost makes me collapse with relief. In my bag, my mobile phone pings. A message has arrived, but who would be texting me at this time in the morning? I drop Charlie's hand to reach for the bell on Freya's door.

I press my finger on the buzzer and, at the same time, out of instinct I pull out my phone.

The message is from Chloe. I see her name first; I've saved her number in my contacts. She's on the other side of the world, a whole time difference apart; now the timing of this text makes sense.

I've remembered the name of Sarah's cousin, writes Chloe.

But what does Chloe's message matter now? I'm not looking for answers any more. I'm going to leave all that behind. I'm going to tell Freya that she was right. I'm so aware of the huge glass window behind me, the pale light shining on the horizon. I press the bell again; I've done it now. In a matter of moments, she will wake up and the door will open.

I glance down at Chloe's text once more; once more before I'll choose to delete it. I can hear footsteps inside the flat. Freya is up, she is coming, she's just on the other side of the door. I take Charlie's hand again in mine and pull him to me, huddling him against my ribs.

I can hear the sound of the door being unlocked. In a moment it will open.

I have to scroll down to see the last part of Chloe's text, the final part where she has written the name.

I hear the click as the door opens and then she is standing right there before us.

I see the words, so stark on my phone.

I feel the floor beneath me upend. She is standing right there in front of me.

Sarah's cousin's name is Freya, the text says.

Chapter 35

'Freya,' I say.

I want to burst into tears with the shock. It feels as though a hundred walls are collapsing within me, flood banks crumbling, a tidal wave of pounding water breaking through.

'I know ...' The words fall out of me. 'I know who you are.'

She looks at me with shock on her own face, and then – what else? – is it fear?

Everything is spinning backwards, my whole world rearranging itself. I lift Charlie up, holding him to me. He is so heavy yet so tiny in my arms. I have come to the person who I thought would help me, who would protect us, who would save Charlie. Instead, she has been lying to me all along. The twisting wrench of it sends a flare of pain through my head and it feels as though it is blinding me. Is this what it feels like when your mind finally splinters, when it finally breaks irreparably in two?

I have no idea what is going to happen now as I stand there, arms wrapped around my son. She never expected me to turn up here. How could she? I should never have had her address. She would never have known about the licence card I stole from her, that impulsive, crazy move in Starbucks. Even I didn't know what I was doing at the time.

Here we both are, face to face with each other, so many things falling terrifyingly into place. And so many questions still so nakedly unanswered.

'I'm sorry,' Freya says. 'I really am sorry.'

In my arms, Charlie begins quietly to cry. To my amazement I can see tears forming in Freya's own eyes.

I dig in my pocket and hold the pale pink driving licence out to her, as though that explains everything about why I'm here. She takes it from me without a word. I'm suddenly aware of how freezing I am. Neither of us in coats and it's so cold. Freya is in a dressing gown and pyjamas, warm from her bed, but I am cold right down to my bones.

Freya opens the door wider. 'Why don't you come in?'

Charlie is tiny, exhausted and cold. We are miles away from our home. Her flat is bright and open and warm. I don't know what else to do. I feel so weak; my legs are trembling. I don't know how long I can keep standing for. I can't imagine climbing back down all those stairs. I've used the last of my energy just to make it here. What other choice do I have?

Against my better judgement – but honestly what judgement do I ever have? – I step forwards.

The warmth envelops me like a blanket. Charlie slides down from my neck and leans against me, slipping his hand into mine.

'Come through here,' says Freya. We follow her down a white hallway. 'I'll make something for you, just sit down in there.'

There is a pale yellow living room, a blue sofa. I can see through to a pretty little kitchen. It's the strangest reversal of when Freya came to visit me. I sink onto the sofa and pull

Charlie onto my lap. The cushions are so soft under us. He curls against me, bewildered, too tired to try to make sense of it. He slips his thumb into his mouth and closes his eyes. For sure, he has stopped shaking now. In the warmth, all of his muscles relax. I wrap my arms around him, like a shield. I can hear Freya in the kitchen. I am dizzy with tiredness, with all the weight I've lost. It takes an effort to even sit upright; it takes such an effort to hold up my head.

There are vases of flowers set all around the room. The whole place feels like some strange bower. Or a shrine.

I give in to it then. What else can I do? There's nowhere left for me to go.

*

We sit across from each other on faded sofas. Charlie has fallen asleep like a dead weight in my arms. My joints ache from the effort to hold him against me. My throat is dry, my whole body feels dry, empty.

'I didn't want anyone to know,' Freya says.

Somehow I manage to make myself nod. *I know.* 'You were the relative who refused to get involved.'

The drink she's made is pale gold. The water shimmers in the cup, or maybe it's my vision that's flickering. Steam rises like a strange mist between us, mingling with the heady scent of the flowers.

Freya leans forward and places a small photograph in front of me. Faded, a little creased, like something you've kept at the back of a drawer. The girl is young, so much younger than when I knew her, only a child, but it is impossible not to recognize her. That gap in her front teeth. Sarah.

And another girl with her. Hazel eyes.

Freya.

I can see the resemblance between them now.

'She came to stay with us,' Freya says, 'as a child. When she was seven and I was nine. After her mother died and her father went to prison. Her parents were my aunt and uncle.'

I have no other choice but to listen. I want to close my eyes and disappear, but I haven't the strength to even stand from this couch. The pieces are jamming themselves together in my mind. The parents who died. The relative they couldn't engage. I have the connection in front of me now: Sarah Jones and Freya were cousins.

Freya goes on. 'My parents never talked about what happened. The fact that her father murdered her mother. It was too horrible a thing for my dad to acknowledge. Such an awful, black stain. My parents … never spoke about anything like that. I was so naïve. I didn't understand.'

All her words, the flowery perfume in the air; I feel dizzy picturing the family they once were. Perfect on the outside. So warped on the inside.

'You told me Sarah lied about her parents.' Freya shakes her head. 'But you see, to her it was never lying.'

The pain in my head is worse than ever. I reach forwards, slipping an arm from underneath Charlie. I try to lift the cup of tea but my arms are too weak. My hands shake and I spill it. I have to set the cup back down. All the while, Freya watches me. I press the heel of my hand to my eye; the pain crouches there, plucking at my eyeball. Charlie stays, wrapped in at my side.

Freya stands up and, instinctively, I flinch back. She's not that tall and she can't be that strong, but …

She holds up her hands. 'I'm sorry. I don't mean to startle you. You're here … you've come here, that has to mean something. I want to explain it to you. I need you to understand why I did what I did.'

On the dresser, there is a little contraption, a circle of panels, tiny figures painted onto each one. She carries it over and sets it on the table between us. 'Do you know what this is?' she says. 'Have you seen what it does?'

Silently, I shake my head. The movement gives me vertigo. I don't know what she is trying to show me.

'When we were kids,' she goes on, 'this was Sarah Jane's favourite toy. A zoetrope. This isn't the one we had back then. That one got … damaged. But I bought this one. To remind myself. To remember.'

She pushes a finger against the panels, setting them revolving. She keeps pushing so that the panels spin faster and faster. For a moment, there's nothing but mess and blur, nothing coalescing, nothing making sense; but then I see it. The tiny figures flow together and become one: not a series of images but a single dancing figure, swaying, gliding, animated.

'I told Sarah Jane … she could imagine anything she wanted. She only had to think of it, and we could make it real. I thought that was how you were supposed to do things, how you made the world okay. My parents – my father especially – controlled everything that way.'

Beside us, the zoetrope slows, the dancing figure fragmenting, splitting. Falling apart. But Freya sets it spinning again and the little figure dances back to life.

'I thought it didn't matter what was real and what I made up. It was only later that I learned how dangerous that could be. I was lucky enough to have someone set me straight. A psychologist, would you believe.' She gives a wry smile. 'But it was different with Jane – with Sarah – because she never really had anyone to help her. And because she had such a lot of reality to suppress. With her, the game got completely out of hand.'

I can't tear my eyes away from the zoetrope, and its spinning feels as if it is spinning everything inside my head, so fast, so violently that I can't get a grasp.

'She was there when it happened,' says Freya. 'Sarah Jane witnessed the whole thing. Her father … the hammer … She had nightmares about it; she couldn't get those images out of her mind.'

And then Freya tells me about the night with her cousin, up on the roof.

'Back then,' she goes on, 'I was only trying to help her. And later, after the accident, I honestly thought she would stop. But years later, when my own parents died, she came to their funeral. I was crying and she put her arms round me and hugged me. I knew very little about what had happened to her since we were children. I knew she grew up with various foster families. But she came to the funeral, and put her arms around me and hugged me, and she whispered to me: *It's all right, Freya, remember? It's all right. You can just Make-Believe that they're not really gone.*

'And then I met you and you told me about the table laid out in her flat and I realized …' Freya drops her head into her hands. 'She never stopped, did she? I don't think she ever stopped playing my game.'

Through my dizziness and vertigo, I see it. The pieces slide into a heart-rending picture. 'Those plates,' I blurt out. 'The meal she was preparing, the table set for two guests. It was all in her mind, wasn't it? Nobody was ever going to come.'

Freya can only nod. 'After you found her, the police tried to reach me, but I just couldn't do it. I couldn't speak to them. Because I understood at once why no one found her and I knew, in the end, it was all my fault. She cut herself off from everything, everyone, lost herself in her fantasy world. And it was all because of what I had taught her. Our Make-Believe game had gone far too far. So I hung up every call from the police. I refused to answer even when they came here, to my door. Like you have now. I wouldn't let them in, but you ... you weren't going to stop. You wanted to know, and I didn't want you to expose me.'

It's obvious and I'm sure of it now. I have a pain in my chest, as though all the muscles around my heart are cramping. 'You wrote that text message. You pushed all those pages through my door. You already had my address, my contact details from the CMHT, and you dug out that old entry from my psychiatric file. You used what you thought happened with Charlie against me – to threaten me, to scare me. You tried to make me feel so crazy I would stop.'

'I'm sorry. I am so sorry. I was scared. There's a report about me, a terrible report about what happened between me and Sarah as children. If it had got out, if any of those details had got into the newspaper ...' Freya puts her face in her hands. 'It would have ruined all my ambitions and jeopardized my whole career.' She looks up again. 'And honestly, I was only trying to help you, Jennifer. I mean, look at what all this searching has done to you. I was only trying to steer you away. For your own good. For your own health.'

I put my own head down. I grip my knees and force myself to take a breath, drawing the air right to the very bottom of my lungs.

I think of Sarah and the truth she couldn't face. The world of dreams she made for herself.

I think about those plates set out, ready and waiting for the imaginary guests who would never visit her: those perfect parents who lived and breathed in her mind. She had created a fantasy as solid as real life. With Freya's dangerous, misguided help.

I understand. I understand everything. All I've been doing is trying to get to the truth and instead I've become tangled in falsehood after falsehood, layers of fantasy, layers of lies. And I've fallen victim to the biggest falsehood of them all.

'It's wrong,' I gasp out to Freya. 'You say you want to help people, but that isn't helping. You lied to Sarah, and you did even worse to me … You haven't changed, you haven't learned. You've done the same thing all over again.'

Beside me, on the sofa, Charlie is stirring. He stretches, blinks; he is waking up. 'Mummy?' he says, reaching for me. 'Mummy, where are we?'

But darkness is seeping into the edges of my eyes, dragging a curtain of black across my vision. I can't feel my limbs; my whole body has gone numb. All I can feel is my heart, hurling itself against the walls of my chest, lurching, stuttering. I can't control it, I can't even breathe.

Stumbling, I try to get to my feet. I need to get me and Charlie out of here, but the pain in my chest is blinding.

I can't see anything, or feel anything, except the shuddering of my heart. A total darkness is descending on me. I reach out a hand, try to grasp hold of something, anything, but there's nothing there.

Somewhere, far away and very faintly, I think I hear a siren wail.

I fall into the blackness for seconds, for minutes.

I fall into the blackness for what feels like days.

Chapter 36

When I wake up, there's a white ceiling above me. Rows and rows of white tiles. Under my head, there is a soft pillow.

I close my eyes.

When I open them again, I'm still in the same place. I move my hands, and my palms brush against a blanket. Soft and real, under my touch.

There's a familiar smell. For a split second, it sets my stomach roiling. Then it eases, because I know it's all right this time.

I'm in hospital. I am lying in a hospital bed.

When I turn my head to the side, I glimpse the drip in my arm, the metal pole, the clear bag above me. I'm careful not to move too suddenly, not to dislodge anything. I can't tell how fragile I still am.

I see someone, too, at the side of my bed.

Alastair.

My lower lip splits when I try to smile. My body has been suffering. I feel everything now. The pain is in every sinew and joint.

'It's all right,' he says. 'Just take it easy.'

But I try to push myself upright in the bed. 'Where's Charlie?' The words catch in my dry throat.

'Right here.'

He beckons to someone down at the end of my bed. Tears come into my eyes when I see my son. He pushes up to me, drops his weight onto me, burrowing against my neck. I manage to lift my bony arms and wrap them around him, a bandage holding the drip needle tight. How on earth have I got so unwell?

'Charlie,' I whisper. 'Charlie, I'm so sorry. But it's all right now. All these people are going to look after us. Charlie, I promise you, I'm going to get well.'

A nurse comes to adjust the things around me that need fixing. I lie there and let her. I'm so unbelievably tired.

She leans over me as she straightens the blanket. 'You suffered a terrible collapse,' she says. 'You're very, very malnourished, and your potassium levels were something awful. But we've put you on a drip, and you're already looking pinker. Before long, you should be right as rain.'

Alastair tells me I've only been here since last night – or rather, the very early hours of this morning. To me, though, it feels as if I've been out for weeks. He explains that he rang me, and Freya picked up and told him where I was. She was the one to call an ambulance. Alastair tells me he came as soon as he could.

'I thought you'd lied to me,' I tell him. 'About being at university with Sarah.'

'I'm sorry,' he says, 'that I let you think I was there. I was so ashamed. I never made it to any university. I was struggling with anxiety, even back then.'

'You shouldn't be embarrassed,' I say. 'And I should have told you that I knew Sarah, once. We worked together, very

315

briefly.' I fill him in with what tiny details I have. 'She really was as lovely as you said.'

Now the facts are all out in the open. Almost all of them. It feels better. It feels really good.

The sun slides round the window of the ward: morning, midday, afternoon. A different nurse brings round a tray of food, and helps me to sit up and eat. It feels as though I haven't eaten in years. With each mouthful, I can feel my cells getting stronger.

A doctor comes to tell me I should be able to go home this evening, after just one more check of my bloods. I'll be discharged for follow-up through my GP. Alastair takes Charlie to the canteen for a hot chocolate, leaving me to get a little more rest.

*

Once they've gone, the ward door closing softly behind them, for a few moments I lie there, staring at the ceiling again. I think of everything I have learned about Sarah – Sarah Jane, or Jane, as Freya knew her; all the pieces of the picture that I have collected up and can now set out, like frames of a film, ready to roll. I let the story all come together in my mind; all the thoughts and words are there.

I think too about the email she once sent me. That casual phrase, *Stay in touch!* But in the end, it was Sarah who cut ties. She did it with Marianne, with Alastair, with Chloe. With everybody in the end. Retreating into herself and her own world. Telling her stories only to herself. It must have grown exhausting, to be out there in the world, so full of spirit and life, with colleagues, with friends, with a boyfriend. Being around people, keeping up the pretence. Wondering when it would all fall apart.

I close my eyes, and open them again.

After eating something, I feel stronger. I think maybe I feel strong enough.

I roll over and lift my phone from where someone has set it down on the bedside table. The screen is tiny, not like on my laptop, but it will have to do. I want to do this now, before I leave here, while I'm in this safe, clear space. I open up the Notes application, a fresh blank screen.

I think about my previous effort at a narrative for the inquest: that empty page, my thoughts a total blank. This time, I pour out everything. I don't care that it is emotion-filled and unprofessional, or that it feels like trying to describe a dream. It was a dream life that Sarah Jones was living. I conjure up the composite Sarah I have pieced together, and I try to tell the story of her life. The best way I know to explain the circumstances of her death.

It isn't professional, but it's what I need to write down. It is what I want people to know. I want to set the panels of her life out clearly, and tell a story people can try to understand.

Share a lesson perhaps for all of us to learn.

It's just after 6 p.m. when I send the document off. I email it to the address the coroner's officer gave me.

In there are all the answers I can give. I know these answers apply to me too.

I know some day soon, I will have to set my own record straight.

Chapter 37

3 weeks later

What do you wear to an inquest? I stand in front of the mirror in my small bedroom, holding items of clothing up against me. At least I have regained most of the weight I lost. My clothes fit me again. Just about.

I settle on a pale cream blouse and a pair of dark grey trousers. Some smart shoes, a smart jacket. When I look at my reflection in the mirror, I'd like to say I look like my old self. The outfit is one I could easily have worn to work, and my hairstyle and make-up haven't changed. But I am different. I am changed. I can see it, clearly. I feel it in the way that, these days, I'm always trying to look myself right in the eye.

I have gained back the weight, but I am still weaker than I should be. I am aware that I tend to move more slowly. I still have some recovering to do. Part of me wonders whether I should even attend this inquest. But most of me knows that I have to see this through to the end.

When I saw my GP after discharge from the hospital, she wanted to refer me back to the mental health team. Small wonder, knowing my history, seeing the state I had got myself in. But I felt something shift in me after that night with Freya. Something that has never shifted before. So maybe I will need the mental health input again but, for now, I've managed to arrange a compromise: I've agreed to keep seeing my GP every week. And if she still wants to refer me after a month, I won't say no.

I took Charlie to see the GP too, and all the tests she did say that he's just fine.

The inquest is being held at Southwark Coroner's Court. Abayomi has allowed me time off to go. He thought, in fact, that it would be good to have a representative of our Housing Association there, so I can go while Charlie is at school. He's doing better in class now than ever. His normal teacher is back, recovered from her surgery. She tells me Charlie seems happier and brighter than ever. And I don't tell her how things went while she was gone.

I'm going to the inquest, but I won't have to speak. Mike Bernard, the coroner's officer, has said there is no need for that. I can go there and just listen to what others have to say. To see what sense they have made of this for themselves.

Mike Bernard has drawn my notes up into a statement, a neat-looking document that he posted to me to sign. He had taken out a lot of my scribblings. Just stuck to the pertinent facts, just the part I contributed to Sarah's sad fate.

Alastair has told me that he will be there. When I rang her, Marianne too said she will come. Chloe is on the other side of the world still, but she sent me a message this morning. She is thinking of Sarah. She will be there through her thoughts.

And Freya.

I can't stop wondering whether Freya will be there too.

I stand for a last look at myself in front of the mirror. I look at myself square-on. I'm ready. As ready as I can ever be.

I take the bus towards the centre of town. April sunshine beams in through the scratched windows of the upper deck where I sit. It warms the interior so much that I have to take off my coat. I get off at the stop that TfL tells me is the right one and I pull up the address again to check the directions from here. There is a text message on my phone from Alastair: *I've just arrived. See you soon.* I read it through twice, three times, before pushing the phone back into my pocket.

The coroner's court is on Tennis Street, only a couple of minutes' walk from the bus stop. I at once see the figure of Alastair, standing outside. He touches me, gently, on the arm when I join him, and tells me that I really am looking better. I tuck my loose hair behind my ears and my chin into the collar of my coat.

From the pavement, I look up at the building that looks so ordinary, like a dozen other council buildings. I can't help wondering how many stories have been told here. How many truths have been dragged into the light.

Alastair checks his watch then turns his wrist to show me. 'Shall we go in?' he says. It is ten to the hour. I nod.

Inside, there's a little desk, a sort of reception, and I explain that we've come for the inquest into the death of Sarah Jane Jones. The man on the desk has grey hair clipped short and skin lined with thick wrinkles. He gives us a book with a sheet to sign and we put our names down, one above the other. I can see from the page that Marianne is already here. She has come, just like she said she would. I spot PC Delliers' name in there too.

Alastair and I go in.

Inside, the court is small and hushed. The walls are plain beige, and the furnishings kitted out in smooth, pale wood. There is no sense of grandeur, just efficiency. Well-meaning people doing their jobs. There is no judge or jury but I make out the coroner right away. She looks wise, kindly. I wonder what she makes of my statement and whether it has been of any help to her at all.

PC Delliers sits in the very back row. She gives me a smile and a nod as I pass. Then I spot Marianne, sitting near the front. When she sees us, glancing over her shoulder, she stands up and comes over, leaning heavily on her crutch. She leans in to hug me, just like old friends. I wonder how much this day will cost her, how hard it will be for her to learn Sarah's reality, unpick the gold-edged image she's held and let it go.

'This is Alastair,' I tell her. 'The man you told me about, Sarah's ex-boyfriend.'

I've set Marianne straight about Alastair; she was suspicious of him, though only looking out for me, but now I know that Marianne and Alastair are both people I can trust. Now when I introduce them, she hugs Alastair too. I think of the funeral that no one came to. The difference this time. Friends of Sarah's are here. Maybe even family too.

I look around the room again, but I still don't see Freya. Instead, there is a scattering of people I take to be journalists. Maybe now there will be full articles about Sarah. I imagine now they will release her name. I try to imagine what kind of stories they will print. Macabre stories, or compassionate ones. I think again about the statement I wrote. Whether any of that will form part of their truth.

Freya isn't here and I'm taken aback by the weight of disappointment in my chest. Usually, in inquest cases, I've learned, it is the family who are so desperate for clarity. So much of an inquest is for them. They are the ones, normally, who so need answers. Instead, this time, it was Sarah's only family fighting tooth and nail to keep things hidden.

And then I see her, slipping in at the back. When she sees me, she smiles, her eyes meeting mine, but I find myself unable to smile back. Instead I turn away. I wonder what I can possibly say to her. I feel as though I have so much, and so little.

But before I can wonder any further, we begin.

*

The first witness is the pathologist who carried out the post mortem. He describes how the body – Sarah's body – was identified from her dental records. The coroner's officer reads from Sarah's medical records. Her history of allergies to wasp stings; tallying the dates of when she last renewed her Epi-pen. Not recently enough.

A police officer who attended the scene of the flat attests to the set-up in that tiny space. I recognize him, vaguely, as one of the first officers who arrived on the scene. It brings those moments back to me. The cold wall against my shoulder as I leaned in the hallway outside the bedsit; that thick, sandy smell in my nostrils; the thin file of papers clutched to my chest. It all began from there, the shock, the trauma of it. The not-sleeping, not-eating. And the more I searched and searched for answers, the worse it became. A downwards spiral, all those layers of fantasy and falsehood. All my threads of reality breaking down.

They show a picture of the bedsit as we found it. The stark reality of how it was. So different from the fantasy Sarah created for herself. Like the zoetrope rising up to speed, I see it suddenly all coming together.

Chapter 38

BACK THEN

Sarah Jane Jones

After the accident, falling from the roof, Jane was in hospital a very long time. Weeks and weeks went by while they fixed her leg. It hurt a lot, but she tried not to cry.

She was never supposed to cry, she knew now.

A few times, Uncle Brian and Aunt Susan came to visit. When they did, they didn't bring Prin. For some reason Jane's cousin wasn't allowed to see her. And Uncle Brian and Aunt Susan never stayed very long.

There were other people who came to see her too. Fiona, the social worker she remembers from before; once, a police-man. When they talked to her, they used her proper name. She ended up being *Sarah* all over again. The grown-ups had lots of discussions. She could sense them making important plans.

When Jane tried to think about what happened on the roof, the pictures were all fuzzy in her head. She remembered stars and Prin and flying. She didn't remember what came after that.

And if she thought too much, other pictures came up. Ones she couldn't stand, and couldn't get away from.

Not when she was lying in a hospital bed.

In the hospital bed, she could hardly move. She could only lie there and think her thoughts. Terrible memories going round in her head.

She had to find a way to stop them. That's when she remembered what Prin had taught her. *You only have to believe it and it's real.*

That was where the real game began.

Lying in that hospital bed for weeks by herself, Jane had a lot of time to practise. There were a thousand details she could create.

The more she practised, the more real it became, and by the time she was well enough to leave and go home – to a brand-new home all over again – what happened really seemed like nothing but a dream.

And her Make-Believe life felt completely real.

*

Almost twenty years later, Sarah unfolds the little table in her bedsit flat. The flat isn't big enough for a proper table, one that would be out all the time. She has to make use of the space as best she can.

She's bought flowers from Tesco, garishly bright. She unwraps them and arranges them in a vase. In the kitchen is the on-offer bottle of wine she bought from the Sainsbury's Local near the station, plus all the ingredients for a recipe she will follow.

It is late April and there's a mini-heatwave in London. Sarah clambers up on the draining board to open the little flap window in the kitchen, to get some air in. The kitchen is dirty; she hasn't cleaned for quite a while, but Sarah simply ignores the dirt. This window opens out to a scrubby patch of grass at the back, away from the noisiness of Brixton Hill and the main road. The air that comes in creates a breeze, and on the current of air a clumsy wasp slips in too, confused by the unseasonable heat. It lands on the table, its wings iridescent in the afternoon light.

Sarah puts the radio on, the same station she has listened to for years. Capital FM. It's old-fashioned to have a radio, but she uses her phone so little really. It's easier without it. That way there's nothing to disturb her scene. Life has been so tiring for her lately: all those friends she's made at the office where she temps. Sometimes she loses track of what she's told them. So often, she can't remember who knows what. She likes them all, is glad for the company, but other people always, always make it less real. Sometimes, she just gets exhausted. Needs a little time for herself. This time, she feels it more than ever. So much so that she's ended up deleting all the numbers from her phone and all the contacts from her email account.

She just isn't sure, this time, that she'll have the energy to go back.

Up until now, she's had a little money to see her through: the inheritance from her aunt and uncle. It's been enough over the years that she doesn't have to work all the time, so long as she's careful and lives as cheaply as she can. It's allowed her to take time out, now and then. But now that money isn't far off running out.

Not long now until her guests arrive. It's going to be so wonderful to see them. They've been with her for such a long time. But she doesn't always get to spend time with them like this.

Just for a moment, she feels something tugging at her, like a whisper, as though she is dreaming and – far away – someone is trying to wake her up. A flicker of screaming, blood.

But Sarah ignores it. Nothing matters except for right now. She sets the fold-out table with plates and cutlery. The glasses she puts out are smudged with fingerprints, but the sun makes them sparkle; from a distance they look fine. She removes the sauce from the heat, switches off the cooker for now and sits on the little sofa in the living room, sliding down so that her head rests against the arm.

The radio plays, the sun dazzles in through the tiny window. It's hard to see clearly against the glare. It's easier if she simply closes her eyes. She thinks of that summer as a kid, with her cousin. Spinning the zoetrope, turning cartwheels on the lawn. Above her, the wasp traces lazy lines through the hot air of the flat. Sarah can hear it buzzing over the sound of the radio. She should probably be scared, but she isn't really. To be honest, she isn't scared of much any more. Maybe in some ways, it would be a relief. The wasp lands gently on the arm of the sofa. Sarah feels its tiny legs tangle in her hair.

It is so peaceful, lying here in the April warmth. When she feels something brush at her neck, she doesn't mind. She pictures her guests arriving any minute: her parents, the ones she made from the stars. She focuses on how much she loves them, how much they love her. Nothing between them has ever been wrong. The world out there … but she lets the thought extinguish. She refuses to be anywhere else but here.

She can feel the wasp, softly tickling, on her neck. She reaches up a hand – but not to brush it away. With her palm, she makes a little cup over the creature. She feels it vibrate against her skin. It wants out, and she should let it go, but what if …?

What if?

She tightens her hand a little, trapping it. Hugging it close to her neck.

She just wants to sleep, honestly. Sink into a dream. That's all she's ever really wanted from this life. She knows the truth is that she never faced what happened. Never came to terms with it, never had the chance to try. She had to just cover the whole thing over, weave a dream life in which she could live. But it's so tiring to keep all the pieces stitched together; she's always, always at risk of falling through.

But if she could sleep – if she could sleep for ever … How glorious it would be to never have to wake up.

The sting, when it comes, feels far away and faint. Moments later a mugginess sweeps over her, thickening her tongue, her throat. Distantly – so distantly – Sarah knows what is happening. She knows how dangerous this is. But here and now, all she knows is that the door of her flat is opening and a man and woman are stepping inside. They have come. They're here. She is drifting, everything around her is fading, but here and now there's a lovely mother and father with her, just the way she's always wanted.

A perfect moment she has created. A perfect Make-Believe of a life.

And nothing to wake her up from the dream.

Chapter 39

After just two hours, the coroner reaches her conclusion. An open verdict. She is satisfied, she tells us, that there was no foul play: so much of the evidence points towards natural causes. Only there is not quite enough evidence to rule more conclusively. And so, that is her finding on the cause of death: an open verdict. And it is not her job to go much further than that.

Around me, I'm aware of people getting up and leaving the courtroom. And yet I find myself unable to move.

'I just need a minute,' I tell Alastair, and quietly he slips away. I will get up in just one second – it's not long until I have to collect Charlie from school – but I need a moment. At some level, I already know what I must do. It feels as though this has been the point of this whole journey. Maybe, in the end, that was why I was the one to find Sarah. It's maybe why from the start I needed so badly to know what had happened. I almost lost my mind on the way, almost sacrificed my health in the process. But maybe I had to walk through that fire, that long dark tunnel to reach this point.

At last I stand, my legs stiff, and make my way out of the courthouse into the pale April sunshine. Alastair and Marianne are waiting for me outside. And Freya too.

Freya steps forward. I can tell at once that there is something she wants to say to me. I let her approach, and push my hands into my pockets, waiting to hear what she has to say.

'You were right.' Her words are quiet but direct. 'And I just want you to know, I'm not working with the team any more. I'm not going to pursue a psychology career. I can't do it. It wouldn't be right. Not after everything I did.'

I look at her, and meet her eyes. 'You told me that you wanted to help people. But you do that by giving them the truth. Instead you tried to mess with my reality too.'

'I know,' she says. 'I know that. And I'm really going to change.'

And now it's time I took my own advice.

*

I head home. When I reach the flat, there is still a little time left before I need to go and collect Charlie. In the kitchen, I open the cupboard under the sink. The recycling bag is still here, with those pages of notes stuffed deep inside. They are real, after all. It's weeks since I dumped them in there. Right then, there was no way I could look at them. They were my worst nightmare, the thing I had been running from for years, thinking I could keep it at bay by punishing myself in my own bizarre ways.

I know now what I have to do.

I wonder if at some level, Dad had been fighting for this all along. Trying to find a way to talk to me about it. But for all these years, I didn't want to speak about it, and then Dad's first loyalty was always to Mum. No doubt the conflict inside ate him up over the years. There's a reason he needs those small tablets that live in a drawer by his bed. In the end, it would have to come down to me. I think the reality is, I've been needing this the whole time.

I pull the bag out and empty it, laying all the pages out on the kitchen table. I fetch a thick dark pen from the living room, plus fresh paper and a biro, and set them on the table as well, ready.

I take each sheet of notes and order them as best I can, checking dates, checking the timeline of appointments and events. They go a long way back. My whole history.

Back then, my mother was only trying to help. Just as Freya was only trying to help her cousin. Freya stumbled on the power of the mind. She knew what a difference an alternative narrative could make. But that power can be such a danger. We can be so blinded by what we try to make ourselves believe.

I finally find the page I am looking for. An old entry, from eight years ago.

Mrs Arden (client's mother) explained that her daughter fell asleep with her infant son on the couch at home. The child slipped down and became trapped against the cushions and suffered a degree of asphyxiation. Mrs Arden discovered mother and baby, woke her daughter and called an ambulance. Doctors examining the child report no observable damage, but Jennifer Arden has been presenting as highly agitated and distressed.

Freya would have seen this entry in my file, and – for her needs – that narrative already contained enough guilt. She fired off an anonymous accusation, confident of it landing: *Jennifer Arden, I know what you did.*

*

I stare at the typed words for a really long time. It's even longer before I can pick up the pen, but I do it.

If I have learned anything from all of this, it is that we need to face it: our truth, our whole truth and nothing but. That is what truly protects us from madness. Facing and dealing with the things in our lives that have happened, or that we've done. Dealing with the parts of ourselves that we are most frightened of.

I draw a thick heavy line through all of those words, erasing them, redacting them, blotting them out.

Then I write the true words in their place.

Chapter 40

I met Charlie's father the summer I returned home from university. Uni had been a stretch for me. I didn't cope very well with being away from home. Growing up, I'd been so used to doing everything Mum's way. I didn't know how to think for myself. Afterwards, that June, I came back to the same house, back to my parents. My old school friends had moved on, or I hadn't kept in touch. It was a hot summer, a heatwave. There was very little to do except wait for my exam results.

I didn't know what I wanted to do next in my life. My thoughts about a career drew a blank. The whole summer stretched ahead of me, emptily.

Most days, I took the train into Brighton, meandered along the seafront. I met Charlie's dad – Luke – there.

I remembered him vaguely from school. He had been in the year above me. He remembered me vaguely too: enough to recognize me but not enough to really know anything about me.

We hung out together all of that summer. Come July, we were officially dating. Come August, I had got my results: a 2:2.

Bit of a disappointment, really.

I got a job, working in a local café. Luke was working in his dad's business, a timber yard on the outskirts of town. He usually smelled of sawdust when we met up. We were together for the whole of the next year. He had a flat that I stayed at most of the time, taking the train back at weekends to see my parents. The following February, we put my name on the lease.

I think I got pregnant because I didn't have any other plans. We both had steady jobs, we lived together. Sometimes we'd talk about getting married, but Luke's dad had been married three times, so he didn't believe in it, he said. So we made a baby instead. I just couldn't think of what else to do in my life.

I liked being pregnant. I really did. It was a proper project.

My parents were happy, too. My mum had often talked about grandchildren. A sort of second chance for her, maybe. As a mum, she had never got things quite right.

Over the next winter, my stomach grew and grew.

We set up a nursery in the flat. Luke worked longer hours at the timber yard; he said he was trying to save extra money. It meant we didn't see so much of each other, though. He felt a little distant, but that was okay. It was only going to be for a while, just to save up a bit and get ahead. It was all ways of planning for when the baby came. Luke worked extra hours and I sorted out the cot, the baby clothes, the nursery, all of that.

My waters broke on the first of May. Luke was at work; he didn't answer his phone straight away. Mum was the one who drove me to the hospital.

At the hospital, things moved very, very quickly. Maybe there would never have been enough time for Luke to get there.

334

My labour had started in earnest when his text came through.

Sorry. I can't do this, it said.

Everything just fell apart then. The whole picture I had set up for myself. My life with Luke, a future, a family. A pretty picture-postcard my mum could enjoy. And now none of it was going to be real.

I moved with Charlie back into Mum and Dad's house. Luke stayed in his same flat in town, then moved away, to Scotland, a few months later.

I couldn't stop crying. That was the first sign that something was wrong.

Nobody saw it though, somehow. Perhaps Dad assumed I was just upset about the break-up. Maybe Mum just pretended that I was only missing Luke.

Mum told her friends and neighbours that he had had to take a job up north. She didn't tell anyone that Luke had left me.

I was not coping well with Charlie. He was only a baby, but I got angry with him all the time. It felt as if he knew exactly how to time his bouts of crying so as to tip me over the edge.

I didn't talk to anyone about it. I didn't really have anyone to tell. My uni friends had all moved on. The mums from my NCT class were all coping fine. Dad was in the background, happy as always to let Mum take the lead. And Mum just kept saying what a lovely baby he was, picking him up and pinching his cheeks.

I'm not sure how long exactly Charlie had been crying for that night. In my mind, it was six, seven hours. Non-stop.

Everything was a haze for me. It was as though I was standing outside myself, watching. Seeing exactly what I was about to do, but utterly, completely powerless to stop it.

Still now, in my dreams sometimes, I can see myself lifting up the cushion. I can hear the wave of silence and relief as I press it down.

Mum found us. Thank God Mum found us.

At the hospital, she lied. She told them a much more palatable story. One she could share with the neighbours, if she had to.

Just an accident. Just a mistake. Nothing to do with me being unwell.

My mother helped look after Charlie a lot more after that. She took him off me most of the time. And I fought my way up through the blackness. I managed to break free of it, not talking to anyone, just fighting interminably upwards on my own.

I think it cost me a great deal to do it like that. I think it left me with strange mental scars.

*

There came a day when I made it out. I remember the exact moment. It happened one morning, quite out of the blue. I went through to Charlie's room to lift him from his cot and the early morning sun was shining in at the window, dazzling him a little in his eyes. I lifted my hand, to make a shade for him, and he opened his eyes wide, looked up at me and smiled.

He smiled.

In that moment, my whole world righted itself.

From that moment, I loved Charlie in a way that made everything else fall away, everything that had gone before.

I loved him with a violent, soul-bending love.

And I have never fallen out of love with him since.

Chapter 41

The day after the inquest, Friday, I head into the office. Emma is there, same as always, scrolling through the dozens of updates on her phone. I listen more carefully to her this time, though, to what she says when she tells me about all her online friends, people she knows from all over the world, who like her posts and put hearts for her kitten pictures and cry-laugh emojis at the silly things she says.

People she has never met. People she only knows online.

As we switch off our computers at the end of the day, I do something I never have before. I ask her if she has any plans for the evening. Before, I've always assumed she has so many friends. In my mind she was always rushing across London for parties.

But: 'Oh,' she says with an awkward laugh. 'No … Bit of a quiet one for me tonight.' She looks really quite small, standing there in the office doorway, with her coat done up right to her chin, her phone still clutched in her hand, like a lifeline to the world.

'Do you fancy an after-work drink then? I don't have to pick up Charlie until later.' Charlie is on a play-date with Molly until six thirty, and right now it is only just after five.

Emma's eyebrows lift in surprise but a smile follows quickly behind. 'Thanks,' she says. 'That would be ... really nice. It can be a bit lonely, you know? Nights you're home alone.'

I smile back at her. I think of all the assumptions it's so easy to make. I nod. 'Yeah. I know.'

We turn off the office lights and set the alarms. I wait for her at the top of the stairs as she locks the office door behind us. Then we head down, into the hubbub of the city together.

*

On Saturday, it's a clear spring day; mid-April. Charlie and I go to the park. The sun is bright, and it's warm enough that Charlie has stripped down to his T-shirt. Warm enough that I am not shivering. I've got a takeaway hot chocolate in my hand, thick with cream and chocolate sprinkles. I got it from the new coffee shop that's opened up round the corner from us. Another trendy café in Brixton. Soon we'll head back to the flat for lunch where the fridge is stocked with all kinds of wholesome foods. I'm doing better now. I've put on quite a bit of weight.

In front of me, Charlie runs in circles, burning off all the energy he has. The air is so clear and my head is clear too.

It is quite easy for me to see him properly now.

'Watch me!' he shouts. 'Mummy, watch me!'

His birthday is coming up in just two weeks. He took the invitations into school yesterday and he tells me almost everyone's going to come. It's a lot better at the school gates now, ever since I called up Molly's mum and explained about my anxiety and why I behaved how I did. She said she totally, completely understood – funnily enough, she used to suffer depression. Then she must have had a word with the other school parents, because it's pretty much back to normal now at the gates.

I'm thinking too about calling Alastair later. Inviting him along to the party. It's probably not Marianne's kind of thing, but I'm going to call her as well, to suggest we meet up for coffee and cake. It's about time I started making an effort. Stopped keeping my whole life to myself.

Charlie climbs to the top of the slide, the metal glinting in the April sunshine, bright as a blade. He shrieks as he catapults down, landing awkwardly at the bottom, scattering wood chips. For a moment, my heart trips over itself, losing all coordination. Then Charlie scrambles back to his feet and I draw a sharp breath, scraping the air back into my lungs.

He is healthy. He is fine. Isn't that what the GP said?

I hold up my phone and take a picture of him. For a moment my fingers hover over my contacts, then I select Dad's email and forward the photo to him. Since my unannounced visit, he's been calling more often and even got Mum to finally come to the phone. Those conversations are brief and stilted. But at least, I tell myself, it's a start.

'The slide, Mummy?' shouts Charlie. 'Can I go on the slide?'

I hold my phone camera up again. 'Of course!'

Sarah chose to live in a fantasy. A fantasy partly of Freya's making. And in trying to unravel that fantasy, I came close to losing my own mind. It sent me on that downwards spiral until I didn't know which way was up. But I was vulnerable already, of course I was.

Because of my own fantasy I was living.

But crossing those words out in my file and writing the real ones is what has freed me. Facing the awful, painful truth. I wasn't well back then, and I should have had help. The rift in my reality began right back then.

Now I am sound in body and mind. I can tell what is true now and what is false. Now I have Charlie, safe with me, happy in the light of this bright spring day.

I shiver. A cloud passes over the sun, and sunlight and shade blur in its shadow. How easily it can happen, I think. To layer one reality over another. How powerful the mind is. How fragile. But I wrote the truth in my own hand in my notes, and I keep that page with all my other strategies and tools. On the top. In case, like Sarah, I should ever be tempted again.

I pull my jacket a little more tightly around me as Charlie runs up to me, takes my hand in his. I look down at him, straight on, and smile. I know what I did to him, long ago. I can look that too, now, squarely in the face.

So that's what I have to remember from here on. Not to forget. And not to look away.

I squeeze Charlie's hand in mine. The sun comes out, shining bright again, almost too bright to properly see by.

'All good?' I say to him, screwing my eyes up a little in the glare.

Charlie looks up at me, his face so open, his smile only ever-so-slightly lopsided. 'All good,' he tells me. 'One hundred per cent fine.'

And I keep smiling back, my heart skittering in my chest, and tell myself that I really do believe him.

Acknowledgements

Safe and Sound was inspired by the true-life case of Joyce Carol Vincent, a woman in her thirties who died at home in late 2003 and whose body was discovered in 2006. In 2011, filmmaker Carol Morley created a deeply moving docudrama about Joyce's life and death, based on interviews with those who knew her. I first saw *Dreams of a Life* around 2013, and have remained emotionally haunted by it ever since.

Writing a book is hard and writing a second book can be even harder, but many people have helped me with this terrifying task. Firstly, my agent Sarah Hornsley, who always knows what I'm trying to do and sets me straight when I zoom off course. *Safe and Sound* (like *Little White Lies*) required a 'massive re-write', but Sarah, I know it is all the better for it. Also to my brilliant editor Cicely Aspinall, whose enthusiasm has buoyed me all the way and whose astute feedback made *Safe and Sound* shine. It has been such a pleasure to work with you, Cicely, always knowing I am in safe hands. Thanks go to the whole team at HQ/HarperCollins, both in the UK, and in the US and Canada. You have all worked so hard to champion my books and I feel so privileged to have such an amazing team supporting me. Special thanks go to copy editor Penny

Isaac, publicist Isabel Smith, and designer Anna Sikorska for *that* incredible cover.

I would also like to thank Louise Wilkinson, Head of Information & Learning at the Child Brain Injury Trust, who helped me with my research, and also The Children's Trust for the amazing resources on their Brain Injury Hub. Both of these charities provide invaluable research, information and support for children and families; if you would like to donate you can do so here: https://childbraininjurytrust.org.uk/donate/ and here: https://www.thechildrenstrust.org.uk/donate. Thank you as always to Stuart Gibbon who has again helped me with the police-y bits of this story. All the errors and liberties are mine, and thank you as well, Stuart, for all the re-tweets!

I am so grateful to all the wonderful readers, reviewers and bloggers out there. Your support for *Little White Lies* was a constant motivation as I wrote this second book, and I am thrilled that you have picked up *Safe and Sound* too. It's readers that I write for: my words are just words, but you are what make the stories matter.

Love and thanks to family and friends who have encouraged me on this journey with such enthusiasm. In particular, my lovely in-laws: Misako, Jenny, Liana and Rob, and Chiyo. It means so much to me that you have read my books and I'm even more thrilled that you enjoyed them!

Navigating the world of writing and publishing has been made a hundred times easier and more fun thanks to my fellow Debut 2020 authors, all of who are incredible writers and whose friendship has been one of the best things to come out of this tumultuous year.

Once again, my sister Katherine has been an amazing first

reader as well as a huge source of end-of-the-phone support. My parents, Brian and Claire, continue to run great PR for my books as well as plugging the plot holes from my sh*tty first drafts. And finally and as ever, all my love and thanks go to my husband Dan, to whom all my books are dedicated in my heart.

p.s. Oh – and thanks to Mimi, my cat.

ONE PLACE. MANY STORIES

Bold, innovative and
empowering publishing.

FOLLOW US ON:

@HQStories